Nebraska
Coast

Books by

CLYDE BRION DAVIS

THE ANOINTED

"THE GREAT AMERICAN NOVEL—"

NORTHEND WILDCATS

NEBRASKA COAST

Nebraska Coast

Clyde Brion Davis

decorations by
Edward Shenton

Farrar & Rinehart
New York   Toronto

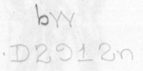

Foreword

In gathering material for NEBRASKA COAST I have drawn from many histories, not only of early days in the West, but from histories of transportation in the United States and from histories of the American canals.

Particularly, however, I must express my indebtedness to Dr. Addison E. Sheldon, Superintendent of the Nebraska State Historical Society in Lincoln, not only for his historical works, but for my own use of the Nebraska State Historical archives.

I must thank Martha M. Turner, Nebraska State Librarian, and George G. Allanson of Wheaton, Minnesota, whose grandfather, Major Joseph R. Brown, invented the historical steam wagon.

I must thank John Hyde Sweet, owner and editor of the Nebraska City *News-Press,* for use of old files of the *News,* which were invaluable to me in gaining a picture of Nebraska in the early 1860's.

Most of all, however, I am indebted to my father, the late Charles N. Davis, a Nebraska pioneer, who left me an heritage of reminiscences and anecdotes that have become the backbone of this story.

CLYDE BRION DAVIS.

Contents

Part I

York State

York State

I

When I was six years old I thought it would be a good thing if my Aunt Christine died. I never spoke of this to anyone, but I thought she would be much happier dead. I thought I should be happier too, because I didn't like the idea of Tom Brooks coming to our house.

Often I heard Tom Brooks moving around downstairs long after everyone had gone to bed. He made a faint rustling sound like two pieces of paper rubbing together and the sound made me shiver on my husk mattress in the loft. I was afraid he might climb up the loft ladder some night, although there was no good reason for him to do that. He must have known that Aunt Christine would not be in the loft.

Tom Brooks had drowned in the lake four or five years before. His boat had capsized in a squall and he was unable to swim in his heavy coat and boots. They found his body the day before he and Aunt Christine were to have been married and they held his funeral in the Presbyterian Church without taking down the wedding decorations.

Of course I couldn't remember any of this but I had

3

heard it many times and I had seen Tom Brooks's gravestone in the churchyard.

My older brother Alan could remember how Tom Brooks looked and he also claimed to have seen Tom since the funeral.

"It was moonlight and bright," Alan said. "I looked out the loft window and there was Tom Brooks standing thoughtful under the apple tree and looking at the house."

Aunt Christine was tremendously interested in Alan's story. She questioned him at length with a strange light in her reddish-brown eyes. Aunt Christine had red hair which she parted in the middle and drew severely down across her thin cheeks. She was very serious.

Some time after Alan's experience Aunt Christine came to the breakfast table with a flushed face and Father commented on her appearance.

Aunt Christine looked down and said softly in a voice that quivered, "Tom was here last night."

Father's black eyes opened wide. He was in the act of raising a sizable piece of fried salt pork to his mouth, but he laid down his fork.

"I woke up," said Aunt Christine, "and I saw him standing by the foot of the bed smiling at me. I said, 'Tom!' And he said, 'Christine, darling.' "

For a moment everyone was silent, gaping at Aunt Christine. A clammy shiver ran up my neck into my hair.

"Did he," Father inquired solemnly, "get in bed with you?"

Aunt Christine lowered her eyes and said nothing.

Mother's straight, sandy brows merged above her nose. "Jack!" she cried. "Haven't you any decency? Haven't you any decency at all?"

Aunt Christine rose and left the table, looking neither

left nor right. Father's swarthy face wrinkled in a grin. His teeth were big and strong and white.

"Just wondering about spirits," he said. "Just a scientific question, that's all. By grab, there's no sense getting het up about a scientific question, is there?"

I sympathized with Aunt Christine. It was then I decided it would be a good thing for her to die. I thought if Aunt Christine died there would be no necessity for Tom Brooks to come around our house any more. I thought if she died the two spirits could wander contentedly over the hills in the moonlight or float hand in hand with the midnight wind across the lake. I thought that would be nice for them and nice for me too.

Aunt Christine, however, did not die. Instead she went to visit the Fox sisters over in Arcade township. There was a great deal of talk about Margaret and Catherine Fox and the messages they got from beyond the grave, so Aunt Christine went to see them.

From the spirit of a peddler who had been murdered and buried in the cellar of the Fox farmhouse (before the Fox family lived there, of course) Margaret and Catherine got a lot of information about Tom Brooks for Aunt Christine. It seemed he was very happy over there in heaven and he was watching over and protecting Aunt Christine every hour.

Also from the spirit of the murdered peddler Aunt Christine learned that she herself had the power of communicating with spirits and the Fox sisters showed her how to get messages from the world of shadows by means of a cherry-wood table.

So when Aunt Christine got home she held a séance. Present at the session were Mrs. Lownes, wife of Jake Lownes the blacksmith, and Mrs. Pearson, who had driven over from Bristol, and the two Seacoy sisters from

Naples. Aunt Christine invited Mother to take part, but Mother said she had some spinning to do and she sat back in a dusky corner with a tallow dip flickering by her side while she whirled the big wheel and the spindle wailed more mournful than any ghost that ever walked.

Aunt Christine assembled her guests around the cherry table down the room by the fireplace and told them to rest their fingers lightly on the tabletop.   .

"We must be very still for a while," she said. "I calculate it'll take ten minutes or a quarter hour."

So they sat there, Aunt Christine hollow-eyed and tense with her big cameo brooch gleaming in the firelight and old Major, the black-and-white shepherd, asleep by the hearth and Grandpa Macdougall dozing in his chair with his cane between his knees and my brother Alan and sister Eliza and I sitting together on a bench nibbling at friedcakes but pretty much scared by the whole eerie business.

We could hear the heavy breathing of the women around the cherry-wood table and the fire crackled and there was the sweet scent of burning hemlock. Pretty soon Mrs. Lownes whispered, "Did you feel anything?"

"I think so," said Mrs. Pearson.

Then Mrs. Lownes asked, "Chris, did you say they rap once for yes and twice for no?"

"Other way around," said Aunt Christine.

Then the door swept open and Father stomped in.

"Hello, folks," he bellowed. "What's up?"

"Oh, dear," breathed Aunt Christine.

"Shh. We're about to talk to a spirit," said Mrs. Lownes.

"Fine and dandy," roared Father. "I like spirits myself." He pulled an earthen jug from under the cupboard. "Anybody join me?" He laughed at the serious circle of women and the firelight glittered on the small gold earrings in his ears. "No?" He slung the jug across his upper arm, tilted back his head and let the whisky gurgle down his throat. I liked to see Father drink from a jug. He did it with such graceful abandon. But sometimes I did not like to see him when he had tilted the jug often.

With an amused grin on his face Father leaned against the stone mantel and put his hands in his pockets.

Presently the table moved slightly. The end near Aunt Christine raised and then thumped on the floor.

"Did you do that, Chris?" Mrs. Pearson asked in a whisper.

"No, no, I didn't," said Aunt Christine hoarsely.

Then suddenly the table rocked back and forth from Libby Seacoy to Aunt Christine.

"Is there a spirit here?" Aunt Christine asked in a hollow voice.

Bump, bump, went the table.

"That means yes," said Mrs. Pearson.

"Is it—is it you, Tom?" Aunt Christine asked.

The moan of the spinning wheel died as Mother turned her attention to the table.

Bump.

"It ain't Tom Brooks," said Mrs. Pearson.

"Is it Mr. Rosna, the peddler?" Aunt Christine asked.

Again the table bumped once.

Aunt Christine's eyes were wide and ghastly in the firelight and there was a green glow from Tom Brooks's emerald ring on her left forefinger.

"Did any of us know you in your lifetime?"

One more single rap.

"Will you spell out your name as we give the alphabet?"

Bump, bump.

So Aunt Christine gave the alphabet—A, B, C, . . . and at "D" the table rapped twice.

"It's D," said Mrs. Pearson. "It begins with D."

Aunt Christine began over with the alphabet—A, B, C, D, and this time she went clear to O before the table thumped.

Again down the alphabet to L when the table bumped twice and then quickly twice again.

"Do you mean double L?" asked Aunt Christine.

Bump, bump.

"Maybe," said Mrs. Lownes, "the name is Dolly. Is your name Dolly, spirit?"

Bump, bump.

"Yes," said Aunt Christine faintly, "her name is Dolly."

Father reached behind him and took down his copper powder flask that hung beside his shotgun. Cautiously he sprinkled a heavy train of powder across the hearthstone and then hung the flask back on its peg.

"Dolly," whispered Aunt Christine, "do you know Thomas J. Brooks in the spirit world?"

Bump, bump, bump.

"Well," said Jenny Seacoy, "what does *three* knocks mean?"

"Wants to know what spirit township he's in," said Father.

"Shh." Mrs. Pearson looked up angrily.

"Do three knocks mean you know him well?" asked Mrs. Lownes.

Bump, bump.

"Has Tom Brooks got a high standing in the spirit community?" Father asked.

The table was silent.

"Oh, Mr. Macdougall," said Mrs. Lownes, "please don't. You'll frighten her away."

"Dolly," said Aunt Christine softly, "are you still here?"

Bump, bump.

"Please don't be frightened, Dolly. Could you tell me something about Mr. Brooks? Is he—is he happy?"

Bump, bump.

"Could you bring me a message from Mr. Brooks?"

Bump, bump.

With the tongs Father lifted a coal from the fire. He touched the coal to the end of the powder train and there was a blinding flash and whoosh!

Major leaped to his feet barking. Aunt Christine stared at us children on the bench, screamed a long-drawn wail and toppled off her chair to the floor while the firelight glinted through the white billow of pungent powder smoke rising to the ceiling.

Mother rushed across the room and bent over Aunt Christine on the floor. "Help me loosen her stays," she demanded of Mrs. Lownes.

Father came up with his earthen jug. "Here," he said, "give her a snort of whisky. That'll fix her."

Mother glared at him. "You and your whisky—you big blundering lout. That's all you ever think of—whisky and tomfoolery—and maybe you've been the death of her."

Eliza ran and brought Aunt Christine's smelling salts bottle which quickly revived her. But henceforth Father avoided the spiritualist séances.

Aunt Christine became more adept in the art or better attuned to the spirit world as time went on and her sessions were well attended. She was able to bring messages for almost everyone, and once she even brought Grandpa Macdougall a message from Grandma Macdougall. The message was, "Be sure and keep your watch wound."

Grandpa said, "Now what on earth'd she mean by that? I swanney. Never did have much sense when she was alive and I can't say running around with spirits has helped her much."

II

Nominally Father was a farmer. But he didn't do a great deal of farming. He always felt he could have more fun and make more money doing something else than trying to raise crops on the stony hillsides.

A frequent occupation of Father's was charcoal burning. He would make tight wigwams of birch or willow poles over a pile of pitch pine, leaving a hole near the bottom to start a fire. Then he would cover the wigwam with dirt. When the fire was started he would shovel dirt over the vent and throw more dirt on the sides where smoke oozed out.

When the fire had burned down the dirt-covered wigwam would have been converted into charcoal which he would load into our green-and-white sloop *Lily* and transport to Canandaigua. Sometimes he would take Alan or me along. That was always an adventure, going to Canandaigua.

There was such a trip when I was about eight years old. I had learned to steer after a fashion and Father had given me the tiller while he went down in the cabin to see how an earthen jug was riding.

I had taken off my new red-topped boots to ease my feet and had set them up beside me where I could admire them. There was a fresh quartering wind and little whitecaps were popping across the lake, which was blue from the summer sky. Cloud shadows drifted across the high, vine-terraced hills and I was happy with anticipation of what I should do and see in Canandaigua.

In my preoccupation I suppose I let up on the tiller. Anyhow the sloop swung with the wind. Suddenly the sail went slack, then with a crack it billowed inward and the boom came swinging back like a whip.

I dropped the tiller and dove headfirst down the

cabin hatch, startling Father so badly he dropped the earthen jug on his foot and spilled about a pint of rum.

"By holy dang," said Father. "What on earth bit you?"

Then, as the *Lily* heeled over in the wind, he dashed up the ladder and straightened the sloop out. He glared at me fiercely and then, seeing me whimpering from my bruised knees and bumped head, he began to laugh.

"Where my red-top boots?" I blubbered. But I knew without asking. The boom had a scant foot clearance and it had swept my boots into the lake where I also might have landed had I not dived so quickly down the hatch.

"Ought to thrash you for carelessness," said Father. "Ought to thrash you for losing your boots."

I began to cry in earnest.

"Calculate you gave yourself a pretty good thrashing tumbling down in the cabin, though. Saves me the trouble. By gol, you'll have to wait a long time before you get another pair of boots like that. See I can't trust you. Go on forward."

So I went forward in disgrace and lay down in the sunshine and cried. Pretty soon I realized I had been forgiven, however, and dried my tears. Father was booming out a song, rather incongruous for him, in his powerful but not very tuneful voice.

"Down on the canebrakes every day I go,
    Take my bath in the lake below;
If I chance to meet a drunkard,
    Oh, so pale and thin:
Well, how do you do, sir,
    Won't you pray walk in?"

When we got to Canandaigua and Father had disposed of his cargo he took me to Richmond's oyster saloon on Main Street, a dimly lighted place with dark brown wainscoting running higher than a tall man's head and with sawdust on the floor.

On the wall was a brightly colored lithograph of Belle Cameron in tights. There was another lithograph of John C. Heenan, the American boxing champion, stripped to the waist and extending his formidable fists. And next to Heenan was a very spirited picture of the trotter, Flora Temple, stretching her trim legs while her driver's whiskers flowed dashingly over both shoulders. Printed beneath this picture was the inscription, "Flora Temple, world's trotting record 2:24½."

Father and I sat on stools at the counter and the waiter, who was bald-headed and wore an enormous, drooping mustache, came up and rested his fat white hands in front of us.

"Hello, McWalrus," said Father.

"Hello, McInjun," said the waiter. "What'll it be?"

"I think," said Father, "a couple of bowls of raw oysters'd be grateful to our innards. What say, Clint?"

"Yes, sir," I said.

So the waiter brought us two large bowls of raw oysters and Father showed me how to drench them with vinegar and to sprinkle them with black pepper and salt. We made a meal, and a very good meal it seemed, of the oysters and bread. Then Father paid the waiter two shillings and we sauntered up the street.

I was proud of Father that day as we walked up the board sidewalk. I noted how much handsomer and more dashing he was than the townsmen. He was taller than any man we met. His sloping shoulders were broader and he walked with the spring of a foot racer.

Most of the other men wore narrow-brimmed hats with high crowns, but Father's hat was black and broad-brimmed and rakish with a low, flat crown and on this day he was wearing a mottled grouse feather stuck in the band. His wampus jacket was open at his swelling chest as was his blue flannel shirt, and around his bronzed neck was knotted a scarlet kerchief. His gold earrings set off the picture.

Presently we turned a corner into Coach Street and came to a barroom. "Believe," said Father, "I could do with a blackstrap."

We went through the swinging doors into the barroom which, like the oyster saloon, had sawdust on the floor.

"Blackstrap," said Father.

The bartender looked inquiringly at me. "Make him one with milk?" he asked.

"Fine and dandy," said Father.

So the bartender shook up a concoction of molasses and rum for Father and a concoction of molasses and milk for me. Father tossed off his drink, smacked his lips and looked at me. I was struggling with my beaker manfully. It had a strong, disagreeable taste, but I assumed it would make me grow.

"How much?" asked Father of the bartender.

"His is on the house."

"Fine and dandy." Father laid a couple of two-cent coppers on the bar. "Shake me up another."

I wriggled my bare toes in the cool sawdust and thought of my red-topped boots at the bottom of Canandaigua Lake. I wondered if fish made nests and if so if they would utilize my fine boots. That brought up memory of a poem I had to learn in school the winter before. The poem was about some birds that used a silver dish for a nest and about the little birdlings that grew up in it. I sipped on my blackstrap and tried to remember how the poem went. There didn't seem to be much sense in learning poems if one forgot them right away.

Father was listening to three men talking at the bar. He finished his second drink and laid down four cents. "Shake me up another, will you, neighbor?" he said to the bartender.

Two of the men at the bar were wearing long-tailed black coats and dun-colored high beaver hats. The third wore a wampus like Father's and a high-crowned felt hat.

I remembered part of the poem. It went:

> And do you suppose that they arose
> To higher powers possessed,
> Because they knew they lived and grew
> Within a silver nest?

That was the end of the poem. I couldn't remember what went before, except in a general way.

Father now was talking to the three men, but he wasn't agreeing with them.

"Excuse me, mister," he said, "but I don't admit any such thing. I say no government's got a right to take a man's property away from him without paying him for it. And it don't make any difference whether his property is farm land or horses or niggers. That's what I say."

"A human being can't be property," asserted one of the beaver-hat gentlemen.

"By grab, you'd think it was property damn well did you pay a thousand dollars for a darky," Father said.

The gentleman raised his thin-stemmed wineglass and sipped. "I never in the wide world," he said, "could conceive of a man paying money to buy another human being."

"I ain't saying slavery's right," said Father. "But I do say slavery hasn't been against the law, so you can't let slaves loose without paying the owners. The way you look at slaves depends on how you was brought up. Lots of things in this part of the country might look pretty bad to the folks down south. You say slavery ain't human. Well, I think it *is* human."

"In other words, you approve of slavery," sneered the beaver-hat gentleman.

"No such thing. I say it's human because humans

treat each other worse than animals of the same breed treat each other. Never hear of a William Morgan murder amongst cows or horses, did you?"

The beaver-hat gentleman shrugged his shoulders. "My friend," he said haughtily, "you're talking nonsense now."

Father touched a Masonic emblem on the gentleman's lapel. "My talk," he said, "is damn nonsense to a Mason. Your talk would be damn nonsense to a Southerner, by grab."

"We were discussing slavery. Might I ask have you read *Uncle Tom's Cabin?*"

Father laid four cents on the bar. "Shake me up another blackstrap, will you, neighbor? No, I haven't read *Uncle Tom's Cabin.* I'm a busy man without time for reading storybooks. But from what I've heard I calculate it's wrote by a chickenhearted woman who's hell-bent to stir up some trouble."

"Trouble *should* be stirred up," proclaimed Beaver Hat, stamping his cane in the sawdust. "Trouble should be stirred up and plenty of it. These Southern Bourbons are getting altogether too high and mighty. The government should pass a law freeing every slave in America and then send an army down there to enforce the law."

Father grinned dangerously. "They should ought to pass a law," he said, "shutting up the big mouths of lunatics like you."

"What do you mean, sir!" demanded Beaver Hat, stepping forward and jutting out his chin at Father.

"I mean, mister, that loose-mouths like yours are talking sluff talk and trying to stir up a civil war between the North and South."

"Nothing of the kind."

"I mean, mister, if they'd take a dozen selected loose-mouths down south and hang 'em high and dry, and if they'd take a dozen selected loose-mouths up here and hang 'em high and dry, it'd be a fine example for the rest of you loose-mouths and then there wouldn't be any trouble."

Beaver Hat's face flushed. "That's an insult, you galoot," he cried.

"Didn't mean to compliment you much," said Father, taking another draw at his blackstrap. "Might be a good thing to hang that *Uncle Tom's Cabin* woman too."

"Why, you—" Beaver Hat raised his heavy cane. "I've a good mind to crack your crown, you impudent—"

Father didn't seem to move fast. But all at once his right hand had hold of the breast of Beaver Hat's frock coat. As his hand lifted slowly, the slack of the frock coat wrinkled oddly. However, when Father's hand had lifted to the level of Beaver Hat's curly whiskers, the slack was all taken up and the coat held tight at the armpits. Then Beaver Hat, with an astonished expression on his pink face, came up in the air with his polished boots six inches off the sawdust.

With his left hand Father wrenched away the cane and tossed it clattering to a corner. Then he spoke softly into the face of Beaver Hat. "Don't make threats at me, fellow," he said. "I don't take kindly to threats. I'm all for peace and harmony, mister, and I aim to have peace and harmony even if I got to fight for it."

Then he sat Beaver Hat down in a chair with a loud plop and turned to me. "Come on, bub," he said. "We got things to do up the street."

No one said a word as Father and I walked from the barroom. I looked back from the door and Beaver Hat was still in the chair, staring at Father's back.

We then walked up the street to a store where a big black boot hung over the sidewalk.

"Remember me?" Father asked the clerk.

"Why, yes. Yes, indeed."

"Well, last week I bought a pair of red-top boots for
the cub here."

"Yes, sir."

"Well, we want another pair just like 'em."

"Yes, sir. Yes, indeed."

And presently Father and I were striding down
toward the lake and I was wearing another pair of
new red-topped boots. I couldn't find words to thank
Father.

"It's all right," he said. "Now you don't have to tell
your mother about losing the others. She wouldn't like
you steering the boat in the first place. Say no more
about it."

With a good following north wind *Lily* tore over the
lake. Father at the tiller was feeling good. He sang one
of his dog songs that went:

> "Old Rover is the finest dog
> That ever ran a race;
> His ears so quick, his feet so fleet,
> And *such* an honest face.
> My playmate, he, in every sport,
> The moment I begin,
> He's always ready for a race,
> And always sure to win."

III

My brother Alan was five years older than I. My sister
Eliza was two years younger than he.

Alan was always a harum-scarum lad, full of the devil
and all.

One day when we had been out woodchuck shooting
we dropped in Jake Lownes's blacksmith shop, which
was a very good loafing place and where one might hear
about everything that was going on.

Frank Lucas and Ed DeVinney were there ahead of us and Frank Lucas told a story about Alan and him going to old Mom Singer's shanty down at the end of the marsh. Old Mom was reputed to be a witch.

"Al and I was down the swale," said Frank, "and I says to Al, 'Al, let's you and me go see old Mom and get her to tell our fortunes.'

"And Al says all right and pretty soon we comes in sight of her shanty and Al, he says, 'Wonder if the old bitch is home.'

"Well, we're anyhow forty rod from the shanty when he says that just the way you'd talk ordinary and we don't say much of anything more until we get to the door and knock.

"Right away old Mom Singer opens the door and looks out kind of hostile. 'Yes,' she says, 'the old bitch is home.'

"Al's eyes stuck out so far you could knock 'em off with a hoe handle."

"Couldn't have stuck out any farther than yours," said Alan. "I calculate old Mom's a witch, all right. Elseways how could she have known what I said?"

"Shucks," said Jake Lownes, "she heard you. When you talk ordinary a deef person could hear you plain at *fifty* rod."

"Did you get your fortunes read?" asked Ed.

"Well, sort of," said Frank Lucas.

"Couldn't have heard me five rod off," said Alan. "Wasn't talking any louder than this."

"She made out she was reading our fortune," went on Frank, "and she made us pay two shillings before she even started. Then she says Al and I don't rightfully have what you'd call a fortune. Then she give us some slang talk about both of us getting shot dead before we're twenty-one."

Jake Lownes laughed from the dark corner where he

was lazily pulling the forge bellows. "Probably the truth," he observed.

Alan was looking out the door. "There goes old Put," he said. "Drunker'n usual and carrying a jug."

Wizened little Roger Putnam was scuffing along the dusty road, plainly carrying a load of liquor inside him as well as outside.

"Let's have some sport," said Alan, grinning. He picked up his rifle from the corner, put on a cap and cocked the big hammer. Then he steadied the barrel against the doorjamb, took careful aim up the road and fired. The jug in old Put's hand .broke and whisky splashed in the dust.

Old Put stopped and looked at the earthenware handle and fragment of jug in his hand. He looked at the ruin in the road.

"Mysterious," he said.

Then he took off his dilapidated hat, scratched his frowzy head and looked at the sky.

"Mys-*teer*-ious," he said again. He got down on his hands and knees in the dust and carefully picked up a piece of the jug which still contained perhaps a gill of liquor, lifted it to his lips and drained it. Then he rose and staggered on his way, shaking his head sorrowfully.

Alan's laugh was much like Father's. His normally serious dark face suddenly would split in a wide-toothed grin and roaring laughter would shake him to his toes.

When Alan was fourteen Father sent him to the Academy in Canandaigua. But the town boys undertook to haze him. During the season's first snowstorm half a dozen boys attacked Alan with snowballs. In a fury he fled to a woodpile and let go a bombardment of firewood at his tormentors. The battle didn't last long. One of the hazers was down unconscious in the snow with a fracture of the skull and another was howling with a broken arm.

That afternoon Alan was called into the superintendent's office. Gravely the superintendent told him that one boy was in a serious condition in the hospital.

"Too bad some of 'em got away," said Alan evenly.

"You mean you're not sorry?"

"Of course I'm not sorry. They started a fight and I gave 'em a fight."

"Young man," said the superintendent, "I'm afraid you have a vicious nature. A snowball fight is play. Because you were pelted with snowballs was no justification for you to commit assault with clubs of wood. You must learn to curb your dangerous temper or you will end up in prison or on the gibbet. Even now it could go very hard with you if that boy's parents wish to press charges."

"When a gang picks on me," said Alan, "rules don't count. One fellow and that's different. I'll fight one fellow fair if he fights fair. But there's no fairness for a gang to pitch on one boy with snowballs or whatever and I'll fight back with anything I can get hold of. Maybe it was play for them to pitch on me alone because I'm a stranger. But it wasn't any fun for me."

"Then you're not repentant?"

"Not a scratch."

The superintendent pursed his lips. "Macdougall," he said, "I'm afraid I shall have to ask you to leave the Academy."

"Fine and dandy," said Alan. "I don't like it here, anyhow."

At home Mother felt very bad about it all. But Father said Alan had done right.

"By grab," he said, "if that cub's father wants to go to court over that thing I'll make him almighty sick of it all before he's through with it."

A few days later the lake froze over and we all went skating. In the evening a brisk south wind came up and I saw Alan spread his coat like a sail and speed north like an iceboat. When I looked again he was not in sight.

At suppertime he had not returned and Mother began to worry. After the dishes were washed she kept going to the window and, shielding her eyes from the light, peering down at the dark lake.

When it was bedtime she refused to leave the fireplace although Father did his best to convince her Alan was big enough to take care of himself.

I awoke about midnight hearing voices downstairs. I got up, slipped on my boots and went down the ladder with a blanket around my shoulders. Aunt Christine was there with a comforter draped around her and her red hair was hanging in two braids outside the comforter. Her red-brown eyes were wild in the firelight.

"Oh, go back to bed, Chris," Father was saying.

"I tell you," declared Aunt Christine, "it was a vision. I saw him struggling in the icy water. He's drowning in the lake, I tell you. He's fallen through an air hole."

"You had a bad dream," said Father.

"It was a vision. You know my visions don't lie, Jack. I tell you we've got to do something."

"Do what?"

"You could anyhow go out and look," said Mother, beginning to sob.

"Yes, I could go out and look. But the lake's sixteen mile long and it's too dark to see anything."

"All right," said Mother, rising. "I'll go out and look for him myself."

"I'm going," Father sighed. "Just give me some time to get my clothes on."

"Can I go with you?" I asked.

"All right," said Father, looking at me. "Hurry up and get dressed."

I scurried up the ladder and had my clothes on in half the time it usually took me in the morning. But when I came back down Father was dressed and was just lighting one of *Lily's* oil lanterns with a paper squill from the fireplace. He had on his cap with the strings from the earflaps hanging loose. He looked very serious.

"Got your skates?" he asked.

"I'll get 'em. They're in the shed."

"Get mine too."

I started for the back door, but the front door opened before I pushed the latch and there was Alan, carrying his skates and looking very tired.

"Hello," he said.

Father didn't smile. "Just starting to hunt for you," he said.

"Oh, Alan!" cried Mother.

Aunt Christine just stared and didn't say anything.

"Where you been, young man?" Father demanded.

"Canandaigua."

"Canandaigua!"

"Well, you see there was a good wind and I spread my coat and went sailing like a bird. Thought the wind would die down or maybe shift before I had to come back. But the first thing I knew I was clear to Canandaigua and I had to skate all the way back against that wind. That was pretty bad, I can tell you. Like to starved to death. Had to tack like a boat and skate maybe twenty-five miles to get home."

Father blew out the lantern.

"I'll heat you up some supper right away," said Mother.

"Anybody with an ounce of brains," said Father, "would stop to think about getting back before he started on any such tomfool trip."

IV

The spring I was ten Father came home from Rochester
one day and announced he was going to buy a canalboat.
Mother was appalled. "Just another excuse," she said,
"to get out of work." She was sitting in her cushioned
chair darning stockings and she drew her thin mouth
down severely at the corners.

Father laughed. "Just an excuse to make some money,"
he said.

"Money! You could make a good living here on the
farm if you'd work. You could make extra money with
the sloop if you behaved yourself. Then we could lay
by something for our old age."

"Never make anything farming this stone patch," said
Father. "By grab, you know that as well as I do."

"You couldn't make any money canalboating unless
you worked a good deal harder than you do on the farm.
Pastor Rucker said just the other day that canalboating
can't last much longer. All the rotten characters in the
country are being gathered right on the Erie Canal, he
said, and the Lord will be fixing to do something."

"Did he say the Lord would send an army of musk-
rats to dig holes and drain the canal off?"

"He said for one thing that the railroads are going
to take all the canal business because they can move so
much faster."

"That's sluff talk," said Father, "and I don't care
who said it. Nearly five thousand boats on the Erie Canal
last year."

"That's just it," said Mother. "Too many boats. And
because there's so many boats for every pound of freight,
you think it's high time you got a canalboat." She
shrugged her shoulders. "Real reason you want a boat,

I suppose, is so you can hire a female cook like the other canal reprobates."

"If I want another woman I don't have to hire a cook," blurted Father. "Besides all that let me tell you a few things you don't know, and Pastor Rucker don't seem to know, either. Those railroads are run by a bunch of thieves. You buy passage on the steam cars and you don't know whether you're going to get where you're going or not.

"I saw a man in Rochester who'd bought a booking from New York City to Rochester on the steam cars. He got as far as Albany, all right, but when he tried to get on the cars at Albany the captain wouldn't take his bookings. Said the bookings wasn't good on his line. So the man had to buy new bookings on a line boat and stage to Rochester. Wouldn't give the railroads any more money. This man was hopping mad and says he's found out lots of other people have had that same experience not only with passengers but shipping goods.

"Suppose you're shipping a cargo by steam cars and one road won't take another road's bookings. Then your cargo is bogged down some place and you don't know where and you probably lose everything. By grab, I can tell you the steam cars aren't going to close up the canal while that's going on—especially with the rates they charge.

"Then there's something else—when you're riding on the cars or shipping freight you never know when one brigade of cars is going to have a concussion head on with another brigade. When both brigades are tearing along twenty mile an hour they come together at forty mile an hour. Figure out what that'd do to you or your cargo. Hardly a week goes by they don't have a concussion some place."

"Well," said Mother, "I wouldn't get on one of those cars myself, but Pastor Rucker says they'll quit running them so fast pretty soon and then it'll be different. He says going too fast is all that's wrong with the cars. He says sometimes they go thirty mile an hour or faster and a man who'd ridden that way told him it was just a terrible sensation—just like falling."

"Oh, that part's stuff and nonsense. When I was coming back from Rochester the turnpike runs alongside the car tracks for a ways and the steam cars came roaring along just when I got there. They were ringing their bell and whooping it up with their steam whistle and tearing along hell for leather, so I spurred up Annie and we kept right along with them for a mile with the passengers waving out the windows and the pilot pouring steam into his engine for all he was worth. Annie and I was going just as fast as the steam cars and it certainly wasn't any terrible sensation. That part's just stuff and nonsense, but when you're riding a horse there's no danger of running off a track or having a concussion with another horse."

"Well, that's only what the man told Pastor Rucker."

"That," said Father, "don't have anything to do with canalling. But these big and almighty proud railroad companies *do* have something to do with the case. They think they're lords of all creation and can do what they please. But you take canalboats and they're run by little fellows and the little fellows got to keep reasonable honest and careful on account of how much competition there is. Give a canalboat a bad reputation and it ain't going to get much business. The West is building up all the time and there's going to be more and more business taking stuff out to the settlers and bringing grain and tobacco and all east from the West. That's just as plain as the nose on Roger Putnam's face and the railroads aren't going to take that business away from the canal, either."

Mother slipped her china darning egg into the toe of

one of Father's woolen socks and squinted her eyes as she threaded the darning needle. "That's what you think now," she said.

"That's what I *know* now."

"That's what you *knew* when you put fifty dollars in the perpetual motion machine."

"All right," said Father, "bring that up again. But, by holy dang, I still think that machine might work if he had enough money to build the tower higher."

Mother sighed. "Well," she said, "I suppose there's no stopping you."

Father grinned. "You're right that time," he said. "I'm going to get the *Samuel W. Reed* and try her out. Then if I don't like canalboating I can always sell it again. Probably make a good profit too. Business is going to pick up and canalboats will go up in price."

He rose from his chair, stretched and padded over to the cupboard in his stocking feet. Then he lifted his earthen jug from the bottom shelf, drew the cork, swung the jug across his biceps and took a pull. "Whooey!" he breathed. "That's good spirits, indeed."

Father's canalboat was a small one—not more than fifty feet in length. It was a faded yellow canalboat— faded and smeared yellow with rusty black stripings. But before navigation opened Father went up to Rochester and repainted it brilliant red and yellow. The hull was a flaming scarlet and the cabin yellower than a lemon. Then he brought the boat down to Palmyra and we got ready for the season.

It was all very exciting, particularly exciting to me because I was to learn to drive the tow horses and Alan was to learn to steer. Prospects for spring and summer and early fall were gorgeous because we might take cargoes to Buffalo and Albany and perhaps down the Hudson River clear to New York City.

Mother opposed Father taking us boys on as crew

even more violently than she had opposed his buying the boat in the first place.

"Jack Macdougall," she said, "maybe you want your sons to become rough characters and even criminals, but I think I've got something to say about that. You know what sort of folks are on that canal. Think of the things those boys may see and hear. Think of the temptations you're throwing in the path of your own flesh and blood."

"Well, now," drawled Father, "those boys have got to learn sooner or later that the world ain't a Sunday school. If they're bright they know that pretty well already. The sooner they find out about rottenness and crime the sooner they'll be able to look out for it."

"Or the sooner they get mixed up in it."

"Maybe—if they're not the right stock. If a cub's a natural-born crook and liar, he'll be a crook and liar no matter whether he was raised in a hothouse and never heard of thieving and lying. Anyhow, that's the way I look at it. You can't keep a boy or girl nice and innocent all their life by just pretending the world is all nice and lovely. Jeepers! Look at that Rhone girl. Big, overgrown lunk of a girl that thought babies grew on bushes until she had one coming herself. Knowing about things never hurt any cub. Most of 'em stumble into trouble because they don't know how to watch out for trouble."

"I suppose," said Mother, "you'd like to take little Eliza into taverns and other low places so's she'll learn how rotten men are."

"Might do her good. But I ain't trying to say about her. I'm willing you should bring up Eliza, except I'm going to have something to say if I don't think you're doing right. But I'm going to run those boys and that's all there is to it. And I'm going to take 'em on the canal-boat."

Mother sighed and shook her head sadly.

Father had a good general knowledge of canal pro-
cedure, but for our first voyage he hired an old canaller
named Johnny Wormworth to give us pointers.

Johnny first taught me to drive. Two of our work
horses, Bonnie and Alex, were hitched tandem to a
whiffletree and the whiffletree was hooked to a heavy
towrope about 175 feet long. I was to ride Bonnie in
the rear and drive Alex, while Father or Alan sat at the
helm holding the boat in the middle of the canal.

It was all very easy except when we met another boat
and, on our first voyage, being westbound or "upstream,"
even that was comparatively easy because we had the
right of way. Under the Erie Canal law, the eastbound
or "downstream" driver must pull over to the outside
of the towpath and stop. His boat, drifting on its course,
was steered to the far side of the canal. The towrope,
slackening as the boat drifted, would sink to the bottom
of the canal, allowing the westbound boat to pass freely
over as it steered toward the towpath. The eastbound
towrope would be lying slack across the towpath and
the westbound horses would step over it as they passed
between the eastbound horses and the boats.

From Canandaigua we carried over a small cargo of
twenty or so barrels of wood ashes consigned to a Rochester soap factory and a few hundredweight of potatoes
and buckwheat for Buffalo, but Father was hopeful of
picking up more freight en route.

V

We started on a fine spring morning with the sun glistening on the dew-spangled grass and bushes and with a
light fog hanging white in the swales. The night before
we spent in the close, musty little cabin of the *Samuel
W. Reed* and, what with the strangeness and excitement,

I had slept but little. Consequently, I was in that odd, drowsy state wherein the world seems glamorous and dreamy and still uncommonly real.

Spring frogs were creaking in the marshy spots and birds were twittering in the thickets. Bonnie and Alex kept talking to each other with blubbery sighs. Their hoofs thump-thumped in rhythm on the hard-packed towpath, and in my nostrils was the strong smell of horse and the wet, fishy smell of the canal. I was very happy, for I was bound for new places and I was filling an important niche in the world. I was practically a man now, and only ten years old.

Father at the steering sweep also was happy. Presently he began to sing dolorously:

> "Old Grimes is dead, that good old man,
>   We'll never see him more;
> But he has left a son behind,
>   Who bears the name he bore.
> Old Grimes, he had a yaller dog,
>   His tail was red as fire;
> He bark-ed up a mullen stalk
>   And treed an antymire."

Our boat was small, our cargo light and our horses fresh. So, despite a crew of novices, the *Samuel W. Reed* was making great speed—for a canalboat. To show their high spirits, Bonnie and Alex broke into a trot. Delightedly, I looked back and saw the boat throwing up a splendid swell from her blunt bow. Then I saw Johnny Wormworth running forward, waving his arms and yelling.

"Whoa, Alex! Whoa, Bonnie!" I called, and the boat slid in toward the bank. Johnny plainly was excited and was yanking his whiskers with his left hand.

"Great holy jeepers, what ails you?" Johnny shouted.

"What you mean?" I yelled, chagrined.

"Well, you look a little out with those hosses. You'll get us in no end of trouble, does an inspector see you. Hold them hosses down to a walk before you get us all in the calaboose."

"Keep those horses at a walk," ordered Father.

"Yes, sir," I said.

"Hi, stinktybump," yelled Alan, "hold them hosses to a walk."

"Giddap," I said, and clucked my tongue at the horses.

We had been overhauling a big black and red boat. Now, despite my holding our horses down, we still were gaining on it, for Bonnie and Alex were fast walkers and the big boat was moving very slowly.

After an hour we were close behind the big boat. It bore the name *Birdie Fuller, Schenectady* in a fancy gilt scroll on its bulky stern. The three men on deck paid no attention to our approach, made no move to pull over and allow us to pass.

The horses and I were opposite the *Birdie Fuller* amidships when Johnny Wormworth blew on his brass trumpet for a passing. The men ignored him. Johnny blew another blast and the man at the steering sweep waved his hand back with an imperious gesture.

"Stay back where you belong, you dirty slut," he yelled.

Father's bellow could have been heard a mile. "Take this tiller, Wormworth," he shouted. Then to me: "Clint, whip up those horses. Bump the back of their God-damn boat. I'll show 'em if they're running this canal."

I whipped up Bonnie and Alex, who gladly went into a trot again. And, sitting sideways on Bonnie, I saw the bullhead of the prow of the little *Samuel W. Reed* bang into the glossy stern of the big boat.

Two men of the *Fuller's* deck crew came running aft just as Father leaped from our bow to their stern, seized the helmsman by the scruff of the neck, jerked him from

the steering sweep and threw him spinning ten feet away.
The two deck hands were burly fellows and they rushed
upon Father together.

But as they rushed, so did Father. A swinging blow,
lightning fast, knocked one of the deck hands clear over
the rail and he splashed loudly into the canal. The other
ducked under a swing and grappled, but Father's knee
came up viciously and laid him cold.

I had stopped our horses. Their driver, a long-legged
boy whose blue jeans were tucked into his boots, had
stopped their three mules and our boat was drifting
back, away from the *Fuller*.

Father grabbed the *Fuller's* bewildered helmsman by
the front of his jacket. "Now," he roared, "will you pull
this boat over and let us by?" He cuffed the man's jaw
with his open hand. "Or do I lay you out and pull it
over for you?"

I couldn't hear what the man said, but Father let him
go, took up a boat hook and fished the one man out of
the canal.

"Hey, there, Clint," yelled Johnny Wormworth, "pull
up so's your papa can come back home."

"Giddap, there, you Alex. Giddap, Bonnie," I com-
manded, shaking the lines over Alex's back.

We pulled the *Samuel W. Reed* up while Johnny
steered close and Father jumped back. The *Fuller* helmsman, looking fearfully back, steered for the far bank.
The one deck hand was lying doubled up, clutching
himself with his arms. The wet one, whom Father had
fished up with the boat hook, was leaning against the
rail, holding his jaw. As we passed, Johnny Wormworth
blew a derisive blast on his trumpet, but the *Birdie Fuller*
crew didn't even look at us. The long-legged driver,
however, stared at me as I drove Bonnie and Alex past
his mules. Then he cleared his throat loudly and spat
into the towpath.

At Rochester we unloaded our barrels of ashes, but Father was unable to find additional cargo for Buffalo. However, we pushed off the following morning as he believed we could make up for our scant initial cargo with a big eastbound load. We pushed off for Buffalo, crossing the Genesee River on an amazing aqueduct, where the canal actually went across the river on a bridge.

Canalling had lost its glamour for me long before we touched Lockport. I had been riding long hours without a saddle and my backsides had blistered. Then the blisters broke and scabbed over.

Alan spelled me a few hours each day, but not enough to allow my sores to heal, and the night before we reached Lockport I was miserable, indeed. I was sick of Father's cooking, which was oatmeal and tea and stewed dried apples for breakfast, and for dinner and supper, invariably, fried salt pork, boiled beans, fried potatoes and stewed dried apples. I was homesick and weary and sore and I didn't like the way the cabin smelled after we went to bed, for the low-roofed, dank cubbyhole retained the stale odors of cooking and of Johnny Wormworth's pipe.

Father caught me crying on my hard bunk and pulled me out of bed. "What you whimpering about?" he demanded.

"My behind's so sore can't lay on my back."

"Lay on your belly then."

"I don't feel good. I want to go home."

"No Macdougall is a blubberer," Father said. "Reason you're sore is because you're soft. The way to cure that is to ride horseback and get toughened up. Now you dry up and be a man."

At Lockport there was a jam in the canal. Something had gone wrong with one of the five locks and scores of boats were stacked up both below and above.

It was a colorful sight in the gorge where we were resting. Our own yellow and scarlet *Samuel W. Reed* actually seemed drab beside some of the ring-streaked and striped craft that glittered with gilt and enamel.

Most of the canallers were taking the delay good-humoredly and there was a good deal of visiting from one boat to another. There was a fiddler on one boat and when he began to saw out "Old Dan Tucker" he presently was joined by a banjo player who wore a huge coppery beard. They attracted two more with a jews'-harp and a paper-covered comb.

At the sound of the music cooks began to come out of the cabins, hurriedly tying on sunbonnets. Some of them began dancing with their boat captains on deck and the older and fatter ones sat smiling and knitting in rocking chairs. Jugs were passed, sometimes from one boat to another, and there was considerable banter passed with the jugs—especially between the men and the cooks.

"Hey, Mary," one canaller called, "when you coming over and get your red drawers?"

"You're not so cute," another yelled. "Mary don't wear no drawers, red or otherwise."

And the cook shoved back her sunbonnet and shrilled out, "Shut your big mouths, both you stinking sons of bitches."

There was a wooden ramp running up the side of the rock-walled cliff where we upstream drivers led our horses and mules to the west end of the locks and down which the eastbound drivers led their horses and mules to the lower end.

I suppose the ramp was perfectly secure, but I was fearful as I led Bonnie and Alex up the way. Their hoofs made a hollow clumping on the boards which echoed a hollow feeling in my middle.

I was about halfway up when there was a great commotion on the locks. The locktenders had repaired whatever was broken and they were working frantically amid shouts and cheers to clear the jam. Boats were being cleared from one lock to another with surprising speed. One would be taken in from above, the water would gush through the spillway to the lower lock and the boat would drop like a boy sliding down a tree. The gates would open and the crew would pole their craft out while the next upstream boat would be poled into the locks.

Beyond the upper lock there was an open lot or common with hitching racks and here the drivers congregated in the rank-smelling mud to brag and lie and chew tobacco and often to fight.

Most of the drivers were boys, fourteen to eighteen years old, and most of them were dirty and ragged and extremely tough. Their conversation was at least two-fifths profanity and obscenity.

They paid no attention to me, for I was a stranger and the smallest of the group and no doubt unworthy of their notice. I listened to their loudmouthed conversation with some awe, for much of it was about this girl in Rochester and that girl in Tonawanda, but a great deal of their talk was obscure to me because I was unfamiliar with the terminology of vice.

Every now and then a boat would be poled out of the upper lock and someone would yell, "*Red Angel* cleared!" or "*Jenny Bledsoe* cleared!" and the driver of the *Red Angel* or the *Jenny Bledsoe* would hurriedly and profanely get his horses from the hitching rack, leap on one and trot down to the towpath to make his hitch and resume his journey toward Tonawanda and Buffalo.

I had been on the lot for nearly half an hour before one of the boys spoke to me. He was about fourteen and his long, black, greasy hair hung clear over his wampus collar in back. He looked at me with narrowed, unfriendly eyes. "What you doing here, squirt?" he said. "You ain't a driver."

"I am so a driver," I said.

The youth turned his head. "Hey, bullies," he called, "see what says it's a driver."

A taller youth came up grinning. While his body was thin, his cheeks were round and there were yellow streaks of tobacco stain from the corners of his small mouth.

"What boat *you* driving?" he demanded.

"The *Samuel W. Reed.*"

"Never heard of it," said the first boy. "Must be one son of a bitch of a boat."

"It's a *good* boat," I declared.

A group of boys gathered around, most of them grinning.

"Oh," said the taller youth, "he says it's a God-damn good boat. Are you a God-damn good driver?"

"Well," I said, "I guess I aint a God-damn good driver yet. But I will be before long."

The tall boy grinned and seemed quite friendly then. "That's the way to talk," he said. "But you know you got lots to learn yet, don't you?"

"Yes," I said, "I know I got lots to learn."

"Now that's fine and dandy." He nodded his head seriously. "When a cub thinks he knows it all, to the hell with him. But I say when a cub wants to learn we should ought to help him. We always like to help new driver boys and learn 'em something and make men out of 'em. Ain't that so?"

"God-damn truth," said the first boy.

"Now, sonny," said the tall youth, "I'll tell you what. You open your mouth and shut your eyes and I'll give you something to make you wise."

He was chewing tobacco, so I assumed he planned to put some fine-cut tobacco in my mouth. I had never tasted tobacco, but the curlicues of fine cut looked good and I was not averse to experimenting. I shut my eyes and opened my mouth.

At once a hand clapped over my mouth and a horrible, slimy, cold mass squirmed over my tongue. I spat furiously and opened my eyes to see three or four fat angleworms fall wriggling from my mouth to the mud. I retched and drooled and spat while the group of drivers screamed with delight.

With tears of joy running down his dirty cheeks the tall boy slapped me on the back. "Now're you wiser?" he howled. "Now're you wiser?"

I pulled away from him in rage and then, getting control of my sickness, I kicked him in the belly as hard as I could kick. The big boy shrieked and fell on his face in the mud, clutching himself with both hands.

I started to run but two other boys seized me. They started to cuff my ears. Then a very thin, middle-aged man in a long-tailed coat and a dun beaver hat came on a loose-jointed gallop through the mud. "Here, there," he shouted in a squeaky voice. "What on earth's going on here?"

One of my assailants turned to the newcomer. "This whelp needs a licking, deacon," he said. "This smart cub gave Eddie the boot in the belly."

The deacon looked at the tall youth, who now was sitting up with mud smeared on his face, holding his middle and blubbering.

"Did this boy kick you?" the deacon asked.

"He's near killed me, that's what he did."

The deacon looked at me sternly and then took me by the ear. "Did you kick this boy?" he demanded.

"Yes, sir," I said, "I kicked him because—"

"I ain't interested in why," he interrupted. "There's no reason under the sun for kicking another boy like

that. Don't you know you could kill him kicking him
there?"

"Had it coming to him," I asserted.

"Had it coming to him! The very idea. Who are you
and what're you doing on this horse lot?" He gave my
ear a yank.

"Let go my ear. Ow! I'm with my horses and I'm
waiting for my father with our boat."

"What's your boat?"

"The *Samuel W. Reed*. Ow! Let go my ear."

The boys were laughing and circling around us.

"You come with me," said the deacon. He led me by
the ear to the head of the locks just as Father and Johnny
Wormworth were poling the *Samuel W. Reed* out. The
red and yellow craft looked beautiful, indeed, at the
moment.

A lounger who was sitting on the bank whittling a
stick bellowed out, "Hosses for the *Samuel W. Reed!*"

Father sighted us as they poled the boat up by the
towpath.

"Where in tarnation's the horses?" he shouted at me.
"Look alive there."

"Make him let go my ear," I called.

"You shikepoke," yelled Father, "let go that boy's
ear this instant."

"You his father?"

"I'm his father and you let go his ear."

The deacon let go my ear, which felt as if it had been
pulled three inches out of shape. "I want," he squeaked,
"to make sure you give him punishment or I'll attend
to him myself."

Father leaped to the bank. "Who in hell you think
you are?" he shouted, striding up to the deacon.

The deacon stood up very straight. "I," he said, "am
Deacon Throckmorton and it's my business to look after
the souls of these poor boys who work on the canal."

The deacon was tall as he stood there, but Father was half a head taller and looked almost twice as broad.

"You lay hands on my boy again and you'll be sick of your job, souls or no souls," said Father. "If this boy needs a licking I'm the one that'll give it to him and I'll decide whether he needs it. Understand me?" He turned to me. "Clint, what deviltry you been up to?"

"He kicked another boy in the belly," said the deacon.

"Why for?"

"He was twice as big as me," I said, "and he put a handful of fishworms in my mouth."

Father stared at me. "Fishworms in your mouth! Well, by holy jeepers, what you standing around with your mouth open for? Well, by holy jeepers!"

"I thought," I said, "he was going to give me something nice. I thought he had something good and he was about fifteen years old and he said for me to open my mouth and shut my eyes and he put fishworms in it."

Father roared with laughter and slapped his thighs. "Well, I swanney," he said, "if you don't know more than open your mouth and shut your eyes to a strange canal boy you deserve to get fishworms put in your mouth. And a big boy mean enough to put fishworms in a ten-year-old's mouth deserves to get his belly kicked. So I calculate everything's square."

Father turned to the deacon. "Now, sir," he said, "you got no license to lay hands on my boy at any time. You understand? I should ought to pull your ears and let you find out how it feels."

"Aren't you going to punish that boy?"

"I am not. And you even touch my son again and I'll tie you up in such a knot folks will think you're a whoofle. Now you get out of here and mind your own business—if you got any."

Deacon Throckmorton shook his head sorrowfully. The driver boys had retreated to the horse lot.

"Sir," said the deacon, "you'd better learn to control your tongue. I am doing the Lord's work and I can tell you that you've got an accounting to make with the Lord before very long."

"Let me worry about that," said Father. "Now you begone."

Deacon Throckmorton, muttering to himself, ambled loose-jointedly away. Then Father went with me to the horse lot after Bonnie and Alex. The loafing driver boys stared at us, but had nothing to say.

Father *did* make a profit on the season's canalboating before the coming of ice forced us to tie up the *Samuel W. Reed* for the winter and go back to the farm. And before the season was over Father also had several rousing rough-and-tumble fights, none of which he lost.

The most spectacular of these battles came on a hot midsummer day as we were plugging along slowly east past Long Swamp. The mosquitoes were especially bad along there and I had a handkerchief tucked under my hat and hanging down behind to protect my neck while I rode.

Father was steering and Alan was lying in the scant shade of the cabin with his hat over his face to protect it from the bloodthirsty swarms.

We were meeting a long blue boat named the *Thomas Moriarity*, so I pulled Bonnie and Alex to the outside of the towpath and stopped while Father steered to the south bank for the passing.

Three men were sitting on the *Moriarity's* deck with a jug between them. They were plainly Irish and one tall, redheaded fellow stood up as the boats came close. He bowed exaggeratedly and spoke with a thick brogue. "A fine day to you, sir." The other two laughed loudly.

At that moment their boat was just passing over our towline and I felt our tugs tighten out and then fall suddenly limp. Father let out a roar of rage and started running along our deck.

I knew then what had happened. Some crews fitted sharp scythe blades to the keels of their boats in such a manner that the blade ordinarily rode snug against the bottom, but could be released to hang straight down. When passing an enemy or some other crew they believed they could bully, they would lower the scythe blade and cut the other towrope.

In this case the half-drunk Irishers saw our crew was only one man and a half-grown boy and had severed our line for sport. They found more than they expected.

Father leaped to their boat, grabbed the first two men by their collars and banged their heads together so hard it sounded like a handclap to me five or six rods away. Both were limp and senseless when he dropped them to the deck, but the big red-haired fellow sprang upon Father before he could turn to meet him and the impact sent them both sprawling over the low blue rail. They made a great splash and in a moment the dirty water was white with their furious threshings. Water was flying so I couldn't see what was happening, but half a dozen times both Father and the big Irisher went clear out of sight.

Alan dove over the *Samuel W. Reed's* rail and swam toward the fight, but Father's deep voice called, "Alan, you keep out of this—you hear me!" So Alan, treading water, kept away.

A moment later the two men parted and Father swam on his side to the *Moriarity* and hauled himself dripping to the rail. The Irisher was swimming weakly behind and when Father was aboard he put down his hand and hauled his adversary up.

"Now, you skunk," said Father, "I'm taking your tow-rope. You can stay here and try to splice the one you cut."

One of the Irishers whose heads had been bumped was standing up now. "You'll do no such dam thing, be God," he said.

"You want more, do you?" cried Father, and swiftly smote the objector, sending him clumping to the deck. "You got any objections?" he demanded of the big fellow. The big Irisher shook his head and sat down.

Father went to the bow of their boat and unhooked their towline.

"Clint," he called to me, "unhitch from your whiffletree and hitch to their rope."

I was reluctant to obey because I couldn't tell what reception their driver would give me, but I knew it was far safer to face that red-haired boy of twelve or thirteen than it would be to argue with Father at that moment. So I rode up to the boy very unhappy in my apprehension.

His freckled face spread with a grin. "Served 'em damn well right," he said. "Wish he'd give my uncle a good bat for me."

So we traded towropes and we of the *Samuel W. Reed* plodded on east leaving the *Thomas Moriarity* pulled up to the grass-grown bank with its battered crew disconsolately surveying the towrope they had cut. Splicing a towrope was a disagreeable task.

VI

That fall Abraham Lincoln was elected President of the United States on the Republican party's slogan, "Vote yourself a farm." He received only forty per cent of the popular vote and Congress remained Democratic.

For years the government had been in control of the Southern Democrats. The Dred Scott decision and virtually every other action had been in favor of the Southern states.

Lincoln was no abolitionist, but he was feared as an abolitionist in the South, and he was elected by abolitionist support. So a little more than a month after election South Carolina voted to secede from the Union because of the federal government's "outrageous usurpations of power and aggressions on the state's rights."

Before Lincoln was inaugurated five more states voted to secede. A month following inauguration the Civil War was on.

The day after Lincoln called for 75,000 volunteers to "put down the rebellion" Father and I went to Jake Lownes's blacksmith shop to get Bonnie shod. Father had just returned from Rochester where he had ridden to dicker on some canal business and that always meant he was full of a discussion with his old friend, Father Joe Kennedy. Father was no Catholic and, as a matter of fact, he had little to do with any religion, but he had great respect for the priest's views on political affairs.

"Smartest dang man I ever saw," he would say, "until he gets talking religion and there he's blind. Knows everything and agrees with me perfect until he gets on a tangent on virgin births and such sluff talk. If he wasn't a priest that man should ought to be president."

Aunt Christine used to say that for a week after Father got back from a trip to Rochester it would be the "papist priest" talking instead of Father.

On this day in Jake Lownes's blacksmith shop there was Tom Willson, whose farm was over toward Bristol, and also old Roger Putnam, whose whisky jug Alan had broken.

"Old Abe'll learn them Southerners a thing or two," observed Put. "I'm glad this war has come and now, by gol, they can settle things once and for all. About a month and it'll all be over, I calculate."

"Put," said Father, "you're a lunatic—a God-damn lunatic."

Old Put bristled. "What you mean, Jack Macdougall?" he demanded.

"Mean what I say. This war's the worst thing could happen to the United States. May mean the end of the nation. Over in a month! By grab, those folks down south feel this business just as strong and probably stronger than the Northerners do. They ain't going to be licked easy. This war will run a year at least and maybe several years."

Jake Lownes plunged a hot horseshoe into a tub of water and sizzling steam rose in the murk. "Jack," he said, "you ain't for the South, are you?"

"I'm against both sides," said Father. "I'm against both sides of politicians that got us into this thing. I'm against the war and killing thousands of good men because some ignorant old women up here are feeling sorry for the niggers down south. To hear 'em talk you'd think a Southerner beats a nigger to death just for the fun of it."

"Well," said Jake, "I think things is pretty bad down there on the plantations."

Father grinned. "Jake," he said, "if you made your living working horses and horses cost a thousand dollars a head, would you be crazy enough to beat horses to death?"

"I ain't a Southerner," said Jake.

"Southerners are folks. Of course there are mean ones the same as everywhere, but no matter how mean a Southerner might be, he's going to think twice before he works a nigger to death or beats one to death or starves one to death when it's going to cost him a thousand dollars. If he's any kind of a businessman at all, he's going to try and keep those darkies he owns in good shape so's they can do good work. Ain't ever been down in New York, have you, Jake?"

"No."

"Well, you should ought to go down to New York City and see the way some of those factory-working Irishers and Italians live. Lots of them will go to this war and get shot trying to free nigger slaves when the niggers are a lot better off than themselves. In those factories they work twelve hours a day in heat that'd kill a cockroach and make just enough to live in crowded-up hovels with half enough to eat of rotten food for their children and they wear rags and die of consumption and summer complaint in droves.

"It don't make any difference to the factory owners whether their workers die or their workers' families die. They don't own 'em. And there's always plenty more wanting jobs.

"But down south when a nigger baby dies the old master loses money."

"It ain't right to sell human beings like hogs," said Putnam. "It ain't right to snatch a baby from its mother's breast and sell it down the river."

Father ignored him. "There's a lot more to this war than we hear about," he said.

Jake Lownes lifted Bonnie's off hind hoof and gripped it between his leather-aproned knees. Then he went to shaping it up for the shoe with a long rasp file. He didn't say anything.

"Trouble is," went on Father, "us common folks never know what's going on. One bunch of politicians get jealous of another bunch of politicians and both of 'em lie like thieves to try and make the voters line up on their side.

"The South is jealous of the North because the North has got most of the money in the country. All the factories in the North try to get their politicians to slap on a high tariff to protect the stuff they make from competition of factories in Europe. They get a high tariff and they can charge us anything they want to charge for the things they make.

"It's just the other way around down south. Down there it's all farming mostly of cotton and tobacco and corn. They want to buy their factory goods as cheap as they can, of course, and they know a high tariff will raise prices. And they know if we slap on high tariffs the countries in Europe will come right back and slap tariffs on cotton and tobacco and make it tougher to sell their raw stuff over there."

"You better look a little out, Jack Macdougall," said old Put. "You're talking treason and you better look a little out before they throw you in jail."

"Put," said Father wearily, "you ain't got brains enough to pour swamp water out of a boot even if directions was on the heel. If you didn't open your mouth so much, you wouldn't advertise it so much."

"I calculate," said Put, "my mouth won't ever get me in jail."

"Listen," said Father, "slavery ain't what's causing this war—not by a jugful. But, by grab, the Southern Democrats have been holding the upper hand in Washington and they don't want to lose it. They try to get new slave states out west and the Free Soilers try to get more free states out west so's they can have more senators and put over their high tariff. The Free-Soilers have been winning out and that's the big thing that's causing this war. This slavery talk is all hogwash to get good American boys up north wrought up so's they'll go down south and shoot other good American boys and the whole thing is a damn crime and disgrace."

Jake Lownes let down Bonnie's hoof. He slapped his hard left palm with the rasp. "Jack," he said, "there may be some little truth in what you're talking about. But you're just dodging the fact that tariff and slavery and all didn't cause Mr. Lincoln to call for volunteers. The south has started a war to bust up this Union that our forefathers died to make and it's up to patriotic Americans to stop 'em. First place the Southern states pull out of the Union when they've got no legal right to. That was enough itself. But then without a cause in the world they open fire on Fort Sumter. They fire on the American flag, they capture an American fort. You mean to say, Jack, you think we can overlook that? Well, by God, we can't. And I honor Abe Lincoln for calling for soldiers to put down the rebellion and I'm going to join up myself if they'll take me." Jake Lownes whacked the anvil with his rasp.

"Hurray for you, Jake," said old Put. "I fit at Lundy's Lane myself and I'd jine up again if I was ten-fifteen years younger."

Father grinned. "That's all right," he said. "If they'd take old kadates like Put to fight the war, I wouldn't have any kick. And Jake Lownes is old enough to know what he's doing, so if he wants to go to war it's his own business. When a man gets past thirty, if he don't know enough to not be bumfoozled by politicians' talk, why, it's his own lookout.

"What upsets my belly is that parade in Canandaigua with fifes and drums and flags turning young boys' heads so they rush in and enlist without knowing what it's all about."

"You sure your own boy won't be enlisting, Mac?" asked Tom Willson.

Father looked at me and grinned. "I'm glad my boys ain't old enough," he said.

"Don't mean that cub," said Willson. "What about that big boy?"

"Alan? He's only sixteen. He couldn't get in."

"Big as most men," observed Willson.

"He won't try to go," said Father. "He's got too much sense." But his face turned serious. "We better let the South secede and form another country if they want to," he said. "We better forget all about Fort Sumter than throw this country into a civil war.

"In the first place, Abe Lincoln's got no right to call for volunteers that way. That's the job of Congress. He's taking it on himself to declare a war because the Democratic majority in Congress maybe wouldn't vote for it. Abe Lincoln's guilty of a high crime, whether it was just ignorance on his part or not, and Congress should ought to meet immediately and impeach Abe Lincoln and stop this enlisting."

"And you think they'll do that?" asked Willson sarcastically.

"No, I don't think they will. But they should ought to."

"Jack," said Jake Lownes, "I wouldn't talk that kind of slang in front of folks that don't know you."

"It's not slang talk and I'll talk it where I damn please," asserted Father. "I'm against this war. I'd like to help hang Abe Lincoln and Jeff Davis and Bill Yancey and a few others. It should ought to have been done last fall."

"Macdougall," shrilled old Put in a quivering voice, "when they get out the tar kettle for you, I got an old feather bed I'm going to donate for a damn good cause— even if I *am* too old to fight."

Father took Bonnie's halter shank and led her to the broad door of the blacksmith shop. Then he turned and laughed. "Generally," he said, "it's kadates too old to fight that's the most bloodthirsty for a war."

The next morning when I awoke in the loft Alan was not in his bed and his bed had not been slept in. There was a note on the table downstairs. It read:

"Dear Father and Mother:—Frank Lucas and I have gone to enlist in the army. I know Father won't understand, but I don't think I could ever hold up my head again if I don't go in this war. It looks like to me the holiest war ever fought —to free men and women and children who are held in slavery because their skins aren't white. I can't help it, but that's the way I feel and I can't do anything but enlist to save our country. I know Father thinks I am not old enough to know my own mind, but I do know my own mind and this is what I have got to do. The war is not going to last long so do not worry. There will be just about one good battle and then the rebels will see their mistake. I will be back home by the middle of summer to help Father with the canalboat, so don't worry.

Your loving son, Alan."

Mother was crying. "Can't you get him back? Can't you?" she sobbed to Father. "He ain't old enough to join the army."

Father paced back and forth across the room. "Must have lied about his age," he said. "Oh, holy jeepers, why didn't the boy talk to me about it? Why didn't he just come to me reasonable and talk to me and I could have explained it to him reasonable?"

"They can't hold a young boy like that," said Mother. "Jack, can't you get him back?"

"Maybe," said Father. "Yes, I suppose I probably could get his discharge on account he must have lied about his age."

Bulges of muscle stood out on his lean, brown jaws. "But, wife, it would ruin the boy to bring him back now. It would be branding him a liar public. It'd be a terrible disgrace for a boy to have his father come and drag him out of the army. He'd never get over it."

"It'd be better than to have him get shot."

Father shook his head. "That's the trouble. I know that boy and I know it'd ruin him to have us interfere now. He ain't a man yet, but he's elected to be a man and we can't do a thing about it. Wife, I never had anything hurt me so bad in my life. But we just got to let him go and hope for the best."

VII

Two weeks passed with no word from Alan. Then there came a letter from a camp down in Maryland. He was a private in Company B of the 32nd New York Volunteers. Frank Lucas was with him and they were enjoying the business of learning to be soldiers. Camp life was good sport, drilling was good sport, and chasing the rebels back into their holes in a couple more weeks would be better sport.

By this time the war fever had swept the country and there was little friendliness toward Father when he went to Bristol or Naples. There were no more gatherings at Jake Lownes's blacksmith shop because Jake had joined the army and the shop was closed.

It was time to get the canalboat running, but Father was apathetic about canalling, now that Alan was gone. He also was apathetic about getting the spring work under way on the farm.

Late one afternoon I drove to Randall's store in Bristol with Father for some supplies. As we entered the store the group huddled around the cold round-bellied stove became oddly silent. Randall himself, usually voluble, looked at Father darkly as he filled the orders and said nothing until Father asked for a pound of gunpowder.

"Pound of *gunpowder*, eh?" sneered white-bearded Randall.

"Pound of gunpowder," said Father evenly.

The group at the stove stared in silence. Old Roger Putnam spat fluently into the sawdust box.

Father paid Randall. "You take the kerosene can, Clinton," he said, picking up his packages.

I lifted the greasy gallon can and pushed the potato more firmly on the spout. We started from the store and then Father turned back. "Any mail for us, Randall?" he asked.

"Yep, there's a letter for ye," Randall admitted grudgingly. He pawed at his stringy whiskers and walked hump-shouldered and loose-jointed behind the post-office grille. Then he came out with a worn, heavy envelope and handed it to Father without a word. Father took it without a word and put it in his side pocket.

"Is it from Alan?" I asked as we walked from the store.

"No. From Cousin Dave."

"He's way out west?"

"Yes. Nebrasky."

"Wild Indians out there, aren't they?"

Father put his bundles in the back of the buggy. "Yes, I guess there are. But Dave could handle them. Better take the kerosene up front so's it won't slop on things."

We got in the buggy and Father handed me the lines. "You drive and I can read my letter," he said.

So I held the kerosene can between my feet and let old Alex walk down the rutty road while Father ripped open the heavy envelope and began to read. It was a long letter.

Presently he breathed, "Hmm." A little later he said, "Well, I declare." Then he said, "I swanney."

"He say anything about the Indians?" I asked.

"Not yet. I'll read it out loud when we get home."

When Father finally folded the letter and put it back in its envelope, we were in sight of home—a sprawling, weather-beaten frame house with an uneven brick chim-

ney and a lean-to storeroom, bordered with sugar maples
and an immense apple tree in the rear.

"How'd you like to go out to Nebrasky?" Father asked,
looking straight ahead.

"Fine," I said, "but we got to run the *Samuel W.
Reed* and we got to get going pretty soon. You can't run
the *Samuel W. Reed* with both Alan and me gone."

"That's right," said Father and slapped my knee with
his big brown hand.

We unhitched Alex and while Father wheeled the
buggy into the shed I led Alex to the barn, tied him to
his manger next to Bonnie and took off the harness and
hung it carefully on its peg. Then I slapped Alex on the
rump, went out and lifted the kerosene can from the
buggy. Father was standing there with his bundles in his
arms, grinning in a strange way.

We carried the supplies into the lean-to storeroom and
then went through the door to the kitchen where Mother
was taking a pan of fragrant bread from the oven.

"Got a letter from Cousin Dave," announced Father.

"Well," said Mother.

"Very interesting letter," said Father. "Come on in
the other room and I'll read it. Chris and Eliza in
there?"

"Eliza's there. Christine's in *her* room, I calculate."

"Well, call her out. She'll want to hear this. Almighty
interesting."

"Wait until I get this bread out of the pans," Mother
said. Holding the hot pan with a scorched cloth, she
eased the huge loaves out and covered them with a piece
of clean muslin. Then she wiped her red hands on her
apron and followed us into the sitting room.

Eliza, who had Mother's sandy hair, was sitting by the
window with her long legs doubled under her, working
on a sampler. Mother called Aunt Christine, who came
from her room slowly with foreboding in her wide eyes.

"Bad news?" Aunt Christine asked.

"No," said Father. "Just a letter from Cousin Dave. Interesting letter and I thought you should ought to hear it."

"Oh." Aunt Christine sat down slowly and smoothed her voluminous petticoats.

Father, Mother, Aunt Christine, Eliza and I were there. That was our whole family now, for Grandfather Macdougall had died of lung fever the winter before.

Father struck a lucifer match and lit our shiny glass kerosene lamp and then ceremoniously drew the letter out.

"It's written," he said, "from Rock Creek, Nebrasky Territory, and it says:

" 'Dear Jack:—I've been contemplating an epistle to you for a long time, but the recent turn of events impels me to delay no longer.

" 'I know what your feelings are on the recent political developments as well as if we had had opportunity to discuss it at length.'

"You see," said Father, looking up from the letter, "this was written on April thirteenth and he didn't know Fort Sumter was fired on yet."

"The thirteenth is a bad day to write any *important* letter," said Aunt Christine.

"Poppycock," said Father. "Well, Dave goes on to say: 'I am afraid my pen has not the power to describe this Promised Land so you can visualize it as it is. Imagine a country gently rolling, just enough for proper drainage, mile after mile of the richest, blackest soil you ever saw without a stone to block your plow and all covered with lush green grass and wildflowers. No trees to clear, and no trees at all except the groves of forest and wild fruit trees along the streams.

" 'You, Jack, have never seen soil that could approach

this in richness. There is a story here which perhaps may be apochryphal, but still illustrates the point. It seems a Nebraska farmer was digging postholes when he was called away and he carelessly left his posthole auger in the hole. He did not return to his task until the following morning and then found himself unable to pull the auger from the black soil. Finally he was obliged to hitch a span of oxen to the implement before he could retrieve it. Then he discovered the cause of his trouble. The soil was so rich that the iron auger had actually taken root.' "

"That don't seem possible," said Aunt Christine.

Father laughed. "Dave's a great codder," he said.

Aunt Christine tossed her head and turned down her mouth. "Codding or lying," she said, "if he ain't telling the truth about that, how you going to know *when* to believe him?"

"Pshaw," said Father, "Dave's no liar. He just cods sometimes about things anybody with a lick of sense would know was only codding. Matter of fact, Dave sometimes is a preacher. Preaches out there on the Nebrasky coast."

"Well, that's nice slang talk for a preacher, I must say. Iron taking root and growing."

Father chuckled. "Well, let me get on with this letter. Dave says: 'What I'm getting at is this: There are literally hundreds of thousands of acres of this land yet untouched. It is open to anyone to settle on and acquire by pre-emption. That is, you pick out your hundred and sixty acres, build a house of some sort and then pay the government land office a dollar and a quarter an acre.

" 'Jack, after farming the rock quarries of York State, this country would be paradise to you. Sixty to eighty bushels of corn to the acre is no novelty out here.

" 'As you know, I have been out here two years now and I have done remarkably well. I'm not exactly rich yet, but I certainly am well-to-do. I built a stage station at Rock Creek, which proved profitable and then leased it to the stage company. The first of this month I got a patent on that land and now am selling it to the stage company at an excellent profit. But I have a better farm on the Little Blue River where we are living now and I shall retain this place and farm it.

" 'You may have read of some disturbances on the Kansas border, but that is all over now. Of course there is still some trouble in Kansas, but this territory was settled by a different type of person. You may know something about the fire-eating abolitionists who have carried on campaigns of terrorism in Kansas, but we have had none of that here. Nebraska has been settled largely by men who either have sympathy with the South or by men like you and me who have no sympathy with either faction of troublemakers. Thus far we have had no war excitement and I doubt if it will touch us in the event of actual civil war. War does seem inevitable now, however, and I fear it would last for years, bringing much sorrow to you in York State.

" 'I urge you, Jack, to sell your property there for what you can get and emigrate to this great territory. You will find happiness here, and wealth too. This new country is a great place to raise children; my own are as healthy and brown as Indians and I recently have built a schoolhouse and engaged a fine young teacher who could instruct your younger offspring.

" 'I know you are not very religious yourself, so you would not miss a church. However, I do believe religious instruction is invaluable to the younger folks especially, and I am taking steps to found a church as soon as we can find a good pastor. At present we hold religious services in the school on Sunday and I preach the sermons myself.

" 'Hoping I have convinced you and that I shall hear

from you soon to the effect that you are bringing your family to Nebraska, I am as ever,

" 'Your affectionate cousin,

" 'David.' "

Father looked around at us. "Well," he said, "what you think of that?"

"For land's sake, Jack Macdougall," said Mother.

"What you mean—for land's sake?"

"I mean, you're not thinking for a minute of moving your family out to that wilderness?"

"Why not?"

"Why *not!* Out among the red Indians and ruffians?"

"Dave's no red Indian or ruffian. And there must be *some* other decent folks there. Leastways, they're not war crazy."

"Where is New Brasky?" asked Aunt Christine.

"It ain't New Brasky," said Father. "It's Nebrasky— one word. It's out west, past St. Louis."

"I knew it was bad news before you started to read the letter," said Aunt Christine.

"Well," said Father, "we're going. I've just decided. Going to sell this farm and the sloop and the canalboat."

"Jack Macdougall!" cried Mother. "Don't you think we've got *anything* to say about it?"

"Sarah," said Aunt Christine, "the man's lost his reason. If there ever was a time for you to put your foot down this is it."

Father ignored her. "We're going to get away from this narrow-minded, war-crazy community," he said. "We're going to get away from this stone-patch farm that was worked out before I was born. We're going to a new country where I'll have a chance to amount to something and where Clinton will have a chance, and Alan too—if we ever see him again."

"In the first place," said Mother, "how ever would we get out there?"

"The same way other folks go places—on the steam cars and steamboats and maybe stagecoach part of the way."

Mother shook her head. "You'll never get me on the steam cars," she said.

"Oh, yes, we will. You're a good woman, wife, and a good woman always goes with her husband and children. Clinton wants to go to Nebrasky and so does Eliza, don't you, biddy?"

Eliza smiled. "I think I'd like to travel out west," she said.

"Eliza's place is with her mother," said Mother, "and I'm not going out on the frontier. There's no sense in it."

"Sarah and Eliza can stay with me," said Aunt Christine.

"Where?" asked Father. "Have you got a house someplace?"

Aunt Christine started to cry.

"Jack Macdougall," said Mother, "you can sell that canalboat if you want to and I won't have a word to say. You can sell your sloop if you want to. But you haven't any right to sell the home over our heads. And you haven't any right to take my children out to that God-forsaken place, wherever it is."

"God-forsaken," said Father, "and sixty to eighty bushels of corn to the acre? Come on, Clint, we've got to do the chores. This family is going to Nebrasky together or it ain't going at all. Chris, you got a home with us as long as we have a home. Can't force you to come to Nebrasky with us, but you're welcome. Don't know what you'd do here alone."

"I can manage. Don't worry about me," said Aunt Christine, sniffing.

"We're not going out to that place and that settles it," said Mother.

"Come on, Clint," said Father and we went out to the

barn. Father milked while I threw down some hay for
the horses and mixed a bran mash.

"Think Mother will change her mind?" I asked.

Father didn't pause in sending the streams of frothy
milk into the bucket.

"What do you think?"

"Don't know," I said. "Wish she would."

Father rested the top of his head against old Daisy's
red flank. "Clint," he observed, "women has to be
handled in a curious way. You watch things and keep
your mouth shut. Maybe you'll learn something that'll
help you later."

At supper Father remarked, "Of course there are some
drawbacks to going to a place like Nebrasky."

"You *don't* say." This from Mother.

"Imagine it's pretty hard for a man to get a drink of
oh-be-joyful out there."

Mother looked at him.

"Until a year or so ago they had a law prohibiting
drinking liquor altogether. Even now they say it's pretty
scarce."

Mother didn't say anything.

"Calculate it's all in getting used to it," went on
Father as if he were talking to himself. "Drinking liquor
is kind of a habit. If you're where it is you drink it. If
there ain't any liquor around you don't think of it.
Course it's pleasant to have a snort now and then, but I
suppose there might be things to make up for it. Take
that fine rolling land for two hundred dollars to a
quarter section."

"You wouldn't farm it if you had it," said Mother.

"Wouldn't farm it! Of course I'd farm it. I like farming when there's a chance to raise anything. But, after
all, I admit there might be some hardships for you
women. That is, for a while. It might not be all fun until
we got a house built and everything. Of course you could

stay in the nearest town until we got the house built, but you might not enjoy that either."

"That isn't it at all," said Mother.

"Got to be considered," said Father. "Guess I was too brash without considering everything."

"That's nothing new for you," said Aunt Christine.

"Guess you're right," said Father, looking down at his plate. "This war's just made me sick. Guess I haven't been able to think straight for a while. But I'm getting things untangled now. The war's on now and it can't be helped. Calculate I've been talking too much. Folks around here won't hardly speak to me now, they're so war-crazy. They think I'm a traitor because I was against the war.

"Well, as I say, the war can't be helped now and I might as well forget what I know is the truth. If it was just myself I wouldn't give an inch, but I've got to consider my family. I've had my beliefs and I haven't been afeared to speak my beliefs and I've been making it well-nigh impossible for the children to hold up their heads with other children. It ain't right for Clint and Eliza to hear their father spoke of as a coward. It ain't right for you either, wife. Folks don't come and see us any more. Folks hardly speak to me on the road."

"Guess we can stand that, all right," said Mother, her heavy eyebrows puzzling together.

"No, it ain't right. But, by grab, I've decided I'm going to do the right thing by my family. I'll sell the canalboat and join the army."

"Now what on earth are you talking about?" demanded Mother. "I think the same way you do about the war. What do we care about what these folks say."

"No," said Father, "it's all right for me. Maybe it'd be all right for you too, but it ain't right for the children. I'm going to sell the canalboat and join the army. That money will help you get through and Clint can raise a garden and you can get Johnny Wormworth or somebody to help with the heavy work and butcher the hogs. You can get along."

"Now that's stuff and nonsense," said Mother.

"No such thing. I realize now I haven't thought enough about my family. I've been selfish, downright selfish, with my opinions and now I'm going to atone for it. Because I've been so open about saying how wrong this war is, I've become the same as the lowest criminal in the eyes of these neighbors of ours. Only way I can redeem myself and redeem you is to join the army. I'm going to put the boat up for sale tomorrow."

"Maybe you can't even sell the boat," said Mother.

"Oh, yes, I can. This is going to be the biggest season the canal ever saw. The South is blockading the Mississippi River. Freight is coming east already and piling up. Bet I can get a thousand dollars for the *Samuel W. Reed*—maybe twelve hundred. There's talk there may be a draft to get soldiers for the war and boat captains would be exempt. No trouble at all to sell the boat."

"Well," said Mother, "if boat captains would be exempt, *you* would be exempt. It wouldn't be any different for you than for them."

"Oh, yes, it would too. Those exempt captains have all been hurraying for the war. They've been hurraying for our brave boys in blue to march on Richmond. They've been hurraying to hang Jeff Davis to a sour apple tree—what would have been a good idea if they'd done it six months ago and strung up Abe Lincoln and a dozen others alongside.

"Those exempt captains are all heroes and they'll probably set the *Samuel W. Reed* afire some dark night because I'm for peace. No, by grab, I've got to join the army and go to war because I believe in peace. Them that are all for war can stay at home and be honorable and set fire to peace-loving men's houses and boats."

"You don't think," asked Aunt Christine, "somebody might come and set this house afire?"

"No," said Father. "They won't because I'll be redeemed. I'll be in the army right away."

Mother was pale. "Now that's all slang and you know it. How do you think we could get along here with you in the army? What would we do for a living?"

"Same as Mrs. Jake Lownes. Same as other soldiers' wives."

"Mrs. Lownes is a dressmaker. She can make a living sewing."

"Well, you ain't crippled—either you or Chris. You two can run this farm. You've always said a good living could be made off this place and maybe you're right. Besides, the money from the canalboat will help you out. Lucky thing I bought that boat, wasn't it?"

"Jack, you can't join the army and leave us. What's it matter what people say? You got to think about your family. Suppose you get killed?"

"I *am* thinking about my family. That's why I say I've got to go in the army. And I won't get killed. I'm pretty tough."

"A bombshell or a bullet could kill you just the same as anybody else."

"Well, I'm lucky."

Mother sighed. "Do you think you could sell this place?"

"Why sell it? You got to have someplace to live while I'm in the army."

"I mean if we went to—to Nebrasky."

Father surreptitiously winked at me. "Oh, that," he said. "I suppose we could sell the farm if we were going to move out there. Well, maybe not right away. Might have to put it in an agent's hands and let him hold it until he could get a good price. But it could be sold within a few months. Why? Don't think you could stand

going out there, do you, wife? When you get right down
to it, there's a lot of drawbacks to moving west and there
might even be some few hardships for you."

"I've been thinking it over," said Mother, "and I suppose it would be a good thing for you to get away from
these whisky topers around here and then there might
be more opportunities for the children in a new
country."

"Well," said Father reluctantly, "there might be something to that."

Aunt Christine began to cry again. "Don't know
what'll become of me," she wailed.

"Why, Chris," said Mother, "you'll come with us."

"I—I couldn't leave—Tom."

Father covered his mouth with his hand and looked
pensively at the cold fireplace. Mother went over to
Aunt Christine and put her arm around her sister's
shoulders.

"The grave don't mean anything, dear," Mother said.
"You know that. Tom's spirit is what matters and he
would come along with you. He certainly would. He
never would stay here with you gone. He'd come along
with you."

"At no extra fare," said Father.

VIII

True to his predictions, Father had no trouble selling
the *Samuel W. Reed* for $1,000. And to tell the truth,
I had no sorrow in seeing the boat go. I was heartily sick
of driving tow horses, and I was excited over prospects
of going to the wild West.

Father sold the sloop, auctioned the stock and a good
deal of the house furnishings. Judge Tucker at Naples
took the agency for the farm, declaring he felt certain he

could dispose of the property at a good price before the summer was over.

Father originally intended to take some of the live-stock to Nebraska, but it developed he would either have to travel with the stock car himself or hire a man to do so and he finally decided it would be wiser to sell all the animals and acquire more when we had crossed the Missouri River.

Johnny Wormworth drove our big farm wagon laden with our trunks and a plow and other implements and bedsteads and feather beds and Mother's old mahogany sideboard and a few pieces of other furniture and barrels of dishes and kitchenware and pictures, including huge crayon portraits of Grandpa and Grandma Macdougall, to Canandaigua where it all would be loaded on the steam cars. Then Johnny drove the horses and wagon back to Arch Pearson, who had bought them at the auction.

At first the cherry-wood table with which Aunt Christine talked to spirits was to be included in the sale, but Aunt Christine burst into tears and at Mother's sugges-tion Father made her a present of the table.

It was a sunshiny morning late in May when we left our old home. The big apple tree back of the house was in full bloom and so was the purple lilac bush in front.

We all had new clothes for traveling. Both Mother and Aunt Christine had new flowered woolen gowns they called "de lane" and they had smaller hoops than usual and tight bodices. Mother's gown had pink flowers on it and Aunt Christine's had lavender flowers, and Aunt Christine wore her precious blue crystal bottle vase pinned at her left breast with two blue pansies in it while Mother's bottle vase was of plain white crystal with a small bunch of violets and a rose geranium leaf.

Both had small new hats which tied under their chins with broad ribbons. And Aunt Christine was careful to see that her crystal smelling salts bottle was in her reticule to overcome the terrors of riding on the steam cars. She thought Mother should have one also, but when Father laughed uproariously at the idea they decided both could use the same bottle—which incidentally was a gift to Aunt Christine from the lamented Tom Brooks.

Eliza, who was fourteen now, had a lightweight woolen gown, checkered brown and red, which reached to her shoetops. But her sandy hair still hung down her back in long curls.

Father was wearing a new black broadcloth suit and a stiff-bosomed shirt and a silk waistcoat and an immense gray cravat fastened by a pin made in the shape of a woman's slipper. He wore his new black hat at a rakish angle and looked very dashing and handsome, I thought. I myself had a new black suit very similar to Father's, except that it buttoned higher on the chest.

Few of the neighbors came to bid us farewell and Godspeed. We had become pariahs, indeed. The ostracization seemed to center on Eliza and me—or at least it seemed to us that way. Her former chums at school had been shunning her for a month, bringing her many tearful hours at home, and I had been in three or four fights brought on by boys yelling "Copperhead, Copperhead, slimy, stinking Copperhead" at me.

Mother and Father must have felt all this keenly although they said little about it. Father had been born and reared in the neighborhood. Mother had lived on the farm ever since she and Father were married in Canadaigua seventeen years before and almost everyone within miles had been our friends before the war started. So the unhappiness of the last few weeks lessened the wrench of leaving.

Hiram Mann came over from Bristol with a livery rig to drive us to Canandaigua—where we should depart on the Canandaigua and Niagara Bridge Railway for the first leg of our long journey. We loaded our carpetbags in the back of the surrey together with a huge picnic basket filled with fried chicken, cheese, hard-boiled eggs, boiled ham, bread and butter and friedcakes and a quantity of russet apples that had been buried all winter.

Mother and Aunt Christine and Eliza came out of the house carrying their reticules and shawls. Then Father locked the front door. He seemed to have some trouble turning the key. "That lock must have got rusty during the rains," he said. "Seems to kind of stick." His voice sounded odd. Then he came down to the surrey and handed the key to Hiram Mann. "Now, Hiram," he said, "you look alive and don't forget to give that key to Judge Tucker."

"I'll remember," said Hiram. He was sitting on the right of the surrey's front seat, holding the impatient horses with lines tight in his left hand and his long buggy whip in his right. Hiram Mann had stringy, long black whiskers.

Father helped Mother and Aunt Christine and Eliza up to the back seat. Then we climbed in front. Because Father and Hiram Mann filled the front seat snugly, I sat between Father's legs on one of his knees and held to the dashboard.

Hiram Mann clucked his tongue and the horses lurched into a trot. But before we had gone fifteen rods Mother spoke. "Will you kindly stop a moment, Mr. Mann?" she asked.

"Whoa!" called Hiram Mann and pulled the horses to a halt.

"Children," said Mother. Her voice was tense and sad. I twisted on Father's knee and looked at her.

"Look back, children," said Mother, "you may never see it again."

The lake was sparkling and blue in the sunshine and the new cattails grew in a green rank in the marsh to the south. The tall hills were very green and the maple and beech trees were leafed in their soft spring foliage and there were big billows of white clouds floating above.

Our rambling old brown house with its curled, weather-beaten shingles looked forlorn with the curtains gone from the windows and the barn looked empty and the well sweep seemed weary and dejected and a lump of homesickness rose in my throat. Aunt Christine covered her eyes with her handkerchief and Mother said huskily, "Drive on, Mr. Mann."

Hiram Mann said, "Giddap." The horses broke into a trot again and the gravel slithered from the iron buggy tires. Eliza and I kept looking back until the surrey made the turn at the top of the hill and the apple tree was as white as a single white snowball blossom and the last thing I saw of the house two crows were flying slowly over the big brick chimney.

"Good-bye, old home," Eliza said like a lyceum speaker.

Then no one said anything for a long while and there was no sound except the horses' hoofs and the grating of the buggy wheels and Hiram Mann once in a while clucking his tongue.

For the first few miles I kept looking at this familiar hill or that familiar swale and thinking I might be a man before I saw them again. Then we got away from my old stamping ground and were trotting through country I did not know, for I seldom had gone to Canandaigua except by boat.

I was happy now to be on our way toward new scenes and adventure and I heard Mother in the back seat talking to Aunt Christine and saying, "Well, now that everything's as it is, I guess I'm glad we're going away. But I keep worrying about how Alan will find us way out there in Nebrasky when he gets out of the army."

Father looked over his shoulder. "Stuff and nonsense,"

he said. "Alan can get to Nebrasky City just as easy as going to Buffalo."

So, after a while our horses clop-clopped onto the hard streets of Canandaigua and Hiram Mann drove us to the railway depot, although we didn't know just when the next brigade of cars would steam west. Hiram Mann helped us unload our carpetbags and shawls and the picnic basket into the waiting room of the depot. Then he took off his high hat and bowed stiffly to Mother and Aunt Christine and even Eliza and he shook hands with Father and me and wished us Godspeed and good luck, but he didn't seem particularly enthusiastic and I thought that even Hiram Mann was calling us Copperheads under his breath.

We were in the waiting room and Mother and Aunt Christine and Eliza sat down together on a smooth, wooden bench with their shawls folded neatly over their laps and we put the carpetbags and picnic basket in front of them on the floor.

The floor was very dirty and the glass in the waiting-room windows was so dusty and cobwebby that little light entered. In the center of the room there was a huge rusty iron stove setting in a box of sand. The box of sand was spattered with tobacco juice.

There was a strange, irregular click-clicking going on beyond the grilled window and the window had a sign over it reading, "Ticket Agent."

"What's that noise, father?" Eliza asked excitedly.

"Magnetic telegraph," Father said.

I looked through the grilled window and saw a man with a brown beard sitting at a table jabbing away at a brass thing that chattered like a crippled cricket. The man wore a green shade over his eyes and was very intent at his work.

Father came up to the grilled window. "When's the

next brigade of cars for Niagara Falls and the West?" he asked.

"Just a moment." The man spoke sharply without looking up. Father hunched his shoulders, lifted his chin and ran a forefinger inside his stiff, uncomfortable collar. There was an unidentified musty odor in the waiting room that I associated with the magnetic telegraph.

Presently the bearded telegrapher pulled a small lever on the telegraph and quit jabbing the handle. The telegraph sputtered a couple of petulant clicks back and then was silent. Then the man rose stiffly from his chair, snapped up his red sleeve garters and sauntered over to the window.

"What can I do for you, sir?" he asked coldly.

"You can tell me when the cars go to Niagara Falls and the West," Father said.

"Eleven-thirty," said the man.

Father craned his neck to look at a clock inside the office. "It's a quarter after ten now," he observed.

The man looked. "That's right," he confirmed brusquely.

For the first time in my experience, Father seemed a little on the defensive. "All right for us to wait here for the cars?" he asked.

"Why not?" blurted the man. "It's a waiting room. That's what it's for. You just want to *see* the cars or you going someplace?"

"We're sort of going someplace, I'd say. Going clear out to the Nebrasky coast."

The bearded man's manner changed ever so slightly. "Oh," he said, "in that case you want to buy tickets. Cheaper a lot to buy passage here than pay on the cars. Where you say you're going?"

"Nebrasky coast," said Father, putting his hands in his pockets.

The telegrapher reached under the counter and

brought up a map and spread it out. Then with eyes squinted thoughtfully, he traced with a blunt forefinger from the right to the left, muttering to himself. His tongue stuck out the corner of his mouth, surrounded by brown whiskers. "Hmm," he breathed finally, "that's a long ways. Rails don't run but to St. Joseph, Missouri, and they ain't been even that far very long."

"I know it," said Father. "We take a steamboat from St. Joseph, Missouri."

"Oh, you know that already. Well, I can sell you passage from here to Niagara Falls and from Niagara Falls to Port Huron, Michigan, and from Port Huron, Michigan, to Chicago, Illinois, and from Chicago, Illinois, to Hannibal, Missouri, and from Hannibal, Missouri, to St. Joseph, Missouri. You got to look after your own steamboat when you get to St. Joseph."

"I calculate I can do that," said Father.

"How many passages you want?" the man asked.

"I got three grownups and two children."

"How old the children?"

"Girl's fourteen; boy's eleven years old."

"Well, you got to buy a whole passage for the girl. Boy can go for half a passage."

Then the man pulled up a dog-eared book and began to wet his thumb and flip the pages and scowl and write down things on a piece of paper and count on his fingers and cipher and look up at the ceiling mumbling and wet his thumb again and flip more pages and write down things and count on his fingers and cipher and I began to get hungry and went back to Mother and Aunt Christine and Eliza who were sitting very straight on the wooden bench with their hands folded on their laps.

I said, "Ma, I'm hungry. Can I have something to eat out of the basket?"

Mother said, "Well, you can have a friedcake or an apple."

"I'll take a friedcake."

"I'll take an apple," Eliza said.

So Mother unfastened the catch on the basket and dug down through the napkins and the smell of fried chicken and bread came up while she was moving things and she got me a friedcake and Eliza an apple.

I had to sit quietly beside Eliza while we were eating and it seemed something like sitting quietly in church except that one didn't eat substantial things like friedcakes and apples in church, but only a small bite of the piecrust bread and a little sip of the grape wine they served for communion.

I thought about this and thought that, after all, we weren't in church and jabbed Eliza lightly in the ribs with my elbow.

"Ow," Eliza said, and scowled at me under her heavy sandy brows. Then she jabbed me hard with her elbow.

"*Ow!*" I said loudly and jabbed her again.

"You children behave yourselves," Mother said.

"Well," I objected, "she banged me hard with her elbow."

"He banged me first," Eliza said.

Father, who was standing on one foot and then the other by the grilled window, turned and looked inquiringly at us.

"You behave yourselves," said Mother, "or your father will attend to you proper."

I finished my friedcake and licked my fingers. "Ma," I said, "I'm thirsty now. Can I go and get a drink of water?"

"Guess there's no place to get a drink."

"Yes, there is. I saw a pump and a cup right outside."

"Well, don't wander away. Maybe the steam cars will be here any minute now."

"No, they won't. The man said up at the window that'd be more than an hour."

"Well, don't wander away, anyhow. Steam cars don't wait for people."

Aunt Christine turned to Mother, "Oh," she said, "I just wish this thing hadn't ever come up. I just know I'm going to be frightened to death. I just know it's going to be terrible and we're going to have to ride for days."

"Now, don't worry, Chris," Mother said. "It may not be as bad as all that. Lots of people ride the steam cars and live through it. I'm not going to worry a bit."

"Ma," said Eliza, "can I get a drink too?"

"Yes. But hurry right back and see that your brother don't wander away."

So Eliza and I went out the back door to the old wooden pump under an elm tree. I had to pump quite a while before the water came and Eliza insisted on washing out the cup before she would drink.

"My goodness," she said, "you never know who's been using a cup last. Maybe a nigger or Irishman."

So she drank gingerly and I pumped myself a cup of water and it was cool and good. The sun glittered on an array of new lightning rods on a brick building across on Main Street. A barefoot boy came running along rolling a big hoop and the hoop rang like a bell when it bounced over stones.

Across in the back yard of a brown frame cottage was a large willow cage where a dozen or so passenger pigeons were talking sadly to one another. I let the tin cup rattle down on its chain and started across the road.

"Clint," called Eliza, "you come right back here now. Mother said for you not to wander away."

"I'm not wandering away. I'm just going over there to see the pigeons."

"Now, listen. Ma said for you not to go away."

"I told you I'm *not* going away. Just going across road."

I went around a bush to the cage and looked at the

birds, admiring the sheen of their slate-blue backs and red-brown breasts. Then I saw they all were blind. A man was hoeing in a garden near by.

"Why for are these pigeons all blind?" I asked.

The man straightened up from his hoe and grinned at me under his big mustache.

"They're stool pigeons," he said. "I blinded 'em so's they'll call other pigeons to the nets. You see, I got some big clap nets and when the pigeon flights start I sprinkle some corn out in a field next to the nets and put these stool pigeons down and they eat the corn and the flying pigeons see 'em and come down by the thousands and we clap the nets over 'em."

"Why you call 'em *stool* pigeons?"

"Well, generally you tie 'em to stools so the flying birds can see them better."

"You catch many pigeons?"

"Many? Why, bub, we got more than a barrel of pigeon breasts salted away from last year yet. We got so many we fed 'em to the hogs."

"Clin-ton!" Eliza was calling me, standing with one hand on the ball atop the pump.

"All right, I'm coming." I went back across the road and pumped myself another drink of water. Then we went into the waiting room.

Father had completed his transaction with the agent and was sitting back with Mother and Aunt Christine, looking pleased with himself.

The magnetic telegraph was clicking furiously again and the man with the brown beard was leaning over the machine, now and then writing something on a piece of paper with a crayon.

"How I know he ain't a fraud?" Father said to Mother. "Maybe he's above board, but how do I know? Suppose I buy passage all the way for all of us and spend money enough to buy four cows and a span of horses and when

we get to Chicago, Illinois, say, I find the passage I
bought to Missouri is no good. That's happened before
and how do I know it wouldn't happen now? And, by
grab, what would I do then? Couldn't very handy come
back to Canandaigua just to lick this gazabo.

"Maybe it'll cost a mite more the way I'm doing, but
we'll be sure we ain't been horsed. I only bought passage
to Niagara. When we get there I'll buy passage to Chicago, Illinois, and so forth."

"Well, I think that's probably safer," said Mother.

"This railroader was pretty mad," Father went on.
"Asked me if I didn't trust him and I told him I didn't
trust anybody connected with the steam cars and if he
didn't like it he could go soak his head. That shut him
up."

The magnetic telegraph ceased its chatter and the
bearded man opened the outside door and went out on
the veranda that ran beside the steam-car rails.

"Maybe the brigade of cars is coming, ma," I said.
"Can I go out and see?"

"Not a speck of it," said Mother. "You get out there
and they might run over you."

"I'll go with him," said Father.

So we went out on the porch and the telegrapher was
just pinning a piece of paper to a blackboard. He went
back in the door without looking at Father and a group
of loungers gathered around to read the paper.

The paper, scrawled in red crayon, read: "Telegraph
from Virginia. All quiet today along the Potomac. General McDowell expected to move south and crush the
rebellion before the week is out."

"Well, it's about time, I'd remark," one of the
loungers said.

Father and I went back in the waiting room and after
a few minutes we heard a lounger call, "Here she
comes!"

Father stood up. "Well, folks," he said, "they say the cars are coming. Let's go out." Even he seemed a little excited as he picked up three of the carpetbags.

Aunt Christine's face was white and tense as if she were being led to the gallows. "Oh dear," she sighed, weakly.

Eliza and I carried the picnic basket between us and both Mother and Aunt Christine carried small carpetbags, their shawls and reticules. We trooped out on the depot's veranda and, sure enough, here came the cars steaming up from the big brick shed where they kept the steam engine when not in use.

The huge locomotive's bell was ringing loudly while steam blew alternately from one side and then the other with a hissing roar. Black pitch-pine smoke billowed up from the tall black chimney that was bigger around at the top than the water hogshead in Jake Lownes's blacksmith shop. The barrel of the locomotive was glistening black. But in front was a sharp wooden ram made of heavy fence pickets and painted bright red. Also brilliant red was the great reflecting lamp on the front of the barrel and the high iron wheels. But there were two big nubbins atop the barrel, something like big upside-down kettles, that were painted a pumpkin yellow. The brass alarm whistle sprang from the top of one of these kettles and the brass bell hung from a red frame just behind the chimney with its rope running back to the red cabin where worked the pilot and the firetender, roughlooking characters in blue jeans.

The roof of the red cabin extended backward far enough to protect the firetender while he was stepping back and forth from the low red wood car that followed directly behind the locomotive.

Now the depot porch was filled with people, some only down to see the show, but many hurried men and women with carpetbags who were there to take the cars.

With a great bumping and metallic screeching and hissing of steam, the locomotive stopped directly in front of us with the brigade of bright yellow, flat-topped cars strung along behind. On the red cabin of the locomotive was painted in a black-edged yellow scroll "Bertha L." and I caught a glimpse of the florid-faced firetender throwing sticks of wood as long, almost, as fence posts into the blazing furnace.

There was great confusion and yelling. The loungers were all gathered around the locomotive and one yelled up to the pilot, "Say, do these iron hosses blow up often?"

And the pilot spat out nearly a cup of tobacco juice on the depot veranda and said, "Naw—only once." So the loungers all haw-hawed and slapped one another on the back and howled: "They only blow up once. That's pretty good. They only blow up once. Wouldn't be anything left after they blowed up once."

An excited man in a blue uniform with gold around the collar and sleeves skipped along the depot porch yelling, "All aboard! All aboard that's going aboard. All aboard for Rochester, Batavia, East Buffalo, Niagara Falls and points west."

"All aboard the telegraph and a nigger to carry the news!" howled one of the loungers and the rest went into spasms of haw-hawing. "That's pretty dang good," another yelled. "All aboard the telegraph and a nigger to carry the news."

"Come on," said Father, "let's get aboard before we're left."

"Let's get in the back car," said Mother.

"Why?" asked Father. "What for you want to be in the back car?"

"If we hit anything," said Mother breathlessly, "we'd be farther away."

"All right. But get a move on."

Father was striding down the depot porch with his three big carpetbags. Mother and Aunt Christine were almost running to keep up with him and Eliza and I with our big picnic basket were galloping in the rear, pulling and hauling against each other.

"If you'd let me have it alone, we'd get along faster," Eliza said peevishly.

"And if you'd let me have it alone, I'd run," I shouted.

Eliza let go of the basket which swung in and almost knocked my feet out from under me. "Ow!" I yelled and set down the basket and rubbed my shin.

Eliza went on and I got the basket up in my arms and stumbled desperately along the long porch.

Father was down to the rear car and was standing impatiently by the platform. He started to help Mother into the car and then he saw my plight.

"Eliza," he shouted, "help that boy with the basket!"

"He won't let me," Eliza screamed.

"All aboard that's going aboard!" shouted the man in the blue uniform.

"Eliza, you hear me?" yelled Father. "You help that boy!"

So Eliza ran back and got hold of the basket. People hurriedly were climbing aboard the car in front. The bell on the locomotive began to ring lazily, "ding-clang, ding-clang." Father helped Mother and Aunt Christine into the car, dashed out again and lifted his carpetbags to the platform. By that time Eliza and I panted up with the basket and Father reached down and lifted the basket up with the carpetbags.

"By grab," he said, "I should ought to butter and fry you both. Scoot in there now and look alive."

Eliza and I scampered up the stairs and seized the basket again and entered the car. The interior was gaudily painted yellow like the exterior and the seats were red plush. Eliza and I struggled down the narrow

aisle past a dozen or so passengers who already were
seated, toward the rear of the car where Mother and
Aunt Christine were sitting gingerly together. The bellowing voice of the fellow in the blue uniform still was
roaring, "All aboard—all aboard!" outside.

I stumbled over a tin spittoon in the aisle and just
then the car gave a terrible rumbling jerk forward and
I went sprawling. Eliza dropped her end of the basket
and fell in the lap of a plump woman.

"Look alive there!" called Father. I was spread-eagled
over the big picnic basket, but I turned and saw that
Father was grinning and that he had dropped one of his
carpetbags in order to grab the back of a seat.

"Oh, excuse me, please," Eliza said to the plump
woman.

"All aboard the telegraph and a nigger to carry the
news!" yelled the lounger on the depot porch.

I got to my feet but another lurch sent me sprawling
again.

"Low bridge there, sonny," said an Irishman in the
seat next to me.

"Jeepers," I said, "was it a wreck?"

"Not yet," said the Irishman. "We don't wreck until
we go down the Batavia hill."

The car now was bumping alarmingly in short rapid
jerks like a marble rolling down a washboard. I struggled
to my feet in desperation and worried the basket back to
a vacant seat behind Mother and Aunt Christine, slid it
between the seats and climbed over it to the window.
Eliza sat down beside me and Father with his three big
carpetbags took the seat across the aisle from us.

I looked out the window and saw we were actually
moving, moving through the outskirts of Canandaigua,
while dogs chased along barking and small boys stood in
suspended animation watching us. The quick jerking
had ceased and now the car was only rocking in a com-

paratively gentle manner as we picked up speed and the wheels under us roared and clicked over the iron rail joints. The bell on the locomotive was still ringing lazily, "ding-clang, ding-clang," and through the open window drifted the quickening puff-puff-puffing of the engine and the scent of pitch-pine smoke.

Then I heard Mother's voice. "There, there, Christine," she was saying. "This isn't so bad."

"I—I think I'm going to faint," Aunt Christine said.

"Here," said Mother, "where's your reticule? I'm not frightened, Chris—see. Where's your reticule?"

I stood up and saw Mother open Aunt Christine's reticule and take out the crystal bottle of smelling salts. She removed the stopper and waved the open bottle under Aunt Christine's nose. Aunt Christine's head bobbed back. "There," she said faintly. "There, I'm better."

Mother corked up the bottle. "Of course you are. And it really isn't any worse than riding fast in a buggy. Not as bad. You don't get the wind in here."

Now we were out in the country, traveling at a great rate along a valley between high hills covered with maple, beech and hemlock. The bell rope that ran next to the roof along the side of the car was slap-slapping against the wood and the pair of brass kerosene lamps were swaying back and forth on their chains. Up ahead the steam whistle shrilled again and again as we tore across a wagon road and I saw a farmer struggling with a span of white horses that were rearing and plunging in panic while the cars passed by.

Father leaned across the aisle. "This is kind of splendid, ain't it?" he said to Eliza and me.

"Jeepers," I said, "never saw anything like it."

Eliza smiled sadly. "We're on our way," she said, "to the far Nebrasky coast."

Presently the man with the gold-braided blue uniform

came into the car and, bracing himself against the sway
and bounce, began to take up passage tickets and to col-
lect money from those who had not bought passage.
Father handed him our passage tickets and pointed out
our party. "When," he asked, "do we get to Niagara
Bridge?"

"Three-thirty or four o'clock."

Father shook his head in amazement. "Imagine that,"
he said. "Know when we can catch the cars there for
Chicago?"

The man shook his head. "Ain't any cars run from
Niagara Bridge to Chicago, Illinois. You can take the
cars from Niagara Bridge to Port Huron, Michigan."

"Well, there's a railroad runs from Port Huron, Michigan, to Chicago, Illinois, ain't there?"

The railroader looked meditatively at the ceiling.
"They say there is," he observed cautiously. "I ain't ever
rode on it. Ain't ever seen it. But they say there is."

"You know when we can catch the cars from Niagara
Bridge to this other place—Port Huron, is it?"

"Port Huron, Michigan? Well, I think there's a train
sometime early tonight. That's a Canadian railroad and
you cross into Canada at Niagara City. You can find out
all about it there."

"Gol," I said to Eliza, "we're going clear outside of
the United States. We got to go through Canada to get
to Nebrasky."

Eliza frowned. "I don't like that a bit," she said.

"That don't hurt anything. We ain't at war with
Canada. We're just having war with the south part of
the United States."

Eliza shook her head. "Maybe we're not having war
with England and all those English places right now,"
she said, "but we're apt to any minute. Father says England wants the rebels to win on account of cotton and

tobacco and everything and they might decide to have war right when we were in Canada."

"Well, I calculate they won't shoot us. We wouldn't be doing anything but riding on a train."

"No, maybe not they wouldn't shoot us. But they might take us prisoner and hold us for ransom and there wouldn't be anybody to pay our ransom. All the neighbors back home would say it served Father right because he was against the war."

"Suppose they did. That wouldn't be so bad, would it? Not many boys and girls our age ever been a prisoner of war. And you wouldn't have to go to school."

"Well, I like to go to school—or I did up to just lately when the girls got so plaguey mean."

Eliza and I took turns sitting next to the window, feeling the wind blowing cool on our cheeks and smelling the rich pine smoke from the locomotive. It was very fascinating and not a bit frightening when we got used to the bounce and speed.

The country soon got less hilly and more rolling after we left Rochester. Cows in pastures would gaze apprehensively at our approach and then lift their tails and gallop awkwardly away. Crows would race the cars, gaining and then dropping back, cawing wildly for miles. And when we came to towns and stopped briefly to allow passengers to get off or get on the cars, there was always a crowd around the depot verandas, peering at us curiously and plainly envying us passengers for all they were worth.

But despite the excitement I suddenly discovered I was very hungry and appealed to Mother.

"Well, well," she said, "I calculate it *is* time for dinner." She leaned across the aisle. "Jack," she said, "if you'll get up the dinner basket we'll have something to eat."

Father grinned. "Some victuals *would* be grateful to my innards," he said.

He lifted the basket up on the seat and opened the lid. Mother rose to dole out the food, but the cars lurched going around a curve and threw her back, partly on Aunt Christine. Aunt Christine sighed wearily. Mother laughed. "Land of Goshen," she said, "I can't keep on my feet. Calculate you'll have to hand out the food, Jack."

Father sorrowfully shook his head at her and Mother looked around at us, smiling. Her eyes were bright and she seemed to be enjoying herself more than I could remember.

Father lifted out a napkin, put a couple slabs of buttered bread and chicken and cheese on it. "Have some victuals, Chris?" he asked, leaning across Mother.

Aunt Christine shook her head. "Couldn't touch a bite," she moaned.

Mother took the napkin. Then Father gave Eliza and me big helpings of everything and it was very fine, sitting there on the red plush cushions, eating fried chicken and friedcakes and apples and throwing the bones and cores out the window.

When we were through we staggered back to the water tank in the rear of the car and drank water from the tin cup. Then Father and I went out the back door and stood on the platform, holding tightly to the iron railing. There we got a better notion of the speed we were traveling than inside, for the timbers that held the iron rails together were rushing under us so fast they were only a gray blur and the dust rose behind the cars in a choking cloud. There, too, the roar of the brigade was louder as was the screeching steam whistle.

"Jeepers," I yelled, "this is fine. Let's ride out here most of the time."

Father grinned and, letting go the railing with one hand, pulled his new hat on tighter.

Presently the door opened and the blue-uniformed railroader stepped out. He took hold of Father's arm. "Come inside," he shouted. "Want to show you something."

Father and I edged inside the door and the railroader pointed to a picture of a skull and crossbones painted on the door. "That," he said, "is a picture of a passenger who rode on the rear platform. We're coming to the Batavia grade and we go down there like the devil was chasing us. Hit a bump and off you go. Against the rules for passengers to ride outside."

"All right," said Father. "If those are the rules, we'll stay in the car. How fast we go down that hill?"

The railroader shook his head impressively. "Sometimes forty miles an hour," he said.

We went back to our seats and, sure enough, before long we were plunging down a hill at what seemed to be reckless speed, the speed perhaps of a cannonball, with the car rocking violently back and forth and clouds of dust billowing in the open windows. Through the open front door we could see a jeans-clad railroader on the platform of the car ahead with feet braced far apart as he twisted energetically on an iron wheel that applied brakes to the racing car wheels.

"It's running away!" a man yelled from up front. "She's got away from 'em!"

Aunt Christine screamed and fainted, her head falling over against Mother.

"Jack!" cried Mother. "Help me. I can't find her reticule."

Father rose and a lurch threw him across the car. He caught himself on the side of the seat.

"Slap her face," he said. "That'll bring her out of it."

"Is it going to wreck?" Mother asked tremulously.

"No. Of course not. They go down this grade like this all the time. It's all right. The railroader told me all about it."

He stooped and picked up Aunt Christine's reticule and took out the smelling salts bottle. Mother held it under Aunt Christine's nose and her sister opened her eyes, threw up both hands to her temples and screamed again. Mother gave her another sniff of the bottle.

"Oh, I knew it, I knew it!" Aunt Christine cried. People were turning their heads and staring at her.

"Knew what, you goose?" Father demanded harshly.

"Oh, I *knew* we were all going to be killed."

"Killed, hell," said Father, "we were just going down a hill and we're most down now. Sure—it's slowing up."

And, with the screeching of the iron brakes on the iron wheels, the train *was* slowing and presently we were rolling at our usual speed along a flat country with groves of trees here and there. The railroader in blue jeans came through the car, wiping his forehead with a red handkerchief. Then he and the gold-braid railroader came through from the rear platform, going up front.

A bald-headed man passed our seats going to the water tank for a drink and on the way back he paused before Father and said, "Mister, I calculated we were gone for certain that time."

"Ho," laughed Father, "we were just going down the Batavia grade. They always go down that hill like that. Have to."

The bald man shook his head. "Mister," he said, "I been down that grade on the cars half a dozen times, but never like that before and I hope never again. She was running away, neighbor, with the bit in her teeth and headed for the stable. Got going before they could set the brakes and it was a wonder we stayed on the rails. Thought we was gone half a dozen times."

"Well, I swanney," said Father.

"How fast you think we was going there, neighbor?" asked the bald-headed man.

"Don't know. Thought maybe forty miles an hour."

"I bet we was going at least a mile a minute," said the bald-headed man.

The gold-braid railroader came on the run through the car, pushed past the bald-headed man and went out on the back platform. He leaned far out on the step for an instant, then hauled himself back, sprang into the car and pulled the slapping bell rope. Then he rushed back to the platform and began to twist the iron brake wheel with all his might. The train began to slow up more and more and the gold-braid man ran through the car to the front platform where the blue-jeans railroader was twisting again on the brake of the car ahead.

The train was stopping out on the grassy flats, apparently far from any town.

"Get the bucket from that car," I heard the gold-braid railroader say to the blue-jeans railroader. Then he raced back to our drinking water tank, seized a large wooden bucket and turned the spigot to fill it with water.

Eliza was sitting next to the window, but I suddenly climbed over her and stuck my head out.

"What on earth ails you?" she demanded.

"Want to see," I said. And looking down and back I saw a cloud of blue smoke rising from under the car.

"Gol," I said.

"What's the matter?" asked Eliza.

"The car's on fire," I said.

"Oh, my goodness," said Eliza, "we went through the air so fast it set the wood on fire."

Aunt Christine turned suddenly in her seat. Her red-brown eyes were wild. A strand of her red hair had come unfastened and was straying down the side of her pale cheek.

"What's the matter?" she demanded shrilly.

"We went so fast the car caught on fire," I said.

"God have mercy!" Aunt Christine screamed. "We'll be burned to death now." She seized her reticule and sprang to her feet, but the slowing cars lurched and sent her back in the seat.

"Perhaps," said Eliza, "we'd better flee for our lives."

I saw the blue-jeans railroader leap from the platform ahead carrying a wooden bucket with water slopping over the rim. Then, as the cars jerked to a stop, the gold-braid railroader went off the back porch with his bucket of water.

"Take it easy, Chris," said Father, standing up. "We ain't going to be fried here."

A fat woman up ahead—the one Eliza had sat upon as we entered the car—screeched and men started crowding into the narrow aisle from their seats. I climbed right over Eliza, stuck my legs out the window and jumped down to the dirt beside the rails. I landed on my hands and feet and straightened up to see the blue-jeans railroader throw his bucket of water on a flutter of pink flames that were crackling up the yellow boards of the car above the rear wheel.

The fire sizzled out, but there was a brown charred spot disfiguring the bright yellow of the car and the brown spot was surrounded by a darker yellow of blistered paint. The wheel and bearing were smoking hot and the gold-braid railroader threw his bucket of water on the wheel in small quick sluices. The wheel spat and sizzed violently at first, but before the bucket was empty the wheel and bearing apparently were cold.

A tall, important-looking man dropped off the car. "What's wrong?" he asked.

"Dry bearing," said the gold-braid railroader. "Grease ran out and she got red-hot going down the hill."

"Set the car on fire?"

"Yep."

Men and women from the cars began to crowd around. All the windows on our side were filled with people leaning out. They were calling, "Say, there, what's the matter? The fire out? Are the cars busted down? Can they go any more?"

And the people on the ground were calling back, "No danger now. Fire's out. Just went too fast."

And a half-grown boy harrowing a field just beyond the rails wrapped his lines around a rail of a stake-an'-rider fence and came tearing over to see what had happened to the steam cars.

"All aboard, everybody," yelled the gold-braid railroader.

"Can we go? Is it safe now?" a man asked.

"Of course it's all right. We got to go slow to East Buffalo and get more grease on the axle. That's all."

So we all climbed back into the cars and I found Father sitting in my seat and leaning over talking to Mother and Aunt Christine. "Can't see," he said, "why Chris would make such a fuss over being killed, anyhow. Look at all the good spirit friends she's got and you wouldn't think she'd mind becoming a spirit herself. Would think she'd be one of the last persons on earth to be scared of dying."

"I'm *not* scared of dying," said Aunt Christine, very dignified. "But I don't want to be burned to death or torn limb from limb."

"Oh, quit plaguing her," said Mother. "Can't you let her be?"

Aunt Christine started to cry. "He just wants me to die, that's all," she sobbed. "He just wants to get rid of me. I'm just too much trouble and he *wants* me to die."

"Stuff and nonsense," said Father. "If you burned up here we all would be burned up too and that wouldn't have been any fun for me. *I* ain't got many spirit friends."

"Jack!" said Mother sharply and Father went back to his seat. Then the cars jerked and started to run slowly on. Our car made a lot more noise than it had before and seemed to pound more in the rear. We stopped a couple of times before we reached East Buffalo for the gold-braid railroader to get out and look at the wheel. Once he threw another bucket of water on it.

Finally we did get to the East Buffalo depot where several tracks branched off, some going to the lake and Canal Street and another going to Niagara Falls. A number of men came out and looked at the wheel. Then the engine pulled the cars ahead and backed a few times so they could see how it was working.

I made Eliza change places with me so I could lean out the window and watch and finally I heard one big man say, "Well, it ain't any use, boys. The ex is warped from getting so God-damn hot. Have to take this carriage off and put the Niagara Bridge passengers in the carriage ahead. Have to put a new ex and maybe a new wheel on this carriage. God damn, Robinson, you got to quit coming down that grade so fast. I'll be a son of a bitch. Can't you start setting them brakes when you get to the top of the grade? God damn. You'll be going off the rails someday and killing everybody aboard."

The gold-braid railroader was looking down at the depot veranda floor and seemed quite ashamed. He didn't seem very important any more. "Yes, Mr. Fleming," he said. "I'll be more careful about that."

Then the gold-braid railroader climbed on our car and he seemed important all over again. "All right," he shouted. "Everybody for Niagara Bridge get into the car ahead. Plenty of seats up there."

So Eliza and I wrestled the picnic basket up to the next car following Father with the carpetbags and there were seats because of the number of people who had left the cars for Buffalo, but not enough seats so we could be

We crawled across the bridge, with the boiling white-and-green torrent far below, moving scarcely faster than a man would walk.

"And that's Niagara Falls," said Eliza. "Just think—Niagara Falls. I heard of it all my life and now I'm actually *seeing* it."

We clanked and rattled across the bridge and then the hollow bridge sound ceased and we were on land once more, stopping beside a dirty brown building with a British flag fluttering in front. By craning my neck I could look back into the United States and see the straight American Falls roaring white.

Eliza leaned forward excitedly. "Wasn't it beautiful, mother?" she asked. "What you think of it, Aunt Christine?"

"Wonderful," said Mother. "Positively wonderful. Wish we could stay longer."

"Didn't really see it," said Aunt Christine. "Just caught a glimpse and then we were on that awful bridge. Didn't dare even open my eyes while we were up there."

"By holy dang," I said, "you mean you didn't even look while we were crossing the bridge? You mean you kept your eyes shut all the time? Well—"

"Clinton," Mother spoke sharply, "now you mind your tongue."

Two stern-looking men in red coats were coming through the car. They were speaking to all the passengers, one by one, and on two occasions opened up carpetbags and looked inside.

Eliza cringed. "Oh," she whispered, "here come the redcoats. Oh, I wonder if they've declared war on us?"

As they reached us Father held up our passage tickets. "Those four," he said, waving at us across the aisle.

"Don't want your tickets," one of the redcoats said. "Train captain will get them. You all Americans?"

"You bet your boots we are," said Father.

Eliza gasped.

"Where you going?"

"Nebrasky coast."

The redcoat drew his eyebrows together. "Where's the New Brasky coast?" he asked. "That a British possession?"

Father laughed. "It ain't New Brasky. It's Nebrasky and it's a territory out west in the United States."

"Oh. Then you're just going across Ontario to Port Huron."

"That's right."

The redcoat squinted at the tickets Father held in his hand. "All right, then," he said, "but you can't get off the cars."

"Don't want to," said Father.

"Well, it's just my job to tell you."

Unsmilingly the redcoats moved on and Eliza sat up straight again. Presently the engine bell began to ring and the cars jerked and jerked again and we were steaming out of the town of Clifton and westward across the green fields of Ontario.

I leaned out the window and looked ahead at the hazy, romantic blue horizon of a foreign land and at the foreign oak and maple trees along the draws and at the foreign streams and at a couple of foreign Canadian boys standing barefoot in the dusty road waving as our brigade of cars steamed past and I thought that the rebellion in the United States meant practically nothing to these boys. I thought they probably never had heard the term "Copperhead." I thought they might never have heard even of Abe Lincoln because I didn't know the name of their ruler—unless it was Queen Victoria, the same as England.

I thought these boys probably saw me in the car window and took it for granted I was a Canadian boy like themselves, not dreaming I was on my way to the Nebrasky coast. I thought there wasn't a chance of them having heard of my destination because even the red-coats who came in the car didn't know. And then I felt even more thrillingly a traveler than ever before. I settled comfortably on the plush seat and turned and grinned at Eliza. "Jeepers," I said.

"What's the matter?"

"Well," I said, "we're—we're going way out west."

Eliza looked at me and wrinkled her nose. "You goosy-gander," she said.

The cars were running directly into the setting sun and the setting sun reminded me that ordinarily it would be time to drive old Daisy into the barn for milking and that I never would see that old cow again. And thinking of milking reminded me that supper followed.

"Ma," I called ahead. "What we going to have for supper?"

"Fried chicken," she said.

"When?"

"Are you hungry now?"

"Awful."

"Well, ask your father if he's ready for supper and if he is for him to get out the basket."

So I asked Father and he said he was hungry enough to eat a hydrophobia cat raw and got the basket up on his seat.

Aunt Christine said maybe she could eat a very small piece of chicken, so we all had a nice supper, throwing the bones and other leavings out the window as we had done for dinner.

By the time it was getting dark the Canada hills were leveling off and we were traveling at a great clip across a flat, grassy stretch that Father said was just north of Lake Erie and we could hear the locomotive up ahead going chuggety-chuggety-chuggety and ringing its bell and screeching its whistle every time we were coming to a road to warn people that the cars were coming.

And afterwhile the gold-braided captain came in the car and pulled down the two brass kerosene lamps and lit them and they looked very pretty swinging from the top of the car on their chains.

Then the captain told us to shut the windows to keep the unhealthy night air out of the car. Father had to close ours for us because it was stuck and with the windows shut you couldn't see much except your own reflection in the glass and the reflection of one swinging lamp that moved back and forth across the window. But as it grew quite dark big sparks from the locomotive chimney began to race by and it was fun to watch their course and it seemed we were going faster than ever before.

Finally people began to try to go to sleep, sprawling out in their seats and taking off their boots. Father took off his new boots and rubbed his feet where they had been pinched and draped his long legs over the arm of the seat and in no time at all was asleep. Mother and Aunt Christine covered their shoulders with their shawls and their heads disappeared below the top of the seat ahead of Eliza and me.

Eliza and I took off our boots and scrooched down in the seat. I was sitting next to the window and I found I could make sort of a barrel of my two hands, put the outer edge against the glass and my forehead against the inner edge, which would shield my eyes from the light and thus I could look out into the night and see the black trees and fields float by with an occasional faraway light from a farmhouse in view.

At length I grew drowsy. I curled up the best I could and drifted off. Then I awoke with the cars stationary beside some depot and a couple of men talking loudly while they rolled a wheelbarrow along the veranda.

There was a lighted window in the depot and I could see a man inside working at the magnetic telegraph. I had a thought that it would be exciting to work at night on a railroad. Then I went to sleep again.

I woke up with the cars speeding through the night again and the sparks racing past the dark window. Across the aisle Father was asleep with his mouth open and his stiff collar off. Eliza was asleep beside me with her head covered by her plaid shawl.

Two men were snoring loudly above the roar of the car, one slightly faster than the other. The slow snorer had a deep KAAAW! The fast snorer went *wheee!* They would start out, KAAAW-*wheee!* and then blend together for a couple of rips until the fast snorer passed the slow snorer and they were going, *Wheee*-KAAAW! for two or three snores until the fast snorer got farther and farther ahead until he got clear around the track and caught up with the slow snorer so their snores got to be KAAAW-*wheee* again.

The car smelled very close and of cramped human bodies and of feet and of stale food. Up ahead two men were talking languidly about the American rebellion.

"Neither side's got any real soldiers," one of them said. "They won't have anything you could call a war. One side's scared and the other dasn't. Take one regiment of good British soldiers and they could chase all those farmers back to their plowing in two days. That goes for both sides."

The other man yawned. "Guess that's what they need too," he said.

I yawned also and stretched my legs across the picnic basket and went back to sleep.

I awoke with Eliza shaking me.

"What's the matter now?" I demanded crossly.

"Got to get off the cars," she said. "We're there."

I rubbed my eyes and Father was standing up smiling

at me. "Get a move on," he said. "Get those boots on right away."

I started to pull on my boots. The cars were standing by a depot and there was a gaslight burning outside.

"Where are we?" I yawned.

"Port Huron, Michigan," said Father.

"Oh, back in the United States."

"That's right."

I got my boots on and stumbled out of the seat with Eliza and the picnic basket. Father was ahead with the carpetbags and Mother was helping Aunt Christine get her hat on straight.

"I know I look a sight," Aunt Christine said.

"Nobody to see you this time of night," said Mother.

We cast long black shadows across the depot porch from the lamppost as we straggled across to the darkened waiting room. After the close car the outside air smelled cool and sweet. On the wall a big clock was ticking slowly and in the dim light I saw it was a quarter after three.

The ticket window was closed but light shone through the frosted glass.

"Say, there!" Father called. "Say, there inside."

There was no response. He called again while Mother and Aunt Christine and Eliza stood shivering a little in the night chill. Father turned to us from the closed window. "Wait here a minute," he said, and went out the back door of the depot.

Presently he came back. "There's a cab out there that'll take us to the other depot," he said. "Can't raise any of these railroaders and the cabman says it's too far to walk with baggage anyhow. Come on and we'll ride. If he's lying he'll be sorry."

So we went out on the silent street where an old black hack stood hitched to a sleepy white horse and the fat cabman put our carpetbags and picnic basket on top and we went clop-clopping and lurching along the dark, bumpy streets of Port Huron.

"You know when the cars steam for Chicago, Illinois?" Father called to the cabman.

"One train goes about eight o'clock." The cabman's voice was hoarse. "Think that un's the first."

"Can we get in the depot all right?"

"Oh, yes. They got a nice waiting room with seats and all. You can wait there fine and stretch out on the seats and sleep."

The old horse sputtered and slowed to a walk.

The cabman slapped his lines. "Giddap there, Bessie," his voice rasped. Bessie went into her measured clop-clop again.

At last we rattled across some railroad tracks, turned sharply and pulled up before a squat dark building. An immense willow tree hung black over the roof, making the building even darker.

The cabman climbed stiffly down and opened the door. "Here you are," he said.

Father got out first. "Sure we can get in there?" he asked, nodding his head at the depot. The fat cabman reached not higher than Father's shoulder. "Course you can," he said.

Father strode up and tried the door. Then he came back. "All right," he said.

The cabman handed down the carpetbags and basket. Father paid him and we edged gingerly into the musty, black waiting room while the cab horse's hoofs clop-clopped back through the sleeping town.

"Jeepers, it's dark in here," I said.

"Should say it is," agreed Father. "Looks like they could afford to have a light. Wait a minute."

He struck a lucifer match and the flickering blue flame showed three rows of wooden benches. "There," said Father. "There's a lamp in the corner." He went across the room and struck another match and took the glass chimney from a kerosene lamp on a brass corner bracket. He applied the match to the wick and then dropped it as the flame neared his fingers.

"Oh, hell's bitches," he snorted in disgust. "No oil in the lamp. Well, I'll light another lucifer so's you can find benches. Then maybe we can get a little more sleep."

He struck a third match and in its tiny light we sprawled on the hard wooden benches. And the next thing I knew it was daylight and Father was talking to Mother.

"It's an hour and a half until the cars steam," he said, "and I could do with a cup of coffee. I see an eating house across the way there. Suppose we all go over and get a hot breakfast?"

Mother was trying to straighten up her hair. "I'm agreeable," she said.

"I dreamed about Tom," Aunt Christine whispered to Mother.

Mother raised her eyebrows.

"Tom felt bad about us moving away from York State. It was so plain it must have been a vision."

"Oh, it was just a dream, Chris. Think no more about it."

We trooped across the street to the eating house, which smelled of hot rancid grease. Already it was peopled by a dozen or so men, mostly in blue jeans, who were eating breakfast amid noisy conversation.

One lumpy fellow with a wild shock of gray hair was loudly berating General McDowell for inactivity.

"Whyn't he get busy?" he was demanding of four other men at the counter. "He's got a big army down there and he's only a jump from Richmond. Whyn't he get busy and smash right down to Richmond and capture Jeff Davis, that's what I want to know. Why, damn me, it looks like he's just giving the rebels a chance to work up a big army of their own. Why, damn me, it looks like he's afeared of Jeff Davis or something."

"Well, I don't know." This was a very tall and very lean fellow with an agile Adam's apple. "I don't know. Maybe he's just waiting until he can get a big enough army to scare the rebels to death and they'll go back without any fight at all. Maybe he's just smart and knows what he's doing."

"Smart, my eye."

"Well, maybe he is. Maybe what Irv McDowell is doing will save bloodshed. I sort of think he might know what he's about or else he wouldn't be a general like he is."

"Why, damn me," roared the wild-haired man, "I think Abe Lincoln should ought to kick McDowell out and put in somebody that ain't afeared to fight—somebody like this young McClellan. You need young fellers for fighters. When you get old like me you get cautious."

We all sat down at a wide table which was adorned with a very fancy pewter cruet of salt and pepper shakers and an ornate, stopperless vinegar flask. A plump waitress slapped up to the table and leaned on the corner.

"You folks want some breakfast?" she asked. One of her round blue eyes was looking coyly at me. The other was looking straight before her at Father.

"We wouldn't be looking for supper this time of day," said Father.

"Well, you want five breakfasts?"

Father looked serious. "Five?" he said. "Well, let's see." With his long forefinger he pointed at each of us. "One, two, three, four," and then at his own chest, "five. Yes, young woman, there's five of us."

The girl giggled and her strange blue eye wandered up toward the ceiling. "All right, then," she said. "Five breakfasts."

She went back to the kitchen and in the due course of time returned bearing a great stack of pancakes and sausage and a platter of fried eggs and a plate of saleratus biscuits and another plate of butter covered with a wire screen against the flies, and a platter of fried potatoes and a huge syrup pitcher and a dish of watermelon pickles and a bowl of dried peach sauce and tall, thick mugs of coffee.

We took a long time at breakfast and then walked slowly back to the depot, picking our teeth with wooden toothpicks the waitress brought us in a glass. Even Aunt Christine had forgotten her presentiments of evil long enough to eat her share of the pancakes and sausage and eggs.

X

The magnetic telegraph agent had come to work and the passage ticket window was open so the busy, clickety-click of the telegraph instrument filled the room.

"My," said Mother, "I feel grimy. I'd like a chance to wash."

"Guess you'll have to wait until you get on the cars," Father said. "They got a washbowl in the ladies privy, don't they?"

"Yes," said Mother, looking modestly at the floor.

Father went up to the ticket window and finally got the telegraph agent away from his telegraphing long enough to sell passages to Chicago and to say that the cars would be along in half an hour or so. Then Father came back and sat down with Mother and Aunt Christine and told Eliza and me we could play around outside the depot for a while if we didn't try to go see the sights and get lost. So we played tag until we heard the locomotive whistle and the ding-clanging of the bell as the cars steamed up to the station.

On the cars Mother made me go to the men's privy to wash and comb my hair. There was a black iron washbowl that had a hole in the middle and a cork on a chain to stop up the hole. And there was a small iron pump that brought the water into the washbowl from a tank. After you washed, you pulled out the cork and the dirty water ran out the hole onto the railroad track as the cars sped along. Also, the privy seat had no bottom and it was fascinating to look down and see the railroad ties flash past below, so fast they became sort of a gray blur.

There was a lot of wild forest land from Port Huron down to Chicago. I kept a close watch for deer or bear but saw nothing. Likely the roar of the cars frightened all the wild animals far back into the brush.

But by the time we had our dinner from the now-lightened basket, even riding on the cars was beginning to pall. I also was beginning to tire of the cold fried chicken and bread. I went to sleep that afternoon and slept for at least two hours.

At suppertime Mother went through the basket and found several apples that were beginning to rot and dropped them out her window. The chicken was virtually finished, so we dined on the cold boiled ham, hard-boiled eggs and cheese with the bread and butter that definitely was beginning to taste stale.

It was dark when we reached Chicago. Disappointed as I was in not seeing Lake Michigan, I was too weary to protest vehemently, and within a couple of hours we were on our way again, steaming through the night for Hannibal, Missouri. I went to sleep with sparks flicking past the window and the now-familiar click-click, clickety-clack of the wheels over rail joints in my ears. Several times I awoke to find the cars standing by some remote Illinois depot and the mumble of men's voices outside, but I would stay awake only long enough to shift my position on the seat. Finally I really awoke with the cars zippety-zipping through the dawn across a broad green plain where cows grazed and where white breakfast smoke rose from farmhouse chimneys against the pink-and-blue sky.

We started to eat some stale bread and ham and Father looked at it unhappily. He rubbed his hand over the black stubble on his chin.

"Wife," he said, "we'll be in Hannibal, Missouri, in an hour or so. What say we wait for breakfast and go to an eating house?"

"Well—" she said. "Can we afford it?"

"Oh, we can't be too stingy. And besides, we *need* a good breakfast. Another thing, I'm going to have to spend a dime for a store shave. Good Lord knows I can't shave myself on these bouncing steam cars. I'd cut my throat sure."

So we put the crusty buttered bread and ham and friedcakes and cheese back in the picnic basket and in an hour or so we steamed down to the Mississippi River, broad as Canandaigua Lake but brown as mud. We drifted up to the depot at East Hannibal, Illinois, and, obeying the shouts of a swaggering fellow who yelled with a cigar in his mouth, we hurried out to a ramshackle wharf and aboard a little paddle-wheel steam ferryboat which was to take us to the Missouri side of the river.

They lost no time casting loose moorings and, with hoarse whistle roaring, we splashed upstream until we were in the middle of the river and then swung with the current and headed for the village we could see snuggled in the green hills. Downstream were two islands, both covered with a thick and beautifully green growth of trees and around one of these islands came a steamboat, glittering white in the morning sunshine and with black smoke pouring from her two tall slim chimneys while gigantic paddle wheels at each side churned the muddy water to foam.

As we neared the Missouri side I saw a whole line of white steamboats tied up to the wharf and spoke of it to Father.

A man standing next to us grinned at me. "All held up by the war," he said. "No telling when they'll be running again."

We were all very hungry by the time we got to the red brick Hannibal depot, for it was at least half past eight, and we left our carpetbags and picnic basket in the waiting room and went across the street to an eating house.

The waitress was a thin, sallow girl who spoke with a peculiar drawl. "Good mawnin," she said, "would you all maybe like some nice fried chicken for breakfast?"

"No!" roared Father.

"Sorry, sir, I just asked," the girl said. "How about some nice po'k chops?"

"That's the ticket," said Father. "Pork chops and potatoes and maybe some oatmeal."

"You *all* want that?"

Mother smiled and nodded her head. "I think that would be a nice breakfast," she said.

"And some nice gooseberry pie?" the girl asked.

"That's fine and dandy," Father agreed.

So we had a splendid breakfast of oatmeal and thick cream and three pork chops apiece with fried potatoes and cucumber pickles and biscuits and honey and gooseberry pie, which was very good, indeed. But Father grumbled a little when they charged us 25 cents apiece, making a total of $1.25 just for breakfast.

"Back in York State where we come from you can get a whole dinner for ten cents," Father said.

"This," said the girl, "ain't a cheap-John place. We don't have anything but the best."

We went back to the depot and Father found that the next train for St. Joseph didn't leave until eleven o'clock, so he went out to find a barbershop and told us it might be a good idea for us to stretch our legs a little.

The passage agent said it would be perfectly safe to leave our carpetbags and things in the waiting room, that he would keep an eye on them, so Mother, Aunt Christine, Eliza and I took a little walk around the town.

It was a very hilly town, with houses built way up on the sidehills and the main street leading down to the river where the cold steamboats were lined up.

In a vacant common two or three squares from the depot several soldiers in blue uniforms were drilling a party of young men in civilian clothing. Some of the young men had long-barreled muskets over their shoulders, some had shotguns or squirrel rifles and others had only pieces of board cut roughly in the shape of a gun.

One of the soldiers had a sword buckled around his waist and he was giving orders in a gruff voice. While the men were marching this soldier would count, "ONE! two, three, four." He would shout the ONE and count the two, three, four in a monotone, trying to make the marchers catch the cadence and keep step.

The recruits would march across the field side by side in a single line until they were approaching the edge while the soldier with the sword would twist his mustache and yell, "Guide right, there! Now hold it! Hold it! Now, fours right—*March!*" and the column would turn and go back the way they had come.

We stood with quite a crowd of other people and watched. "Now that's right pretty, don't you think?" Aunt Christine said.

I turned in surprise and looked at Aunt Christine. That was the first word of approval she had given *anything* since we left home.

"I suppose," said Mother, "Alan is marching like that down south."

The crowd about us was fully as interesting to me as the marching men. Nearly half were Negroes. Of course I had seen Negroes before; there were Negroes in Canandaigua—two or three families of them. But here in one group were at least twenty, some of them as black as a cookstove.

When we finally moved away I said to Mother, "Ma, do you suppose those darkies are slaves?"

"W-e-l-l," she said looking back at them, "I really don't know. I think I've heard of slaves in Missouri. But there was the Missouri Compromise. Did that free the slaves here, Christine?"

"My land, I don't know," said Aunt Christine.

"Well, if these aren't slaves, I expect most of them *were* slaves once."

I looked back at them. "Gol," I said.

We walked up the street past some stores and Aunt Christine and Mother looked in the windows at the hats and coats and dress material. Aunt Christine shook her head. "Don't have near as good selections here as in Canandaigua, do you think?" she asked Mother.

"Well, no," said Mother. "On the whole, I don't. But I do think that bonnet with the wreath of pink posies is nice."

I got tired of following the women and looking in store windows and told Mother I was going back to the depot.

"Well," she said, "now, if you want to, go ahead. But don't go wandering off and getting lost and missing the cars."

"I won't, ma," I promised.

"Now mind, if you do, we'll go off to Nebrasky and leave you here. You wouldn't want to be left in Hannibal, Missouri, would you?"

"No, ma'am," I said. Then I went on down the hill toward the depot. But I really wanted to go down to the river and look over the steamboats and when I reached the depot I kept on going.

I had gone not more than a square or so from the depot, however, when a broad-faced, hatless boy with long straw-colored hair came out of a side street and stood grinning at me.

"Good morning," I said.

"Oh, good *morn*ing," he said with an exaggerated drawl. "We think we're pretty smart with our la-di-da clothes and our good mornings, don't we?"

"I'm traveling on the steam cars," I said. "Wouldn't travel on the steam cars in jeans, would you?"

"Where you from?"

"York State."

"Oh—*York* State. York State, huh? We think we're pretty smart traveling from York State in our la-di-da clothes and all, *don't* we?"

I stepped up closer to the boy. "What the hell you mean?" I said in Erie Canal fashion out of the corner of my mouth. "By holy dang, I think I'm a deal smarter than you, you dirty little chunk of mule manure."

The boy was taken aback by my language. He spat in the dust to recover his composure.

"Well," he said, "you don't look very smart to me."

"You look like a plumb idiot to me," I remarked.

"Maybe you think you can fight."

"Wouldn't have to fight much to whop you."

"That's what *you* think."

"Yes, that's what *I* think."

"How," he asked, "would you like to kiss my backsides?"

With that I hit him in the eye and he rushed upon me. He was quicker than I expected and had an underhold around my waist and one of his bare, wiry legs twined around one of mine. I tripped and went down hard in the dust with the boy on top and, before I really knew what was happening, he hit me in the face two or three times. Then I got him by the throat and threw him off. I twisted on top of him and, holding his arms down with my knees, pummeled his face until his nose was bloody and he was crying. Then I let him up and he went off weeping.

I brushed the dust off my hat and clothing as best I could and went back to the depot to find Father standing by the door looking anxiously up and down the street.

"Where's the rest of 'em?" he asked.

"Uptown looking in windows."

"Well, by grab, they'd better be getting back." Father's face was closely shaved and a reddish bronze in color. He smelled of barbershop perfume and also of spirits. He looked at me and his eyes opened wide. He leaned forward and put his knuckles on his hips.

"Well," he said, "look at you! Jesus Christ and his twelve disciples, look at you. Where on earth you been and what you been up to? *Look* at those clothes and look at that face."

"Just couldn't help it," I said.

"What you mean, you couldn't help it?"

"A boy jumped on me because I was dressed up. Before I knew what, he'd thrown me down and hit me."

"What'd you do then—get up and run?"

"No, I didn't. Sent him off bawling."

"You telling the truth, Clinton Macdougall?"

"I don't tell lies. You know I don't tell lies."

"Well, you better not let me catch you telling lies. Now get out there to that pump and wash your face off. You got a black eye, I think, but it won't kill you. When you get washed come back here and I'll see can I get your clothes brushed off."

By the time the women got back to the station I was fairly presentable and occasioned no more from Mother than, "My land, I calculate I don't dare let you get out of my sight."

Mother had bought a new loaf of bread and got it sliced and buttered to eat with the cold boiled ham that remained in the picnic basket.

It seemed that a great many people were moving west, for there was quite a crowd on hand before the cars even came to the station. And by the time the bell began to ring every seat was taken and some men were standing in the rear of our car. We got aboard early, so we had our seats together as we were accustomed to have them, but a heavy-set, well-dressed man came up the aisle and spoke to Father across the aisle from me.

"Mind if I sit with you, sir?" he asked.

"Not at all, sir," said Father. "Glad to have you."

The man's rugged, smooth-shaven face was bronzed as if he had spent much of his life out of doors, but he was dressed in neat-fitting black like a parson or banker.

"Going to St. Joseph?" Father asked.

"Well, yes," said the man, taking off his beaver hat. His hair was thick and brown, but graying in front of the ears. "Going to St. Joseph on the cars, but taking the boat there for Nebraska City."

Father grinned. "That's our ticket too." He indicated us across the aisle with a sweep of his hand.

"Homeseekers? Looking for Nebraska land?"

"That's right."

"Well, you'll find it grand land, sir. If you and I are going to be fellow passengers so long let me introduce myself. I'm Joseph R. Brown of Minnesota."

"I," said Father, "am Jack Macdougall of York State and I'm happy to meet you."

By this time the cars had started and we were moving

through a valley between high hills bordering the Mississippi.

"You been in Nebrasky before?" Father asked.

"Oh, yes," said Mr. Brown. "And you've never seen any land like it."

"That's what I hear," said Father, "but some of that prairie back through Illinois looked almighty fine to me."

"Wait until you see the soil on those rolling Nebraska prairies. Where you going in Nebraska?"

"Well, sir, we're going to Nebrasky City first. Then I'm going to get a wagon and a span of horses and go out to Rock Creek. Got a cousin out there."

Mr. Brown stroked his heavy eyebrows. "Rock Creek," he said, "just where is that?"

Father grinned. "Well, to tell the honest truth, I don't know exactly. Can't be terrible far from Nebrasky City, I guess."

Mr. Brown opened a small carpetbag and took out a map. He spread it over his knees and he and Father studied over it.

"Rock Creek," mused Mr. Brown. "Rock Creek . . . Well, here it is. Clear down by the border. Might be better to take the trail up from Leavenworth. It's right on the old Oregon Trail. . . . No, I guess it'd be better to ride the steamboat on if you want to get an outfit. Can do better in Nebraska City and I don't believe you'd have as far to drive either. You'd take the Nebraska City cutoff across the Big Blue. It doesn't show here, but I imagine there's some sort of trail down the Big Blue River. You plan to take a pre-emption down there?"

"I calculated I would," said Father.

"Well, I'd almost take it for granted the land is good down there."

"That's what my cousin writes me." Father repeated

the story of the iron posthole auger that sprouted in the rich Nebraska soil. Mr. Brown laughed. I got out of my seat and looked at the map on his knees and it had lines drawn on it in blue and red crayon.

"What's this line?" Father asked, running a finger on a blue mark that started at Omaha.

"That," said Mr. Brown, "is the old Mormon Trail. Follows the north bank of the Platte. You see the Oregon Trail runs pretty well parallel to the Mormon Trail from just this side of Fort Kearny out to Fort Laramie. This straight red line from Nebraska City is our new cutoff. This light-blue line is the old road that curved up here about forty miles to meet the Platte and then curved south again about forty miles to hook up with the Oregon Trail at Fort Kearny. You can see the old road is crooked on the map, but you can't see the mudholes and deep sand."

"Didn't suppose," said Father, "that there was anything like mudholes or deep sand in *Nebrasky*."

Mr. Brown's deep-blue eyes twinkled. "It's not exactly heaven there, yet," he admitted. "Man wouldn't feel natural if he didn't have *something* to plague him.

"Well, I was telling you about this road. There's a big firm of freighters named Russell, Majors and Waddell that have the contract to take supplies out to the army in the Mormon country—out to General Albert Sidney Johnston's old force."

"General Johnston," said Father. "There's a General Albert Johnston that's—"

"Same one. He and Jeff Davis went to school together or something. Well, this Russell, Majors and Waddell is a tremendous firm. Moving hundreds of freight wagons west a year and driving eight or ten thousand oxen."

"Whew!" breathed Father.

"That's right. Tremendous. They picked Nebraska

City for their eastern terminus and that made great business for Nebraska City and it made the folks up in Omaha pretty unhappy too.

"Well, the Omaha fellows knew the road from Nebraska City to Fort Kearny wasn't any too good so they got to sending delegations to Russell, Majors and Waddell and the Omaha newspapers were printing pieces about wagons getting bogged down on this southern road all to convince Russell, Majors and Waddell they should leave Nebraska City and move up where they could have a good road. This old Mormon Trail—see?"

Father nodded his head. "That was before this new red line here was built?"

"Yes. I'm coming to that."

I went back to my seat but leaned over the aisle so I could hear.

"Then," went on Mr. Brown, "gold was found at Pikes Peak and when a rush started for the mountains the Nebraska City men decided it was high time to do something before Omaha won the argument. Last year Nebraska City sent out an exploration party to Fort Kearny to see if they could discover a better route. They did it. They came back and said a road could be made seventy miles or so shorter to Fort Kearny. It would run practically due west from Nebraska City, going over Salt Creek near the Saltillo crossing and then to the Big Blue. From there on it was smooth prairie almost all the way to the Platte just this side of Fort Kearny, where it would join the Oregon Trail."

"So they built a road along that survey?"

Mr. Brown smiled. "Well, yes and no. You don't exactly build roads out in that country. They hitched a couple span of mules to a big breaking plow and plowed a furrow from Nebraska City to the Platte— about a hundred and seventy miles."

"Plowed a furrow?"

"That's right. A covered wagon with supplies went along. They followed the easiest grades and kept away from ravines and moved along the south side of the divide all the way from Nebraska City to Fort Kearny. Of course some streams had to be forded, but they fixed that so the freight wagons won't get mired down. The crew in the covered wagon picked up glacial rock along the way and dumped the rock in the creek bottoms where they were to be forded.

"The freight wagons followed the furrow and in no time at all they had such a splendid road that Omaha couldn't truthfully criticize it. Otoe County—Nebraska City's the county seat—just voted twenty thousand dollars in twenty-year bonds to build bridges and a good many of them will be outside of Otoe County, even. That shows enterprise, doesn't it?"

"Well, I should remark."

Mr. Brown smiled. "I see no reason why I shouldn't tell you something even more interesting, Mr. Macdougall. But, first, let me give you some advice. Don't buy your pre-emption down there along Rock Creek and the lower Oregon Trail."

"What's wrong with it down there? Isn't the land as good down there as any place?"

"Well, the land may be all right. There are millions of acres of land that are all right. But you take your land down there and you'll just have some land. Your markets never will be any better than they are right now. Well, never is a long time. I'll say your markets won't be any better for many years. You'll be isolated. But you take your pre-emption somewhere along this new cutoff between Nebraska City and Fort Kearny and you'll be rich within ten years. Mark my words—rich within ten years."

Father rubbed his chin and looked at Mr. Brown sharply. Mr. Brown laughed.

"Oh, I haven't anything to sell. At least I have nothing to sell *you*."

Father's mouth opened. "You mean," he said, "that there's a railroad going through on this trail?"

"You're a shrewd man, Mr. Macdougall, but that isn't it—exactly."

"But there *is* a railroad going through sometime, isn't there? Didn't Congress pass something about a railroad to the Pacific Ocean?"

Mr. Brown shook his head, looked down at the map and chuckled softly. "That thing," he said, "has been up before Congress for ten years or so. Somebody is always bringing up that wild scheme with the idea of bleeding the United States out of a hundred million dollars. It's a great idea for the eastern bankers and it's a joke to the men who really know the West.

"Perhaps someday they can build a railroad successfully across the plains and the mountains. Perhaps a hundred years from now after the country has been settled and all the Sioux and Cheyennes either killed off or converted to Christianity they can build such a railroad. But not now."

"Well, now listen," said Father, "if the Indians are as bad as all that, how about a man moving his family out on a farm in that country? Is that very sensible? By holy jeepers, I wouldn't be grateful to a redskin for taking *my* scalp."

Mr. Brown's shoulders shook. "Nor I," he said. "But here—" His finger traced the map between Nebraska City and Fort Kearny. "There's little danger from Indians along here. That's mostly Pawnee country and the Pawnees are the white man's friend. Where there are Pawnees camped the white man can feel safe from attacks. Oh, maybe a couple of Pawnees might slip in at night and steal a chicken or a blanket or something, but that doesn't count. The important thing is that all the other Indians war on the Pawnees and the Pawnees have sided in with the whites against the field."

"But can you *trust* the Pawnees to stay friends with the whites?"

"Oh, I think so. Unless you started some foolishness like building a railroad across their hunting grounds. I wouldn't trust 'em in that case. But the main difficulty in building a railroad would be on the other side of Fort Kearny anyhow. That's where the Sioux and Cheyennes and Arapahoes come in. Those savages would kill off the workers as fast as they came in. To build a railroad as far as the Mormon country you'd need two soldiers for every man with a pick and shovel and you'd have to keep a troop of cavalry stationed along every mile of rails to protect it once it was laid down. Another thing—no man talks about building a railroad across the Rocky Mountains who's seen the Rocky Mountains."

"Well, I haven't seen 'em," said Father, "They much bigger than the Alleghenies?"

Mr. Brown threw up his hands. "Bigger than the Alleghenies? Whoo! Why, my friend, the biggest Allegheny would be just a pimple on the flank of Pikes Peak."

"Well, I swanney," said Father. He thought a moment and scratched his head. "Now, Mr. Brown, you were saying I hadn't ought to locate down there near my cousin, but up here on this strip between Nebraska City and this Fort Kearny, weren't you?"

"That's right," said Mr. Brown.

"But you didn't go into any particular particulars. You just said I'd be rich in ten years did I locate up there. You got *real* reasons for saying that?"

"I've got my reasons, Mr. Macdougall. Yes, I've got *real* reasons."

"You talked at first like it might be a railroad going

through and then you say there can't be a railroad. It seems like you're talking riddles to me, Mr. Brown."

"Not at all. Not at all. To put it bluntly, Mr. Macdougall, I have an invention that will revolutionize the transportation business."

"Oh, *I* see," said Father, raising his eyebrows. "Well, I put some money in an invention once that was going to revolutionize the power business. It was going to put the steam engine out of business and it was going to do away with water wheels. It was a perpetual motion machine and it would work all right for a little while. Then it'd play out. The inventor said he could make it run forever if he had a little more money to build the tower higher. Well, maybe he could, but I myself didn't want to put good money after bad."

Mr. Brown laughed. "Well, Mr. Macdougall, a lot of money has been sunk in perpetual motion machines, but a little study of physics would prove to both the inventors and the investors that perpetual motion is impossible. You can't have motion in this world without a certain amount of friction and where there's friction there's lost power."

"This isn't perpetual motion you're inventing, then?"

"Scarcely. . . . No, it's perfectly simple and I'm not looking for investors. My invention is a steam wagon."

"A *what?*"

"A steam wagon. Well, it's really a locomotive that travels on wagon roads instead of on railroad rails and it pulls a train of freight wagons."

"Hmm," breathed Father.

"I've built two of them that were partly successful and I'm building the third now. I've been back in New York City at the John Reed Manufacturing Company supervising the construction and correcting the weaknesses the first two had."

"Well, I don't know if I exactly get the idea," said

Father. "You're making a steam engine to travel on a wagon road. Now, what I don't see is this: Can a steam locomotive engine travel all right on a wagon road, why'd they *build* railroad tracks in the first place? By grab, I can't see that."

"Of course," said Mr. Brown. "You're quite right. The answer is that a railroad locomotive *can't* travel on a wagon road. A railroad engine has to have smooth rails and easy grades because it hasn't enough power."

Father's eyes opened wide. "Not enough power! Man alive, are you trying to cod me or what? Not enough power? Why, look at the cargoes these engines yank along as fast as a good horse can run."

"That's right. They've got loads of power once they're traveling at a good speed. But let one of the locomotives try to start up with a long train on a heavy grade or even on the level if there's a little oil or grease on the rails. The driving wheels just spin around and the engine can't get a foothold."

"Should ought to have some ashes or sand to put on the rails then."

"They *do* have sand right on the engine and pour it on the rails, but even that doesn't do any good when the engine has a heavy load. But the same engine wouldn't have any trouble with that load once it had it going."

Father nodded his head. "I know how that is," he said. "A team of horses may have the devil of a time getting a canalboat under way but don't have trouble once it's moving."

"That's right. And the driving rods on a steam locomotive are hooked up directly with the driving wheels. They've got to do that in order to run thirty or forty miles an hour. But for pulling real loads the engine should be geared down."

"Geared down? What's that?"

"Well, you know what a *gear* is."

"Lots of kind of gear," Father said loftily. "There's household gear—beds and tables and the like. And some folks call victuals and drink gear."

"No, I mean gear *wheels*. Cogwheels. You know—a small cogwheel meshing into a big cogwheel, the little ones going fast and the big ones going slow, but with more power."

"Neighbor," said Father, "I'm afraid you're getting in pretty deep water for me."

"Not at all. You understand a block and tackle?"

"Have used 'em enough. Ought to."

"Well, then you know that one man can lift what several couldn't budge when he uses a block and tackle."

"That's so—if he's got it hooked up right and has got enough rope."

"Exactly. And gearing a machine down is the same principle as block and tackle. Look—"

Mr. Brown took an envelope from his pocket and with a pencil sketched a big wheel with cogs and a small cogwheel working against the big wheel.

"Now we'll just assume," said Mr. Brown, "that this little gear wheel has sixteen teeth in it and the big one has a hundred and twenty-eight."

"All right, that's agreeable with me."

"Now suppose the power is being applied to the little gear wheel and it's moving at a hundred revolutions a minute. It turns around once and how far does the big wheel turn? Why, it turns only the distance of sixteen teeth, of course. It turns only one-eighth of its circumference. Isn't that right?"

"Sounds right to me."

"Very well. Then the little wheel will turn around eight times while the big wheel is turning around once and consequently the big wheel is turning with eight times the power of the little one."

"Well, I swanney," observed Father.

"That is," went on Mr. Brown, "it's almost eight times as powerful. Some power is lost in the friction of the gears and all."

Father frowned. "Well, now look here, Mr. Brown," he said, "just suppose what you say is so."

"You can see it's so, can't you?"

"Well, yes, except for one thing. If that little cog-wheel was the driving wheel on a locomotive and travel-ing fast enough to take a brigade of cars at forty miles an hour, then that big wheel would be traveling one-eighth of that and eight goes into forty just five times. Why, your cars would be going only five miles an hour. Jeepers, a man can walk that fast if he hustles. That's no good."

Mr. Brown laughed. "That's a very smart observa-tion," he said. "That's very smart. But you've got to take into account the fact that the drive wheel would be a lot bigger than the small gear wheel, so you'd get a lot more speed than that. You'd get maybe eight or ten miles an hour."

"Hmm." Father peered again at the sketch on the envelope. "Well," he said, "if that's so, wouldn't you be offsetting that extra power you got from your block-and-tackle wheels?"

Mr. Brown looked at Father quickly. He stroked his big eyebrows. "You're dead right, Mr. Macdougall," he said.

Father laughed delightedly. "Hadn't you seen that, Mr. Brown?" he asked. "Looks like a plain proposition of the more power the less speed and the more speed the less power."

"Oh, yes," Mr. Brown said, putting his hand on Father's knee. "We realized that all along. I was just a little surprised at a man who's not an engineer and who hasn't been working with machinery catching on so fast."

Father laughed again. "All us Macdougalls are smart folks," he said. "But there's something else I don't understand."

"Well," said Mr. Brown, "let's straighten up this other point first. We *do* get several times the power our engine would deliver ordinarily by gearing it down. And we *do* get eight or ten miles an hour. Eventually we'll have lighter, faster steamers that will make about twenty miles an hour."

"All right," went on Father, "now take in the spring when the roads are all mud. Take when ordinary horse wagons get mired down. What you going to do with an immense heavy thing like a steam engine? Why, it'd sink practically out of sight."

Mr. Brown shook his head. "Not out west," he said. "You'd be perfectly correct, if you were speaking of Minnesota or your York State where the clay soil gets so heavy. It's partly true of eastern Nebraska too. But most of Nebraska and all of the far western states have a sandy soil. You don't get a heavy mud except along the streams. Another thing—the drive wheels on our steam wagons are ten to twelve feet in diameter and about two feet across the tire."

"Whew!" said Father, looking up. "Higher than the roof of this car."

Mr. Brown looked up also. "Oh, a lot higher. That ceiling isn't more than eight feet. But the width of the rear drive wheels keep them from sinking in the mud. We have a double row of studs in each rim to take hold of the road so there won't be any slipping. But of course I'll have to admit there might be a few days in spring when we'd have difficulty operating in eastern Nebraska. I do believe, though, that we can run every day in winter—which is more than the railroads can say. I believe this new steam wagon will be able to travel through any snow that ever fell in the United States. You see, those great wheels will simply tromp it down and go over it like a man on snowshoes."

"Well, I swanney," said Father. "You say you've actually manufactured one of those machines and it worked?"

"Have made two of them, Mr. Macdougall. Both of them worked successfully, all right, but there were some imperfections which I've corrected in this new model. In the first place, they were too slow. Of course, even four or five miles an hour would be a great improvement over the ox wagons crawling along the plains at a maximum of two miles an hour, but our new steam wagon will pull wagons with at least twenty tons of freight across the plains at eight to ten miles an hour. I'm confident of that."

"Ought to get a lot of business if you can do that," Father said.

Mr. Brown beamed. "Business!" he said. "We'll get more business than we can take care of for years. Already I've got a contract with Alexander Majors to take all the freight we can handle. That, I should say, means something. Russell, Majors and Waddell moved about three million pounds of freight last year from Nebraska City by ox team.

"I suppose," went on Mr. Brown, "that I sound like a book peddler or something. But I'm not trying to sell you any stock in the company or to sell you anything. Don't get that idea. I haven't any stock to sell. I don't need any money to finance this business. I'm just talking to you this way because I know all the land along our route will be taken up within the next year or so and I'd like to see men of your caliber become our neighbors. That will mean something to the Steam Wagon Company. And it'll mean wealth to you."

Father nodded his head seriously. "I'm beginning to get the idea," he said.

"Now look," Mr. Brown went on, "we'll have at least twenty steam wagon freighters running on regular routes to Denver City, the Mormon country and California inside of two years. But that isn't all. We're going to build a fleet of lighter, faster steam wagons for the passenger trade. As soon as the road is graded and bridged better we can run these light, fast steam wagons at a fifteen mile an hour average from Nebraska City to Denver City, hauling at least two stagecoaches behind. With that we'll not only get all the passenger business, which is a real item, but we'll get the mail and express contracts too.

"You see what that'll mean? Towns will spring up all along our route—shipping centers. Farmers will bring their produce—their corn and wheat and hogs and all —into these towns to ship by steam wagon to cities in the East and West and, as business increases, these towns, or at least some of them, will become cities themselves."

"Hmm," breathed Father.

"Suppose now, Mr. Macdougall, that you did this: Suppose you established a ranch on the steam wagon route at a reasonable distance from Nebraska City. Suppose you built a nice neat home and had a supply of good food there and your womenfolks could cook tasty dinners. The Steam Wagon Company would be glad to co-operate. We would recommend that passengers eat at Macdougall's and the steam wagon trains would stop there for a breathing spell."

"Hmm."

"And you could have a little store in your living room and sell delicacies and chewing tobacco and gunpowder and shawls and trinkets to passengers. Then you could cut wood from the stream—of course you would locate

near a stream—and the company would buy the wood
for the steam wagon and pay you for having a couple
barrels of water handy for the boiler."

"Sounds pretty good," said Father.

"And not only that," went on Mr. Brown; "all this
would make your farm a station and settlers within ten
or even twenty miles would haul their crops and stock
to your place when they wanted to ship it. So you could
build stock corrals and granaries, and of course you'd
be paid by the other farmers who used them. And
you'd be in a logical spot to build a general store to
supply the needs of the settlers who brought their produce in to ship."

"I swanney," said Father, "that all sounds *almighty*
good."

"Of course it's good. And it's practically inevitable.
Before you knew it the town of Macdougall, Nebraska,
would be established with a post office so the residents in
the district could get their mail there. But that wouldn't
be all. Once there's a town established, other businesses
would be attracted. Here's a plow agency wants a building and somebody else wants to open a saloon and
another man wants to start a newspaper and so on.
Where can they do it? Well, no other place but on your
land—if they want to make a success.

"Then what do you do? Why, you split up a section of
your ranch in town lots, sell what you want and hang
to the rest. You hold to a good share of the choice loca-
tions and then if your town should grow into a city in
ten or fifteen years you, Mr. Macdougall, are a multi-
millionaire, to say nothing of being mayor if you want
to be or maybe go to Congress."

For a moment Father looked out the window at the
green hills of Missouri drifting by. There was a smile
on his face. Then he turned back to Mr. Brown. "That,"

he said, "is a very fine picture you paint. By grab, it *is*. But there's something else I'd like to ask you."

"Fire away," said Mr. Brown.

"Well," said Father, "you take a railroad engine and it's got sides to its wheels to hold it on the track. It runs along and just follows where the iron rails go. That's all right. But I don't see how you're going to keep this steam wagon of yours from running off the road."

Mr. Brown laughed. "Perfectly simple," he said. "Perfectly simple. Take this steam wagon we're building in New York now. The rear wheels are about twelve feet in diameter and two feet wide on the rim. The front wheels are six feet in diameter and one foot wide at the rim. Well, the front axle is on a king bolt just like an ordinary wagon and there's a helm like a ship's helm attached to the front axle. We have a helmsman who steers the steam wagon just as he would steer a ship. Of course he rides right in front and there's an engineer also looking after the engine and keeping up steam in the boiler."

Father nodded. "Of course," he said, "I don't know what conditions are with the savages out there any more than what you say. But suppose the government decides they've got to have a railroad running out to the Pikes Peak mines and to California to bring gold to fight this war with. Suppose they send out enough soldiers to clean out the Indians and build the railroad. Then where's your steam wagon business?"

"My friend," said Mr. Brown, "God forbid that this war should last long enough and become serious enough for such an emergency. But if it did— Well, just *say* that it did. Could they spare enough troops from the war to drive out the Indians? I doubt if they could do the job with much less than a hundred thousand cavalrymen. Consider the expense of that.

"Then suppose they were going to put the railroad through. I'll never grant that they would, and I'll explain just why a little later. But just suppose they *were* going to clean out the Indians and put the railroad through. That wouldn't be good for us of the Steam Wagon Company, but how would it affect you settlers on the steam wagon's route?"

"Well, we'd be probably miles from the cars. We'd probably have to team our crops for miles to ship by the cars."

Mr. Brown shook his head and straightened the map on his knees. "Of course," he said, "if the railroad ran west from Omaha that might be true. But look at the map. Is it logical that the railroad would select a dead town like Omaha for its eastern terminus and run its rails over this swampy oxbow following the Platte River down rather than pick an enterprising community like Nebraska City and put its road straight through? Is it now? If they had brains enough for the actual building of a project like a railroad, it'd be unreasonable to think of them using Omaha for their terminal. No, Mr. Macdougall, *if* a railroad ever is built west, it'll start from Nebraska City. And in that case it would have to parallel the steam wagon road and in that case it would go through Macdougall, Nebraska."

Father looked at the map.

"But," went on Mr. Brown, "that isn't the point at all, at all. The point is they'll forget all about the railroad once the steam wagons get running.

"To begin with, the railroad theory is wrong—economically wrong. It costs too much to keep up those iron tracks and there's too much danger of wrecks. When two brigades of cars approach each other, through someone's error, they can't be steered around one another. Unless it happens to be on a long straight stretch of track and the enginemen can see the other train approaching in time to stop, there is a bad wreck. If one of the iron rails becomes twisted or broken, the enginemen can't possibly see it in time and the train leaves the rails and goes plunging through the trees. A wreck of that kind is almost as bad as a concussion of two trains."

"I calculate you're right," said Father.

"Don't you see?" asked Mr. Brown. "Don't you see nothing like that can happen to steam wagons? There can't be concussions because the helmsman can steer around another steam wagon or any other obstruction. They can't run off the rails and wreck because there are no rails to run off. Passengers would rather ride in the steam wagon coaches because it'll be safer, and it'll be cheaper, too, because it won't cost so much to operate as the railroad cars.

"Why, I predict that in ten years there'll be steam wagons operating all over the United States—let alone the West. The states will build good roads to attract steam wagons because it'll be to their advantage to have passenger and freight lines running through their communities. I don't say the steam wagons will supplant railroads entirely, but I *do* believe they'll be the principal factor in building up the West. I seriously doubt if there'll ever be a railroad west of the Missouri River. There's no reason why there should be."

"By grab," said Father, "you're most convincing. One way to look at it, it seems almighty silly they ever built railroads at all. Curious they didn't think of running steam wagons over the roads in the first place."

Mr. Brown smiled. "They just didn't work out the principle of the steam wagon," he said. "They had to wait for me to think of gearing the power to big drive wheels."

XI

We reached St. Joseph shortly after seven o'clock that evening and, at Mr. Brown's suggestion, took a cab with him to the red brick hotel. The cab was a ramshackle and weather-beaten coach with two woolly, nervous little horses hitched to it. The cab driver was an impudent, bearded fellow with a broad-brimmed, high-crowned hat on the side of his head and a frazzled cigar clamped between his teeth. He didn't bother to take the cigar from his mouth while talking.

We stood at the depot while this cab driver loaded our carpetbags on the roof. The sun was just setting behind the timbered hills across the slow-running river and the sun's scarlet reflected in swirls on the muddy current. Two steamboats were tied at the dock with smoke drifting lazily up from their stacks and a crew of singing Negroes were unloading a cargo from one of the boats.

The steamboat smoke drifting up across the sunset and the cool air of evening and the smell of coffee roasting somewhere near by and the singing of the Negroes all blended and affected me strangely. Everything was so new. And yet it all seemed curiously familiar.

Across the street from the depot several blue-uniformed soldiers lounged in front of a barroom while a Negro slept atop a pile of gunny sacks next door. Two wide-hatted young men strode by with big pistols strapped around their waists. They were talking loudly and angrily about "those sons of bitches up there."

And just before we climbed into the cab an Indian family stalked silently past—the man first with a red blanket wrapped around his shoulders and a long feather in the band of his battered hat; the squat, fat wife next, likewise with a blanket wrapped around her, and three scantily dressed children following in single file, according to size. The largest was a boy slightly smaller than I, who looked at me with unfriendly round black eyes. I stared back at him and then it occurred to me that I was actually Out West. Then the affairs of New York State seemed remote enough to have been in another life.

The woolly ponies took our cab at a trot up the steep hill and then went at a gallop down the other side while the vehicle swayed and bounded over ruts, knocking Aunt Christine's hat askew, and finally it swerved in to the side of the street with the driver bellowing, "Whoa, Buck; whoa, there, Tommy," and we were at the hotel.

"My stars," said Aunt Christine, straightening her hat, "I calculated we had a chance to live if we ever got off those steam cars. But even steam cars are safer than a ride like that."

"Why, that was fun, Aunt Chris," I said.

"Fun! Is that fellow a wild Indian?"

"Indians don't have whiskers," I said. Then we went into the hotel and got rooms. Father and I had a room together. Mother, Aunt Christine and Eliza had another room with two beds, Aunt Christine sleeping alone and Eliza and Mother sleeping together in the other bed.

Father found out that the steamer *Majors* would leave "about" eight o'clock in the morning for Nebraska City and Omaha, so the women retired to their room early to recuperate from the long journey on the steam cars.

Father grinned at me in our room. "Maybe," he said, "we'd better go down in the lobby and see what we can hear."

We went down the dark, red-carpeted stairs and the lobby was busy with men standing in groups talking loudly and cheerfully about the war, the Pikes Peak region, Kansas disorders and the Overland Trail. Father's new friend, Mr. Brown, was sitting on a divan with a broad-faced, heavy man whose blond hair was unruly and

whose side whiskers looked something like those Horace
Greeley wore.

Mr. Brown saw us and called, "Oh, Mr. Macdougall—
I want to make you acquainted with Ajax here—most
important man in Nebraska City."

"I'm grateful to meet you, Mr. Ajax," said Father,
extending his hand.

The man's eyes squinted and his wide mouth twisted
slowly into a grin. He stood up and shook hands with
Father. "My name," he drawled, "isn't really Ajax. It's
Gus Harvey. My friends just bestowed Ajax on me as
sort of a nom de plume."

"Mr. Harvey's editor of the Nebraska City *News*,"
supplied Mr. Brown.

"Most important man in Nebraska City," said Mr.
Harvey, "is Major Brown—when he's in town." His
eyes were still squinted in his quizzical grin. "Where do
you hail from, Mr. Macdougall?"

"York State," said Father. "Calculate on locating permanent in Nebras*kah*, though."

"I'm from York State myself," said Ajax. "Watertown."

"We're from down Canandaigua way."

"Hmm. Well, that's a pretty country. But can't compare with Nebraska."

"That's what Mr. Brown tells me."

"*Major* Brown," corrected Ajax.

Father turned to Mr. Brown. "Well," he said, scratching his head, "I didn't realize and know you were an
army man. I disremember now, but maybe I said some
things you wouldn't like."

"Not at all," said Major Brown.

Ajax smiled his slow smile again. "Don't tell me, Mr.
Macdougall," he said, "that you're not in favor of hanging every mother's son who was born south of the Mason
and Dixon line?"

"I," said Father, "think they could have stopped this war if they'd had a few hangings a year or so ago—if they'd hanged the right ones, both North and South."

Ajax looked at Major Brown and Major Brown rubbed his chin and looked at the ceiling.

"The whole thing," said Ajax slowly, "narrows down to the disgraceful induction into office of that Illinois buffoon. I knew it at the time and I wrote it in the *News* that if the nation could survive the calamity of this clown being put into the presidential chair with a majority of more than a million votes against him, the nation can survive *anything*. He was a sectional candidate. His election was a triumph of sectionalism. Do you know Lincoln received only twenty-six thousand votes in fifteen states of this Union?"

"Didn't know the exact figures," said Father.

Major Brown whistled softly to himself. "What's the news been, Ajax?" he asked.

Ajax winked at Father. "Had you heard that Brigham Young is a widower?" he asked.

"No, I hadn't heard of that," said Major Brown.

"It's a fact. Brigham is in mourning over in Utah. Pretty much broken up. One of his wives died last month and she was the handsomest of all his wives—except six."

"Now that's too bad," said Major Brown.

"Yes, and John Bennet has got his new giant jackass, Henry Ward Beecher, out at stud. Guarantees a foal for ten dollars."

"Think of that," said Major Brown.

"Is its name actually Henry Ward Beecher?" Father asked.

"His registered name," asserted Ajax solemnly.

"Well, I swanney," observed Father.

"And there's a farmer named Frank Barclay lives just north of Nebraska City found a strange cow and calf in his barnyard the other morning. Note tied to the cow's horn asked Barclay to please care for the cow and calf until the owner called for them. In a few days there was a new-born baby left in a basket on Barclay's porch. Note in the basket said the baby was owner of the cow and calf."

"Well, I swanney," said Father.

"Lincoln showed himself to the world as a powerless imbecile when he allowed Fort Sumter to surrender."

"That's a matter of opinion," said Major Brown.

"General Beauregard has requested the removal of women and children from Washington before he starts bombarding the city."

"Very considerate of him," said Major Brown. "How are you and Kicking Bird Reynolds getting along?"

"We've got no differences serious enough to fight a duel over yet. And we're in complete accord on one thing at least."

"What's that, may I ask?"

"Certainly, my dear sir, inasmuch as it concerns you directly. Kicking Bird and I are entirely agreed that Major Brown's steam wagon is not only going to prove the making of Nebraska City, but of the entire West."

Major Brown bowed. "I thank you, Mr. Ajax."

"And, oh, yes," continued Ajax, "while we're speaking of progress, here's something else that'll interest you. Charley Gerber's tearing down his butcher shop on Main Street. Going to put up a fine two-story brick building."

"Good for Charley," said Major Brown. "Now, if you gentlemen will permit me, I shall retire. I have some correspondence to attend to. Shall I see all of you at the steamer?"

"We'll be there," said Father.

"I'll try to make it," said Ajax. "Right now I have a pressing engagement. Must go and see a man about a goat."

"Be careful," said Major Brown, "of this Missouri pop-skull."

The next morning we were at the steamer dock early and Negro stevedores still were loading cargo, carrying stacks of dark slabs on their woolly heads.

"What are those things the darkies are carrying?" I asked.

Father look at me in surprise. "Don't you know bacon when you see it?" he asked.

"Bacon?" I asked.

"Well, Jack," said Mother, "I don't know as we ever had any real bacon since that boy was big enough to know about it."

"What's bacon?" I demanded.

Father laughed. "That's bacon the niggers are carrying. It's pork sidemeat that's been smoked and cured like a ham."

"Is it good?"

"Well, that's just a matter of taste. I, myself, don't care so much for it. Rather have salt pork. Not so strong tasting. But bacon has its points—it keeps good. That's why they have it for soldiers and pioneers. They can move it easy and keep it for years without really spoiling."

"Don't look very good to me," I said.

"Well, you'll probably have to eat it when we get out on our new farm. It ain't bad. Guess some folks would rather eat it than salt pork once they get used to it."

They put down the gangplank for passengers and we went aboard, getting seats on the upper deck where we could see all that was going on.

The *Majors* was a small steamer, not nearly as large as some canalboats, and was driven by a paddle wheel at the stern. Presently the cargo and passengers were all aboard and the mate on the lower deck began to howl and swear and give orders and a bell began to tinkle and the steam whistle boomed twice and ropes were cast off and the paddle wheel turned slowly while the *Majors* backed into the stream. The bell tinkled again and again. The whistle roared hoarsely, echoing back from the willow-clad shore across the river. Then, while passengers on deck waved and people on the dock waved back and screamed, "Don't forget to write, now remember," the long driving beam began to pump back and forth and the paddle wheel pounded the coffee-colored water to a white froth and we started on the last lap of our journey to Nebraska Territory.

The boat was crowded. People were moving about constantly, crowding past our bench in the starboard stern, but we were content to sit there, watching the tall forest-covered bluffs slide past.

"You suppose there's wild Indians living over in the woods?" Eliza asked.

"Don't know how wild they'd be," said Father, "but you can depend on there being Indians hereabouts."

"Buffalo too?" I asked.

"Think you got to get farther west for buffalo now. Seems like I've heard the buffalo are all out on the Great Plains and we're certainly not on the plains yet."

After a while Ajax Harvey came on deck. He seemed to know virtually everyone on board, greeting this one with a wave or a shake of the hand and a dignified bow for the women. When he spied us he came over to our bench and Father introduced him to Mother and Aunt Christine.

"You'll find this country quite different than Canandaigua," he said.

"I can believe that," Aunt Christine said. "I can well believe that."

Ajax laughed. "But I assure you, you'll find it better and more exciting."

"It may be more exciting," said Aunt Christine.

Ajax laughed again. "Mr. Macdougall," he said, "there are several gentlemen below whom you should meet. Do you suppose the ladies would excuse us?"

"Glad to," said Father. He looked neither at Mother nor Aunt Christine.

"Can I go along?" I asked.

"No," said Father. "You stay here with the ladies."

"I'm sure you'll excuse us," said Ajax, bowing to Mother and Aunt Christine.

It was noon before Father returned. He was jovial and red-faced and somewhat aromatic. "Met some very fine gentlemen," he observed.

Mother didn't say anything.

"One especially fine gentleman," went on Father, "name of Jaybird Charley Clifford."

"Indian gentleman?" Eliza asked.

Father laughed. "Not him. He's a white gentleman, all right."

"Well," said Mother, "it's fine that you're finding some drinking cronies so soon. Can depend on you for that. Even before we get where we're going."

"Now, now. How can I do any drinking when we're way out on a farm? Come on, it's dinnertime and they tell me these steamboats set fine tables."

The river twisted and turned like a snake and we seemed to travel three miles for every mile of actual progress. Once the boat stuck on a sand bar and the engine snorted and gasped while the paddle wheel, in reverse, lashed the water for half an hour. Then the *Majors* shook and wriggled herself free and we were on our way dodging snags and other sand bars. And late in the afternoon we finally nosed into the shore at Nebraska City with the whistles roaring out blast after blast.

Across the river were the terraced bluffs of Iowa—four

layers of heavy woods, one above the next with strips
of bright green grass between and a blue river haze laying
over all. Upstream the slick river swung slightly east and
then far to the west. Downstream there was a broad bend
to the east.

The *Majors* splashed slowly in, with Nebraska City
spreading ahead up the high hill—red brick and white
wood and log shacks.

"We're landing on the far Nebrasky coast," observed
Eliza.

Father picked up the carpetbags. "Mr. Ajax," he said,
"advised us to go to the Seymour House until we sort
of get our bearings." We inched along with the crowd
down the gangplank and the dock was a confusion of
activity—clattering trucks, shouting bosses, running
stevedores, passengers greeting people ashore, cab drivers
yelling insistently for patronage.

Straight up the hill the main street ran west from the
docks and it was crowded with ox teams and big-wheeled,
high-sided, canvas-covered freight wagons and with
horse-drawn vehicles and with horsemen and pedestrians
too. The pedestrians were having a difficult time picking
their way through the deep mud and avoiding death
under the wheels. The mud was at least four inches deep
and as black almost as tar.

An eager young man in a buckskin vest rushed up to
Father. "Right this way to the Seymour House!" he
shouted.

An equally eager but bearded man in a frock coat
rushed up from the other side. "Right this way for the
Cincinnati House!" he yelled.

A lank fellow in high boots darted up in front.
"Listen to me, mister," he said. "You can save money
coming with me to the Ludwig House."

"That's right, mister," said the bearded fellow. "You

can save money at the Ludwig House—if you don't mind bugs."

"You're a liar," shouted High Boots. "And they got worse nor bedbugs at the Cincinnati."

"Don't call me no liar, you bastard!" bellowed Cincinnati House. He strode stiff-legged up to High Boots, doubling his fists.

"Come on, mister," said the first youth. "Let 'em fight whilst we go to the clean, comfortable Seymour House."

"Good idea," said Father and we followed the youth to an open hack which was hitched to four horses. The five in our party left only two more available seats. "Just a minute now," said the eager youth after our luggage was piled on behind. "Won't be a minute."

And presently he returned, leading a very fat man who filled both vacancies, and the youth untied the horses and we started on a trot for the steep hill with the mud flying and spattering from our wheels.

"This here's Main Street," the youth shouted. "Seymour House is just beyond the top of the hill." He grinned proudly.

A carriage went splashing down the hill, throwing a spray of mud in our faces.

"Oh, my heavens!" Aunt Christine cried. "That's terrible. Did you ever in the world see such nasty mud? Look at it!"

"Chris," said Father, "that black mud *means* something. It means rich soil, that's what it means. That rich black mud means things grow here in Nebras*kah*. That black mud is grand to a farmer like me."

We swung around a heavy freight wagon drawn by five span of oxen. The driver labored along in the mud on the near side cracking a thirty-foot whip like a pistol shot and bellowing, *"Whoop!* Who-haw!" and just ahead was another wagon, drawn likewise by ten oxen and another "Whoop, who-hawing" driver and three more just like it ahead and some of the drivers cursed us as our hack raced past throwing mud in their faces.

Down the hill came a tawny milch cow in a bawling gallop, pursued by three barking cur dogs, and a man on horseback raced through the mud after them all, swearing at the dogs and lashing at them with a quirt. He cut ahead of the cow and turned her back up the hill as we drew abreast.

Aunt Christine put her hand on Mother's arm. "Did you *ever* hear such language?" she asked.

"Well, I've heard some language even back home," said Mother.

The air was strong with smells—the new black mud, the familiar reek of stock and manure and other strange and unidentifiable odors. Our hack splashed to the top of the first steep hill, but the street stretched on west, now in a gentle slope. Then the hack suddenly cut left across the broad street, swinging ahead of another trotting hack team, and pulled up in front of the Seymour House—four square stories of red brick, with white wooden porches extending across the front and covering the sidewalk at the second and third floors.

A foppish clerk led us up the stairs to the third floor and showed us our rooms on the south side. Our windows overlooked a narrow vacant lot, a one-story flat-roofed building and a two-story frame building with a gable roof and a black sign reading, "Wine and Liquors at Wholesale."

Father took off his coat in our room, rolled back his sleeves and poured some water from the pitcher into the big pink-flowered washbowl. He dipped his hands into the water. Then he turned and grinned at me. "Well, bub," he said, "here we are."

"Yes," I said, "here we are." I was sitting on the edge

of the bed with the big carpetbag at my feet. I felt let down and tired and unhappy and somehow lost. From out on Main Street came the bellow of the ox team drivers yelling, *"Whoop!* Who-haw!"

Part II

Nebraska Coast

The Nebraska Coast

I

We stayed in Nebraska City several days while Father
hunted and dickered for a team of good horses and a
wagon in which we could travel to Cousin Dave's place
on Rock Creek. He also extended his acquaintanceship
and heard many strange things.

Everywhere he found enthusiasm for Major Brown
and his steam wagon and he became more than ever
convinced that it was logical to take a pre-emption on
the route which the prairie steamers would take.

During these several days I saw little of Father and
I resented not being taken with him. I felt that now we
were in the wild West I must act like a man and probably do a man's work. And I felt therefore I should be
treated like a man.

So I wandered alone and unhappy around the streets,
looking in the windows and watching the great freight
wagon trains entering the city and leaving, bound for
the romance and adventure in and beyond the Rocky
Mountains.

The windows held displays fascinating to any boy.
There was Rotton's gun store with the windows filled

with rifles, muskets, shotguns, bowie knives and pistols. And there was the harness shop of W. M. Hicklin that had a gigantic saddle hanging as a sign above the door and in the window fine saddles, bridles and whips and spurs more handsomely decorated than any I had ever seen before. And Hawke and Nuckolls outfitting store with a great banner across the front, "HO! FOR PIKE'S PEAK!" and everything inside that the miner or pioneer or freighter might need, from barrels of lard to dried apples, wire nails and bluegrass seed. And in their window was a handsome lithograph of a manly-looking fellow wearing a splendid brush of brown beard and beside his face was printed in red ink: "DO YOU WANT WHISKERS?"

This placard declared that the times and this country called for *real men,* that it took real men to grow real whiskers, that real whiskers were a badge of real manhood. Further, the sign stated, "Warner and Company's Grecian Compound will force whiskers like these to grow on the smoothest face or chin."

I pondered over this advertisement. I realized I was young to grow such a fine beard under ordinary circumstances, but these were no ordinary circumstances. If I *did* have a magnificent beard Father would be obliged to recognize me as a man and take me with him instead of leaving me home with the women.

I went into the store. It was a busy place but clerks were finding ample time to gossip with customers. There were smells of camphor and woolens and leather and oil and the sad sweet odors of dried fruit in the air.

I came up behind one group and a clerk was saying to them, "Heath Nuckolls got a hundred mules in St. Louis for a hundred a head. Worth a hundred and fifty of any man's money."

"I still say," one of the customers declared, "that mules ain't worth a damn for freighting. Maybe better nor horses, but you got to feed 'em grain anyhow and oxen can keep up strent on plain grass."

I went to another counter and a customer was insisting loudly, "Snake charming is a tarnal impossibility. Just wait a minute. Don't care what anybody says."

The man was fumbling in his wallet. "You look a snake in the eye to charm him and he'll charm *you* just as sure as hell's hot. Most dangerous thing you can do is to look a snake in the eye. I got it right here some place. Here it is right out of the *News* and if you don't believe me, why don't you ask Kicking Bird or Ajax? Now listen here:

" '*Horrible Experience.* London, England, April 20— A young man here is dying as a result of looking too long at a serpent. The young man stared at the serpent in a London museum for some minutes. Then bladders of blood an inch long swelled out on his eyelids.

" 'Apparently the young man was unable to remove his fascinated gaze from the reptile's beady eyes and his own eyes disintegrated into a black, jelly-like mass. The young man now is dying in terrible agony.' "

"I still don't believe it," another customer said.

"All right, *don't* believe it. But here it is, right out of the Nebraska City *News*. If you want to call Ajax Harvey a liar go on and do it to his face."

"I ain't saying Ajax Harvey is a liar. Somebody sends this piece to Ajax from London or he cuts it out of a London newspaper and prints it again. Because it ain't true and because Ajax prints it don't make Ajax a liar. It's just the Englishman is a liar and I reckon there's liars aplenty in London just the same as Nebraska City."

"You're just ignorant, that's what's the matter with you. Ain't you ever heard of mesmerism?"

"Sure, I've heard tell of mesmerism. I reckon when they was passing out the brains *you* didn't get all there was on the plate. I'll grant that a man that knows how can mesmerize another man because I seen it done on the stage. I grant a snake can mesmerize a bird because I seen that done too. But I don't grant a snake can mesmerize a man and turn his eyes into black jelly and kill him like that says."

"How about Adam and Eve?" asked the clerk. "Seems like a snake did some mesmerizing in the Garden of Eden."

"Never mesmerized no man. Mesmerized a woman, maybe."

"And the woman mesmerized the man, huh? That's a good one," said the clerk.

I had pushed up against the counter and the clerk finally saw me. "You want something, sonny?" he asked.

I leaned over the counter and spoke softly. "How much," I asked, "is that Grecian Compound?"

"That which?"

"That Grecian Compound you got a sign about in the window. You know." I motioned with my hand, indicating a full beard on my face.

"Oh," said the clerk. "You mean the whisker grower?"

I nodded my head.

The clerk burst into a roar of laughter. "Tommy," he gurgled. "Hey, Tommy and Ben—look. Haw-haw-haw. Look who wants to get some whisker grower."

The two who had been arguing over the serpent howled and slapped each other on the back and their roars attracted more men who came hurrying up wanting to know what was funny and the clerk would say, "Why—haw-haw-haw—look who wants to buy some whisker grower," and the newcomers crowded around me so I couldn't get away.

"Hell's afire," I blurted, "I never said I wanted that stuff for myself. I just asked this jasper how much it cost. Maybe I don't want it at all. Maybe I want it for my aunt for all he knows. Maybe I want it for my aunt for all *you* know. All I did is ask this lunk how much is Grecian Compound and he goes off like a laughing jackass. Now you can all go to hell."

I pushed my way out of the crowd and I heard one of the men say, "That there boy don't need no whiskers."

Then someone seized my arm. I turned and it was Father.

"What's all this about?" he demanded. "You coming in here and making a laughingstock of yourself?" He led me from the store.

"I wanted to get some of that whisker-growing stuff," I said, "so's I can be a man."

"What in tarnation you want whiskers for? By grab, I'm a man, ain't I? And I don't go around with a horse's tail hanging on my face."

"Yes, but you're big. If I had whiskers I'd look like a man and you'd let me go around with you."

"Clint," he said, "looking like a man don't make you a man. You'll grow up soon enough and have a man's troubles."

"I have troubles now," I said.

"Well, maybe you've been kind of lonesome around here, but we'll be going west now. I've got a fine team of horses and a strong wagon with a canvas top and I'm just getting supplies. Calculate we can start out for Cousin Dave's place tomorrow morning. You run on back to the hotel now and tell Mother and the girls."

We did set out the following morning in the new wagon. It was a sturdy, tight wagon with moderately high sideboards and bows covered with new white canvas. The horses were strong-legged bays named Doug and Frank, used to the western country.

As our goods had not arrived yet from Canandaigua, Father made arrangements for them to be held until we came back. He had bought a supply of blankets and bedticks filled with clean new straw, tin dishes and cups, a couple of iron kettles, a frying pan and an ingenious iron frame that could be set over a campfire to hold the frying pan, coffeepot and a small kettle all at once. We had a cask of drinking water, an ax, a long-handled shovel, a new shotgun and powder and shot flasks. Our provisions included a slab of blackish bacon.

With the canvas sides of the wagon tied up, we had only a roof over us. Father and Mother sat on the wagon seat while Aunt Christine, Eliza and I sat on the straw ticks very comfortably in the bottom of the wagon. Even Aunt Christine seemed to be in good spirits when we pulled out of Main Street on the Overland Trail cutoff, westward bound.

Doug and Frank were eager apparently to be on the trail and insisted on trotting downhill despite the considerable load they were pulling, so in no time we were out in the open country with the prairie breeze, sweet with bluestem grass, rippling the canvas.

For a few miles there were farms and new orchards. Then the road, or trail—for at times it was not an actual road but half a dozen parallel wagon trails—went through unfenced pasture land, heavy with tall, waving grass. The country was virtually treeless, except along the valleys there grew heavy groves of oak, elm and black walnut. The hills were low and broad and when we mounted to the crest of a rise it seemed we could look away for fifty miles.

Father was entranced. "Look at that country!" he exclaimed over and over, waving his whip. "Just look at it. You'll never see a farming country equal to that if you travel the whole world."

Then he began to sing:

> " 'I've roved over mountains,
> I've crossed over floods,
> I've traversed the wave-rolling sand;

> But though the fields were as green
> And the moon shone as bright,
> Yet it was not my own native land.'

"By grab, my own native land never was anything to compare with this. Look at that sweep. Just enough slope for fine drainage. And I'll bet there ain't a stone to hit your plow in that whole slope there."

Then he began to sing again:

> " 'Lay down the shovel and the hoe,
> Hang up the fiddle and the bow;
> There's no more work for poor Uncle Ned,
> 'Cause he's gone where the good niggers go.'

"Giddap, Frank. And would you look at that grass. By grab, did you ever hear of such wild grass? Wouldn't that fatten up cattle, though?

> " 'Lay down the shovel and the hoe,
> Hang up the fiddle and the bow' . . .

"Well, Cousin Dave didn't lie. Nobody lied when they talked about this country. They couldn't lie. Why, I *believe* that story about the iron posthole auger taking root now.

> " 'There's no more work for poor Uncle Ned.'

"Say, maybe we ain't in Nebraska after all. Maybe we all stumbled into heaven in a covered wagon."

"It ain't heaven," said Aunt Christine.

> " ' 'Cause he's gone where the good niggers go.'

"How you know this ain't heaven, Chris? Your friends don't say it's any better farming country than this, do they?"

Aunt Christine slapped at a huge, bronze-backed fly. "They don't have such flies as this in heaven, you can be good and sure," she said.

"Ha!" Father chortled. "Should be a song in that. Let's see. They got no flies half this size in the skies."

To the tune of *Sweet By and By* he began to sing:

"They got no flies half this size in the skies;
   Got no flies half this size *in* the skies;
They got no *flies* half this size in the skies;
   Got no flies half this size in the *skies*."

"Jack," said Mother, "I can't see any reason to get sacrilegious about it."

"Sacrilegious! By grab, I think I was giving heaven the best of it—admitting it could beat *this* country in any way. Look at that sweep. As far as you can see."

"I'm looking at it," said Mother. "It's all right, I guess. But compared to York State it looks pretty dreary to me."

"Dreary! Woman, what're you talking about? Dreary!"

"Well, right across there you can't see a tree for miles. Who ever would *want* to live in a place like that?"

"Giddap, Doug," said Father. "Plenty of trees as far as I'm concerned. If you're going to farm you're just saved cutting down the trees and grubbing out the dang stumps. Too many trees breed chills and fever too."

"You certainly don't have the nasty black mud in York State," said Aunt Christine.

"Nasty black mud. Well, Chris, I calculate there's no use talking to you about that any more. You know by now that black mud means fine soil. And it's all dried up practically now, ain't it? Don't see any nasty black mud along here, do you?"

"Not right here, no. But there's nasty black mud at the bottom of every swale."

"Well, I swanney." Father spat over the wheel in disgust. "What you think of this country, Clint?"

"Fine and dandy."

"What you think, biddy?"

"It's all right, I calculate," Eliza said, "but it'd seem more romantic like if there were some lakes."

Father clucked his tongue at the horses and shoved his hat to the back of his head. Meadowlarks whistled in the grass beside the way and sometimes fluttered up and away as we approached. Now and then some large brown birds, which we took to be prairie grouse, sprang up in coveys with a whirring of wings. Later we learned these birds were prairie chickens.

"See those fat grouse?" Father called to me. "Look at the size of 'em. By grab, we'll just have some of those grouse for dinner, that's what we'll do. No use letting things like that go to waste."

I got the new shotgun up from the wagon bed for him and found the powder and shot flasks. While I was doing this a caravan of a dozen eastbound freight wagons came in sight over the hill, each wagon drawn by six oxen. While they were at least half a mile away we could hear the bellowed "whoops" of the drivers. And the train made a pretty picture against the green grass and the distant blue hills with the sun shining on the wagon canvases.

Father measured powder and shot and loaded both barrels of the shotgun while Doug and Frank pulled the wagon slowly on. He had just finished when we were drawing up to the wagon train and he greeted each successive ox driver with, "Hello, there, neighbor!"

Some of the drivers merely held up a hand in greeting. Some yelled, "Howdy." Some surly ones trudged along, paying no attention. But a mustached young fellow on horseback came galloping up from the rear and doffed his hat when he saw Mother.

"How far west you going?" he asked.

"Just to the Big Blue. Then turning south."

The young fellow, tanned as dark as an Indian, smiled. "That's all right, then," he said.

"What you mean?" Father asked.

"Injuns kicking up beyond Fort Kearny. Not so safe for one wagon to go alone past Dobetown. Just going to advise you to join up with a train when you get to Fort Kearny."

"Well, much obliged. That's kind of you, but we ain't going as far as Fort Kearny. No danger getting scalped between here and the Big Blue, is there?"

"No, you're all right here. Safer than Nebraska City. Nebraska City's death on bullwhackers." He waved his hand and galloped off.

"Clever fellow," observed Father.

"Yes," said Mother. "He had very nice eyes."

"But I calculate his loud-mouthed bullwhackers scared all the grouse into the next county."

Five minutes after the last freight wagon was past, however, another covey of birds whirred out of the grass.

"Here, wife," said Father, "you take these lines. I'm going to get us a dinner. Whoa, there."

I went over the tailboard and joined Father in the tall bluestem. We were on the top of a rise and my first impression was one of awe at the immensity of the sky. I stood transfixed, gazing up and off at the gigantic, cream-colored clouds banked in billow after billow in the bright blue above.

"What's the matter?" asked Father.

"Well," I said, "it's the sky. There's so much of it."

Father laughed. "Grand, ain't it? Well, you're not hemmed in with hills and trees like you're used to. And smell that air. Fresh and sweet and nobody ever breathed that air before." He swelled his big chest and hit it with his hand. "Come on, let's see what these prairie grouse look like."

We had walked less than two rods when eight or ten of the birds roared up and away. Father fired both barrels and three birds dropped into the tall grass.

"Get 'em quick!" he yelled. "Maybe some are just hurt and will hide away."

I dashed through the grass and the breeze blew a whiff of the strong powder smoke in my face. I kicked around in the grass and finally found all three birds. They were brown and barred with black and nearly as large as Plymouth Rock pullets.

Father felt of them. "Mister," he said, "they're fat as butter. Nobody ever need to starve to death in this country with critters like that flying around."

"Going to get any more?"

"No. That's all we need for dinner. No sense killing something you don't need."

He skinned and cleaned them quickly and put them in the wagon against dinnertime. Then we got back in and went rumbling westward.

Now and then we would sight a cabin, usually a hundred rods or so from the road. Father pointed to one such with his whip. "See that house?" he asked.

"You mean that shanty?" asked Aunt Christine. "Don't tell us you mean to move your family into such a place."

The building, if you could call it a building, was indeed a squalid hut with long grass growing on the roof.

"The Macdougalls," said Father, "won't be living in a sod house. Leastways, that's not what I'm counting on. No, I was just going to tell you. I heard all about those sod houses in Nebraska City and they say they're not so bad as they might look. They cut big slabs of this thick sod and lay them flat one on top of the other. They say they're warm in winter and cool in summer."

"And nice and dirty the year round," said Aunt Christine.

"Don't know about that."

"Being a man, you'd never think about that," said Mother.

"Well, I don't calculate we'll live in such a place. I calculate the thing for us is to find a nice spot near a nice stream. There's timber along all these creeks and we'll get enough logs to build a fine log house and I'll bring enough lumber from Nebraska City to finish it nice and with some real shingles for the roof."

"Just think of living in a house with *real* shingles on the roof," Aunt Christine said.

"Calculate folks living in those sod houses would think it was pretty fine."

"Your family," said Mother, "isn't used to living in mud houses, though."

"Giddap there, Frank," said Father. Then he began to sing:

"Down on the canebrakes, every day I go,
Take my bath in the lake below."

II

We passed the stage station and stable at Nursery Hill—two long low log buildings at the crest of a rise that gave us a view of miles and miles of rolling hills to the south and west, hills that were brilliant with June, fading in the distance to a lavender blue. Then down the slope and presently we came to the little Nemaha crossing where the wagon trails converged into a single road to use the limestone ford which had been placed in the stream's bed.

Here were the black scars of many old campfires, and

on the far side of the little river we stopped for our first meal on the trail.

Father chopped some wood, built a fire and placed the four-legged grill over the flames while Mother sliced some of the bacon and put it in the frying pan to make grease for frying the prairie chickens.

I went to the stream with the shiny new tin coffeepot and dipped up some water. There was difficulty in getting water even passably clear, for the stream was shallow at the bank and even at best was muddy and quite unlike the clear brooks of New York State.

While I was making repeated attempts to dip the coffeepot half full without scraping silt up with it and trying to avoid dipping pollywogs or wrigglers or skaters with the water, a long-tailed bird somewhat larger than a robin flew low across the river, screeching loudly at me. He landed on a limb and looked down impudently. He was mostly blue in color, but was marked with white and a little black and he had a crest on his head.

I made a motion as if to throw something at him and he flew back across the stream crying, "Screech! screech!"

I stooped to make another attempt to fill the coffeepot with clear water and the bird came screeching back again. This time I did throw a stick at him and he went upstream shrieking libel about me to the whole world.

By the time I got back to the camp the bacon was sputtering in the frying pan and giving off a delicious odor.

"Say," I said, "that stuff smells good."

Mother looked up from poking the slices around with a fork and pushed back her sunbonnet.

"Of course it smells good," she said. "You think I'd cook you something that wasn't good?"

"No, but, jeepers, I thought that stuff was probably just something you could eat if you didn't have anything else."

Eliza was rolling pieces of the prairie chicken in flour and Mother scooped up the slices of bacon onto a tin plate. "Just wait," she said, "until you get some of this fine grouse."

Aunt Christine took the coffeepot from me and started to put in the ground coffee. Then she looked at me and pursed up her mouth. "Well, my stars," she said, "that water looks like weak coffee already. What do you mean, to bring up water like that?"

"Gol," I said, "I did the best I could, Aunt Chris. Honest, I dipped and dipped but it's all kind of muddy. That was about the tenth potful I dipped and all the others were just as muddy or muddier and some had pollywogs."

"Well, I won't make coffee out of stuff like that."

"Well, you better go down and see if you can get any better water."

"What's the matter here?" demanded Father.

"Well, look at the water this boy brought up to make coffee out of."

"I didn't make the water. Jeepers, you'll have to talk to God about that."

Father squinted into the coffeepot. "Ain't very clear, is it? Well, come on, bub, and we'll see what we can do about it."

He reached in the back of the wagon and brought out a long-handled shovel. We walked down and in the mud bank of the stream he dug a hole a couple of feet wide and equally deep. Water seeped in rapidly, which he dipped out with the coffeepot. It was just as muddy as that I had dipped from the river.

"See there," I said; "you can't do anything about it."

"Oh, yes, I can," said Father. "This here's an Indian well. The first you dip out is always roily, but you just wait and we'll have water just as clean as if it came out of our well at home."

He kept dipping the water from the hole as it seeped in and after half a dozen pots were thrown toward the river, he stood up and grinned. "Look there," he said.

I looked into the coffeepot and the water was clear and sparkling.

"Well, I swanney," I said.

"When you can't do something, you come and ask your papa about it," he said.

So we went back to the camp and Mother was putting golden-brown pieces of the grouse on the tin plates. Aunt Christine took the coffeepot.

"That's better," she said.

"I'll bet you ten cents you can't find water like that," I asserted.

"I don't bet," said Aunt Christine loftily.

Father winked at me.

We sat under a huge cottonwood tree for our dinner—fried prairie chicken and bacon and fried potatoes and bread we had bought in Nebraska City and I thought I never in my life had eaten anything so nearly perfect. The grouse itself seemed better than any game or tame fowl I had ever tasted and I was entranced by the bacon.

"Maybe," I said, "bacon ain't very clean with niggers carrying it around on their heads, but I calculate being fried cleans it up all right."

"Cleans it up perfect," said Father. "And I don't believe we need bother raising any tame chickens or ducks with birds like these flying around wild."

"Hmm," Eliza shook her head. "They're awful good. But what would we do for eggs without some hens?"

"That's right, biddy. We'd have a hard time running around the prairie trying to find where these fellows do their laying. Guess we'll have to keep a few laying hens anyhow."

We had unhitched the horses to allow them to graze during our dinner and now I led them down to the stream for water while the women cleaned the dishes and Father swabbed out his shotgun and reloaded it. And the sun was glittering down through the leaves on the little river while the horses splashed and blubbered. And when the horses had drunk all they could hold I pulled them around and the long-tailed blue bird came swooping back again yelling "Screech! Screech!" at me.

All afternoon we rode with the sun bright on the canvas above us. I leaned over the wagonside, watching the slowly changing country, listening to the chorus of meadowlarks and quarreling with Eliza while Aunt Christine took a long nap stretched out on one of the straw ticks.

Perhaps half a dozen wagon trains passed us eastbound that afternoon and several separate wagons, while we overhauled and passed four or five trains and an equal number of single ox-drawn wagons.

One of these single wagons had "Pikes Peak or Bust" rudely painted in tar on the canvas cover. The driver was a thick-legged fellow with a short black beard. Tramping along beside the near ox, he grinned up at us through his whiskers.

"Going to Pikes Peak, neighbor?" he called to Father. "Better trade those hosses for oxen if you be."

"No," answered Father. "I ain't a miner, neighbor. Not looking for gold. Just looking for a good farm."

"Well, you're in the right place to find it, I reckon. No need going further, if you like farming. Myself, I can't be excited about a farm when you can dig a million dollars a year out of a mountain."

"It's all right if you find it," said Father. "Well, luck to you, neighbor."

"Same to you, neighbor. I'll show you the gold on our way back to Iowa."

Doug and Frank went into a trot on the downgrade

and a woman and little girl on the wagon seat waved to us as we left them behind.

We camped that night on the banks of the Big Blue. Across the river and upstream from our camp was the Big Blue settlement where we might have stayed, but Father thought it better to camp.

"Haven't much confidence in the looks of that place," he said. "Don't want to take Cousin Dave a present of some bugs."

"He might not be a stranger to 'em himself," said Aunt Christine.

"Chris," said Father, "it says in the Bible, take thee not bugs to thy neighbor nor thy neighbor's maid-servant nor ox nor anything."

Mother said, "Jack Macdougall, when are you going to quit talking such slang? How do you think that sounds to the children? Suppose they went out and made a statement like that to somebody. What would you think of that?"

"What you mean?" Father asked innocently. "You mean maybe you don't think that's in the Bible? Is that what you mean? Well, I disremember the exact book and verse or you could look it up yourself."

"Stuff and nonsense," said Aunt Christine.

"Well, anyhow," went on Father, "I wouldn't be grateful for some bugs even for myself. If you insist on getting bugs, you two, why, I'll take you up to the station. Clint and I will sleep down here. Eliza's a Mac-dougall and seems to have pretty good sense. Maybe she'll stay here with the Macdougalls. What say? Want to go? Mind you, I don't even say you'd get 'em. Mind you, I didn't say I *saw* anything up there. I just say if *I* was a bug and I came along and saw that place, why, I'd say, 'Here's *my* happy home. I don't need to go a step farther.' "

"Just like you and this Nebrasky land," observed Aunt Christine.

"Just like me and this fine Nebraska land. And if I ain't mistook, our farm is going to be back there a few miles on that pretty creek we passed this afternoon."

"I calculate we can sleep comfortable in the wagon," said Mother.

"Oh, I'll be glad to take you all up to the station if you want," Father said. "Just speak the word and it'll take only a minute to hitch and drive you up."

"I calculate I'll sleep in the wagon," Eliza said. "I think it'd be kind of romantic sleeping in a wagon like a gypsy."

"Oh, we'll all sleep in the wagon," said Aunt Christine.

"Scarce room for all of us in the wagon," said Father, "but you women can have the wagon and Clint and I will get along on the ground. The ground is fine for men. I've slept on the ground before this."

"And in gutters too, probably," Aunt Christine said.

"No." Father pushed his hat back and scratched the side of his head. "No, not gutters. To tell the truth the nearest I ever come to sleeping in a gutter was once when I'd done a long hard day's work and—"

"When on earth was that?" Aunt Christine interrupted.

"I'd had a long hard day's work," went on Father, "and I was very tired and walking home and there I saw your brother George terrible drunk and asleep in a gutter. Well, I woke him up and I said, 'Come on, George, and I'll take you home.' And George, he didn't want to come and tried to fight me and finally he says, 'Tell you, Jack, let's compromise. You lay down here and take a little nap with me and then I'll go home with you without no trouble.'

"Well, as I say, I was awful tired and I admit I was

tempted to take up George's offer because I knew otherwise I'd have to carry him all the way home. I admit I
was tempted. But my nobler nature won out and so I
picked up George and carried him home. That, Chris,
is the nearest I ever come to sleeping in a gutter."

"Stuff and nonsense," said Aunt Christine indignantly.
"You know there's not a single word of truth in that
whole slang story. George Rogers hardly ever even takes
a drink of spirits, Jack Macdougall, and you know he
was never drunk in his life."

"Depends on what you call drunk. I admit I never
saw George when he couldn't blink his eyes."

"If Clinton ever told a story like that," said Mother,
"you'd likely take a horsewhip to him."

"Yes, wife, you're right. I'd lick him to learn him to
take care of himself. Boy his size could ruin himself for
life carrying a big fat man like George Rogers. Could
get a rupture or hurt his back or whatnot. Listen to me,
Clinton Macdougall, don't you ever let me hear of you
carrying George Rogers around no matter how drunk he
is—not until you're eighteen years old. You hear me?"

"Yes, sir."

"Come on, Chris," said Mother, "let's hear no more
of his slang talk. Let's go to bed."

So Father and I rolled up in our blankets and lay out
under the stars and he showed me how I always could
find the North Star by running a line along the Big Dipper. The horses were tied to trees so they wouldn't wander off and they made comfortable noises grazing in the
lush grass. And once in a while a prairie wolf would
howl off in the night and be answered by dozens of his
kind and sometimes the night wind would bring the
sounds of laughter down from the settlement upstream
and there were three dim lights that glowed from windows up there.

And little frogs were singing down on the riverbank

and sometimes a dog in the settlement would get excited at the howls of the prairie wolves and would bark a dozen times and then go off into a howl himself. And our fire would crackle into a bright flame and then die down to a glow and then a piece of wood would break and fall with a tiny shower of sparks and the fire would blaze up again. And the prairie smelled very sweet under the night dew and when I awoke the eastern sky was red with the most brilliant dawn I had ever seen.

III

It was late that afternoon when we pulled up before the Rock Creek stage station. There was one narrow main building, thirty feet long or so with a lean-to on the south side, a smaller building and a good-sized barn and there was a stone well in front of the larger building.

Immediately after crossing a small bridge Father drove off the road to the beaten, grassless path that led to the barn. A tall slim young man stepped from the barn and peered at us curiously with no greeting. His blue jeans were stuffed into muddy boots. His limp-brimmed gray hat was turned up fore and aft.

"Say, neighbor," called Father, "can you tell me how to find Dave McCanles's place?"

The young man did not answer at once. He walked with rather short mincing steps to our wagon and put his foot on the hub of the front wheel. He had a curious face—an extraordinary nose that curved far out and down so far that it almost hid his thin, small mouth behind its downsweep.

"Well, I tell you," he said unsmilingly, "it ain't hard to find. You just take that road that follows the creek and go right antegoglin south for about three mile. Big house and bunch of buildings just before you get to the Little Blue River. Can't miss it."

"Much obliged, neighbor," said Father.

"You're welcome," said the young man seriously, and took his foot from the hub.

Father drove on the trail indicated, through a heavily wooded ravine and along the creek's winding course until we came out on a fertile, broad valley. And there, sure enough, were the buildings at the end of our long journey.

Cousin Dave sighted us from his barnyard and came on the run up the road followed by a boy about my size.

"Well, well," Cousin Dave shouted, "and here you are at last! Welcome to Nebraska! Come on and pull right up to the house. I'll have a man take care of the team and bring in your duffel."

Father put down his hand and Cousin Dave grasped it energetically, giving it a yank as if to pull Father off the wagon. Cousin Dave was a big dark man, almost as big and dark as Father himself. His black hair was long, curling down back of his black hat nearly to his shoulders. He wore a thin black mustache that curved slightly past the corners of his broad mouth. His eyes were black and, while they now were wrinkled with good humor, I sensed they could be fierce eyes, indeed.

"Well, I'm almighty glad to see you, Dave," said Father.

"Well, I'm glad to see you all, I can tell you. I certainly am. How'd you stand the trip, Sarah?"

"Good as could be expected," Mother said.

"It's been a terrible trip," said Aunt Christine.

"Pshaw," said Cousin Dave. "Why, you came practically all the way by steam cars and boat, didn't you?"

"Well, what of that?" said Aunt Christine. "You think traveling on the steam cars is a picnic?"

"I'd sure think it was a picnic," said the boy. He was a round-eyed, serious boy and I liked his looks.

"Hey, Jim Gordon!" Dave yelled. A stocky man in jeans came to the barn door. "Come and take care of Jack Macdougall's team, will you, Jim?"

We all were climbing down from the wagon when Jim Gordon came up grinning. "This," said Cousin Dave, "is Jack Macdougall and his family, Jim. This is Jim Gordon, folks. He works here along with another Jim—Jim Woods, who's out somewhere looking after the cattle. Say—" Cousin Dave took hold of Father's shoulder— "where's that big boy, Alan?"

Father's lips tightened. "Down in Maryland, Dave."

"Oh, I felt sure you'd get him out. He's only sixteen, isn't he?"

"That's right—he's only sixteen. But I wouldn't do that. Wouldn't try to bring him back. That'd likely ruin him. Best to let him go and hope for the best."

Dave nodded his head. He helped Mother and Aunt Christine down from the wagon. "Guess you're probably right, Jack," he said.

A large, sturdy woman came to the door of the house.

"Oh—so you finally did get here," she called. "Well, my land."

"We finally made it, Mary," yelled Father.

The woman came down the path, wiping her hands on a blue apron, followed by two yellow-haired little girls. She was a stern-looking woman, but handsome, and her light-brown hair was drawn straight and plainly down and back where it was tied in a sizable knot at her neck.

"Say," said the boy to me unsmilingly, "want to come down to the barn and see my horse? I got a good horse of my own."

"Sure," I said.

"Can you ride?" he asked.

"You bet your boots I can ride. I used to ride tow horses on the Erie Canal. Used to ride until I had scabs on my backsides bigger'n a dollar."

"Well, that'd be no fun. Say, I've heard your name all right, but I disremember it."

"Clinton Macdougall."

"Of course. Well, I knew it was Macdougall all along, but I disremembered the Clinton part. My name's Monroe. Named for President James Monroe—mighty fine president, too—I guess."

"Calculate he was. Must have been better than this Abe Lincoln."

"I'd hope he was. You named for anybody?"

"Was I named for anybody! Well, I calculate I was named for somebody about as great as President James Monroe. I was named for DeWitt Clinton."

"Never heard of him."

I stopped in my tracks. "Never heard of DeWitt Clinton? Well, by holy dang, I can't believe you. He was governor of York State and he built the Erie Canal what was about the biggest job ever done in the world, I guess."

"Bigger'n the Tower of Babel?"

"They never finished the Tower of Babel and they *did* finish the Erie Canal. I calculate DeWitt Clinton could have been President of the United States if he'd wanted the job."

"Aw."

"I calculate he could. He was an awful big man."

"I reckon *any* man would be president if he could."

"I don't know. There's Horace Greeley. I calculate he could be president if he wanted."

"Well, I bet he'd give a cooky to be president any day. Say, do folks back in York State think this Abe Lincoln is so fancy?"

"Most of 'em do, I guess. Father didn't and so the boys would yell 'Copperhead' at me."

"Well, I'd hit 'em in the nose if they yelled that at me."

"I did hit some of 'em in the nose. But you can't be fighting all the time and then there'd be a gang with some big gazabos you couldn't lick and the little ones would yell 'Copperhead,' and you'd start to lick them and the big ones would take a hand."

"I'd fight 'em anyhow. That's what I'd do."

"Well, I *was* fighting most of the time before we left as it was. What they think of Abe Lincoln around here?"

"Not so fancy mostly. But there ain't many boys hereabouts. You see Pa just built a school here last year. The Helvey brothers got some children up the road a mile, but there's only one boy about ten named Joe and another baby boy and four girls and then Jim Gordon who works for Pa has a boy about seven and a girl five or six and then I got two sisters ten and seven and two little brothers not big enough yet to go to school. Pa got a teacher name of Mr. Brown who's a pretty good jaybird for a schoolteacher, but you'll know all about him later. You'll go to school to him come fall. You'll be living up across the creek there, I reckon. Pa's picked out a tract for your pa to get a pre-emption on. How you think you'll like Nebraska?"

"All right, I calculate. Haven't seen so much of it, but it looks pretty good to me. How you like it?"

"Fine and dandy. Well, you see we been here over two years. I like it fine. I got a horse and a shotgun and I'm going to have a deer rifle pretty soon. They kick pretty hard but I can handle 'em."

"How old are you?" I asked.

"Twelve. You're a little bigger'n me, I guess."

"A little, maybe. But I'm big for my age. I'm eleven."

"Dad burn. You *are* big. I thought maybe you'd be

nearly thirteen. I'm big for my age myself. You ever chaw tobacco?"

"No. But I'm going to try sometime when I get a chance."

"Well, I'll get you a chance. Doc Brink, he's the stock-tender at the stage station, he'll give you a chaw. He gives me a chaw sometimes, but don't you dare tell Pa. He'd whop the life out of me if he knew."

"Is Doc Brink the fellow with the big funny nose at the stage station?"

"Oh, him! No, he's just Doc Brink's helper. Come up from Kansas a few months ago. Name's Jim something or other, but Pa calls him Duck Bill on account of his nose. Makes Jim madder'n all getout when Pa calls him Duck Bill and I've seen him walk back to the stable cussing to himself about it. Reckon he'd try and fight Pa if he had the gumption."

"Can your pa fight much?"

"Can he fight much? Listen, I bet he can whop any-body in Nebraska Territory."

"Maybe," I said, "he could whop anybody in Nebraska Territory before *my* pa got here."

"Whoo," whistled Monroe. "You think your pa is such a fighter?"

"Could whop anybody on the Erie Canal," I boasted, "and they're rough gazabos on the Erie Canal."

"Well, boy, if you think they're rough on the Erie Canal, just you wait until you see some of the freighters around these parts. Boy, they're wild and woolly and full of fleas and never been curried below the knees."

"My pa can curry 'em," I said.

"Maybe you think," said Monroe, "that you could curry a few yourself."

"Maybe I could," I said, "I'm sort of rough."

"Well, just suppose you try it with me."

"You're my cousin," I objected. "We're visiting you and I'd get whopped if I had a fight with you right off."

"Don't have to fight mad," said Monroe. "Can wrestle a little without getting mad and bloodying noses, can't we?"

"All right. Where do we do it?"

"Right here." Monroe rushed at me surprisingly fast and grasped me around the waist. I seized his head in the crook of my arm the way Father had shown me and with my left fingers clamped into my right fingers, squeezed in on the back of his neck for all I was worth. But Monroe wrapped one of his legs around one of mine and pushed me back. I tripped and we fell hard with him on top and before I could bring any real pressure to bear with my chancery, my shoulders were pinned to the dirt.

"You win," I said.

He released me. "Well," he said, "I'm older and should ought to win. But that's a dandy hold you had on my neck. Ouch."

"You were just too fast," I said. Privately I thought I could throw Monroe with my neck hold if given another chance. But it seemed better to let matters stand as they were, inasmuch as I was his guest and he was older.

He brushed off my back. "Say," he said, "we started out to see my horse, didn't we?"

So we went into the dark and manure-smelling long barn and a bay-and-white spotted pony nickered in a stall.

"Well, hello there, Charley," called Monroe. "How's my boy, there?"

The pony put out his nose and wrinkled his upper lip while Monroe stroked it. "This here's Clinton, Charley," said Monroe. "Yes, sir, old boy, this here's my cousin Clinton. Yes. Yes, it is, Charley, old fellow. And maybe Clinton'll want to ride you and you be a good horse to him, won't you, Charley, old fellow? You won't throw him off very *hard*, will you, Charley? Here, Clinton, you rub his nose so he'll know you."

I put out my hand and the pony jerked his head back.

"Come on, Charley," went on Monroe. "He's all right, Charley. Didn't you hear me say he's my cousin? Well, a cousin of mine's all right, ain't he, Charley?"

The pony lowered his head and I softly stroked his velvety nose and then rubbed his sleek neck while he nuzzled my face.

"See, he knows you already," said Monroe. "You must be a pretty good fellow or he wouldn't make up with you so quick. Lots of people he won't have a thing to do with. That's a fact."

We looked over the other horses for a while and then a bell began to ring up by the house.

"Dad burn," said Monroe, "there's the supper bell and I ain't done my chores all yet. Have to do 'em after we eat."

We ran to the house, Monroe bounding in an easy, deerlike stride that I kept up with only by exerting myself. He pumped me a tin basin of water and another for himself and we washed on a long, low bench, using soft soap from a small bucket and drying on a spotty roller towel. Then we went into the big kitchen, steamy with food odors, where Cousin Dave and Mary and the four younger McCanles children and Father and Mother and Aunt Christine and Eliza and the man Jim Woods already were sitting down.

"About time you cubs were getting in," said Cousin Dave. "Got your chores done?"

"Well . . ." began Monroe.

"All right," said his father, "you just see you don't forget them after supper."

"Oh, I was going to do them after supper."

"Clint can help you," said Father. "I calculate he hasn't forgotten his way around a farm yet."

An Indian woman, with face as expressionless as a cow's, was waiting on table and now she brought an immense platter heaping with fried chicken and another platter of smoking ham. Already there were dishes of mashed potatoes, turnips, dandelion greens, hot corn bread and smaller platters of fresh radishes and green onions.

"Looks like, Cousin Dave," observed Father, "that you live pretty well out here."

"Not starving to death, Jack. Were times when I didn't know how long it'd be, but the Lord provided."

"The Lord helps them that uses elbow grease," said Father.

"Will you say grace, Cousin Jack?" asked Dave.

Father rubbed his chin. "Tell the truth, Dave, I'm a mite out of practice."

"Well, you're not opposed, I trust. I've made it a habit and I think it's a good habit to acquire."

So Cousin Dave said a short prayer, giving thanks for the food and for our safe arrival and then began to pass the food while the Indian woman stood with a brush of long turkey feathers on a stick and shooed the flies away from the table.

"Yes, Jack," Dave said, "we've done mighty well here. Mighty well, indeed. And, Jack, you'll do just as well. Things are just beginning to open up here. The East is torn by war and we'll have to produce the grain and meat for the army out here."

"Not going to hurt your conscience, then, growing food for a war?" Father asked.

"Why should it? Somebody's got to grow it—why not me? You know I was opposed to the war. I'm still opposed to it. But the war's on now and there's nothing we can do to stop it."

"Well, I hate to support it."

"I know. I know how you feel, Jack—especially with your boy in it. But we've got to look at this thing sensibly. There's a lot of truth on the Southern side. There's a lot of truth on the Northern side too. It could have been settled without a war if there'd been some way to muzzle the fools.

"But the war's on now and we've got to admit that the South must be beaten. If the South should win and the Union should be broken up, we'll be two weak nations and it won't be long until England or some other European country comes over to cut themselves a piece of pie. England's moving in that direction right now. You can see she wants the South to win, not only on account of cotton, but because she wants the Union broken.

"Let the South win and see how long it'll be before England makes some pretext to jump on the North and move the Canadian boundaries down. No, I tell you, Jack, now that the war's on we've got to help the North —much as I hate to side in with those bloody Jayhawkers across the Kansas border here."

Father looked at his plate. He twisted one of his ear-rings. "Yes," he said slowly, "I know and realize there's a deal of truth in what you say. I got to admit it. But right now, by grab, I'm more interested in the affairs of Nebraska Territory and getting Jack Macdougall's family settled. If I put in my time worrying about the government I can't count much on the government putting in its time worrying about me. The government's got a war to worry about. I got to worry about getting a Nebraska farm. Calculate we both got enough on hand to keep us busy."

IV

"Nothing to worry about as far as you're concerned on a farm," said Dave. "This is about the finest valley in the whole territory and I've picked out a quarter section for you right over there across the creek that's better if anything than my own farm."

Father took a drink of tea and grinned. "I've got some ideas," he said, "that may not fit in with that."

"They will when you see this land. We'll go look it over tomorrow morning. You simply can't lose in this district. Take me. We came in here two years ago this spring. Settled up there where the Oregon Trail crosses Rock Creek and built a house and barn and dug a well there next to a fine grove of trees. You noticed those fine trees, didn't you?"

"Couldn't miss 'em," said Father.

"Well, I began breaking prairie and all the summer of 'fifty-nine travelers were streaming by on the trail, bound for the Rocky Mountains or California or Oregon and we had a new bunch camped under our trees nearly every night.

"I built the bridge and charged ten cents for a wagon to cross and I stocked up on supplies and made a tidy bit selling to the travelers. Well, we had a lot of sport too—quoit pitching and wrestling and debates and dances pretty often with me fiddling and calling off. I made a little money doing that too. Sometimes there would be quite a crowd on Sunday that didn't think it was moral to travel on the Sabbath and then we would hold church services. Yes, I preached. Wouldn't say I was a good preacher, but I *do* know my Bible pretty well and I reckon it was better than no preaching at all."

Father laughed. "Afraid fiddling and preaching are two things I couldn't compete with you on."

"Especially preaching," said Aunt Christine.

"Well, Dave's no Henry Ward Beecher," observed Cousin Mary.

"You ever hear Henry Ward Beecher?" demanded Dave.

"No," said Mary, "but—"

"Can't see how you can come out point-blank and make a statement like that, then."

"Have heard you, though, Dave. You remember that."

"Humph!"

"Oh, Susie," Mary called to the Indian woman, "you might bring in some of that pumpkin butter."

"Pumpkin butter?" said Mother. "Never heard of such a thing."

Cousin Mary's straight, thin mouth smiled. "It's the commonest sauce in Nebraska," she said. "You'll be making it, all right enough. Of course we have some wild plums along the creek but everybody isn't that lucky."

The Indian woman brought in a jar of brown substance which looked vaguely like apple butter.

"Just try some on corn bread," invited Cousin Mary.

We all tried it and found it fairly palatable. "Well," I said, "it's all right but I like grape jelly better."

"Why, Clinton," said Mother, "I'm ashamed of you."

"Ashamed of the boy because he won't tell a lie for manners," said Father, nodding his head at Mother. "Now, me, I think pumpkin butter is wonderful. Much better than dried-apple sauce."

"I think it's kind of nice," said Mother. "I really do, Mary. How do you make it?"

"Well," said Mary, "it's quite simple. You just cook up the pumpkin and mix it with vinegar and sorghum and cloves and cinnamon. If you don't have any other sauce you'd be surprised how they do eat pumpkin butter."

"I'll have to remember that," said Mother. "It's different, anyhow."

"Well, let's see," said Dave. "I was talking when Henry Ward Beecher and pumpkin butter came in, wasn't I? Well, the Overland Stage Company from Leavenworth got to using my place more and more and I built a bunkhouse for them. Then they wanted to buy my property. I talked away from that because I hadn't got my patent on the land yet. Of course I didn't tell the Overland I didn't have the patent. Take a company as powerful as the Overland Stage and you can't tell *what* they might do if they got the upper hand, except that you'd come out the little end of the horn. So I didn't say anything about not having a patent yet and told the company I wanted to hold that property but would give them a lease.

"That suited them all right, so they moved in on a lease last fall and I was pretty glad to move down here. We'd had a bad drouth last summer and I could see the grass down here on the Little Blue was better than up there. Don't think there was much more rain down here, but the soil is better and the slope is better and you can take advantage of the rain. This is a lot better place to farm even if it's a better place for business up there."

"This looks pretty good to me down here," said Father.

"It's perfect. And we've had plenty of rain this year so far. Well, as I was saying, I got my patent on the Rock Creek tract this April and when the Overland made me a better offer than they had last fall I told 'em, all right, I would sell.

"They'd sent a man named Horace Wellman and his wife to take charge of the station and a fellow named Doc Brink as stocktender. Wellman's got a high standing with the company and they'd given him authority to deal with me, so Wellman agreed to give me one-third of the price down, which he did, and he promised to pay the balance in three monthly payments. That's the only thing that's worrying me now."

"Aren't they paying up?" Father asked.

Dave shook his head. "But I'm safe, I reckon. I retained title to the land as security. But when I called for the first payment on the first of May, Hod—that's Wellman —said the money hadn't come yet and he couldn't understand it.

"I didn't need the money particularly and I didn't want to look overly anxious, so I didn't say anything more about it until the first of this month.

"Then I went up and said, 'Well, Hod, there's another payment due and the first one hasn't been made yet.' He was pretty flustered and said he knew it and he couldn't understand why a big company like the Overland would act that way. He said he had written them once and hadn't got a reply, but he would write them again that night. I told Hod to speak right up and tell them I won't stand for nonsense, to tell them I've got to have my money immediately or I'll take possession of the station again."

"What happened then?"

"Nothing—yet. Wellman says he hasn't got a reply to his letter yet, but he's writing again. He said that last night. Well, he'd better get an answer pretty soon. Here it is nearly the middle of June and the last payment is due on the first of July. If they don't pay up in full by then I'm going to take possession."

"Well, by grab," said Father, "I certainly would. Under law I calculate you could take possession now. Maybe the company has been sending the money all right, but this Wellman is keeping it. Did you ever think of that? Maybe one of these nights Wellman will strike off with the money and you'll never see him again."

"He wouldn't be stealing from me. He'd be stealing

from his own company. I haven't been paid and I've given no receipts and I've still got the title to the land. No, I hardly think Wellman's dishonest. But he *has* acted queer, I must admit. No, I think he's just embarrassed by the way the company is acting."

"Guess you were sheriff long enough back east so's you know something about the law," said Father. "Guess you know how to go about taking possession."

Dave laughed shortly. "Well, I don't know. The law is a pretty sketchy thing here in Nebraska yet. There's a justice of peace up the river, but he doesn't know any law or much of anything else. I just hope the company pays up all right. You know—I hate to have that sort of trouble. Well, I suppose if it came down to that and I went to Hod Wellman and told him I was taking possession and he'd have to move out, he wouldn't make trouble. Wellman's no fighter."

"How about the other fellow—what's his name?"

"Doc Brink?"

"I suppose so. Fellow with a funny nose that directed us here."

"Oh, no—that's not Doc. That's just a stable hand working for Brink. He's been around four or five months. Name's Jim Hickok. Harmless and not very bright. I call him Duck Bill just to see him boil."

Father laughed. "Good name for him, all right. Never saw such a beak on a man. But I don't like his eye."

"Well—Duck Bill's all right. He cleans out the stable and does Doc's dirty work. Jim Gordon says Duck Bill's a rabid Unionist and was with Jim Lane's Redlegs, but he's behaved himself all right around here. Oh, they're good boys at the station."

"If," said Father, "you're expecting any trouble, maybe you'd better tell this Wellman to move while I'm here. I'm a pretty handy fellow when there's trouble."

"What do you mean—while you're here? You didn't come to Nebraska just on a visit, did you?"

"Oh, no," said Father, "I'm going to get myself a farm."

"What're you talking about then?" demanded Dave. "While you're *here?* You're going to take that quarter section across the creek there."

Father shook his head, smiling. "No, Dave, don't calculate I will. I guess I've got a spot picked out on the other road on a stream the map calls Medicine Creek."

"Don't want to be near us, eh? Well, of course if you feel that way about us—"

"Not that at all. Matter of fact, when you hear what I've got to say, you'll move up with us."

Dave shrugged his broad shoulders. "I suppose now you're going to tell me you discovered gold on the way down here. Well, Father always did say the Macdougalls were crazy."

Father shook his head good-humoredly. "In a way, Dave," he said, "I suppose I *have* discovered gold. Anyhow, I'm convinced I'll make my fortune up there on the Nebraska City cutoff."

"Make your fortune! That's why I say you're going to settle here. That's why I wrote you to come out. Did you ever see any better land than this?"

"Haven't looked this land over very carefully yet, but shouldn't be surprised if it wasn't just as good as that up there on Medicine Creek."

"Then what in the name of all that's holy are you talking about, you loon? Here is as fine land as ever God made and right close to the Overland Stage line—right on the main road to Leavenworth and only a good step to the road from Nebraska City."

"Things is going to change, Dave," said Father.

"Of course they're going to change—change for the better. Ten or fifteen years will see this country settled up as close as York State and it'll settle along this valley first. You get a hundred and sixty acres for a dollar and a quarter an acre and it'll be worth ten or fifteen dollars by the time that cub is old enough to vote."

"Part of that I believe, Dave," said Father, "but did you ever hear of the steam wagon?"

"You mean the railroad?"

"No—the steam wagon. It's going to put the railroad out of business. They're building a steam engine that'll run on wagon roads and snake a whole brigade of big wagons across the plains as fast as a horse can run."

"Go on," said Dave.

"Well, that's it. They've built a couple of these machines and they work. Now they're building another better one and pretty quick they'll start hauling wagon trains to Pikes Peak."

"What kind of tomfool talk is that? Who you been listening to, Jack?"

"Not tomfool talk, Dave," said Father seriously. "It's a fact. Nebraska City folks can't talk about much of anything else. Man named Major Joseph R. Brown invented the machine and the Nebraska City folks have raised money to grade the road and build bridges. Don't you ever get to Nebraska City?"

"No," said Dave. "I go to Brownville when we need supplies. But all that doesn't sound reasonable to me. I admit I don't know much about railroads, but it stands to reason that if a railroad engine could run without a railroad track they never would build tracks in the first place."

"I know," said Father. "It struck me that way at first too. But they explained it all to me. Now look—"

Father then outlined to Dave the gear principle of the steam wagon as Major Brown had given it to him.

"That's all right," said Dave reluctantly. "It sounds all right, but I'm no engineer and I'd have to see it first.

You're not investing any money in a thing like that, are you, Jack?"

"Not a red cent. They didn't ask me to invest because they've got all the money they need. It don't cost me a red cent and they'll make my place a station if I locate where I'm going to locate.

"You think you did pretty well with your little bridge and station on the Overland Trail. Well, inside of ten years there'll be a steady stream of steam wagons running over that road north of here, to and from Nebraska City. It's inevitable, Dave. Settlers who locate on that line at proper spots will be rich. Down here it'll be just a still-water eddy."

Dave shook his head, smiling.

"Look, Dave," went on Father, "why don't you move up on the main road too? We'll get pre-emptions about fifteen miles apart and open stations where the passengers can eat and maybe get a snort of oh-be-joyful and start stores with supplies for farmers and be shipping points for the farmers to send out their produce to Nebraska City and the first thing we know towns will spring up around our stations. And you'll be mayor of McCanles, Nebraska, and I'll be mayor of Macdougall, Nebraska."

Dave laughed uproariously. "He just never grew up," he said. "Jack just never grew up."

The conversations on the steam wagon were not finished at this session. For the two days we remained at Cousin Dave's place each mealtime was the signal for renewed discussion.

"Have you ever *seen* this steam wagon work?" Dave would demand.

"You know I haven't seen it. But I've talked with men who have."

"And you believe everything you hear."

"No, I don't believe everything I hear. But I don't

disbelieve everything, either. A man that shuts his ears
to everything and won't listen to argument is just a plain
dang fool. Why don't you subscribe to the Nebraska City
News and find out about things? Man named Ajax
Harvey is editor of that newspaper and about the smartest man I ever saw—unless maybe it's this Major
Brown."

"Well, I guess Abraham Lincoln is a smart man too.
But I don't believe everything he says or writes."

"I don't even admit he's a smart man."

"Well, don't talk about it—not too much. I think
most people in Nebraska Territory hold the same
opinion you do. But, after all, this is going to be a free-
soil state in all probabilities and the authorities are
mostly pretty strong Union. Somebody might make
trouble for you, Jack."

"I'm not afraid of trouble."

"Well, neither am I. But I've got a family to think
about and so have you. It doesn't pay to go out looking
for trouble. Pretty easy to shoot a man out here and
claim he was stirring up mischief against the Union."

"I can handle my fights with my fists."

"So can I. But I don't go looking for fights. Enough of
them come your way in a new country without carrying
a chip on your shoulder."

"I know," said Father. "The Erie Canal wasn't exactly
a quilting bee."

"All right, Jack, I'll grant you probably can take care
of yourself—physically. But right now that's beside the
question."

"Oh, you think I need a mental guardian."

"When you get on this steam wagon tangent, I do.
You say it isn't costing you a red cent. All right, it isn't
costing you a red cent in cash. But it *is* costing you something in opportunity. All right. Now, here's an opportunity for a fine pre-emption on the Overland Trail.

You can't possibly lose on it. But you prefer to take a gamble and move up there on a side road that'll continue being a side road unless this harum-scarum idea of steam oxen is successful."

"No," said Father, "I can't see your argument. I get a good farm down here. I get a good farm up there. And everything points to a dang lot more than a good farm up there. I can't lose down here. I can't lose up there and, by grab, I stand to make a lot more than a farmer's living up there by all the signs."

"The whole thing in a nutshell," said Aunt Christine, "is that Jack thinks maybe he can get out of farm work up there."

"Stuff and nonsense," said Father.

Dave threw up his hands. "I give up," he said. "No use trying to talk sense into a Macdougall."

After supper Jim Gordon and his wife, a small woman who looked too frail for frontier life, came over and Cousin Dave played his fiddle a while. Then Aunt Christine, who had discovered a small table that looked like cherry wood, brought up the subject of spiritualism and she, Mother, Cousin Mary and Jim Gordon and Mrs. Gordon grouped around the table to see if the spirits worked as far west as Nebraska. Father, Dave, Monroe and I went outdoors.

In the twilight Monroe and I ran a race to the barn, with their black-and-white shepherd, Rover, barking beside us. Monroe beat me easily.

"Well," I said, "I'm better running long distances. I'll run you right back to the house."

But Monroe ran with the ease of an antelope, outdistancing me more than before. Dave and Father were grinning when we pulled up panting at the house and Rover danced around with delight. Dave nodded his head at Monroe. "That's my son," he said.

"I calculate," said Father, "he's a better man than his paw."

"What do you mean—better man than his paw? Any McCanles always could beat a Macdougall."

Father grinned widely and stripped off his jacket. "It's a race," he said.

Dave pulled off his coat and dropped it on the wash-bench by the door. "You start us, Monroe," he said. "We'll run past the far end of the barn."

"All right," said Monroe, "I'll say one, two, three and yell go. You start when I yell go."

Father and Dave stood together—both big dark men, but Father was more than an inch taller. His shoulders also were broader, but more sloping.

"All right," said Monroe. The two men crouched slightly, Father with his hands on his thighs.

"One, two, three—GO!" yelled Monroe shrilly.

They were off together, with Dave, if anything, slightly in the lead. Never had I seen anyone run so fast. In the twilight it seemed their feet weren't even touching the ground. They seemed to be two huge, low-swooping swallows darting toward the earth, neck and neck. Half-way to the barn Father had pulled a little ahead. Then Dave's shoulders hunched up and he drew a little ahead of Father. Then Father's great long legs drove him up and they seemed to be abreast when they passed the end of the barn.

Monroe and I galloped down and Rover, barking wildly, came to meet us.

"Oh, I think it was a dead heat, all right," said Dave, wiping his forehead.

"No," said Father, "I'd say you was about two hands ahead. Jeepers. Hadn't any idea you could run like that."

"Hadn't any idea. Haven't forgotten me nearly beating you when I was a cub and you practically had your growth, have you?"

"That's it," said Father. "I'm always forgetting I'm almost an old man. I'm thirty-eight years old and you're just a young squirt—almost three years younger than I am. You ain't so fast. I'm just slowing up."

"Well," I said, "if it was so close, why don't you race back to the house?"

"That's an idea," said Dave.

So I trotted back to the house and Monroe started them off again. And this time Dave came in half a stride ahead of Father.

"Just your youth," said Father, panting and extending his hand. "Can't beat Father Time."

Dave laughed and shook hands. "It's just a clean life out here in the healthy Nebraska air," he said.

Father squinted his eyes and looked at him. "What," he asked, "does this clean life in this healthy Nebraska air do to your tussling ability?"

Dave slapped his own broad chest. "Haven't been toppled since I was old enough to vote," he said.

"Well," said Father, "if you don't mind getting your pants dirty, you're about to lose that record right now."

I looked at Monroe and grinned. He grinned back. "I bet you," I whispered, "a two-cent copper on Father."

"It's a bet," he said.

"We'll just see about that," said Dave. "Hate to humble you in front of your son twice in one night, but you asked me to do it."

He rushed at Father, grabbing for an underhold, but Father blocked him with his arms and with a rip like a splintering board the sleeve of Father's flannel shirt was torn from shoulder to cuff, revealing a huge brown arm with straining muscles knotted and crawling like a nest of fat snakes. Dave lunged forward, trying a quick trip, but Father leaped loose and brushed his long hair from his eyes.

"You're not as easy as you look," Father observed maliciously.

"I look easy, do I?" Dave rushed in.

Father ducked low and, moving so quickly that I couldn't see the process, suddenly had one hand in Dave's crotch and Dave swung off the ground, kicking and clear over Father's head. Father stood a moment, holding Cousin Dave at arm's length above his head.

"Oh, you look *pretty* easy," he said. "Maybe I should ought to bang you down on your back, but that ain't good for the innards." He swung Dave down easily to his feet.

"I'll be dad burned," said Monroe.

Dave dropped his hands and stared at Father. "Almighty God," he said, "I still don't believe that was possible. Do you know I weigh fourteen stone?"

"About that, I'd say," said Father calmly. "You want to go on tussling?"

Dave walked over to the bench and picked up his coat. "I only tussle with human beings," he said. "Anybody who can do that to me isn't human."

Father laughed. "I tell you, Dave, it's just clean living and healthy Erie Canal air."

"You can go ahead and move up on your steam wagon road," said Dave. "Then I can still be wrestling champion of Gage County."

Eliza came running out the door and saw Father's shirt. "What on earth happened?" she cried. "Father, are you hurt?"

"Not very serious," said Father. "Cousin Dave's been tussling me."

"Looks like," she said, "he tussled you too hard."

"He did," said Father, "a lot too hard."

"You go hang," said Dave, putting on his coat, "you gorilla, you grizzly bear."

"Well, I just wanted to tell you," broke in Eliza,

"Aunt Christine's got the spirits bobbing that table something awful. She's all excited because Tom Brooks has come out to Nebraska with her."

"What's all that?" asked Dave.

"Stuff and nonsense, that's all," said Father, "and, biddy, I don't want you getting your head all filled up with that hogwash."

"Well, listen," said Eliza, "I don't say I believe any of it because I don't, but it was awful creepy. This Dolly spirit that talks to Aunt Chris so much was talking and Aunt Chris asked if there was a message for anybody here and Dolly said yes. And she asked if the message was for her and Dolly said no. And she asked if it was for Mother or for Mary or for Mr. and Mrs. Gordon or me or for any of the children and Dolly said no. Then she asked if it was for you, Father, and Dolly said no. And then she asked if it was for Cousin Dave and Dolly said yes."

"For me, eh?" said Dave.

"Yes. So Aunt Chris asked for the message and all Dolly would say was, 'Water, water.' And Aunt Chris asked Dolly to go on and that was all she would say, just 'Water, water.'"

Dave laughed. "Why didn't you get the poor spirit a drink?" he asked. "She just thought I would get her a drink of water."

"Oh, you—" said Eliza.

"Speaking of water," went on Dave, "I could do with a drink myself. How about you, Jack?"

"Could do with a drink of *anything*," said Father. "You go back and tell the spirit, biddy, that if it's worrying about Dave getting drownded, there's not enough water in the Little Blue to drown even a McCanles and, besides, folks born to be hung don't have to be afraid of water."

"Oh, you—" said Eliza and stamped her boot and started for the house.

"Hey," yelled Monroe, "ask the spirit when am I going to get my deer rifle?"

V

So, despite the arguments of Cousin Dave and his demonstrations of how fine the land was on the quarter section across the river, we ended our visit one bright morning and started back north in our wagon. We cut into the main road at the stage station with the dew glittering in the thicket along the Rock Creek ravine. A thin streamer of smoke was rising from the kitchen chimney and at the rattle of our wagon the slim young man with the big nose stepped from the near-by bunkhouse door.

"Good morning, neighbor," called Father, waving his hand.

"Morning," replied the young man without changing expression.

We clattered over the little bridge and up to the Big Blue settlement, then turned east on the Nebraska City cutoff. That night we camped on the banks of Medicine Creek near the road and Father proclaimed that here was the site of the future city of Macdougall, Nebraska.

"You may not realize it, wife," he said, "but this is probably the most important day in your life—outside your wedding day, of course."

Mother was rolling pieces of prairie chicken in corn meal and I had just brought up a perfect buffalo skull, complete with arching horns, that I had found near by.

"You really think we'll locate here?" she asked.

"Think? Why, of course we're going to locate here. Why not? Ever see a finer stretch of land than this? Just look." He swept his arm in an arc to include the east bank of the creek and northward.

"Yes, it's very good," she admitted.

"Then what you talking about, woman?"

Mother looked down at the tin plate of corn meal. "Can't help but think," she said, "that there may be a lot of truth in what Dave says."

Father patted her on the back. "Now, wife," he said, "you just let me do the thinking. I know what we're about. If I could get a government guarantee that I would be worth twenty thousand dollars in ten years by just turning over my hand, why, I wouldn't even bother to turn it over. That's just how sure I am."

"That's just the trouble," put in Aunt Christine. "You're not willing to turn your hand. That's why your whole family will probably starve to death out here in the wilderness."

"Wilderness!" blurted Father. "You call *this* a wilderness. Tom Brooks is out here, ain't he?"

"Jack!" Mother spoke sharply. "Now don't you start that again."

Father laughed and I took advantage of the pause to approach him with the buffalo skull. "Look," I said, "there *are* buffalo right here on our land. They'll probably come through here in the fall like the passenger pigeons or wild ducks and we can get a lot of them."

Father shook his head. "No, I guess not. Dave tells me they're drove pretty well farther west. Says you got to go out to about Fort Kearny before you see buffalo any more. That suits me just as well, because where there's buffalo there's wild Indians and we don't want wild Indians coming in on us some night. I think we can get along without the buffalo, all right."

"Well," said Eliza, "I wish the mosquitoes had followed the Indians."

"Mosquito never would bite an Indian," said Father. "Indian's hide's too tough. Mosquito busts off his beak any time he tries to get through to an Indian. Dave was telling me how the Indians run around practically naked in zero weather. White man asks an Indian if his body don't get cold. The Indian says, 'Ugh, white man's face get cold?' And the white man says, 'Of course not—my face don't get cold much.' And the Indian says, 'Ugh— Indian all face.'"

"Well, my land," said Eliza.

"Dave says, too, if an Indian comes monkeying around just yell 'Puckachee!' at him. That means to get to the hell away from here in Indian talk."

"Oh," said Eliza, "I wouldn't want to say for him to get to that word away in any language."

Father scratched his chin. "Well, it don't mean exactly to get to the hell, but it means to get away and it's pretty emphatic."

"Hmm. What was that word again, Jack?" Mother asked.

"Puckachee. Dave says they'll git if you yell that— unless, of course, there happened to be a lot of 'em."

"Puckachee," said Mother.

"Puckachee," said Aunt Christine.

"Well," said Eliza, "I expect they'd go about as fast if you just yelled scat or shoo."

Father laid out the approximate position of our proposed house and barn and well, which Mother approved, and the next day we left for Nebraska City. The plan was to rent a house there and leave the women while Father and I and a carpenter went back to the land with tools and some finishing lumber and shingles to put up the buildings.

Our goods had arrived from Canandaigua, so Father found a vacant house on Otoe Street, one square south of Main Street, rented it and moved our goods in. Then with a handyman-carpenter named Albert Striker and a load of planed lumber, cottonwood shingles and glass windows, Father and I went back to our pre-emption.

In the early stages of building I was of small value, except for fetching and carrying. But, as the house progressed, I was able to relieve Father and Mr. Striker of much work, such as nailing, finishing and especially could I nail shingles on the "L."

The house sat back from the road about seventy-five feet and was approximately thirty feet long, paralleling the road, and with a one-story L branching back from the east end. This L contained two bedrooms. The house itself was a story and a half, the upper portion containing two rooms—one large bedroom, which could be partitioned by a curtain and a smaller room joining the big room by a door.

Downstairs, about sixteen feet of the length was devoted to the living room and fourteen feet to the kitchen. The steep stairs to the upper bedrooms led up from the living room.

Father originally had planned on a big fireplace in the living room, but Mr. Striker advised against it.

"Costs too dern much out here," he said. "Take back in Indiany and rock don't cost too much. Then you can have a fireplace if you want. But when you get down to rock bottom, what you want a fireplace for anyways? Stoves make better heat and don't use up so much wood or coal or cobs or whichever you're burning."

"I gots lots of wood," said Father, waving at the timbered Medicine Creek.

"Have now, sure enough. But what about twenty year from now? Can't tell what you might want with that timber. Some pretty good saw timber in there."

Father looked off at the horizon, probably visioning the timber needs of the city, Macdougall, Nebraska.

"I calculate you're right, Striker," he said. "We'll use stoves."

Late one afternoon a wagon pulled off the road on our side of the creek. I paid no attention, for freighting traffic had been fairly heavy and frequently there had been campers at the creek. I was holding a window while Mr. Striker nailed on a molding.

"Hello, Clint," said a voice at my elbow and there was Monroe McCanles dressed in good clothes and grinning at me.

"Monroe," I said, "where on earth did you come from?"

"Coming right along with a house, ain't you?" said Monroe.

"Gol," I said. "Hey, father—Monroe's here!"

Father came around the side of the house carrying a saw. His eyes opened wide when he saw Monroe. "By the twelve holy disciples," he said. "Is your pa here?"

"Nope," Monroe grinned. "I'm just here with Hod Wellman. We reckoned we'd camp on your land if you don't mind."

"Mind! Of course we're tickled to have you, boy. But I don't understand. What you doing up here with Wellman?"

Monroe looked back over his shoulder at the light wagon where Wellman was unhitching the horses by the creek. "Well," he said, "we're going to Nebraska City."

Father raised his eyebrows.

Monroe grinned again, enjoying the suspense. "You see, Hod had to go to Nebraska City to get supplies and to get money for Father." He lowered his voice importantly. "You see, the stage company owes Pa for the station and they were supposed to pay up yesterday or lose the station back to Pa."

"I understand that," said Father: "So Wellman's going to get the money?"

"Yes, that's right," said Monroe. "So he was going to be in Nebraska City over the Fourth of July and there's going to be a big celebration with parades and fireworks

and everything, so he said to Pa could I go with him to
see the fun and Pa said I could."

"Jeepers," I said.

"That's fine," said Father. "Our folks are living in
Nebraska City while we're building the house here and
you can go and stay with them. We'll show you how to
get there so's you can't miss it."

"Well, listen, Cousin Jack, I was wondering if maybe
Clint could go with me. That would be nuts for me if he
could."

Father rubbed his chin. Then he grinned. "Well," he
said, "Clint's been a pretty good boy around here lately.
I calculate he deserves a holiday."

"Yeow!" I yelled. I grabbed Monroe by the shoulders
and we danced around in front of the house.

"Now wait a minute," said Father. "Work ain't over
for the day yet. This is the second of July and you'll be
gone three or maybe four days—if you go. So if you want
to go, by grab, you'd better look after your work today."

"Oh, you bet," I said. "I'll see you right after we get
through work, Monroe."

"I'll help you now," offered Monroe.

Father shook his head. "No, Monroe, I calculate you'd
better go and help Wellman. He's taking you, you know.
And, besides, I calculate one boy is one boy and two boys
is just half a boy and three boys is no boy at all."

Mr. Striker looked up. "Which?" he asked.

Monroe frowned. "I don't understand that exactly,
Cousin Jack," he said.

Father laughed. "Well, you just figure it out for yourself."

"One boy is one boy," said Monroe. "Two boys is half
a boy—that it? And three boys is no boy at all."

Mr. Striker chuckled. "By cracky," he said, "that's
pretty dern good. Never heard that one before."

"I catch on," said Monroe, giggling.

"You tell Wellman to come up here for supper," said Father. "Tell him we're expecting him."

Horace Wellman was a short, stocky man who seemed nervous. He stammered and had little to say at supper. But he ate his bacon and beans with gusto, mopping his plate repeatedly with a piece of corn bread.

Finally he looked up from his plate. "Wonder-wonder how that m-m-meeter will be tonight?" he said.

"Which?" asked Mr. Striker.

"Oh," said Father, "that ain't a meteor. That's a comet."

"All-all-all the same, ain't they?"

"Oh, jeepers, no. A meteor's just a shooting star. Zip and a streak of fire and it's gone. A comet is a big tramp planet that goes wandering around the sky for years and years. Going so fast there's a long tail of fire behind her, but they go for centuries before they burn out. This comet ain't such a much. When I was a boy the size of these cubs there was a real comet. Had everybody scared pink back in York State. They was holding prayer meetings every night to keep it from hitting the earth."

"By cracky, it'd make an awful squash if it did hit us," observed Mr. Striker.

"How many c-c-comets is there?" inquired Wellman.

"Loads of 'em, I guess," said Father. "Haven't an idea what they call this one, but that big one that showed up when I was a boy was called Halley."

"Well," said Mr. Striker, "if they're just tramp stars and running away, there ain't nothing to keep 'em from running smack into the world sometime, is there?"

"Guess not," said Father, "unless God's guiding them away. But there's an awful lot of space for 'em to run around in up there. Would be sort of like a blind man shooting a rifle across the prairie and hitting a pinhead twenty rod away—only more so. Not much danger, I'd think."

"I heard tell," said Mr. Striker, "a comet coming in the sky always means bad luck. That's what my old grandmother used to say. Reckon it was the big comet you speak about, Macdougall, that came when my grandfather fell down the well and was drownded."

"Certain amount of bad luck bound to come along," Father said, "comets or no comets."

When it grew dark the comet was blazing brightly in the northwest heavens. We all stood for a long time on the hilltop back of our house looking at it and the prairie breeze was wonderfully sweet. We speculated on the length of its tail, which varied from Hod Wellman's "ten mile" to Father's thousands of miles. Then we walked back through the bluestem grass to where our campfire glowed and we all turned in.

Hod Wellman, Monroe and I started shortly after sunup in the morning. We let the tail gate down and Monroe and I sat in the rear of the wagon with our legs hanging down. He had his little shotgun along so we tried banging away at prairie chickens without leaving the wagon. It was difficult shooting because they were so far from the road by the time we saw them, but in a dozen or so shots we did manage to bring down two. Hod Wellman stopped the team while we retrieved and cleaned them.

It was evening when we reached Nebraska City and Mr. Wellman took Monroe and me to our house on Otoe Street.

"Probably won't se-see you tomorrow," he said. "Fourth of July. Got-got-got business for Friday. You be ready by noon-noon-noon, but maybe have to stay over until S-S-Saturday."

VI

Monroe and I rose early on the Fourth, hearing the banging of guns and the ringing of church bells and the roar of anvils being shot down by the steamboat landing. We didn't wait for breakfast, but dressed hurriedly and ran all the way down Otoe Street to the river and over to Main where the anvil shooters were.

Two groups of men were holding a contest to see which could load and fire their anvils faster. Each group had heavy brass rings about three inches in diameter. They would place a ring on the smooth face of an anvil, which sat on the dirt road, pour a quantity of powder into the ring and then run a train of powder from a notch in the ring out to the edge of the anvil. Then they would lift another anvil upside down and place its smooth surface on top of the ring.

Both groups had fires burning in the street a short distance from the anvils, with several iron rods resting their red-hot tips in the flames. When the anvils were loaded one of the men would take one of the iron rods and touch its glowing tip to the powder train. The explosion was like a cannon shot and the upper anvil would be thrown into the air in a cloud of white powder smoke. Then the men of that group would yell.

Tied to the landing and flying numerous American flags were two steamboats—the *Florence* and the glittering new *Sam Gaty* and members of their crews stood on the decks watching the anvil shooters.

Monroe and I stood by watching until one of the brass rings burst and a piece of the brass embedded itself in the gunner's neck. Then we followed the crew up Main Street while they led the bleeding fellow to a doctor's house.

After breakfast Monroe and I fired his shotgun from

the front porch of the house, loading it heavily with powder only, until my shoulder was bruised and aching. Then it was nearly time for the parade and we went downtown.

By then it was blistering hot and the sun was blazing down on the streets lined with people dressed in their best—the ladies in ruffled white and the men in their Sunday black clothes, but with brightly striped shirts.

Presently a band began to blare out "Yankee Doodle" and here came the parade led by a handsome and dignified man riding a big horse that pranced sideways most of the time. The man was wearing a tall black stovepipe hat and a red, white and blue sash draped over one shoulder and a shiny sword bounced at his flank. Everyone on the street seemed to know him and they were yelling, "Hi, there, Ike. You look scrumptious, Ike." And little boys ran along the street calling out, "Hello, there, Mr. Coe." But Mr. Coe acted as if he were in church and the minister was praying. He didn't look this way nor that.

Following Mr. Coe came the band, sweating in their red and yellow uniforms, and blowing for all they were worth. Then came the Rough and Ready Rangers, and they were serious and hot too, but having considerable trouble to keep step. And then came the Zouave Guards. They wore red baggy pantaloons and tight blue jackets with white belts and they marched much better than the Rough and Readies.

Then there were the Nebraska City Guards in regular blue soldier uniforms and an old man waved his cane and yelled, "Them's the boys that can show Jeff Davis a thing or two!" And another old man turned to that one and pursed his lips and went "br-r-r-p" at him.

Then came at least a hundred men on horseback led by a handsome man they said was Colonel Bell and all of them were riding very straight and fine and keeping their horses right in line.

After the horses was a great crowd of little girls all dressed in white and carrying small American flags and then a crowd of little boys also carrying flags and half a dozen women, very flushed in the face, holding their hoopskirts up out of the horse manure with one hand and trying to keep the little girls and boys lined up with the other.

Everyone followed the parade out to Majors' Grove and it was cooler under the trees, even though there were thousands of people milling around. The band played several pieces and then Parade Marshal Coe introduced Reverend H. W. Giltner, who gave a prayer.

Reverend Giltner thanked God for our forefathers who fought to give us liberty and thanked God for our glorious Union and asked God to show the light to those who now would break that Union asunder, and if it came to a battle to lend His hand to the side of righteousness and to aid in freeing from slavery those brothers and sisters who have black skins but souls as white as any, and he thanked God for the bounteous wheat crop, which even then was being harvested, and for the hot weather, because, while uncomfortable temporarily to mankind, it still made the corn grow. And he thanked God for the fine wild raspberries which were so plentiful this season and for the heaping dish he, Reverend Giltner, had enjoyed for breakfast, and he thanked God for leading all present to this new Promised Land, this modern Garden of Eden—Nebraska.

Then William H. Taylor, who was a delegate to Congress or something, rose in a long black coat and read the Declaration of Independence and the crowd cheered and the band played "Columbia, the Gem of the Ocean," and Mr. Coe called on M. W. Reynolds, "famous journalist and statesman," for an address.

When Mr. Reynolds stood up on the platform there was great cheering and the bass drummer beat the drum and a man near Monroe and me yelled out, "Hi-yi! Kicking Bird Reynolds for president!"

Then Mr. Reynolds spoke, telling how the United States was founded and of the ordeals of the founding fathers and of George Washington at Valley Forge and of how they all depended on the calm counsel of Benjamin Franklin.

He said the present times were no less parlous than the days of 1776 and called attention to the counsel of Stephen A. Douglas who had implored the fanatics of the North and the hotspurs of the South to "bridle their passions and to quiet their inflammable zeal for unloosing the dogs of war."

"The civil war still has not gone so far but it could be arbitrated," he said. "But it depends on the people—such people as you assembled here in Majors' Grove—in every city, town and hamlet of these United States, whether the conflict shall go on until those two great armies being assembled on the Potomac and in Virginia shall be hurled at each other's throats, and whether the war thus launched shall go on and on until both sides are exhausted and the lives of hundreds of thousands of young men have been sacrificed."

He quoted Douglas again and urged the people of Nebraska to bridle their passions and not to allow civil war to break out in their own neighborhood.

There was a lot of handclapping for Mr. Reynolds. Then Mr. Coe called on Lieutenant Matthies for toasts and a flashing-eyed, handsome young man in uniform sprang to his feet, drew his saber, held it glittering aloft with one hand and raised a glass with the other.

"Let us drink in wholesome lemonade," he cried, "to the patriots who were not afraid to fight and die, if needs be, to form this glorious Union of states."

There was great cheering.

"And let us drink," he called, "to the new patriots who are not afraid to fight and die, if needs be, to preserve this glorious Union and to keep faith with the memory of our fathers."

This brought even more cheering.

"And," shouted Lieutenant Matthies, "let us drink to this Union itself—to this Union of states, attacked as it is by the degenerate sons of worthy sires."

Then the crowd showed they hadn't been cheering at all before and the band began to play and people started singing with the band, "The Union forever! Hurrah, boys, hurrah!" And Lieutenant Matthies began to beat time with his saber and sing, "Yes, we'll rally round the flag, boys, we'll rally once again, shouting the battle-cry of freedom."

Kicking Bird Reynolds sat back on the platform, not joining in the demonstration, but trying to smile and not doing a very happy job of it.

When the crowd finally quieted a little, the lieutenant offered his last toast—"To the ladies, God bless them, who hide their tears when they send their sons away to fight, to fight that slavery may be wiped from the face of the earth."

Then, when the cheering died out, the band played again and most of the people went home, while those who had driven in from farms got out baskets and had picnics under the trees.

That night Monroe and I went to Houdin's show, for which the city was heavily placarded. Houdin, it appeared, was the master of Heller and Anderson in the black arts. His daughter, Mlle. Caroline Houdin, performed unbelievable acts of second sight while under Houdin's mesmerism. There were to be numerous acts of drollery, acrobatic skill and melody and last, but not least, there was to be the grand weekly drawing of

"Treasure Night," wherein those who had attended the show during the week might come with their numbered tickets and perhaps win one of the treasures the placards listed below.

The treasures consisted of: first, a span of horses worth $500; then a riding horse worth $250; a cow and a calf worth $40; a gold (Beasley) hunting watch worth $40; a revolver worth $35; and last, a dozen kits of mackerel worth $4 a kit.

Both Monroe and I were entranced by the show—entranced and dumfounded. The acrobats, who performed amazing feats of ability and balance, were better than any I ever had seen in a regular circus. So were the trained dogs.

The Negro clown, who sang a lugubrious song about his girl named Susanna, whose "head was like a coffee pot, her nose was like the spout; her ears was like the handle for to pour the coffee out," made us laugh until our ribs ached.

But the most astonishing thing of all was Houdin himself. A dark, satanic gentleman in black with a white shirt front that gleamed under the torches, Houdin appeared most certainly to have supernatural powers.

Before our eyes he turned glass flasks of water to wine. He called a small boy to the stage and before his bewildered eyes reached into his mouth and took out egg after egg until he had a large basketful. He borrowed gold watches from gentlemen in the audience and, despite their horrified protests, beat them to pieces with a hammer. Then he found the watches intact and ticking right in their owners' pockets.

He performed dozens of feats just as impossible as these and then brought his beautiful young daughter to the stage and, by murmuring incantations and waving his long white fingers in front of her eyes, placed her in a sound sleep or state of mesmerism.

While Mlle. Caroline Houdin sat stiff and white in a chair, Houdin came down in the tent, passing among the audience, inquiring what different men and women wished to ask of the mademoiselle.

"This lady, mademoiselle," he called, "wants to know what became of her ruby ring."

"The ruby ring," replied Mlle. Houdin in a dead monotone, "was stolen by a dark young man who entered your home in broad daylight while you were downtown. He picked it up from your bureau and you will never see it again."

"This young man," called Houdin, "wants to know why he hasn't received a letter. Can you tell him, mademoiselle?"

"I can tell him. The young man's fears are groundless. His last letter to her was lost in the mail. She is worrying about him, but is too modest to write before she receives an answer from her last letter. You should not be so suspicious, young man. You should write her again at once."

The young man, who sat only a few seats from Monroe and me, was blushing scarlet but plainly was very pleased and the people around him were laughing and craning their necks.

"Here, mademoiselle," said Houdin, "is a man who does not believe in your powers. He believes he can ask you a question you cannot answer. He wants you to give the number inside his watch case."

"The number," she droned, "is seven-six-three-nine-eight."

"That right?" demanded Houdin.

"Well, wait a minute," said the man, who was wearing blue jeans and high boots. "Wait until I look."

With his thumb nail he pried open the back of his watch. "What was that number again?" he asked.

"Please to repeat, mademoiselle," requested Houdin, evenly.

"The number is seven-six-three-nine-eight," said Mlle. Houdin again.

"By thunder!" cried the man. "By thunder, she's right. Look here, she's right!" He stood up, holding out the open watch and several near him peered in the case and shook their heads in wonder.

Mlle. Houdin answered the questions of a score or more, apparently with complete satisfaction, and then the "Treasure Night" raffle was held. An apparatus like a barrel churn, only larger, was brought out on the platform, the sides of the tent were raised so all holders of numbered tickets from earlier in the week could crowd in.

Houdin now picked up a megaphone and spoke in it loudly so all could hear. "Ladies and gentlemen," he called, "in this drum is a duplicate number for each and every number issued with admissions during the last week. The drum will be spun to mix the numbers thoroughly and I should like to ask some little girl to come to the stage to assist in the drawing. She will be blindfolded and will pick the numbers from the drum one by one. The first number selected will win the first prize of a five hundred dollar span of horses. The second will win a two hundred and fifty dollar riding horse and so on. Now will some little girl kindly step to the stage?"

While Mlle. Houdin, now out of her trance, rapidly spun the big barrel churn, a little girl with long yellow curls and a blue sash came up to the stage and Houdin blindfolded her. Mlle. Houdin ceased spinning the churn.

"Now, sweetheart," said Houdin to the little girl, "will you reach in this opening and pick out one ticket?"

The little girl fumbled into the aperture of the churn and brought out a slip of pasteboard. Houdin looked at it and called through the megaphone, "The first number and winner of the five hundred dollar span of horses is E-nine-nine-four-two—E-nine-nine-four-two."

Monroe and I nervously looked at our numbers. His was E-723 and mine was E-724.

"I got it! By thunder, I got it!" a man yelled and stood holding his ticket aloft. He was the same man whose watch number had been read by Mlle. Houdin. He went down the aisle toward the stage in great glee. "Can't tell you how much I need a new span of hosses," he shouted. "My best hoss just died of blind staggers."

Houdin took his ticket and compared it with the slip the child had drawn from the churn, "It's correct," he proclaimed. "Here is the winner of the span of horses worth five hundred dollars. What is your name, sir?"

"Hiram Snider."

"Where do you reside, Mr. Snider?"

"Lancaster County."

"Well, Mr. Hiram Snider of Lancaster County, let me congratulate you. Here is an order on Murphy's corral and they will deliver the horses to you tomorrow morning."

"Thank you, sir. Thank you and God bless you. I can't wait to get home and tell my wife Miranda how you and the good Lord have blessed me."

A man sitting behind me leaned forward and touched the shoulder of the man next to me. "Joe," he said, "I think there's something rotten in Denmark."

"By golly," said the other, "I wouldn't be surprised."

"Just a little strong for her to read the number of his watch and for him to win the first prize both."

"I got a feeling something ought to be done about this Houdin."

"This is pretty strong, all right. But what you going to do? Couldn't prove anything."

"Could tell Marshal Hickey he ought to look into this fellow's business. He's taking a lot of money from Nebraska City folks."

"Hickey'd have a sweet time doing anything with a man as smart as this Haskell."

"Haskell?"

"Yes. That's Houdin's real name."

The drawings went on, Houdin passing out tickets to the fortunate for the riding horse, and the cow and calf. The gold watch itself was handed out to a portly, dignified man. Then came the revolver and when the number was called a heavy-set fellow in a tight-fitting blue suit ambled forward.

"Oh, Joe," the man behind me called. "See that?"

"Yes, I see it," said Joe grimly.

"Reckon Marshal Hickey will get after this Houdin, all right, now."

Houdin on the platform presented the winner with the shiny new revolver, asked his name, smiled and shook hands. Then he introduced the winner to the audience as Marshal Hickey of Nebraska City. The crowd burst into a roar of applause.

I missed winning a kit of mackerel by a single number. My number was E-724 and E-725 won the mackerel.

VII

The next day we were ready at noon for Hod Wellman, but he didn't appear.

"Well," said Monroe, "I didn't hardly expect him. He thought he might get held up until Saturday."

But Wellman didn't show up Saturday, either, and I began to worry.

Sunday morning I said to Monroe, "Jeepers, I've got to get back to our land. Father will be madder'n a wet hen if I'm not back by tonight."

"Well, Pa probably will be worrying about us too. But what can we do? Can't walk clear back to Medicine

Creek, let alone Rock Creek. Hod will be along today. Nothing can be holding him on Sunday because folks don't do business on Sunday."

But Sunday night came around with no Wellman. Monday we took turns going around Main Street looking for him while the other stayed at the house waiting. I inquired at several saloons, but no one knew Wellman nor had anyone seen a man answering his description. I said nothing about it to Monroe because I didn't want to worry him, but I began to suspect Wellman had got the money from the Overland Stage and had left the country with it.

Tuesday noon great thunderheads were piling up in the northwest and as we watched the storm's approach Wellman drove up in front of the house. Monroe and I ran out to the wagon.

"Gol," said Monroe, "where you been all this time? Thought we were going back Friday or Saturday."

"G-g-got tied up with stage business," Wellman said. "Had to t-t-take steamboat to Leavenworth."

"Well," I said, "we ready to start now?"

"Ready. But-but-but look at them clouds. Going to rain cats-cats-cats and dogs in a minute. Got to wait until the storm's over. I'll b-b-be back."

He drove away and in a few minutes we were in the worst thunderstorm I ever saw. The flashing lightning and rolling thunder came in salvos and volleys, one banging into the echoes of the last. The wind lashed great limbs off the trees and a veritable river roared down Otoe Street. For at least two hours the storm raged, then paused for an hour and resolved itself into a steady rain.

When Wellman came to the house next morning he was on foot. "Can't-can't-can't start this morning," he said. "C-c-couldn't get across the fords and probably Wilson's bridge is gone."

It rained hard again that afternoon, but the following morning Wellman came with the wagon. "Allow we can make it now," he said. "Hurry up and g-g-get in." His eyes were pouchy and he didn't seem to be feeling well.

There was no particular difficulty in reaching Medicine Creek that evening, although the mud did make for slow travel. Heavy freight wagons had cut deep ruts, but we generally followed trails not frequented by the big wagons except at the fords.

Father and Mr. Striker had made great progress with our house, having all the doors and windows in and the spaces between logs largely filled with plaster.

Father wasn't very friendly with Wellman. "If you hadn't got here tonight," he said, "I was going to ride to Nebraska City to see what had happened to you."

"Awful sorry, Mr. Mac-d-d-dougall," Wellman said. "Just couldn't help it. Tied up with business. Had to go-go-go to Leavenworth and the storm hel-hel-held us up."

Early the following morning Wellman and Monroe left for home, Monroe exacting a promise from me that I would come and visit him just as soon as we got moved in our new house.

I worked hard all that day, trying to make up for my long holiday—worked at chinking between logs with plaster. So I was tired at night and took to my blankets early. Once I awoke and saw that embers still were glowing in the campfire. Then I drifted off to sleep again.

I woke up with a start, hearing the pound of a horse's hoofs close by. Over the knoll to the east the sky was dull lavender, streaked with pink. A fresh morning breeze was blowing.

Then I heard a hoarse, sobbing voice calling—"Jack —Clint! Where are you?"

"What on earth?" Father said. "That you, Clint?"

I sat up. "No," I said. Shivers ran up my back.

Then the dim shape of a horse and rider came up the turf from the direction of the road. The horse stumbled and nearly fell. The rider rolled off, tumbled to the grass and then rose to his feet.

"Who's there?" Father yelled.

"Cousin Jack!"

Monroe McCanles staggered up to us and then toppled over on his face, sobbing.

Father picked him up. "What's the matter, boy?" he demanded. "What's happened to you?"

Monroe gurgled in his throat. "Pa," he moaned.

"What's wrong with your father? Quick. Can't you talk, boy? Here, Clint, get me that bucket of water. Then get me the jug of whisky out of the wagon."

Father poured some water into Monroe's mouth from the dipper while Mr. Striker built up the fire. Then he gave him a swallow of whisky. Monroe coughed. His eyes were wide and staring in the new firelight. A meadowlark began to trill near by in the grass.

"Now can you tell me, Monroe?" Father asked.

"Pa's dead," said Monroe in a whisper. He gulped. "He's killed."

"What!"

"Duck Bill killed him. Shot him with Pa's own rifle." Monroe began to cry again.

Father squatted beside Monroe with his arm around him. The fire was flickering up now and the flames leaned into the wood with the morning breeze.

"Now, now, Monroe," Father said. "You sure you know what you're talking about. That just *can't* be so."

"It *is* so. I saw it. I saw everything. Jim Gordon and Jim Woods are dead too. They tried to kill me."

"Jim Gordon and Jim Woods tried to kill you?"

"No, no. Hod Wellman tried to kill me. He'd have killed me only I ran and got away. I ran all the way home and got Charley and rode up here. They killed Jim Woods with a hoe, I tell you. I was there. I saw it all."

"Now, son," said Father, "can't you calm down a little bit? Can't you start at the beginning? Try to tell me what happened."

"Duck Bill shot Pa," said Monroe, "and Hod Wellman killed Jim Woods with a hoe after Duck Bill shot him."

"Here," said Father, "you want another drink?"

"Yes," said Monroe. He took the dipper and gulped water greedily.

"Now, boy, can't you tell us what happened? Can't you start at the beginning?"

Monroe's wild, round eyes stared at Father. "Cousin Jack," he said, "couldn't you go back there with me right away?"

"Of course I can. Of course I will. But you got to rest a little first. And you see can you tell us what you saw."

Monroe rubbed his eyes with his fists. "Well," he said, "I'll try to tell you everything from the start. You see, Hod Wellman and I got back to the stage station along late in the afternoon. We drove up and I saw three of our horses hitched down near the station and I reckoned Father was there. So I hopped off the wagon and ran over and there was Pa and Jim Gordon and Jim Woods.

"Jim Woods saw me coming and he said to Pa, 'Well, look, Dave, here he comes now.' So I came up and Pa says, 'Well, where in the world have you been all this time?'

"I says, 'Nebraska City, pa.'

"And he says, 'Well, you ought to know the place pretty well by now. Why'd you stay so long? We were getting terrible worried.'

"So I told him about Hod Wellman being all tied up with business for so long and then about the storm and he says, 'Did he get the money? Do you know about that?' "

"*Did* he get the money?" Father asked.

"Don't know. That's what I told Pa. I told him I didn't know. Hod Wellman didn't say anything about it and I didn't want to ask him. So by that time the wagon had pulled up to the barn and Doc Brink came out and started unhitching the horses and Hod Wellman jumped off the wagon and walked fast over past the bunkhouse and in the kitchen door of the station.

"Pa watched him and then looked funny at Jim Woods and Jim Gordon. Then he says, 'Guess I'd better go up and talk to the son of a bitch and find out what's what.'

"Jim Gordon grinned at Pa and he says, 'Well, all right, Dave. We'll go down and see Doc Brink. Do you want us, you just holler and we'll come arunning.'

"And Pa says, 'That's a good idea. You go down to the barn. Don't want it to look like I'm using force. But if I got to get rough with Hod Wellman I don't reckon I'll need any help.'

"So Pa and I walked to the station and he put his arm kind of around my shoulders and asked me if I had a good time and I told him about Clint going with us and that we had a fine time and I told him a little about the Fourth of July parade and the speeches and Mr. Houdin's show and he says, 'Well, I suppose that was all very fine, but you ought to have stayed at home. Your papa made a Fourth of July speech himself and that must have been pretty fine too.'

"And then he says, 'Did you bring me anything from Nebraska City?'

"And I thought he was talking about the money, maybe and hadn't understood me and I said, 'What do you mean?'

"And he says, 'Well, every time I go away you expect

me to bring you something when I come back. Seems to me turn about is fair play.'

"I didn't know what to say about that and he gave me another little squeeze and by that time we were up to the kitchen door on the west end of the station and Mrs. Wellman came to the door. She didn't smile or anything. She just stood there in the door with her hands on her hips.

"Pa looked at her and then says, 'Will you tell Hod I want to see him?'

"Mrs. Wellman shook her head. Then she says, 'Hod ain't here.'

"Pa says, 'Not here? What you mean he's not here? I just saw him go in that door.'

"Well, Mrs. Wellman shook her head again and she says, 'It don't make no difference. Hod won't come out. He don't want to see you now and he won't come out.'

"When she said that Pa's face got red and I knew he was getting awful mad. He says, 'By God, you tell Hod Wellman if he don't come out on his own accord in one minute I'm coming in and will drag him out.' "

Father's eyes were squinted as he stared at Monroe and his fists were clenched. There were pouches under Mr. Striker's eyes in the dawn and the meadowlark kept singing and singing in a bush two rods away.

"You remember," went on Monroe, "how that stage station is? You remember there's a curtain about halfway down the room and the bunks are back of the curtain?"

"Never was in there," said Father, "but I know how it might be."

"Well, when Pa said that to Mrs. Wellman this curtain moved and out came Duck Bill, looking not friendly and not unfriendly. Just no expression on his funny face and he came to the door slow and Mrs. Wellman moved back.

"Pa said, 'Hello, Duck Bill.'

"Duck Bill didn't smile or anything. He just said, 'Hello,' back at Pa.

"And Pa looked at him and says, 'I don't know why you're coming in on this, Duck Bill. We're friends, aren't we?'

"Duck Bill says, 'Not when you call me that name.' He said that very serious but Pa laughed then and says, 'Well, all right, Jim, but there's so tarnal many Jims around here they get mixed up. But we *are* friends when I call you Jim?'

"Duck Bill looked at Pa and says, 'Yes.' That's all he said—just, 'Yes.'

"Then Pa laughed and says, 'All right, if we're friends will you give me a drink of water?'

"Duck Bill says 'Yes,' again in his funny way and turned around and dipped up a dipper of water out of a bucket and handed it to Pa. Pa drank the water and looked at Duck Bill over the top of the dipper. Then he threw the leavings on the ground and handed back the dipper and Duck Bill put the dipper back in the bucket and all of a sudden moved back quick and behind that curtain.

"Pa stepped away from the door and then almost ran to the other door. You know, the door on the lean-to, and he looked like he was excited. I didn't know why, but I guess something happened I didn't see, and Pa yelled out, 'Listen here, Jim, if you got anything against me come on outside and fight it out square.'

"He hadn't any more than yelled that than a gun blazed from behind the curtain with a terrible roar and Pa grunted and fell backwards off the doorstep and landed flat on his back in the dirt. Then he raised up sitting and saw me and started to say something and I ran over to him, but he fell back before I could make out what he was trying to talk about.

"I caught a glimpse of Duck Bill standing beside the

curtain holding the rifle Pa had loaned Hod Wellman. Then I squatted down and picked up Pa's head and he was bloody all over his chest and I guess he was dead right then because he didn't move or make a sound.

"I was crying and talking to Pa and not noticing what was going on inside the house, but I could hear some loud talking. And then here came Jim Gordon and Jim Woods running from the barn and one of them yelled, 'What in the hell's happening here?'

"Just then Duck Bill stepped out the door with his long hair flying and he's got a big navy revolver in his hand. He shot it quick, bang-bang, and Jim Woods stumbled and turned and started to run around to the north of the station and just then Hod Wellman, cussing and screaming and not stuttering a bit, ran out the door right past me with a big hoe in his hands and Jim Woods fell down and Hod Wellman was right on top of him with the hoe, chopping his head in.

"Jim Gordon turned and ran the other way, past the well, and Duck Bill's gun went bang-bang quick again, and Jim Gordon half fell, but scrambled up again and yelled out, 'Oh, Jesus!' and went running doubled up for the brush down on Rock Creek and Doc Brink came running out of the barn with a shotgun and he yelled, 'I'll get the son of a bitch.'

"And Mrs. Wellman was in the doorway and she yelled, 'Kill all of the bastards!' So Hod Wellman quit chopping Jim Woods's head with the hoe and came running at me where I was squatted down holding Pa's head and I never saw anybody's face look so wild and terrible.

"He made a chop at my head with the hoe and I dodged and got up on my feet and he chopped at me again and I ducked and ran as fast as I could around the building and south to the ravine and bust into the thicket.

"Just then I heard the shotgun boom out and Doc Brink yelled, 'I got Gordon!'"

"Then I pushed through the thicket and ran all the way home as fast as I could go and told Ma and she didn't know what to do and was terrible scared and finally she said I'd better saddle Charley and ride to get Cousin Jack as soon as it got dusk. So I did. Can you come right away, Cousin Jack? I don't know what Ma's going to do and maybe they come in the night and killed her and the children."

"Bloody crucified Christ," said Mr. Striker.

"Monroe," said Father softly, "did your father have a gun with him?"

"Gun?" said Monroe. "Of course not. He didn't have anything. He didn't have a chance. Duck Bill just shot him down."

"Did Gordon or Woods have guns?"

"No. Leastways I never saw any guns. Listen, Cousin Jack, can't you go right back with me? Ma is scared to death and don't know what to do and Pa's probably still just laying there outside the door."

"You think you can stand riding horseback all the way back?" Father asked.

"I can stand it, all right," Monroe asserted.

"Well, we'll have some breakfast and start right out. Your pony is played out and you'll have to ride one of our horses. You and I will go and see what it's all about."

"How about me?" I demanded. "Can I ride on behind one of you?"

"No," said Father. "No need of you going and it's too long a drag to ride double. You stay here with Striker and I'll be back as soon as I find out what's what."

"Listen here, Macdougall," said Mr. Striker, "if you're going to brash right in with them cutthroats, you take my revolver."

"Don't need any revolver."

"They're pretty damn quick to shoot an unarmed man, Macdougall. You better take my gun for protection."

"I ain't any gunfighter. They must have had some kind of a reason to shoot Dave, but they got no reason to shoot me. They don't owe me any money. And if they make a false move in my direction I'll break their God-damn backs."

After a hurried breakfast Father and Monroe rode away on Doug and Frank.

VIII

Mr. Striker and I puttered around the house for five days, doing what work we could do.

On the afternoon of the fifth day I kept arguing that I should take Monroe's spotted pony and ride to Rock Creek to see what was going on.

"No, sirree, dang it all," said Mr. Striker. "You ain't going to do any such thing. Your father's all right and even was he not, you couldn't do ary thing about it. You're going to stay right here with me and if he ain't back in a few more days we'll go out and stop the stage and go to Nebraska City. Then I'll get a man or two to go with me and we'll go out there."

But that evening Father came back, riding Doug and leading Frank. He looked more tired and older than I had ever seen him and he had little to say until we sat down to our board table for supper, except that Cousin Dave truly was dead and buried.

At supper I said, "What's Monroe and his mother going to do?"

"Going to give up the farm," said Father. "Going back to her folks in Carolina. Tried to tell her she could hire men to work the farm and would be better off here, but she wants to get away. Well, you scarcely can't blame her much."

"What about them murderers?" Mr. Striker asked. "They arrested?"

"Yes and no," said Father. "The Overland Stage seems to run things in that country and Wellman and his gang belong to the Overland Stage.

"First people I saw down there was three brothers name of Helvey. They'd gone over to the station and found the three bodies—Dave and Gordon and Woods— and they buried them. Everything was the way Monroe said. Dave on his back in front of the door, shot through the heart. Woods around to the side with his head chopped in and Gordon down in the brush across the road. No guns on any of 'em."

"Jesus Christ," said Mr. Striker, "what was it all about?"

"Well, I've got my ideas why they killed Dave. Don't know about Woods and Gordon except that they worked for Dave and were with him.

"I got an idea Wellman got away with the money he was to pay Dave and he was scared to death of what Dave would do. I got an idea he told this dim-witted Duck Bill some cock-and-bull story and Duck Bill did the killing, maybe even thinking he was doing the right thing. Duck Bill's story sounds like that."

Mr. Striker swabbed corn bread in his bacon grease. "What'd Duck Bill say?" he asked.

"Well," said Father wearily. "I'll tell you the whole thing. I asked these Helvey boys where there was a sheriff and a court of law and they said there should ought to be a sheriff up in a settlement to the north called Beatrice. So I rode up there and found an old sot named Coulter who was supposed to be justice of the peace and I swore out a warrant for the arrest of Duck Bill and Doc Brink and Wellman. Couldn't remember Duck Bill's right name so I made out the warrant for just Duck Bill, but they got him all right. Found out later his name's Jim Hickok and then remembered that was what Dave said it was.

"So they had a hearing in a cabin of an old man called Pap Towle and this Coulter sat at a table and ran it. Wouldn't let Monroe testify. Said a minor's testimony couldn't hold water in law. Well, I don't know much law, but I do know I've heard about minors testifying in York State. Tried to tell this Coulter so and he said he'd have me arrested for contempt of court."

"Well, I'll be switched," said Mr. Striker.

"Yes," said Father, "only testimony they had was from Wellman and Duck Bill and Doc Brink and Mrs. Wellman. She was the only one testifying except those doing the killing."

"What'd she say?"

"Said Dave and Gordon and Woods came up and attacked 'em. Said Dave was trying to steal the company's horses."

"Steal the company's horses?"

"That's right."

"Well, I'll be switched."

"Wellman and Duck Bill and Doc Brink all testified to the same thing—said Dave and his men came up and tried to take the company's horses. Said they were going to ship 'em down to the Southern army. By holy dang, I don't see how Coulter figured they were going to get horses down to 'em, but that's what they said. And they'd carried that story to all the neighboring ranches and I found out the stage drivers had spread it all along the line that a whole army of Southern sympathizers attacked the station with everything short of cannons."

"Well, Almighty God, this judge didn't find 'em not guilty, did he?" Mr. Striker asked.

"Couldn't do that very well, but I calculate he'd just

let the thing drop entirely if I hadn't been there. Of course I couldn't testify, but I stood up on my hind legs and talked anyhow. This Judge Coulter bound 'em over for trial on charges of murder at the next term of court, all right. But then he turned 'em loose."

"How could he do that?"

Father shook his head and drank coffee. "Coulter says they ain't got a jail and would have to hire guards to guard Wellman and Duck Bill and Brink for the next two years. Next term of court ain't for two years, he says.

"I said to Coulter, 'Well, if you got to hire guards, why don't you do it?'

"He says, 'Got no money in the treasury and it's already cost fifty-six dollars and sixty cents for guarding and feeding the prisoners and a hundred forty-one dollars and ninety-five cents for sheriff and witness and justice fees. I done bound 'em over for trial and reckon they'll come in all right to clear their names. Don't seem to be much evidence against these men nohow.'

"I said, 'You haven't heard but their side of the story. Jeepers, why don't you listen to the boy? He's the only one that's not an interested party.'

"And he says, 'How you know he ain't interested? He came up with his paw, didn't he? He's big enough boy to help steal hosses if they *was* stealing hosses.'

"And I said, 'You're a God-damn fool and probably a crook to boot,' and he threatened again to arrest me for contempt of court.

"So a man named Johnson, and a smart clever fellow, came up to me and he says, 'Mr. Macdougall, I know what you're figuring on doing and I want to tell you, don't you do it. Personally, I wouldn't blame you at all. Matter of fact, I think it should ought to be done. But you kill those fellows and you'll hang for it just as sure as hell's hot.'

"That's what he said. Then he said, 'This Overland

Stage Company runs this country. Nobody up here knew
your cousin, so when the Overland Stage Company says
he was trying to steal stage horses and ship 'em down to
the rebel army, that goes. You or nobody else around
here has got a chance bucking against the stage company.
You shoot one of those ruffians and you're done. You're
just automatically a murderer and a rebel to boot and
you'll be hung higher'n Haman before another sunrise.'

"That's what this fellow Johnson said and he looked
like he knew what he was talking about.

"So I just went up to Wellman and Duck Bill who
were together and I says, 'Look here, you sons of bitches,
I know what you did and you know what you did and
that's enough. I know you never calculate you'll come
to trial and there ain't any way to force you, as far as I
know.

"'All right. But I'm telling you two and you can tell
this Doc Brink to *get out of this country.*'

"And Duck Bill sort of swelled out his chest and says,
'You can't tell *me* what I got to do.'

"And I said, 'I *can't,* eh? Well, I'm telling you, you're
a dog and a coward that shoots down unarmed men, but
you got no gun on you now and I'll smear that big nose
all over your face and break your God-damn neck if you
talk back to me.'

"I'd have done it too, and, by grab, he saw I'd do it
and shut his face.

"Then I said, 'I'm telling you to get out of Nebraska
Territory, both of you.' And I took hold of Wellman
and lifted him a little off the ground to show him I
meant business and I says, 'If I ever see any one of you
three in Nebraska again as long as you live I'll break
every bone in your filthy bodies.'

"Then I let Wellman down and his face was red and
he pulled his coat down and says, 'Come on, Hic-Hic-

Hickok,' and they went off and several men that saw it all came up and shook hands with me."

"Will you kill 'em if you see 'em again?" I asked.

Father looked at me fiercely. "I'll come almighty close to it," he said.

"Don't you go and get yourself hung, now," I warned.

"No danger. I know that breed of cattle. They're on their way out of the territory by now. They're on their way down to Kansas where they belong."

The next day we all went to Nebraska City to tell the women what had happened. And when Father got to the point in the story about Cousin Dave asking Duck Bill for a drink of water, Aunt Christine's mouth opened.

"You remember that warning?" she asked. "You remember, Sarah? It was a warning he didn't heed. When Dolly said she had a message for Dave, the message was 'water, water.' You remember, Sarah?"

"I remember," said Mother.

"Oh, stuff and nonsense," said Father, "If it was meant for a warning, why wasn't it made in a way a person could halfway understand?"

Aunt Christine shook her head sadly. "If Dave had only believed," she said, "he would have thought of the warning and been on his guard when he asked for water."

The next day word was spread over Nebraska City that there had been a pitched battle between the Union and Southern armies. Then the *News* came out and everyone on the street had one. I was downtown with Father and he bought a copy and we rushed home to show the family.

The war headline read: "TERRIBLE FIGHT—The Rebels Defeated at Bull Run."

Then the account followed: "That a brilliant victory has been won by our gallant troops there is no doubt. General McDowell telegraphs, 'Enemy completely routed from Bull Run and retreated towards Manassas, leaving their batteries in possession of our troops.' "

Then there was a short eyewitness account from the New York *Herald* correspondent which closed with, "When I left the field of battle I saw the rebels fleeing in great numbers."

"I wonder," said Mother, "if Alan was in it? Does it say whether any Union soldiers were killed?"

"Doesn't say," said Father. "Probably not many."

"Well, if there were *any*, he might have been killed or wounded."

"Now, don't worry about that, wife. Of course he's never exactly safe as long as he's in a war, but everybody is in more or less danger all the time. Look how many get killed in runaways every year. Look how many get drowned. All we can do is hope for the best and it's a good thing this battle finally came off and turned out the way it did.

"Now the Northern army has got the South on the run and they won't let 'em stop running. That's the way to fight any battle. If you get the other side backing up, just keep 'em backing up. These trained generals know how to fight. That's their business. They'll get to Richmond in a week or so now and Alan may be out here by the last of August or first of September. And we'll be needing him then, too."

I had an odd impression that Father scarcely believed what he was saying, that he was talking largely for Mother's benefit.

Mother shook her head. "Well, we can just hope and pray so, I suppose. Any other news in the paper?"

"Well, here's a piece about some Indians kicking up a little a week or so ago out along Salt Creek and Captain Pearman and Sergeant Laboo and Heath Nuckolls, H. R. Newcomb, J. H. Maxon and John Arthur, Esquires, of the Nebraska City Guards went out to look over the trouble and found everything quiet.

"What's this? Oh, great holy jeepers. Captain Pearman's scouting party brought word of a shooting affair at Rock Creek a hundred miles southwest of Nebraska City. It says a band of desperadoes headed by an outlaw named *McCandless* attacked the stage station and that a Mr. Heacox used a navy revolver and fired but three times, killing his man instantly with each shot.

"Oh, poor Dave! Listen here—McCandless, who has been a terror to the road, banded eight or ten desperadoes together to commit depredations on settlers and travelers and boasted of a rebellious attitude toward the nation."

"Oh, I've got to go down to the *News* about that. Ajax is out of town or it never would have happened. Here it says, 'Brink, Wellman and Heacox, who were together in the defense of the station, were acquitted on examination before a magistrate.' "

Father let the paper fall to the floor and shook his head sadly. He looked first at Mother and then at Aunt Christine.

"Poor Dave," said Mother. "And poor Mary too."

"Just hope," said Father, "that she never sees anything like this. Well, I guess she won't. She was driving to Leavenworth right away to go back home. Now I calculate that was a good thing."

"You going down to the newspaper office?" Mother asked.

Father rose and picked up his hat from the table. "Yes," he said, "but it can't do much good now. This captain fellow heard a story from a stage driver or some other stage company man and brought it in as the truth. I'll go down and tell them what really happened, anyhow."

"Be back in time for supper," Mother said. "It won't be much over an hour."

However, it was not more than twenty minutes before Father returned. His face was sallow and bloodless. His shoulders were slouched forward. He walked with drag-

ging feet into the house and slumped down in the big
armchair, took off his hat and dropped it on the floor.

Mother came in from the kitchen and started as she
saw him sitting there.

"Jack!" she cried. "What's the matter? Are you sick?"
Father shook his head.

"Is it—is it Alan?"

"Yes," said Father.

"Oh," said Mother and dropped the hot-pan holder
she had in her hand.

"Thousands killed," said Father. "They're getting a
list of names at the *News*. His name is on it—Corporal
Alan Macdougall."

Mother sat down and a tear rolled down each cheek.
"But, Jack," she whispered, "he wasn't a corporal. Maybe
it's somebody else. He was a private. That's the way we
wrote to him—Private Alan Macdougall, Company B,
Thirty-second New York Volunteers. Maybe it was somebody else."

"No," said Father. "It's him. He must have got promoted since we heard from him last. The first paper was
all wrong. The Union didn't win the battle. The South
won and the Union troops ran. Looks like General
Johnston may capture Washington."

"I'll bet," I said, "that Alan didn't run."

Neither Father nor Mother looked at me.

Aunt Christine started to cry. "I knew it. I knew it,"
she sobbed. "I had a dream and I didn't tell you because
I didn't want to worry you. But I saw him laying stark
and dead on the battlefield."

IX

By the middle of August we were moved out to our new
house on Medicine Creek. There was a fine new smell

about the place that was very exciting. As a matter of fact, there was a fine new smell about everything out there—especially when Father started breaking prairie and the rich black soil turned up shining from the big plowshare for the first time since the world was made.

Father had bought two oxen at Nursery Hill for the work and paid seventy-five dollars for them and named them Buck and Joe. But he didn't love them. He recognized their worth on the prairie as compared with horses, but he frequently loosed volleys of profanity at the stupid, stolid beasts.

To Father, an ox had no soul. An ox didn't even seem to understand good wholesome cussing. An ox had no spirit and made practically no complaint even over breaking prairie.

But Father had to admit they were economical because they could keep strong on native grass alone. And they were stronger than horses and just as fast when it came to breaking sod, which was slow work at best.

Actually there was no part of breaking prairie that Father liked, but he kept doggedly at it for two weeks. Then came a development which gave him great satisfaction and caused him to hire John Peterson, the broad-shouldered young son of Pete Peterson, to break prairie on our land for two dollars an acre, with Father supplying Buck and Joe and the plow. The Petersons had moved to a pre-emption a half mile northeast of our place and we could see the smoke from their sod shanty from our loft windows.

The development that relieved Father and gave employment to young Peterson was that freighters began to stop at our house at mealtime for food cooked by Mother and Aunt Christine. The meals were not at all fancy—usually fried bacon or ham with thickened gravy and corn bread and boiled beans and potatoes boiled with their jackets on and dried-apple sauce. But it was better food than the freighters could cook for themselves on the road and the freighters, usually having money, were glad to pay the silver dollar Father charged them for the meals.

Our new house *did* look neat from the road, neat and inviting. And the women kept it very clean, except that in the new lumber there had been small flat bugs, pale and almost transparent yellow in color, and these pale bugs infested the house and soon grew surprisingly active and a dark, reddish brown in color after they discovered the Macdougalls were nutritious. It took Mother and Aunt Christine the best part of a year, fighting with kerosene and paint to clear the premises, for not only did they hide in the joints of our bedsteads, but they squeezed in crevices of the floors and walls.

It was after the third party of freighters had petitioned for meals and had been fed at a dollar a head that Father became cognizant of the opportunity.

"By grab," he said, "it looks like we don't have to wait for the steam wagons to get running to make money. By grab, we can make *some* money out of these freighter bullies right now."

So he hired the Peterson boy to break prairie and took me with him to Nebraska City in the wagon. There he bought a barrel of whisky fitted with a spigot and a stock of cigars and tobacco. Then we called on Ajax Harvey at the *News.*

Mr. Harvey pulled his side whiskers when he saw us and grinned.

"How're things out Medicine Creek way?" he asked.

"Fine and dandy so far," said Father. "Got a fine house and barn and we're all settled. Ought to come out and pay us a visit."

"By golly," said Ajax, "I might do just that. Have been thinking about getting away for a buffalo hunt out past Fort Kearny."

"Fine," said Father. "You could stop off with us awhile and if things were right maybe I could go with you. I'd like to get a few buffalo robes myself."

"Well, I can't get away now, but I hope to before winter sets in. If I can't, I'll do it sure in the spring."

"We got to do that," said Father. "Haven't heard any more about Wellman or Hickok, have you?"

"Oh, they've gone, all right. Probably down in Kansas where they belong. Don't know for sure about Wellman, but young Hickok isn't with the Overland any more. He used to be with Jim Lane's Redlegs, you know, and he's probably gone back to guerrillaing in Kansas or Missouri. Mac, I do feel sorry about that piece we printed about your cousin."

"Say no more about it," said Father.

"You can see how it happened, Mac. Even if I had been here, I didn't remember McCanles's name. And when Captain Pearman came in with the story he'd picked up, the boys just took it. You see, it's impossible to verify any report that far away."

"I know." Father's lips drew in a hard line. "Sometimes I think I should ought to have killed those dogs when I had 'em in Beatrice."

Ajax shook his head. "You'd just have been hung," he said. "Can't buck the Overland Stage out there."

Father looked out the window. "Well, Ajax," he said, "what I really wanted to ask you about, what's the news on the steam wagon?"

"Too late now this year," said Ajax. "Major Brown is back in New York now and found they'd got something wrong. Not the right gear ratio and now he's decided he needs a bigger boiler. So we won't get it out here until next spring."

Father frowned.

"Oh, that's all right. There'll be a whole fleet steaming between here and Denver City before next summer is over. They can build the engines pretty fast once they know exactly how they should be built. The county commissioners are going to grade the road and we'll be going like a house afire by the Fourth of July."

"Well, I'll be ready for 'em," said Father. "My business is starting already with the freighters."

"That's great. Well, if I can get away for the buffalo hunt I'll send you a note beforehand by stage. But I'm tied up now with some United States land surveys besides the work I have to do as city recorder. That's saying nothing about trying to run this newspaper."

"Well, try and make it."

"You bet your boots. I'll let you know."

The barrel of whisky was set up in the back of the wagon together with a glass case filled with boxes of cigars and packages of tobacco and other supplies. When we had driven past the outskirts of the city Father pulled up the horses at the bottom of a grade.

"Whoa, there," he said. "Whoa."

"What's the matter?" I asked.

"Just thought of something," he said. "Just thought about that barrel of whisky back there. Haven't tested it and maybe it's no good. Maybe I better test it before we've gone too far. Might want to take it back if it's no good."

He climbed down from the wagon and dug into a box of glasses he had bought, took the paper from one and wiped the sawdust out. Then he turned the spigot on the barrel and filled the glass with brown liquor. He tasted it with pursed lips. Then he tossed off the glass.

"Is it all right?" I asked.

"Seems so offhand," he said, looking seriously at the sky. "But I'm not one to make snap judgments."

He filled the glass again and drank that. Then he wrapped the glass back in paper and returned it to the box. "Yes, Clinton," he said. "I believe that liquor will do. Maybe it's not quite as good as some I have tasted, but then, by grab, it ain't the worst, either. On the whole, I believe it will satisfy those freighters."

We climbed back on the wagon seat and Father clucked to the horses. "You know, Clinton," he said, "you need a shotgun, living out there where the prairie chickens are so thick."

"I know it," I said. "I need a shotgun pretty bad—a little shotgun like Monroe's."

"Well, it looks like business might get pretty good out there. Looks like maybe we might be able to get you a little shotgun—even before the steam wagons get running."

"That'd be fine and dandy," I said happily.

Father began to sing:

"Down on the canebrakes every day I go,
    Take my bath in the lake below;
If I chance to meet a drunkard,
    Oh, so pale and thin,
    'Well, how do you do, sir,
    Won't you pray walk in?' "

It had taken two men to raise the barrel of whisky into our wagon, with considerable grunting and gasping. But Father lifted it down by himself and rolled and carried it into the kitchen.

"Now look here, sir," said Mother, "you can't have that thing in my kitchen."

"Why in the world not? Don't want it in the parlor, do you?"

"Put it in the barn, if you want, but I'm not going to have a barrel of whisky in my kitchen."

"Put it in the barn! Woman, how you talk. Put that fine whisky in the barn where every Tom, Dick and Harry that comes along can help himself? I should say not. That whisky is going to be sold at two shillings a drink, that's what's going to happen to it."

"You'll probably," said Aunt Christine, "drink half of it yourself."

"Chris," said Father, "you're just like your sister— only more so. You know I won't drink any part of that whisky—any part you could measure. But you just got to talk. And you ought to remember the Scripture says something about not denying a mouthful to the ox that tramples out the grain."

"Fine one you are to quote Scripture," said Aunt Christine. "And you're doing precious little trampling out grain. You're counting on your poor wife and sister-in-law slaving over a hot cookstove to feed freighters. That's the way you're counting on making a living."

"Chris," said Father, shoving the barrel of whisky into the corner, "you surprise me. You really do. You know as well as I do that we're going to get rich here and as soon's the steam wagons get running we'll hire a whole army of servants to do the work and I'll dress you and Sarah in the finest of satins. Yes, sir, the very finest of satins. That's what I'll do and you know it."

"Bah," said Mother, "and I told you that barrel of whisky couldn't be here in the kitchen."

"Wife," said Father, "we'll enlarge this place and turn it into a fine eating house and hotel. We'll build another grand house up there on the hill surrounded by morning-glories and roses. It'll not be a log house, but a board house—a white board house with green blinds and a roof that goes up this way on four sides. You'll have the finest carriage in all the land with a pair of spanking blacks and a silver-trimmed harness and a nigger in uniform to drive you." He gave the barrel a final shove.

"Now that's all out of the way and won't bother anybody. When some galoot wants a drink of whisky for two shillings, I'll just come out here and get it in a glass.

Here, Clint, give me one of those new glasses and I'll show you how."

He took a glass and turned the spigot, then held the full glass to the light. "There, wife," he said, "ain't that pretty? Don't you think a weary freighter would be happy to pay two shillings for that? Pretty good to the taste, too." He drank the liquor and smacked his lips.

"You were coming out here," said Mother sternly, "where there wouldn't be much drinking. You were going to get away from your evil cronies around Canandaigua Lake."

"Was I?" Father scratched his chin and looked at the ceiling.

"You were coming out here where there was fine soil and no stones and you were going to farm the land and be decent. Now what do you do? You hire a man to do the plowing and you buy a whole barrel of whisky. Jack, I don't know what to make of you."

"Wife," said Father, "I don't know what to make of *you* sometimes. Breaking prairie with oxen gives me a crick in the back and it deadens my mind. Jeepers, you know I got to keep an active mind if we're going to get rich out here. Nobody ever got rich following a plow. You got to use your brain to make money in this world.

"Now, for instance, I've got an idea right now. There'll probably be some freighters in here for supper. I'll step out and shoot some prairie chickens and you fry 'em up nice and those freighters will be sure to come back when they're this way again. They'll remember the Macdougalls with pleasure. Especially when they're eastbound and thirsty and they know they can get good whisky here—even if pretty high priced."

"You'll have a gang of drunken louts around here every night," said Aunt Christine.

Father shook his head. "Not at two shillings a drink," he said. "Not many freighters going to get very drunk at two shillings a drink. I thought that all out when my mind was free and I wasn't breaking prairie with oxen." He took his shotgun and powder and shot flasks down from the wall.

"Are you going to move that barrel of whisky out of my kitchen?" Mother demanded.

Father grinned. "No, wife," he said. "That barrel of whisky ain't bothering you or anybody else there in the corner. There's no other place for it, so there it stays. Want to help me carry the chickens back, Clint?"

"Bet your boots," I said.

The prairie grass was brown with autumn and waving languidly in the breeze, except for the twenty acres or so Father, with the help of John Peterson, had cut for winter hay.

I had an old grain sack to carry the birds in and I followed closely behind Father. We had no more than passed out of the hay stubble into the waving grass when a covey of chickens rose on whirring wings and Father let go both barrels. Three hens fell.

I ran and picked up the birds and put them in the sack while Father reloaded. He pounded the rammer down on the wadding with an easy motion of the wrist.

> "Ram your powder, but not your lead
> If you want to kill them dead,"

he said.

We moved no more than eight rods when another covey rose. Again he blazed away with both barrels and brought down a pair of chickens. In less than a quarter of a mile he had a dozen birds and turned back.

At the barn we skinned and cleaned the chickens quickly and threw the entrails to the hogs.

"This," said Father, "is a man's way of doing things. Take a woman and give her this dozen of birds and

what'll she do? She won't skin 'em. She'll do the same as
she does with a tame chicken. She'll up and scald each
bird and probably scald herself doing it and then she'll
go to work and pick each separate feather off and then
she'll light a paper and singe off the pinfeathers and
probably burn herself again and mess around cleaning
'em for a couple of hours and by the time she's finished
a half day is gone and she'll be way behind with her cooking or washing or ironing and she'll fuss and fume about
that."

"Yes," I said, "women ain't much good for most work.
Think Ma may do something about our barrel of
whisky?"

Father straightened up and his black eyes snapped at
me. "What you mean—*our* barrel of whisky?" he demanded.

"Well—*your* barrel of whisky."

"You just let me catch you touching that barrel of
whisky and I'll lick you within an inch of your life.
Understand? You let me catch you drinking *any* whisky
before you're eighteen years old and I'll lick the hide off
you."

"Yes, sir. I didn't mean I was going to drink any
whisky. I don't want any of the stuff. Don't like the smell
of it."

"Well, whisky's not for cubs. Too much of it ain't
good for a grown man, either. But I hold that a little
good spirits now and then keeps a man young."

"All I was saying was I wondered if Ma would do anything about you putting the barrel in the kitchen."

"Ho! What can she do? Too heavy for her to move."

"She could turn the spigot and draw it off in buckets
and throw it away. She could do that."

Father laughed. "Never in the world," he said. "She
knows we can get two shillings for a little glass of that
whisky and she knows what you can buy with two shil-

lings. Never in the world would she throw away money like that, not even if I put the barrel in her bed. Here, you go draw a bucket of water so's we can wash these birds."

That evening a dozen eastbound freight wagons camped across the road on Medicine Creek and Father sent me down to tell the men they could get chicken dinners at a dollar a head at our house and fine whisky at two shillings a glass. Several men let out a war whoop and ten followed me to the house.

Father sold them $5.25 worth of whisky, three cigars and several packs of tobacco, making a total intake of more than $16 for the evening.

"Wife," said Father at bedtime, "that was a splendid dinner, if I do say it myself. Those freighters will remember that dinner."

The freighters had gone back to their camp and the tin dishes and pots and pans had been washed and Mother and Aunt Christine were sitting in the living room with a tallow dip between them as they did some mending.

"Yes, sir," said Father, "those freighters will remember that dinner and that whisky and they'll drop in next time they're along and bring more with them. Mark my words, they will. And, by grab, I don't know any easier way to make money than this."

Mother smiled, but didn't say anything.

X

Father was right about the freighters. As autumn progressed into winter there was scarcely an evening that our house wasn't filled with bearded, loud-talking bullwhackers. The table in the kitchen couldn't begin to take care of the diners, so we built a long, rude board table for the living room where they took their turns for supper, objecting vociferously if Aunt Christine or Eliza attempted to take the dirty tin plates and knives and forks back to the kitchen to wash them.

"Hey, there," they would bellow, "none o' that, sister. I'm hungrier nor a bitch wolf with nine pups. Bring on the victuals. I ain't particular about dirty dishes and I'm afeared you might not bring 'em back."

"Naw," another would yell, "nothing left on this plate but a little clean food, nohow. That's what I'm paying to get, ain't it?"

"Sure don't have to worry about washing this yere plate," howled the third. "Buck cleaned it up as neat as was he a dog."

"Me," said the man next to him, "I wouldn't care particular about following Buck Beedle. He's a kind of a sickly cuss and you might catch his complaint."

This one knew well that Buck Beedle was standing directly behind him, ostentatiously smoking one of Father's ten-cent cigars.

"What the Billy be damned you mean, Buck Beedle is sickly?" he bellowed. "Why, you white-livered, splinter-shanked coyote, you're so sickly a louse won't even stick with you."

"Oh, he won't, heh? Let me tell you I got stouter lice nor ever you supported."

"Oh, you have, heh?"

"Yes. I have, stouter and faster runners."

"Got money to back that up?" demanded Buck.

"Got ten dollars that an Abbott louse can beat a Beedle louse in a tin-plate foot race."

"Only ten dollars? Well, if you're that hard up you better save your money for your old age. It'll be on you soon enough."

"Ten dollars an Abbott louse can beat any Beedle louse."

"I hate to take your money 'cause you ain't got a chance. Let me tell you so you don't forget—a Beedle louse has been fed on the richest, finest food in the world. They're the fastest runners, the best fighters and the hardest biters this side of the Boston water front. Before you throw your money away, stop and think on what chance is a skim-milk fed Abbott louse got with an old he-louse off a Beedle chest?" He changed his cigar to his left hand and pounded his chest with his right fist.

"Fifteen dollars on a thoroughbred Abbott louse just picked at random against the best Beedle louse you can find. And I mean right now."

"You're on!" roared Buck Beedle. "Here, gal," he called to Aunt Christine, who was coming in with another platter of bacon. "Here, gal, fetch this yere man a clean plate. Livestock'd get tangled up in that gravy."

Aunt Christine looked at him a little fearfully. She took the tin plate away and presently came back with a clean one. "We don't expect people to eat from dirty plates at all," she said. "If anybody'd just wait a minute, we'd be glad to wash them."

"All right, gal. This plate's for a sporting business before eating business. Now, bub," Beedle called to me, "fetch us that there tallow dip. And you, Abbott, let's see the color of your money."

Abbott pulled out a leather pouch and fingered up a ten-dollar gold piece and a five.

"I'll hold stakes," said the man on his left. "I'll hold stakes and I'll add a fiver on Abbott's hoss, if they's any takers."

"You're covered," said Beedle. "I put in five more on the Buck Beedle thoroughbred."

I brought over a tallow dip, which Abbott set in front of himself.

"Hey, you ain't going to conduct this here race," objected Beedle.

"I'll run it," offered the black-bearded giant on the left.

"No, you don't," yelled Beedle. "You got a bet against the Beedle dandy. Uninterested party got to operate this race."

"I'll run it," said a red-mustached freighter.

"Lewis all right with you?" asked Beedle, poking Abbott with his thumb.

"Anybody's all right with me. And don't poke me that way."

"All right, Lewis, better start heating up that plate."

"Wait a minute," yelled a black-eyed fellow across the table, "I'll bet a few shillings on the Beedle louse."

"Four dollars on the Abbott louse," called a man standing behind him, "and here it is."

"Done." The black-eyed man dug into his pocket.

While the red-mustached Lewis balanced the tin plate from his finger tips and held it over the candle flame, both Beedle and Lewis opened the bosoms of their flannel shirts and, with faces contorting, started exploring with their right hands.

"Ow!" yelled Beedle. "Oh, there I had a honey. I had a real honey, but he was too slick for me. Got away."

"Better get the best you've got," advised Abbott. "You'll need your best."

"Against them skim-milk critters of yours—haw! Well, here's one that'll show you."

Beedle brought his hand out from under his arm, holding a louse between thumb and forefinger.

Abbott's quest also was successful. "Well," he said, "here's my run-of-the-mill Abbott horse, ready to take on all comers."

Beedle craned his neck and peered at the rival vermin. "Hmm," he observed, "pale little critter, ain't he?"

"Pale!" roared Abbott. "He's full of spirit and rarin' to go."

"All right," said Lewis. "Plate's hot enough. Get ready to put 'em down facing to my right and loose holts when I yell go. May the best louse win."

Beedle and Abbott leaned over the hot plate while everyone in the room pressed in closer for a view.

"You ready?" asked Lewis.

"A Beedle louse is always ready."

"The Abbotts are rarin'."

"All right, now. No excuses. One, two, three—GO!"

Beedle and Abbott simultaneously spread their thumbs and forefingers. The two lice struck the hot tin and paused momentarily in surprise. Then they started a frantic scramble around the rim with the Beedle louse, which indeed was slightly larger and darker in color than the Abbott louse, a little in the lead.

"Come on, Beedle!" yelled the black-eyed fellow from across the board table.

"Hustle up there, you Abbott," bellowed the man who had covered the bet. He leaned across the table holding a tallow dip aloft to light the race better.

As the hot plate began to scorch his body the smaller, paler Abbott louse struck into a sprint and was gradually overhauling the big Beedle louse while the cheers of the bullwhackers brought Mother and Eliza to the kitchen door, wide-eyed and apprehensive.

All at once the Beedle louse quit running. He turned and began an ineffectual attempt to climb up the steep rim of the plate.

"Come on there!" shrieked Beedle and stuck out his finger as if to push his louse back on the track.

"None of that, now," warned Abbott.

"Hold your hosses, there, Beedle," said Lewis. "Hands off."

The Abbott louse had passed the Beedle louse and was scurrying at a great rate right around the rim. The Beedle louse slid back on the track from his attempt at the impossible climb, made a quick survey of the situation and took out after the Abbott louse as hard as he could go. He seemed to bow his back like a wild running horse and his legs flew over the hot tin. But the Beedle louse had dallied too long in his vain attempt to climb up the rim. He now tried to make up for his dalliance by superlousean industry, but the race was too far along. The Abbott louse crossed the finish line a good inch and a half the winner, while everyone but Beedle and his backers cheered.

Abbott seized his champion. "Skim-milk louse, huh?" he cried.

"Sure, skim milk," said Beedle. "Mine was just too well fed. Too smart, that's all. He wasn't going to run all the way around that plate without he was sure there wasn't another way out."

The bullwhackers roared.

Abbott collected the gold pieces and clinked them together. "Maybe," he said, "it's smart to try to do something you can't do," he said, "but I'll take a good runner."

"Yes," moaned Beedle, "his smartness just cost me twenty dollars." He picked up his louse and dropped it in the candle flame where it shriveled in a quick puff.

Abbott, howling with laughter, made as if to kiss his louse. Then he tenderly put it back inside his shirt. "Charley's got a home for life now," he said. "Yes, sir, I'll keep Charley like he was a fine lady." He clinked the gold pieces. "All right, you bullies, who's for having a drink on Charley?"

"Here, here, here!"

"Hey, Mr. Macdougall, will you bring whisky for all that wants it? Whisky on my boy Charley."

Father brought on 23 drinks of whisky at 25 cents a drink, making $5.75 to him on the louse race.

Beedle held up his glass. "Well," he said, "here's to

your God-damn skim-milk louse. And it just goes to show, if you're a skim-milk louse, that you can get along better without too much brains."

That was the first louse race held by freighters in our house, but not the last. Most of the men were astonishingly dirty and they held as great pride in the quality of lice they supported as in their own strength of arm or skill with the bull whip.

Mother and Aunt Christine complained bitterly when some of the parasites would desert their bullwhacker hosts and take up residence on softer skin. But Father took it good-naturedly.

"A louse never killed anybody," he said. "It ain't pleasant, but you got to expect a *few* hardships out here at first. But suppose you had to live in a sod shanty like the Petersons.

"We got to look to the future and think of the things to come. Why, if things keep up the way they're going, we'll build our new house up on the hill next summer. I say keep up but, by grab, they're going to get better—a lot better.

"The steam wagons will be running next summer and we'll have servants to do all the work. You women won't have anything to do but set around and pare your fingernails. You can set around all day dressed up in the finest satins paring your fingernails and reading *Minnie Hermon, or the Curse of Rum* while I look after the business."

Father discovered many of the emigrants had forgotten certain necessities and that the freighters also were often in the market for hardware and articles of clothing. So he went to Nebraska City again and came back with a wagonload of tinware, knives, blankets, powder and lead and percussion caps, a new stock of tobacco, physic and ague cure.

Before Christmas the original barrel of whisky was getting low and Father did some calculation.

It was after the last of the freighters and emigrants had left for the night and he sat by the living-room stove with a notebook and stub pencil. When Father ciphered he stuck his tongue out the corner of his mouth and chewed on it with every down stroke of the pencil.

Finally he looked up. "By grab," he said, "she objected to me getting that barrel. Hey, wife!" he called and Mother stuck her head out the kitchen door.

"What you want now?" she asked.

"You know what I paid for that barrel of whisky?"

"No," said Mother, "but whatever it was, it was too much."

"Well, it was forty dollars."

"Forty dollars!" exclaimed Mother. "You mean to tell me you paid forty dollars for that whisky? Jack Macdougall, I give up."

Father grinned cheerfully. "Well, wife," he said, "to tell the truth I thought it was sort of steep myself. By grab, I did. But I just been doing some ciphering— adding up what we've took in on that barrel of whisky and you know it's five hundred and seventy-four dollars and two shillings."

Mother gasped.

"Yes, sir. It's five hundred and seventy-four dollars and twenty-five cents. I got it all down right here in the book. And that's not counting for evaporation."

"What about the liquor you drank yourself?"

"That," said Father, "comes under evaporation. And you subtract the original forty dollars and it makes a total profit of five hundred and thirty-four dollars and twenty-five cents on the barrel of whisky, to say nothing of what's left, which is enough to run things for a few days.

"Out of that whisky alone in three months we've made

enough money to pay for this pre-emption almost three times over. We've took in over a thousand dollars on meals, which is at least eight hundred dollars profit, and made, I calculate, fifty-sixty dollars profit on tobacco and notions. Wife, we're getting rich, even before the steam wagons start. And I got to go get another barrel of whisky. Maybe I'd better get two barrels this time."

Mother shook her head. "I think," she said, "one barrel at a time would be enough. If you got two barrels you'd lose that much more from evaporation."

"Wife, that may be so." Father nodded his head.

"If you don't get so much at a time," I said, "we can go to Nebraska City oftener."

Father lowered his head and looked at me under his heavy black eyebrows.

"It looks," he said, "like you better start staying here more when I'm away. Need a man on hand to look after business."

Eliza sniffed. "A fine man he'd be handling those freighters. When you're away I think you'd better get John Peterson over to look after 'em."

"Oh, so that's the way it is!" exclaimed Father, looking at Eliza with wide-open eyes.

"No, that's not the way it *is*. But he's a big strong young man and he could look after the freighters a lot better than little Clint or us women."

Father nodded seriously. "Eliza, there may be something in what you say. There may at that."

"The thing that worries me about Clinton," said Mother, "is his schooling. Here we are out in the wilderness with no school for maybe forty miles and the boy hasn't even got through fractions. It's bad enough for Eliza, but she at least has got as much education as you or me."

"Nothing to worry about," said Father. "Missing school for a year ain't going to hurt any girl or boy. Prob-

ably be good for 'em. This here's going to be a settled
community pretty soon—it's getting to be a settled community already, and I'll see that there's a school next
fall. Here we come in and there's not a house for miles.
Right away here's the Petersons taking up land and now
their Bergstrom friends from Wisconsin with two
young'uns and there'll be a lot more by next fall.

"And," Father went on, "I was just thinking. That
Bertha Peterson is a big strong lunk of a girl. What's
wrong with hiring her to work here? She could do a lot
of work and make it easier for you womenfolks."

"Nothing wrong with it—if we can afford it," said
Mother.

"Afford it!" Father laughed. "Of course we can afford
it. And I'll hire John Peterson to come over and hand
out the drinks and look after things when I'm away."

So both Bertha and John Peterson came to be permanent fixtures in our household.

Consequently, when Father went to Nebraska City for
the new barrel of whisky, I went along. And after Jim
Ellison had given Father several samples from the wholesale stock, Father felt rich enough to take me to Rotton's
gunshop and buy my longed-for shotgun.

It was a beautiful little double-barreled gun with arching hammers and a polished wooden ramrod that fit
beneath the barrels.

Then it became my pleasant duty to assist Father in
providing prairie chickens for ourselves and the freighters. The gun was my life's greatest treasure. I kept it in
my bedroom, which was the small loft room which originally had been intended for Eliza, but now was given to
me. Since Alan never would come home, Eliza had the
large room which Alan and I were to have shared.

I spent hours oiling and polishing my shotgun, fon-
dling it as a miser fondles gold, thrilling at the decisive
click-clack of the cocking hammers. And when the cotton-

wood shingles on the roof warped, letting the wind-
blown snow drift into the room, I sacrificed one of my
much-needed blankets to keep the snow off my gun.

With the advent of winter freighting did not seem to
decrease. Certainly the business at Macdougall's Crossing
increased.

There was one evening in mid-December when a
northwest gale brought heavy snow and bitter temperature. Early in the evening a train of twenty eastbound
wagons pulled up on our side of Medicine Creek and
shortly afterwards a Smith and Galbreth forty-wagon
train drew in west bound. Nearly 150 half-frozen, hungry
and thirsty bullwhackers stormed our house.

It was almost midnight by the time Mother, Aunt
Christine, Eliza and Bertha Peterson had supplied them
with food. In all they consumed more than $200 worth
of food, whisky and tobacco from our store.

While two tables were crowded with eating freighters,
the others stood around talking loudly and boisterously
with the air so full of tobacco smoke it was like a dense
fog. They bragged about how great men they were, howling about their adventures in Nebraska City, expurgat-
ing some of the details only when one of the women was
in the room. They drank quantities of whisky that
Father, John Peterson and I brought them and once in
a while a group would burst out singing:

> "I feel, I feel, I feel;
>   I feel, I feel, I feel
> Just like a morning star."

Then:

> "Shoo fly, don't bodder me,
>   Shoo fly, don't bodder me;
> Shoo fly, don't bodder me,
>   For I belong to Company G."

There were two louse races that evening for stakes well over a hundred dollars.

Outside, the snow was still blowing and the wind whistling steadily around the corners of the house, and when the dishes were washed Father stepped into the center of the living room.

"Listen, you men," he shouted. "Listen to me a minute. If you quiet down and behave yourselves as many can stay in this room and the kitchen as can find a place to lay down. But I don't want any commotion or rowdy stuff. Understand? All right. You can bunk here on the floor, and in the kitchen too. The rest will have to go out to your wagons and the barn. But I want it understood there's no smoking in that barn. I'll kill the man that sets my barn afire."

"That's fine. Hurray for Mac," some of the men yelled.

"You're all welcome," said Father. "But settle down here right now. No more rumpus. Us folks got to sleep because we got work to do early in the morning. I'm going to blow out these lights in a minute."

There was a mad scramble for places on the floor and in less than a minute every inch of the living room and kitchen was covered by sprawled-out men. But there were more who couldn't find places than those who could. The unfortunate ones bundled themselves up in mufflers, pulled their earflaps down, hauled on mittens and bellowing out that Bill and Sam and Gotch-ear were too lucky bastards to live, they went out into the storm where they built huge fires along the lee of the grove and practically circling the house. The light from the fires twinkled into my room after I had blown out my candle and lay shivering in my bed.

Because of the storm Bertha Peterson was staying with us and was sleeping with Eliza. I could hear the girls, weary as they were from feeding this army of freighters, giggling to each other on the other side of the partition.

Snow seeped down through the warped cottonwood shingles and tickled my face. I pulled up the blanket and went to sleep.

I awoke hearing Eliza scream, "Clint—Clint!" Then her voice seemed to be muffled.

I leaped from bed, struck a lucifer match and lit my candle. Then I lifted the blanket from my shotgun and, with candlestick in one hand and shotgun in the other, pushed through the door into Eliza's room.

Two bearded bullwhackers were there. One was struggling with Bertha Peterson on the bed. The other was holding Eliza, with his hand over her mouth. Quickly I set the candle on the frosty floor and click-clacked both hammers of my shotgun.

"You sons of bitches get out of here!" I yelled. "Get quick or I'll blow both your heads off. Git!"

The one released Bertha and she struck him a resounding slap across the face. Eliza pulled away and ran crying into my room.

"Careful, you cub," one of the men said, "that gun might go off."

"You're damn right it might go off," I said. "And it's going off twice right now if you ain't outside of this house in half a jiffy."

"Now, now, boy," the other said. "Hold your hosses. We was just playing a little."

"Well, *I'm* not playing." I swung the gun toward him and started to count, "One, two,—"

"We're going. . . . Come on, Smitty," said the other man.

They started down the stairs and I picked up the candlestick with my left hand and held it alongside the shotgun barrels. I followed them down the cold stairs in my bare feet and freighters began to sit up here and there over the living room.

"What's the matter here? What's going on?" several called.

"These sons of bitches come upstairs and were getting funny with my sister," I said. "I'm running 'em outdoors and should ought to kill 'em."

A big burly fellow rose up near the stove. His beard was tucked down inside his flannel shirt. "After that little girl?" he roared. "Well, God damn me, they ought to be killed. Get out of here, you skunks!"

Leaping over the bodies of several freighters, he flung the outside door open, grabbed the first fellow and kicked him so hard that he landed on his face outside in the snow.

"Listen, Baker," the other began, "we never done nothing—"

"Because this young'un was more of a man nor you," cried Baker, and kicked him likewise into the snow. "You sluts better take off on foot down the trail," he yelled out. "When old Macdougall hears about you, he'll chase you down and break your stinking necks." Then he slammed the door.

"Whyn't you shoot 'em, bub?" he asked me.

"Well," I said, "my gun wasn't loaded."

Bullwhackers around me roared with laughter.

"But," I said, "I'm going right back upstairs and load both barrels with buckshot in case any more of you bastards got funny ideas."

Baker slapped me on the back. "That's the way to talk to 'em," he said. "They understand that kind of talk and not much else."

After I loaded my gun and went back to bed I lay awake a long time. The freighters' oxen kept up a continual bawling of protest against the storm. The wind whistled and the fires flickered and cast cold shadows on my wall.

The next morning Eliza begged me not to tell what

had happened. But I thought Father at least should know. Besides, I was somewhat proud of my own part in the affair.

Father's eyes blazed. "By holy dang, I wish you'd have yelled for me," he said. "But I'm proud of you, Clint. I'm proud of you and I'm glad I got you that gun. Now I'm going to get you a pony—the first good one I see at a decent price."

XI

The winter dragged on. During storms, which sometimes lasted three days at a stretch, we would have the house full of freighters each night. Eliza took to sleeping with Aunt Christine in the room back of Father's and Mother's on the ground floor, while Father turned Eliza's big room over to the men. He charged them fifty cents apiece for the privilege of sleeping on the floor, and they were glad to pay it.

Often, after the work was done at night, Mother, Aunt Christine and Bertha Peterson would gather around the cherry-wood table in Aunt Christine's room for what Father called a "stuff and nonsense session," for since Alan's death Mother had become more interested in spiritualism and was partly converted to the idea that the dead could communicate with the living.

Aunt Christine's "control," Dolly, brought Mother numerous purported messages from Alan. The gist of these messages was that he was very happy in heaven and was watching over our family—which seemed to be the stock message of spirits. Several times Mother asked Dolly if Alan couldn't be brought forth to speak directly to her.

"Not yet," Dolly would bang out with the table. "He's not strong enough yet."

"Well," said Father, at this information, "if he ain't

strong enough as a spirit to talk yet, by grab, he'll do a hell of a lot of good watching over us and protecting us."

But Alan supposedly *did* send us some advice and warnings. For instance, one cold night the table whacked out a message "to be careful or thunder will crack the vinegar barrel."

This message didn't seem to make a great deal of sense. We didn't have a vinegar barrel, in the first place, and then violent thunder seemed only remotely possible in January. And, besides that, the message seemed vague as to how we could mitigate thunder by taking care.

Aunt Christine's explanation was thus: "You got to remember," she said, wrapping her Paisley shawl around her shoulders, "these spirits are in heaven and of course they talk something like God. You know the Word of God in the Scriptures generally don't come out flat-footed and say something. The Word of God talks in parables and you got to be right with God before you're given the light to see and understand."

"And," said Father, "nine folks that're right with God will see and understand the Word of God in nine different ways."

Aunt Christine shook her head seriously. "No," she said, "it ain't that way at all. And this message from Alan don't mean a thing about a vinegar barrel. That's where ignorant people make a mistake—trying to believe the letter of spirit messages."

"Great holy jeepers," said Father, throwing up his hands. "Well, Chris, I suppose you ain't ignorant and maybe you're right enough with God so you've got the light to see and understand."

Aunt Christine looked at the floor. Then her strange, reddish-brown eyes raised to Father. "I believe," she said, "that I have the light in a small way."

"What you say about this vinegar barrel business, then?"

"I'd interpret it something this way," said Aunt Christine slowly. "I'd say Alan was telling us that no matter how hard things are, we should ought to be cheerful and hope for the best."

"What!"

"Yes. We hadn't ought to go around with sour faces like vinegar barrels or God is apt to strike us down. You see, thunder and lightning are God's own weapons and they stand for God Himself. In other words, if we are always sour like vinegar barrels, when the harder things come along we'll break."

"Chris," said Father, "you win the heat, watch and race."

Late in January there came such a blizzard early one morning that John Peterson couldn't get over. As a matter of fact, the snow was blowing so hard we couldn't see more than a rod from the kitchen door.

In an effort to get out and feed the stock, Father tied the clothesline to the door handle and paid it out while he struggled through the snow in the general direction of the barn. He was gone about 20 minutes and then came floundering back with frost-bitten cheeks, pulling himself in with the line.

He stumbled into the kitchen gasping. "No use," he said. "Either the barn ain't there any more or the clothes line wasn't long enough. Couldn't find it. Well, if it lets up by night the stock won't suffer much except old Kate will need milking pretty bad."

By night the storm *had* abated enough for him to reach the barn and milk the cow and feed the horses and oxen. He found that the clothesline was more than long enough to reach the barn, but that he must have strayed far to the east or west. When he got back to the house the bucket of fresh milk was frozen over.

That night only about a dozen freighters reached our house. Half of them were suffering from frostbite. They believed that scores must have perished on the road. But as far as we could learn later, only two men froze to death and they were poorly equipped gold seekers bound for Colorado with a mule-drawn wagon.

Winter finally did break with a thaw that sent Medicine Creek roaring down its bed like a mighty river. It flooded our grove and made our ford impassable. So, for four days, we had a party of ten freighters and two gold seekers with us. The gold seekers were two young men of German birth who spoke English with scarcely an accent. Both apparently were in their early thirties. The more voluble gave his name as Casper Diercks and that of his partner as Sebastian Muller.

Both were jovial and sang songs in German which apparently were very humorous, because they often had to pause between verses to howl with laughter and call for Father, whom they termed "mein host," to bring some more schnapps.

Diercks had wide blue eyes that could look most innocent and a ruddy face which grew even ruddier after two or three glasses of whisky. He and Muller kept themselves immaculately clean and plainly were averse to getting too close to the louse-ridden bullwhackers, so they smiled their way into eating with our family and they made our meals much more enjoyable.

One evening Casper—we quickly had come to call him Casper and Muller "Bass"—opened a discussion of the wonders performed by the Austrian, Mesmer, and of the cures wrought by animal magnetism, of mind reading and other occult phenomena. Aunt Christine was entranced.

"Is Mr. Mesmer still living in Paris?" she asked.

"Oh, no," said Casper. "He's dead now for many years. But his teachings, they go on. Now I myself, for instance, I could read the mind of one not too mature, under proper conditions. For instance, a half-grown boy, I could read his mind."

"Aw," I said, "I bet a cow you couldn't read *my* mind."

"Now, my friend," said Casper, "have you a cow to bet?"

"No," I admitted, "I ain't got a cow, but maybe I could borrow old Kate."

"No, sirree," said Father, "you can't borrow old Kate for that kind of a bet. What mind you got should ought to be pretty easy to read."

"Well, then," said Casper, "we shan't bet. But suppose we make a test. You don't mind if I try, then?"

"Go ahead and shoot," I said. "But I still bet you can't do it. I saw mesmerism by Mr. Houdin in Nebraska City and I think it's mostly bosh and buncombe."

Casper smiled. He was quite handsome when he smiled. He picked up a candlestick and stepped to my side of the table.

"Now," he said, "you will see whether it's all bosh and buncombe. Will you please move back a little bit? That's right. And I must have a clean tin plate. You see, it is all very particular and I must have my hands warmed just so or my own animal magnetism and the boy's animal magnetism will not—how can I explain?—will not mix together. You understand?"

Aunt Christine handed him a clean tin plate and he held the bottom over the candle flame much as the bull-whackers did for the louse races.

"It might be," went on Casper, "that this boy may deny his thoughts—if he, indeed, thinks wicked thoughts. But that will do him no good. You see, I shall tell enough of his thoughts for his family here to know I do, indeed, speak the truth."

I began to feel ill at ease and to comb my mind for thoughts I should not care to have exposed. I found some, well enough, but banished them with a feeling of certainty he never could dig them from my mind.

"Well, I'm not afraid," I said. "I don't believe a word of it. Read my mind—hah!"

"Now you must relax," said Casper softly. "Don't be so stiff. You must relax in your chair."

He was holding the brightly polished plate face toward me and gently stroking his hand on the back of it.

"My hand is warmed and magnetic now," he droned, advancing on me. "You must close your eyes."

I closed my eyes and felt his warm hand on my brow. It stroked soothingly across my forehead and then down over my nose. I felt a strange tingling up my spine. "Now," he said quietly, "my magnetism and your magnetism are meeting. They are becoming one."

Eliza giggled sharply.

"No, no," warned Casper, "the young lady must not laugh. Perhaps it should break the spell."

His hand left my face and I opened my eyes to see it again moving in a circle on the back of the plate.

"I must rewarm my hand," he said softly.

Father's face was red and his lips drawn solemnly tight. Eliza had her hand over her mouth. Mother was biting her lower lip.

"Now you should close your eyes again, Clinton," whispered Casper. "Very soon now we shall be ready and my mind's eye shall see what rests in your mind."

I closed my eyes and the warm hand again softly stroked my face, around the eyes, down my cheeks and chin. "Just one moment—just one moment," went on the smooth, sleepy voice.

Then Eliza burst out laughing hysterically.

"No, no, no," began Casper.

"Oh, I can't help it!" Eliza cried. "I just can't."

Then Father roared and slapped his thighs and I opened my eyes. Mother and Aunt Christine were laugh-

ing and laughing with tears running down their cheeks.
Bass sat solemnly at one side. Casper also was very serious. "Oh, please, please," he urged.

"By dang," I said, "what's so awful funny? He ain't
read my mind any. I don't see anything to laugh about."

"Oh, haw-haw-haw!" howled Father.

Casper stepped back, tipped his head to one side and
regarded me critically.

"Now," he asked, "doesn't he really look nice? Don't
you think?"

Eliza gurgled helplessly. A strand of Aunt Christine's
red hair came down over one cheek. "Oh, I'll die," she
screamed. "Oh, I know I'll die!"

I began to get mad. "Go ahead and laugh your heads
off," I blurted. "By dang, laugh your heads clear off. I
don't care. I'm going in with the freighters. Maybe they
got lice, but they got good sense anyhow."

"Oh, don't go in there, Clinton," advised Bass Muller.
"They'd make fun of you."

I had risen from my chair. "*They'd* make fun of me,
huh? What in tarnation is there to make fun of *me*
about? He never read my mind. He said he could and he
never did. What'd he read out of my mind—tell me
that!"

Both Muller and Casper now joined in the uncon-
trolled laughter and Bass said something to Casper in
German.

"All right, you laughing hyenas," I said, "go ahead
and laugh if something is so all-fired funny." I started for
the living room.

"Oh, Clinton," Mother called.

I looked and she was drying her streaming eyes on her
handkerchief.

"Before you go in there," she said, "go in my room and
look at yourself in the mirror." Then she went back to
her laughing.

I picked up a candlestick and stalked into Mother's room and stared at the reflection in the looking glass. Then I laughed too.

My face was blacker than any Negro's I had ever seen —solid black with huge white lips and staring eyes. I saw then what had happened. Casper had held the tin plate over the candle flame until the back of it was covered with soot. On the pretext of warming his hand, he had rubbed the soot off on his fingers and had transferred it to my face when he was "merging our personal magnetisms."

But Casper Diercks was not all fun—apparently. He professed an intense interest in Aunt Christine's table tippings. Together, with Mother and Bertha Peterson, they spent hours over the cherry-wood table and Casper developed a "psychic power" also.

To him came a control named Little Freddie and Little Freddie seemed to be a deceased second cousin of Casper's. Once this control brought a message directly from Casper's grandfather, Colonel Bruno Diercks, whose bones rested on the field of Waterloo—proving the power of spirits to cross seas and international boundaries at will. Grandfather Bruno Diercks was very happy in heaven and was watching over and protecting Casper here in America.

Aunt Christine was much impressed with Casper. Her eyes brightened, her step became lighter. And in his presence Tom Brooks did not send her a single message.

Casper apparently was as well impressed with Aunt Christine. They talked and talked for hours on end. And when the flood went down so the Medicine Creek ford was passable and Casper and Bass left for Colorado to find, they attested, a mountain of pure gold, Casper asked Aunt Christine if she would answer his letters if he wrote her about his experiences and Aunt Christine joyfully promised she would.

XII

So spring finally came with violets and fragile spring beauties blooming in the thick grass along the creek, and when Father went to Nebraska City for another barrel of whisky and other supplies he brought home many bundles of seeds.

He brought seed corn and wheat and oats and seed potatoes and beans and peas and garden vegetables such as turnips and parsnips and onions and spring radishes and carrots and cabbages and cucumbers and pumpkins to be planted between the corn rows and watermelons to be planted a long way from the pumpkins to keep them from mixing. He brought a big stack of switches, which were to become orchard trees, if all went well—apple, plum, cherry, pear and peach trees. And he brought, also, packages of flower seed for Mother. There were big, wrinkled nasturtium seeds and portulaca, which would grow low and spiny and bloom with bright flowers something like a wild rose, and morning-glories and sweet williams and pansies.

But best of all—far best of all—trotting along behind the wagon was a bay pony for me. And in the wagon was a small saddle and a rifle. It was no toy rifle fit only for shooting rabbits and woodchucks, but a real gun with a short stock, a gun powerful enough to kill deer or possibly buffalo—if one were close and shot at exactly the right place.

I was nearly hysterical with delight.

"Now you look alive," said Father. "You got to take care of that pony, and take *proper* care too. And you got to take good care of that fine rifle, I'm here to remark."

"Oh, I'll take the best care that was ever taken of anything," I promised.

"And more than that, there's going to be a deal of

work for a boy around this ranch and I want to see that you do it proper."

"Father, I'll do everything you want, and more too."

"Well, you see that you do. We're going to have a terrible busy time around here for a while, setting out our orchards and getting that seed in. We got no time to lose, because I saw Ajax and he's coming out this way in a few weeks for that buffalo hunt. You work the way you should ought to work and maybe you can go with us, taking your new rifle and pony. Mind you, that's not a promise. I just said maybe."

I grabbed Father around the waist and hugged him.

"Well," said Aunt Christine, "if the work wasn't in shape I wouldn't let that worry me when I was going hunting. If you don't get the seed in this year, there's always next year coming."

Father didn't say anything. He looked at me and nodded his head toward Aunt Christine. That made me feel even closer to him.

We did work hard. We worked from dawn to dusk. I didn't even take time to try my new rifle, which seemed to be an almost superhuman bit of self-restraint.

Eliza and I cut seed potatoes and planted them. I carried water for the new fruit trees and dropped seed in drills until my back felt as if it never could straighten up. John Peterson plowed from daylight to dark with the oxen and Father harrowed with the horses.

Each night found me so tired I could only stumble to bed after supper, pausing only long enough to fondle my new rifle and my not quite so new shotgun. But long after I was asleep Father and Mother and Aunt Christine and Bertha Peterson were busy feeding and supplying liquid refreshment to freighters and emigrants.

So when the stage at last dropped off a letter from Ajax Harvey saying that he and a friend named Chauncey Loud were starting in a couple of days for the

long-anticipated buffalo hunt, we had forty acres in seed
—all that Father intended to cultivate that year.

Both Ajax and Mr. Loud, who oddly enough was a
very quiet man, were wearing broad-brimmed sombreros,
buckskin jackets and riding boots when they appeared on
the evening of the second day. Ajax led a pack horse,
laden with a tent and supplies. They were very jovial.

In preparation for their arrival I had killed and
cleaned more than a dozen prairie chickens. And while
Mother was frying the birds Father and Ajax and Mr.
Loud tapped the barrel of whisky a couple of times each.

"Well, Mac," said Ajax, "you seem to have a mighty
fine setup here. All ready for the steam wagons?"

"By grab," said Father, "I don't know whether I am or
not. Got so much business already with the freighters it
looks like I'll be obliged to enlarge."

"Well, that's certainly great," said Ajax. "It is for a
fact. Don't feel hostile toward Major Brown and me because we insisted that you settle on this road?"

"Hostile? I'm everlasting grateful. Here's to the steam
wagons."

They tossed off their whisky.

"Think maybe I'd better come out here and take a
pre-emption myself," said Mr. Loud. He was a small,
gray man with a straw-colored mustache and pale-blue
eyes.

"Lots of land open," said Father. "Whyn't you do it?"

"Going to be a town here sure as preaching," observed
Ajax, "as soon as the steam wagons have been running
awhile."

"What's the news of the steam wagon?" asked Father.
"You heard from Major Brown?"

"Yes. Heard from him a couple of weeks ago. He'll
be along with his first steamer by June probably."

"Everything all right?"

"Fine as silk."

"Any more talk about a railroad?"

"There's always talk about a railroad. Will be until the steam wagons are running regularly and people can see there's no need for one. Every once in a while the railroad business comes up in Washington when some promoters get busy. They argue they could bring gold from California quicker if they had a railroad—which is true, of course."

"Could bring it quicker with steam wagons too," said Father.

"Exactly. Well, there's talk about a railroad in Omaha all the time. Omaha figures she'd get the railroad and take the freighting business away from us. Of course that's ridiculous. Even if the railroad were put through nobody would think of running it down from Omaha over the Platte swamps. The route for railroads or freight wagons or steam wagons or anything is marked out so clearly by nature that nobody could miss it— straight from Nebraska City west, incidentally passing through Macdougall, Nebraska.

"Funny thing—and rather pitiful too—the way Omaha is grasping at straws and making a drive for freighting business. The press up there is proclaiming that Omaha is the place to outfit for the West and how their freighting business is growing by leaps and bounds. But murder will out. Last week they printed a long item about the biggest train of the season starting from Omaha—ten wagons. Imagine that! Why, we're getting so we don't even call it a train if it's less than fifty wagons."

Father laughed and set down his glass. "What's going on in the war—if anything?" he asked.

"Not much really, as far as I can make out. McClellan is still sitting on the Potomac—waiting for it to hatch, I reckon."

"I heard," said Father, "about a Union general named

Grant or something who's been wading in down along the Mississippi River. That amount to anything?"

"Oh, not much," said Ajax. "The war's got to be fought out in the East. This Grant's captured a couple of little forts down in Tennessee, but that doesn't mean much in the whole picture. The Northern newspapers have taken hold of those fights and made a lot of them because they haven't anything else to crow about.

"As I see it, the most important thing about the present war situation is that young McClellan is commander in chief of the Union army and he's afraid to attack. He's afraid of another Bull Run and if he sits there long enough he'll get just that. Johnston eventually will come up and probably drive McClellan back into Washington."

Ajax smiled at me. "How'd you like to go buffalo hunting with us?" he asked.

"Fine and dandy," I said. "Guess I'm going, ain't I?"

Ajax looked at Father. "Think he's big enough to stand it?" he asked.

"I calculate he can stand it if we can," Father said. "He's quite a hunter already, that boy. He's got a new rifle and he's aching to baptize it on a buffalo."

Ajax laughed and stroked his side whiskers. "What have you hunted?" he asked.

"Oh, everything there is to hunt around here. I got all the prairie chickens you're going to eat for supper."

He slapped me on the back. "Well, that's great," he said. "We'll be glad to have you along. Hope you get a buffalo or two."

We started early the next morning, Father riding Doug and leading Frank as a pack horse. I was riding my pony, whom I had named Bob, and had my rifle in a crude gun boot on the saddle. I had made the boot myself from a piece of heavy old canvas, sewing it laboriously by means of an awl. And to make the rifle doubly safe, I had a thong tied to the ring on the side of the lock and attached to the saddle horn.

Bob traveled at an easy rocking-chair lope, much easier than the pounding trot of Ajax's horse, but the pony kept up very well and we made good time.

Within half an hour we had passed the wagon train that had camped at our crossing the night before and started shortly after dawn. And presently we sighted the dust of the eastbound stage. They were approaching with all four horses on the gallop and the stage bowling over the smooth road at a great rate. On the box was Tommy Ryan, a driver who had been very pleasant about dropping mail off for us, and both Father and I yelled at him.

"Where you think you're going?" he called, but before we could answer the stage was gone in a cloud of choking dust and a rattle of wheels.

"That's Tommy Ryan," said Father to Ajax. "Clever fellow and smart as a whip."

Ajax laughed. "You know," he said, "that's the first time I've heard the word 'clever' used to mean good-natured since I left York State."

"Hell," said Father. "How you use 'clever' out here?"

"Well," said Ajax, "you know the real meaning is skillful or smart—that sort of thing."

"Humph," Father snorted. "Old-fashioned meaning is good enough for me. When a fellow is clever, he's obliging and good-natured and—well, he's just clever."

"That's the way they use it in New York State, all right," agreed Ajax, "but the dictionary says a clever man is smart and witty and skillful and all that."

"Usually," said Father, "a clever man *is* smart and witty and all. When you get right down to cases, one of these fellows that go around glum and laying awake nights to think up something mean to do or say, they aren't very smart."

"That's right," said Ajax.

"Maybe," said Father, "that's how they got to using the word 'clever' to mean smart out here. A clever man's generally smarter than a mean man."

"Well," said Ajax, "maybe it was the other way around. Maybe the folks in York State got to calling a good-natured person clever because most clever persons were good-natured. Maybe it was that way."

"How far," I asked, "you think we got to go beyond Fort Kearny to find buffalo?"

"Can't tell, sonny," said Ajax. "Maybe not far, maybe fifty miles. Maybe we won't even find any—if the Indians have been chasing 'em pretty bad."

"Well," said Father, "I don't think it was that way at all. I think they always called an obliging fellow clever. My father always did and I calculate my grandfather did too."

"I," said Mr. Loud, "never before heard 'clever' used the way Mr. Macdougall uses it, but I'm willing to grant he's right."

"Jeepers," said Father, "you never heard of a *clever* man?"

"Oh, yes," said Mr. Loud, "but it was always used the other way—to mean a smart and witty person."

"By grab," said Father, "where'd you say you come from, Mr. Loud?"

"Don't call him Mr. Loud," said Ajax. "Just call him Chan and he came from St. Louis, where they don't know much anyhow. He's just a lawyer and a college professor, but he's going to be a farmer now, I suspect."

"Say, Chan," said Father, leaning over and touching his knee, "you're just the man we want. We're getting a lot of settlers with young'uns and we're going to need a school. Suppose you get a pre-emption across the road from us. Couldn't get finer land in the whole territory. Then you could teach school, if you're a college professor, and maybe teach the cubs some Latin and Greek and fancy things besides just ciphering and reading and spelling. You could make enough that way so's you wouldn't have to farm so much. Farming's pretty rough work at best."

Mr. Loud smiled shyly. "I think," he said, "you might have a good idea there. I'm convinced the thing to do these days is to accumulate some land and I've never seen any better than this."

"Certainly worth thinking over," said Ajax. "Westward the course of empire takes its way."

We crossed the Big Blue early and I looked south at the trail that would lead down to Rock Creek. I thought of Monroe as I had last seen him and I wondered what he was doing now. Father had received no word from Mary; we didn't know whether they had got back to her people safely, even.

Late that afternoon we came upon a party of Indians traveling north. They were a forlorn and disreputable crew, men, women and children. There were about sixty all told, with the men riding in advance armed with bows and arrows and rusty old rifles. Then the dumpy and greasy women riding mangy-looking horses with tepee poles dragging at each side and the poles lashed together behind and piled high with luggage and small Indians.

When I saw their leader call a halt in front of us I was more than a little nervous.

"Think they're Pawnees," said Ajax. "They're peaceful, anyhow."

We rode up and Ajax raised his right arm. "How!" he called.

The leader raised his bare, cordy arm. "How," he returned.

The chief was a skinny man, past middle age and bare to the waist except for an elaborate necklace of beads and wolf teeth. Two feathers were stuck in his greasy black hair. His fierce black eyes looked at us without expression.

"You Pawnee?" Ajax asked.

"Good Indian," said the chief. "Pawnee. Good Indian."

"Where buffalo?" Ajax asked.

The chief's upper lip twitched. "Long way," he said. He waved his brown arm westward. "Pawnee get antelope."

"Don't you like buffalo?" Ajax inquired. "Why don't Pawnee go get buffalo?"

Again the chief's upper lip twitched slightly. "Buffalo now in Sioux country," he said. "No good go in Sioux country. Sioux not good Indian."

"We," said Ajax, indicating the four of us, "go for buffalo."

The Indian shook his head. "No good white man go in Sioux country," he said. "Pawnee good Indian. You got present for Pawnee?"

Father grinned and spurred Doug forward. He reached in his pocket and brought out a cigar. "Here, Pawnee," he said. "Maybe I'll be wanting your vote some day."

The chief took the cigar and looked at it. "How," he said solemnly, and put the cigar in his mouth.

We camped that night by a creek where the vicious mosquitoes forced us to keep damp wood and grass on the fire to raise an eye-watering smudge, and Ajax told us how the Sioux came to be "bad" Indians.

"The Mormons started it," he said. "Well, really it was a silly kid of an army lieutenant. Before that the Sioux were friendly to the whites and arrangements were being made to pay the Sioux for running this road through their territory. Out west near Fort Laramie there was a huge camp of Sioux—several thousand, I suppose—and their chief was a great warrior named Old Bear.

"Well, this Mormon party came along and trailing their caravan was a fellow driving a cow out to Utah. Some commotion frightened the cow when they were passing the Sioux settlement and she ran off the road in between the Indian lodges. I suppose little Indians yelled and maybe threw sticks and old bossy went galloping and bawling as hard as she could go.

"The Mormon followed her a ways and then got scared of so many Indians around him and let his cow go. He went on back with the Mormons and the next day they reported to the commander at Fort Laramie that the Indians had stolen their cow. In a way it was true. After the Mormon had gone back with his party a young Indian caught the cow and decided it was a shame to let good beef go to waste. He butchered old bossy and he and his friends ate her.

"Of course the commander at Fort Laramie couldn't let theft go unpunished. He knew if he let the Indians steal once they'd steal twice, and presently the pleasant relations between the whites and the Sioux would be at an end.

"So the general sent out a party of troops—twenty-nine soldiers, as I recall—and a lieutenant. This lieutenant was a boy from New England, just turned twenty-one, and I suppose he was pretty well impressed with his own importance. His name was Grattan.

"This Lieutenant Grattan and his troop went out to the Sioux camp and took a couple of cannon with them. Grattan sought out Old Bear and had a powwow with him.

"'You've got to find this Indian that stole the cow,' says young Grattan. 'You got to find this thief and turn him over to us.'

"Old Bear wasn't too excited over it all. He puffed

his pipe and looked at the cub lieutenant. Maybe he
was a little contemptuous, I don't know. Some of those
dignified old chiefs could look contempt plainer than
most men can talk it. Anyhow, Old Bear finally says,
'I'll find the cow thief and send him in to the fort.'

" 'No,' says the lieutenant. 'I've been sent out here to
get that thief and I want him. I want him now. You find
him and turn him over to me right away.'

"Old Bear puffs on his pipe and looks at the cub lieutenant. 'No,' he says. 'No good for white soldiers to take
Indian away. Make all Indians mad. No good. You go
back to Fort Laramie. I find man that steal the cow and
send him in to you.'

"Then the lieutenant gets up his dander. 'Look here,
you,' he shouts at Old Bear. 'You're not to tell *me* what's
to be done. I'm telling *you* what's got to be done. You're
going to turn that thief over to me now. Not tomorrow
or next week, but now!'

"He turned to a sergeant who was with him and
ordered: 'Sergeant, have those cannon wheeled into position at the brow of that hill and trained on this camp.'

"The sergeant left to follow the order. 'Now look,'
Grattan said to Old Bear, 'you hand that man over to
me right away or we're going to open fire on your camp
with cannon.'

"Old Bear shook his head. Then he stepped to the
door of his lodge and waved his hand at the lodges
stretching as far as you could see—thousands of Sioux,
warriors, squaws and papooses. 'You,' he asked, 'would
shoot at *this* camp? Look. All of these that you can see—
all are my people.'

"Well, the cub lieutenant told Old Bear that he could
bet his boots if he had any that the soldiers would open
fire with the cannons in about ten minutes unless the
cow thief was turned over.

"So Old Bear looked at the cub lieutenant again, and

he must have been pretty contemptuous this time, and he said, 'Young man, when you talk like that you must be crazy in the head.' Then he stalked back into his lodge and young Lieutenant Grattan rode back to his twenty-nine men where they had placed the cannons on the hill crest.

"Lieutenant Grattan turned to the sergeant. 'Open fire,' he says.

"So the soldiers blazed away with the cannons and muskets. They killed quite a few Sioux—firing that way into the crowded camp—and among the dead was Old Bear.

"The Indians went wild, as Old Bear knew they would. Before the soldiers had time to reload the cannons, the Sioux had killed every one of them with arrows and bullets.

"They knew they were in for it then. Before the shooting was over the squaws were rushing around, taking down the tepees and packing them on their travois."

"On their what?" Father asked.

"Travois. That's what they call those tepee poles they lash to the ponies' sides.

"They knew there was a store of goods in a warehouse near by that was to be distributed to them by a government agent. They knew the government agent never would distribute the goods now. So they raided the storehouse and took everything, and the whole nation fled northward.

"Next year General Harney caught a party of Brulé Sioux on Blue Creek near this trail west of here and gave them a bad drubbing. That quieted things for a while, but there's bad blood between the Sioux and the whites yet. Probably will be until all of them are wiped out."

"We," said Mr. Loud, "are going hunting right out there in the Sioux country, are we? Did I understand that correctly?"

Ajax laughed. "Not really," he said. "Might be some few Sioux around there, but those that are looking for trouble will keep farther away from Fort Kearny than we're going."

"Well, that all should ought to be a lesson to the whites, I'd remark," said Father.

"How do you mean, a lesson?" Mr. Loud asked.

"Well, professor, the trouble is that seldom you'll find a man with any brains being a soldier in the first place. Take this fort commander Ajax was telling about. Sweet-scented hairpin he was."

"How do you mean?" Mr. Loud asked. "It wasn't the fort commander. It was the young lieutenant."

"The fort commander was to blame for sending out a half-baked cub in the first place. That was a job for a man with some diplomacy. It needed a man with judgment—not some hotheaded cub."

"Mac," said Ajax, chuckling, "I wonder if you're noted for your calm diplomacy under stress?"

Father grinned. "Unless I'm certain I can lick the other party," he said, "I'm always diplomatic."

"Maybe this lieutenant felt certain," said Mr. Loud. "Maybe he had too much confidence in his artillery."

"Just what I said, professor," insisted Father. "He was a raw cub that hadn't ought to have been given that much power. If he thought twenty-nine men could lick ten thousand Indians, two cannons or no two cannons, that old chief was right—he was crazy in the head."

"I didn't say there were ten thousand Indians," said Ajax.

"Well, thousands—make it six or seven thousand Indians. It don't make any difference. I still think that business with the old chief was a lot more important than whatever the old general himself was doing back at the fort. It was his job to be boss. Why didn't he go out and look after this affair himself?"

"After all, he didn't know how serious it would become. It was just a case of a cow theft," said Mr. Loud.

"That don't change it. The general thought it was important enough to send out a couple of cannons with twenty-nine armed men. It was dealing with a big army of savages. Taking those cannons and all was threatening war against those Indians and still this general stayed back at his fort so he wouldn't get his shiny boots dusty.

"I'm arguing," went on Father, "that this whole trouble was the fault of the United States government for sending out a lazy general to take charge of a fort like this—sending out a general that would let a half-baked cub go out on such an important job and not only get himself and his men killed, but bring on a war and kill off God knows how many more."

"That's true in a way," said Ajax, "but of course the general couldn't know this boy would take the bit in his teeth like that."

"Didn't know. Well, by grab, it was his business to know about a fellow he'd send on that kind of a job. And he knew the cub was taking a couple of cannons along, didn't he? What'd he think the cannons were for? To hold a revival meeting with, maybe? I myself think the United States government owes the Sioux Indians an apology and should ought to pay for every Indian killed in this ruckus and that includes all of them killed by this General What's-his-name you were telling about—the one that caught 'em on that Blue Creek."

Mr. Loud yawned. "I, personally," he said, "am willing to admit that Mr. Macdougall is right."

"No argument," said Ajax. "Let's turn in and get an early start."

I was kept awake for a while by a company of prairie wolves yapping and yowling near by. I wished it was light enough so I could get a shot at one with my new rifle.

XIII

We reached Fort Kearny the next afternoon and I found it a fascinating place. On the south bank of the Platte River in a wide, grassy valley, it was surrounded almost every night by dozens of freight wagons and caravans of emigrants, who had converged to the Oregon Trail from Leavenworth and from Nebraska City and Omaha.

The fort walls and inner buildings were constructed of gray, sun-baked bricks called adobe, and just to the west of the fort itself a settlement had grown up—built likewise of these big drab bricks—which was called Dobetown.

Dobetown provided the sort of entertainment designed to appeal to soldiers and freighters. True, there also was a store or two that sold supplies—bacon and powder and flour and clothing—but most of the establishments offered women, liquor and gambling—three masculine staples.

We camped to the west of Dobetown near the river, picketed the horses and pitched our tent.

"Now," said Ajax, "I want to go to the fort and see a captain I know. He can tell us where to go after buffalo and what the outlook is. But somebody'll have to stay here in camp or these Dobetown bullies will come out and steal us blind."

"I'll stay," offered Mr. Loud. "I'm tired anyhow."

"Well, don't go to sleep until we get back," said Ajax. "And you'd better load your gun. I wouldn't trust these folks an inch. They're worse than the Indians."

"I saw a lot of Indians," I said.

"That's right," agreed Ajax. "Of course they'd probably steal anything that was loose, but they're mostly harmless. They're relatives of the squaws that're in favor with the army. When an officer takes in a squaw—just

to wash his clothes and cook his meals, you understand—
it seems he has to take in her father and mother and
brothers, and maybe cousins too."

"By grab," said Father, "looking at the squaws, I'd say
it was hardly worth it. Ain't there any white women out
here?"

"Oh, yes," said Ajax. "Quite a few white women in
Dobetown and they're wilder than the savages and not
near as pretty. Well, wait. You'll likely see some when
we walk through Dobetown."

"No treat to me, mister," said Father. "They couldn't
be any worse than some of the specimens on Canal
Street in Buffalo."

"I don't know," said Ajax. "Syphilis is the least thing
most of these wenches have got. If one of 'em brushed
against me on the street I think I'd burn my coat."

"Nice people," observed Mr. Loud. "Yes, I think I
shall stay here with Clinton and watch the horses."

"Look here," I objected, "I ain't going to stay here.
I want to go to the fort."

"Clinton," said Mr. Loud, "it's barely possible I may
become your schoolteacher. In that case I suggest that
you say 'ain't' altogether too often."

"Well, jeepers, I want to see the fort."

Ajax looked at Father.

"Sure he can go," said Father. "That boy's no lily of
the valley. He's seen things. I always say the best way
to keep a boy from stumbling to hell is to give him a
whiff of brimstone."

Ajax laughed and we started off for Dobetown and
the fort.

The streets of the settlement were narrow and rutty
and there were no sidewalks except in front of the largest
saloon, which also boasted a wooden awning for shelter.

"Too early yet for the gambling dives to be open,"

said Ajax, "but the saloons and bawdyhouses run twenty-four hours a day."

The streets were almost deserted. Three soldiers in wrinkled uniforms leaned against the mud wall of a gambling house. A large roulette wheel could be seen through the window. The soldiers looked discontented and stared at us with no friendliness.

"Maybe," said Ajax, "we ought to get fortified for going through the other end of town."

"Good idea," said Father.

So we entered the door of the saloon with the wooden awning in front. Inside was a disagreeable odor of mustiness and stale liquor. The bartender was almost as dark as a Negro, but had long straight hair. He was fat with heavy pouches under his sullen eyes.

Father and Ajax stood before the near end of the bar and the bartender came languidly forward.

"What you want?" he asked.

"Whisky," said Father.

"Whisky," said Ajax.

The bartender nodded his head at me. "Anything for him?"

"What you got?" asked Ajax.

"Bottle beer."

"No," said Father.

"Got ginger beer."

"All right. Give him ginger beer."

So I got a bottle of ginger beer, which I didn't like very well. It was hot and stung my tongue.

Four men were at the other end of the bar. Three of them were bearded and one thin, sallow fellow was smooth-shaven. He had a very long upper lip, but still his front teeth protruded, and he was arguing in a nasal whine.

"That's what you say," he declaimed, "but by God and by Jesus, I know what I'm talking about, I do. There was gold because I seen it. He had gold dust in a belt around his waist."

"You was drunk and you don't know *what* you seen," said one of the bearded men. He had a heavy revolver slung from his bulging waist.

"I wasn't drunk. But drunk or sober I allow I know gold dust when I see it."

"Suppose he took off his belt and poured out the gold dust to show *you*," drawled another of the men.

"That's what I said, and by God and by Jesus I'm telling the truth."

"Poured it into *your* hand?"

"No. I never said that. He poured it into his own hand."

"What happened then?"

"What happened? Well, he says, 'That there's Coloraydo gold.' I says, 'Let's see it.' And he let me poke it around in his hand with my finger. It was gold, all right. What's the matter, don't you believe there's gold in Coloraydo?"

"Oh," said the fellow with the revolver, yanking up his belt, "there's gold in *Colorado* right enough." Then he looked at the other bearded men and laughed.

I was glad to get out of the saloon and into the bright sunlight again. The dirt street was baked hard and smelled of the sunshine.

We went on down the street toward the fort and presently some women began to speak to us from open windows. Some were white women and some were Indian and, as Ajax said, the Indians were more comely. Once a door opened and a slim Indian woman stood in the doorway stark naked. She said nothing, but her thick lips spread in a knowing grin. As we passed she shut the door again.

A few doors on in this long, crooked, one-story mud building, another door opened and a white woman stepped out. She was a fat woman with a fluffy skirt that reached no lower than her knees. She wore red stockings and was quite knock-kneed. Her cheeks and lips were painted very red and when she smiled she revealed a gap where two front teeth were missing.

"Hello, there, boys," she greeted. "Out for some sport?"

"No, sister," said Ajax solemnly. "Deacon Jones and myself are just out looking over the location for our new Methodist-Episcopal church in Dobetown. I am Reverend John Niles and I'm seeking the redemption of you poor sinners. Won't you promise me that you'll attend my services and bring some of the other sisters in sin with you?"

"If you're a preacher," said the woman, "then I'm the Virgin Mary. Come in to one of *my* prayer meetings sometime."

"Not until we get the church built," said Ajax. "And you got to come to my prayer meeting first. I asked you first."

"Maybe we can make a deal," said the woman.

"Yes," said Father, "he can show you the way to heaven and you can show him a hell of a time."

"If he," said the woman, "can do his part as good as I can do mine, he's a better preacher than *I* ever seen."

"You're just bragging," said Father.

"Come on, deacon," said Ajax, "we've got to look after our church site."

"See you again, reverend," said the woman. "See you again, deacon."

We walked down the street.

"Clever whore," said Father.

"That's what *she* says," said Ajax. "Rather good-natured too."

"Are all these Indians around here Sioux?" I asked.

"Yes," said Ajax, "but there are a lot of tribes among

the Sioux and I suppose their particular tribe isn't on the warpath now."

"That's what *I* said," put in Father. "*She* didn't say she was clever."

Ajax cocked his head on one side and looked at Father and then we went into the fort and found Ajax's friend, Captain Matthewson. He was a short man with a stubby, sandy beard and his face, where not protected by hair, was burned a strawberry red.

When we entered, the captain was engaged in a heated discussion with a younger officer about some mules that hadn't been taken where they belonged or had been taken where they didn't belong.

The captain dropped the discussion when he saw Ajax. "Well, hello, there, Gus," he called and rose from his desk. "What you doing out here?"

"How are you, cap," greeted Ajax. "Oh, we just came out to see whether you've got things under control. Abe Lincoln sent me out to look over the situation."

"Tell Abe," said the captain, "that he ain't very popular hereabouts and he'd better keep his flunkies back in Washington."

"I'll tell him. But I doubt if he'll like his soldiers talking that way. Meanwhile, how's the buffalo hunting? The Macdougalls here and another friend of mine think they need some buffalo robes. Meet my friends, the Macdougalls, Captain Matthewson."

The captain shook hands with us. "I don't know just where the buffalo *are* using now," he said seriously. "Sit down and make yourselves at home. Lieutenant Graves, we'll take that up later."

"Very well, sir," said the lieutenant, and clumped out of the room.

"I reckon," went on the captain, "that you can find plenty buffalo if you go to the right places within forty or fifty mile of here. Maybe a lot closer."

He sat down and swung his spurred boots over the edge of the table. "This your first trip west, Macdougall?" he asked.

"First trip *this* far west. I'm living back on Medicine Creek."

"Oh, yes. Well, you ought to go on a ways if you really want to shoot some buffalo. Ought to run out past Fort Laramie. Thousands of them out there. I don't know—maybe millions."

"Any Indian trouble lately?" Ajax asked.

"No, the savages been pretty quiet lately. Never can tell when some damn emigrant will stir 'em up again, though. And if they try to run through that railroad they're talking about, it'll be plain hell."

Ajax laughed. "Needn't be afraid of that, Matt," he said. "That's just talk. I don't think they'll ever try to build a railroad across this country. Not for fifty years anyhow. And there won't be any need for a railroad two or three years from now."

Captain Matthewson raised his eyebrows.

"Steam wagons will be pulling trains of freight wagons past your old fort this summer," said Ajax. "In two or three years there'll be half a dozen each way every day to and from the California coast."

"Well, I've heard some talk about a steam wagon. Anything to it?"

"There's *everything* to it, cap. It's a fact."

The captain laughed. "I'll be looking for 'em," he said. "That kind of business might work. But these Sioux would go plumb crazy if they tried to lay rails across this country."

Ajax nodded his head. "No danger for us to push around off the trail out west of here, is there?"

"Oh, I don't think so. Wouldn't want to write you a guarantee, you understand. It's never as safe as a Sunday-school picnic. But there's no trouble right now."

"That's what we wanted to find out," said Ajax.

"I tell you about Indians, Gus—and you too, Macdougall. They're something like strange dogs. You act scared in front of a strange bad dog and you stand a good chance of getting bit. You act scared in front of a bunch of Sioux out on the prairie and you stand a good chance of getting your hair lifted—whether there's any trouble on or not. You act timid and as if you didn't quite know what you're doing and your relatives are pretty apt to get some bad news.

"Now a party of men can go through the Sioux country and be pretty safe if they act self-confident and bold, but keep a sharp lookout. If you run into a Sioux hunting party, just act like you were their bosses. Not too bossy, you understand. Just act superior, and talk to 'em in—well, in the way an officer talks to a private, if you understand what I mean."

Ajax laughed. "I understand," he said. "That's good advice, cap."

The captain laughed also. "Don't know why I should be giving *you* advice about Indians, though," he said. "You've been around enough of 'em on your surveying."

"Well—I didn't know the present situation. And that talk of yours ought to have a good effect on the cub here."

Captain Matthewson smiled.

"When you going down south to fight the rebs, cap?" Ajax asked.

The captain looked serious. "Don't know," he said. "Never, I hope. This out here is bad enough for me. Seeing that they've got to keep troops out here, why shouldn't I stay? I know the situation."

Ajax and Father rose. "Well," said Matthewson, "drop in and see me on your way back. Tell me what luck you had."

"Maybe we'll bring you a chunk of meat," said Father.

Matthewson shook his head. "No, thanks," he said. "I've got all the buffalo meat I can stand. But if you see a nice bowl of stewed oysters out there you might bring *them* in."

So the next morning we rode out beyond Fort Kearny and, after about twenty miles, we left the Platte and the trail and cut down through the sand hills in search of buffalo.

Sometimes there would be patches of fine sand six or eight rods in extent—rabbit sand, Ajax called it. The grass was shorter and less luxuriant than back in our section. It was a coarse grass and inclined to be curly.

Riding along on Bob, I kept sweeping my eyes over the horizon, hoping to be the first to sight a herd of buffalo, but throughout the morning I saw no animals except two coyotes loping easily along beyond gunshot, several jack rabbits, that would stand on tiptoe with their astonishingly long ears upright until we came close, and numerous villages of prairie dogs.

There was no wood where we stopped for a snack at noon, but Ajax built a fire of buffalo chips.

"Polite word for it," Mr. Loud said, "is 'bois de vache.' That's French for cow wood."

"They burn just as good," said Ajax, "if you call them buffalo chips. Make a pretty good fire—see. Not terribly hot, but perfectly all right for cooking and making tea."

"By grab," said Father, "I'd calculate it wouldn't be extra good for the victuals."

"Oh, it's all right," declared Ajax. "There's no stench. . . . Hey, there, boy!" he called to me.

I looked up from investigating a bright green plant with fat oval leaves. "Don't touch that," he advised. "It's prickly pear, and if you get those spines in your fingers we'll need tweezers to get 'em out."

"Prickly pear?" I said.

"That's right—cactus."

"Well," said Father, "I suppose it's all right to cook with, but I never heard of that before. It's great stuff for medicine, though."

"Medicine!" Mr. Loud frowned.

"That's right. Best stuff on earth for a wound. If it wasn't for cow manure, I'd be a one-legged man right now."

Ajax looked up. "How's that?"

"Well," said Father, "when I was a cub I stepped on a rusty spike once and it went clear through my foot. The wound was so full of rust and corruption that it just oozed a little bluish blood front and back. Hurt—by grab, nothing could have hurt worse. Well, I hobbled home and my old grandfather Macdougall took one look at it and he says, 'Just one thing'll save that boy's leg and maybe his life. Get me some soft cow manure right away.'

"So somebody rushed out to the barn—I think it was my sister Sophie—and got Grandfather a shovel of soft cow manure and he made a poultice of it and strapped it all over my foot."

"Heavens and earth," said Mr. Loud, "I'd have thought that would give you blood poisoning sure."

"Blood poisoning? It saved me from blood poison. Sucked the blood right out of the wound and it was well in no time. That's a fact. I've used it lots since that. Saved my oldest son once. He cut his hand bad on a rusty sickle and I made a cow-manure poultice and slapped it on. Sucked the poison right up. Healed up in no time, by grab, and hardly left a scar. That was the boy that got killed at Bull Run."

"Hmm," breathed Mr. Loud.

"Horse manure work just as well?" Ajax asked.

"Don't know," said Father. "Don't know why it wouldn't, only it ain't soft enough. Really need a cow and there's always a cow around someplace."

"Well," said Ajax, "I knew a man once that cut his foot chopping in a stable and he died of lockjaw. They said it was because horse manure got in the wound."

Father shook his head. "Could have saved that man's life with cow manure," he said.

"I wouldn't let anybody put that kind of poultice on me, anyhow," said Mr. Loud. "It just isn't reasonable."

"Just reasonable enough to save your life, is all," Father blurted. "Of course if somebody is so pernickety he'd rather die than have something around that don't smell like a violet, that's something else again. That's a horse of a different color, by grab."

Ajax scratched his side whiskers. "Let's have some tea and jerky and go look for buffalo," he said.

So we drank hot tea and chewed on the dried buffalo meat they had bought in Dobetown. It was tough and stringy and had a strange, wild flavor. But it was edible and, according to Ajax, very nutritious.

We camped that night by a little stream that trickled along a haphazard course through a wide sand flat. The next morning we set out again in the bright sunshine over a country that seemed to offer exactly the same scenery and same experiences as the day before.

However, by midmorning I sighted two black specks near the brow of a faraway hill.

"Hey," I called, "what are those two things way up there? They buffalo?"

Mr. Loud was riding next to me and he peered intently. "No," he said, "I don't think so. Buffalo go in herds. Don't believe you'd see two together that way."

"Where?" asked Ajax.

He pulled up his horse and looked. "Don't know what else they could be," he said. "Maybe there are more on the other side of the hill. Let's see—what way is the wind? That's lucky—coming *from* them. Let's circle down to that creek and tie the pack horses and go investigate."

By the time our two pack horses were tied I really was excited.

"Your gun loaded, bub?" Ajax asked.

"Yep. But no cap on it."

"Well, everybody better get his gun capped. I think those are buffalo, all right. We'll ride up after them and drive 'em over the hill. If there are more we'll run up alongside and fire into them. You all understand how. Get close as you can and let them have it just behind the left shoulder and aiming down. After you shoot you can drop back and reload and take after them again. If there are just those two, you, Mac, and the cub can have the first shots. If you don't drop 'em, Chan and I will finish 'em off."

"Fine and dandy," said Father.

We capped our rifles, let the hammers down carefully on the caps, mounted and rode up the hill. Bob shied and a rattlesnake burred sharply to my right. He was coiled next to a fat prickly pear and was all ready for business.

"Rattlesnake," I called. "Shall I get him?"

"No," said Ajax shortly.

"Don't bother with any snakes now," said Father. "Jeepers."

"All right," I said, "but maybe he'll bite somebody later on."

"Not likely anybody but a freighter or an Indian and we can spare a few of them," said Ajax.

Now we could see the animals truly were buffalo. We could make out their huge, shaggy humps as they grazed placidly on the hill. We circled up to approach them from the rear.

Ajax spoke a little breathlessly. "We'll drive 'em over the brow before you shoot," he said. "If you shoot on this side of the hill it might stampede anything that was on the other side."

I pulled my rifle from its canvas boot and looked at the lock. The copper percussion cap was in place and the big hammer rested against it.

Twisting in the saddle, I tried the gun to my shoulder, aiming to the right. The safety thong I had attached from the saddle horn to the ring on the side of the gun lock seemed to hamper my freedom, so I hurriedly untied it from the gun and wrapped the thong around the saddle horn.

We circled up on a slow trot. Father also had his rifle ready. He was riding in front of me and the sun glinted on his gold earrings. It occurred to me that I didn't remember seeing any other man in Nebraska wearing earrings.

We were within ten rods of the grazing buffalo before they raised their heads and began lumbering over the hill in an awkward gallop.

"Pull up alongside!" yelled Ajax.

I spurred Bob and by the time we swung down on the other side of the hill I was close behind the rear buffalo and was reining to the left. Father already was up to the first buffalo.

A few scrubby trees grew along the brow of the hill, several of them bearing white blooms. The buffalo skirted the trees and there ahead were at least thirty more grazing giants. At the clatter of our approach they threw up their heads and started off down the valley.

Ajax came racing past me, his side whiskers rippling in the breeze. He was grinning and pulling his rifle from its scabbard. He waved the rifle at me. "Let him have it!" he shouted.

Bob now was in a wild run. He plainly didn't want to get too close to the buffalo, but I managed to pull him within a rod and a half of the beast. I could see the mangy wool on the buffalo's hump, shedding for the spring season. I could even see small fragments of the dark-brown wool break loose from the hump and sail back on the wind.

I gave the reins a twist around the saddle horn, hooked my thumb on the rifle hammer and clacked it back. Then I twisted in the saddle and brought the rifle to my shoulder. Twice I tried to catch the front sight in the V of the rear sight, but I couldn't. So I merely squinted down the barrel at the brown hulk of the buffalo, brought the gun slightly behind the shoulder and pulled the trigger.

The stock reared against my shoulder terrifically. It rammed me sideways so that my right foot lost its stirrup. And just then Bob, outraged by the rifle's roar in his ears, leaped straight into the air. I let go the rifle and grabbed desperately for the saddle horn. My fingers slipped off and I toppled off the near side of Bob, twisted in mid-air and landed violently in a sitting position.

The fall knocked the wind from my body and I sank back in the bunch grass gasping. My shoulder ached cruelly and I finally sat up and moved my arm to see if it was broken. Apparently it was only a bad bruise, no more severe than that on my posterior where I had landed.

The buffalo I had shot was stumbling and falling and trying to rise again six or eight rods away. In a cloud of dust, Ajax and Mr. Loud were riding beside the buffalo herd. Ajax's gun banged. Then Mr. Loud's. Father was dismounting down the hill beside a brown hulk on the ground. I hadn't seen him shoot.

As Father dismounted, Bob came trotting along in an aimless fashion with the stirrups bouncing and Father leaped back on Doug again and peered back under his hand. I stood up and waved and Father came galloping toward me. Despite my aches I couldn't help noticing how beautifully he sat a horse.

He galloped up to me. "Whoa, Frank!" he called and pulled Doug to a halt. It struck me that Father must be pretty excited not to know which horse he was riding.

"You hurt?" he demanded.

I limped toward him. "I ain't clear killed. Calculate I didn't break anything, but I'm kind of bunged up."

"What on earth happened?"

"Well, the gun sort of kicked me loose from the saddle and Bob jumped and I fell off."

"Where's your gun?"

"Oh, jeepers! I don't know. I must have dropped it."

"Well, hustle around and find it again. I was going to hurry up and get another buffalo. But we got two. No need to be hogs. I'll go round up Bob."

He trotted off after Bob, whistling shrilly—whew-whew-whew-whew—and I began looking for my rifle in the grass. My buffalo seemed to be dead. I remembered hearing that one should slit the throat of a slain beast so it would bleed, but I had nothing but my jackknife and decided I would wait until Ajax came back with his hunting knife.

I found my rifle, apparently not damaged. Luckily, it had landed on the stock and had not filled the barrel with dirt.

Ajax, Mr. Loud and Father all laughed at my being kicked from the pony by my rifle, but all said I was fortunate not to get another kick from Bob as I fell.

"Maybe," said Father, "it'll be a lesson to him. I've told him plenty of times to hold a gun tight to his shoulder."

"I had it tight to my shoulder."

"You couldn't have or it wouldn't have hurt you that way. Now load her up and shoot at that little tree."

"Aw," I complained, "my shoulder's too sore."

"That'll be good for it. Go ahead now."

So I loaded the rifle and held it very tightly to my sore shoulder and fired. It jarred me and hurt the shoulder, but it was not nearly so vicious a kick as it delivered when I was on horseback.

"All right, now," said Ajax. "Suppose Clint rides down and brings up the pack horses while we get busy on these buffler."

So I rode Bob back down the hill, upbraiding him on the way for throwing me off, and brought back the lead horses. The men skinned off the hides of the four buffalo, took the tongues and strips of steak from the humps. They packed the meat inside the buffalo hides and lashed the buffalo hides to the pack horses.

That night we camped by the little stream at the foot of the hill. Coyotes, scenting the dead buffalo, called their relatives from all neighboring townships and held a noisy feast all night.

Part III

Steam Wagon Road

Steam Wagon Road

I

By summer the freighting business was more active than ever. And we had two new neighbors, making a total of five families in our immediate vicinity.

Of course our first neighbors were Pete Peterson and his family, which consisted of Mrs. Peterson and John and Bertha. Next were Mr. and Mrs. Hans Bergstrom, old friends of the Petersons, and the four Bergstrom children, Martha, Ole, Willie and Peter.

Then in the spring, Albert Striker, the carpenter who helped build our house and barn, had taken a pre-emption to the east of us and had moved in with his three children, Albert Jr., Susie and Mabel. And Sime Phillips, broad-shouldered young blacksmith from Nebraska City, came out and took land across the road where he set up a blacksmith shop to do wagon repair work and shoe horses, mules and oxen for the freighters and emigrants. Phillips had a boy and a girl, Harry and Tish, which made a total of ten children of school age in the neighborhood, not counting Eliza, who had put up her hair and declared herself a young lady.

So when Chauncey Loud and his wife did come out

and take a pre-emption, Father donated land near the road and on high ground farthest from the creek and Bergstrom and Phillips contributed for lumber and Mr. Striker built a one-room school in which Mr. Loud could teach us after the summer work was over.

The newcomers all were mightily pleased with their land, but nevertheless they were disgruntled. That was because of the Homestead Law.

Under the pre-emption law, they had paid or had agreed to pay $1.25 an acre for their 160 acres. They had been convinced the Homestead Act never would be passed. And even after Congress had voted approval, they still did not believe President Lincoln would sign it. True, Lincoln had been elected on a "Vote yourself a farm" platform, but the newspapers printed predictions that the President never would allow the Homestead Act to become a law, that he would either veto the bill or let it die on his desk as President Buchanan had done with a similar Homestead Bill two years before.

There were many arguments to back up this position, but the principal one was that the government needed money so badly to fight the war that Lincoln certainly never would give up any source of revenue like the sale of public lands—at least not until after peace had been signed.

The war was going in unhappy channels for the North anyhow. General McClellan finally had got up gumption to make a move on Richmond, but had been scared right back again. General Pope had made another move into Virginia, but was badly defeated and had retreated almost to Washington.

Nevertheless, Lincoln *did* sign the Homestead Act into a law and our neighbors found they could have obtained their 160 acres without the $200 they had agreed to pay, simply by living on the land for five years.

Father comforted them. "Now look," he said, "that

law don't even go into effect until the first of the year. You can have title to this land by then, and do you want a homestead there's nothing to stop you taking another hundred and sixty acres. Maybe you can even get adjoining land and have a whole half section. And there's a clause in this new law that you can get the new land the same way you got this. I mean you can pay off a dollar and a quarter an acre after six months if you want without waiting five years to get free title on it.

"Another thing—maybe had you waited for this law you wouldn't have got just the land you wanted like you've got now. By grab, there's going to be an almighty rush for homesteads, come New Year's Day."

Then privately to the family, he said, "I'm glad we didn't start building the new house, wife. I'll be in Nebraska City right up at the head of the line when the land office opens on the second of January.

"First of January is a holiday and the office won't be open then, but I'll be right up at the head of the line when it *does* open and I'll try to get my filing on the hundred and sixty directly back of this place. This place will be our business and that place our home. We'll plant trees around the house and be a quarter mile away from the road. I calculate it'll be pretty noisy down here when the steam wagons are puffing through tooting their whistles."

Already our house on the road was becoming to look more like home with the flowers blooming around the house, but in truth it *was* noisy there even now, with the bellowed whoop, whoo-haw! of the bullwhackers sounding practically all day long and now the clang-clang of Sime Phillips's hammer and anvil across the road. Also, in dry weather dust from the freight wagons covered everything.

Preparing for the rush of a higher class business when the steam wagons got running, Father built an addition to the L on the house—a bedroom for Eliza. The big upstairs room adjoining mine was converted into a dormitory for those freighters who were willing to pay 75 cents for shelter. In Nebraska City he bought some more glass showcases and placed them in the living room to display tobacco, knives, tinware, blankets, colored handkerchiefs, striped sticks of peppermint candy, writing paper and pens and ink, bottles of ague cure, New Testaments and other articles we had for sale.

Being so busy with all these things, Father had scant time for farming and now John Peterson was working every day on our place. John was rankling over the Homestead Law because he would be only twenty on the first of the year and not eligible to take out land.

Along in June John came to Father with a plan. "Look, Mr. Macdougall," he said, "Eliza and I are in love and want to get married."

"Crucified Christ!" said Father. "What sort of stuff and nonsense is that? Eliza's just a little girl. What she know about being in love and getting married?"

John scratched his blond head. "She ain't no little girl, Mr. Macdougall," he said. "She's going to be sixteen come winter and lots of girls get married when they're sixteen."

"They shouldn't ought to," said Father firmly. "Eliza's just a little girl, sixteen come winter, or no sixteen come winter. She's got to go to school this winter and learn some more ciphering and maybe Latin. John, you're a good boy and if Eliza wants to marry you when she grows up I'll give you no objections at all. I'll be glad of it that she's getting a good strong, honest chap like you. But she ain't old enough to know her own mind now. Maybe when she's eighteen or twenty she wouldn't even want to marry you. Girls change a lot, John. You wouldn't want to be married to her three or four years from now if she didn't want to be married to you—now, would you?"

"No," said John, looking down. "Course I wouldn't want that. But I don't think she'll change. I know I won't change."

"Boy, you can't know a thing of the kind."

"Well, I do. I know I've been in love with Eliza ever since I first saw her and she says the same thing about me. That's been a long time."

"Man alive, she was just a child in pigtails then."

"That don't make any difference."

"Well, it does make a difference. If you two are really in love it ain't going to hurt cubs like you to wait a few years, to wait until you got something to support a wife on. I'm not going to have my daughter marrying some man who hasn't got a home or a red cent."

John grinned sheepishly. "That's just it," he said. "Did I marry Eliza this winter when she's sixteen, then I'd be head of a family even if I ain't twenty-one yet. Then I could get a fine homestead."

"Oh," said Father, "so that's it."

"Well, that's why I don't think we should ought to put it off."

"It don't go, John. When you're twenty-one there'll still be loads of good homesteads. You get your land then. And, after a couple of years or so, if you and Eliza still want to get married, I'll have no objections."

"But," said John, "we wanted to get a homestead right here so we'd be near you and my folks. Then I could work for you the same as now and work on my homestead in my spare time."

Father shook his head. "Sorry, John, but there's no use talking. You're the kind of fellow this community is going to need. I'd like to have you around here. But there's no use talking any more about it. Eliza's just too young."

II

Shortly after the Fourth of July Tommy Ryan, the stage driver, dropped off a letter from Ajax Harvey.

"You'd better come down to Nebraska City next week," Ajax wrote Father. "Major Brown is bringing his steam wagon in by steamboat and there's going to be a celebration that will make history. Maybe you should bring the cub too. He could ride the first steam wagon train back to Medicine Creek and he wouldn't be as likely to fall off a steam wagon as a horse. It would be something for him to tell his grandchildren."

Father read the letter aloud. I whistled. "Jeepers, father," I said, "can we go? Can we, father?"

"Well, I don't know," said Father. "We're apt to be pretty tarnal busy about that time."

"Busy!" Aunt Christine sniffed. "Clinton, you don't know your father very well yet. If you knew him like I do, you'd know wild horses couldn't keep him away from Nebraska City if there's anything like that happening."

"Chris," said Father, "that's sluff talk and you know it. If I go to Nebraska City it'll be because, all things concerned, I think it's better business to go there than to stay here."

But we *did* go to Nebraska City, Father riding Frank and I riding my pony, Bob.

We rode in on Main Street and were on the point of turning over to Otoe, where Father had located a boarding house that served good meals at a reasonable price, when Father sighted a man he knew.

"Hey, Ernie," he called, "the steam wagon in yet?"

"You bet she's in," said Ernie. "Come in on the steamer *Omaha*. They got her unloaded and are putting her together down at the foot of Main Street. I just come from there."

"Come on," said Father, and we went on a gallop down the long levee hill.

Long before we got there we could see an immense crowd down by the river. More than a thousand people were crowded around a huge black and red something and there was a sound of hammering.

When we rode up we could see the top of the engine over the heads of the people—the smokestack and top of the boiler, which set vertical instead of horizontal like a railroad locomotive. We also could see the top of one huge drive wheel, which was twice as high as most men in the crowd.

"Let's hitch and look it over," said Father excitedly.

We turned our horses and looked for a hitching rack, but every available space was taken by teams and riding horses. We rode up a block and the same situation held.

"By holy dang," said Father in exasperation, "we might as well left our horses back home and walked in."

We trotted south on a side street and nearly a block from Main finally found a vacant hitching post and tied our horses. Then we hurried back to the levee.

The crowd was excited, men, boys and a few women and many dogs, moving this way and that way, trying to press in closer so they could get a better view of the engine. The hammering continued and then a man's voice called out, "Please move back a little, folks! Give us a chance to work or we'll never get this engine together."

We were on the outskirts of the crowd, uphill from the engine.

"Dad burn," a man close to us said, "look at the size of them big red wheels. That thing ought to run a sight faster'n a railroad enjine."

"Let's get up and look at it, father," I urged.

Father shook his head. "Can't do it," he said, "without

walking on top of a lot of people. We'll get plenty chance to look it over, I calculate."

"They say there's six more of 'em on the way," a man said.

"Yep," confirmed another. "But six won't be a circumstance. They'll have fifty of 'em running to Denver and San Francisco before this time next year."

Over at one side the crowd undulated like a wheat field in a wind and a familiar voice was calling, "Coming out—please let me get out, folks." Then the crowd opened and Ajax Harvey emerged with his hat shoved over one ear.

"Hey, there, Ajax!" Father called.

Ajax looked around him, spotted us and grinned. He started around the crowd and we met him and shook hands.

"See you got here all right."

"Yes, we got here. But now what?" Father asked.

"We can't get down there and see the engine," I complained.

"Don't see why not. You could take hold your pa's coat-tails and a big strong man like him could plow right through without killing more than a dozen. Well, they haven't got it together yet anyhow. Crowd will thin out later and you can get your eyes full. I tell you, Mac, there's going to be a big banquet at the Seymour tonight for Major Brown. You two will have to be there. Brown will want to see you. He's got two engineers with him—a Dave Osborn and Charley Sloat."

"Well, I don't know," Father hesitated. "We ain't scarcely dressed for banquets."

"Oh, don't worry about that. Lots of folks won't be dressed up, either. Come on and walk up to the *News* with me."

"Well—" said Father, "we got our horses tied over there a ways."

"You can ride Bob," I offered, "and I'll ride behind Father."

Ajax laughed. "That's all right. I'll take you up."

So we walked down the side street to where our horses were hitched. "I calculate," said Father, "it won't take more than a week now to stop all this railroad talk."

Ajax shook his head. "Don't know," he said. "There's been an awful lot of railroad talk of late. Haven't you read about it?"

"Well, no," said Father, "I guess I haven't. We don't take a paper now."

Ajax stopped and looked at Father. "Man alive, you mean to say you don't take the Nebraska City *News?* I'm shocked and hurt."

"Well," said Father, "you see we don't get mail very regular out there. Only when Tommy Ryan happens to get it, I guess. I've been figuring on subscribing to the *News*, but calculated I'd wait until the steam wagons got running and maybe we had a post office."

"Oh, you can get the *News* all right now. Might be a couple of days late sometimes, but you'd generally get it eventually. I'll put your name down for a subscription when I get back to the office."

"Well," said Father, "all right. I guess I can't say no."

Ajax grinned and then his face turned serious. "You were asking about the railroad," he said. "Well, there's been a lot moving on the railroad question since I last saw you. An almighty lot."

"They trying to get a bill passed?"

Ajax looked up at Father. He half smiled and shook his head. "No, Mac," he said, "they aren't *trying* to get a bill passed. They've already passed it and Lincoln has signed it."

"Great holy jeepers!" said Father. "You're not codding me, are you? Well, didn't anybody explain to 'em the truth about a railroad and this country?"

"Oh, yes. But a lot of others explained that it *would* work, and some of the explainers were so-called engineers that the promoters had hired, I suppose."

We had reached our horses and Father stood scratching Bob's nose.

"Yes," went on Ajax, "and they've practically given the country to the railroad too."

"What do you mean?"

"Well, they're giving each alternate section of public lands to the railroad for ten miles each side of the track."

"Oh, jeepers. That probably would take the land I'm calculating to get under the Homestead Act. That probably would take the land where I calculate to build our new house. Can't file on it until the first of the year."

"Now hold your horses," said Ajax. "I don't think they'll even get a survey run. Certainly if they did run a railroad past your land it would whoop the value up. But there isn't any *certainty* yet that this proposed railroad would start from Nebraska City. Omaha has got a lot of influence in Washington and Nebraska City has a reputation of—well, of not being such a strong Yankee town, to say the least. Perhaps yours truly, Augustus Harvey, had a little to do with that reputation."

"They wouldn't dream of running it from Omaha?"

"That's what Omaha thinks. Lincoln himself is going to decide the eastern terminus of the line."

Ajax grinned and took hold of Father's arm. "Mac," he said, "last week I wrote a piece on that subject. If you took the *News* you'd know about it already. Anyhow, I said that the hand of nature already had marked out the route for *any* line westward—whether it was railroad, steam wagon or what. I said, 'Omaha's arguments are like a moonlight view of an old maid,' and sent a marked copy to Abe Lincoln himself. Don't know whether he'll ever see it."

"Now look here," said Father, "don't they know about Major Brown's steam wagon?"

"They don't pay any attention to it. I tell you, Mac, the whole thing is a dirty Republican party steal. They don't really plan to build a railroad. But the government has agreed to lend the company sixteen thousand dollars a mile to lay the rails across the prairie and forty-eight thousand dollars a mile for laying them across the mountains. That's what the promoters are after—the money and the land."

"By holy dang!"

"That's why I'm so anxious for the steam wagons to get running right away. When the steam wagons actually are making regular trips between Nebraska City and Denver City, there can't be any further argument for a railroad. Then the people will force Congress to drop this crazy scheme to give away perhaps an average of thirty thousand dollars a mile from here to the Pacific coast. Estimate it to be two thousand miles and that probably would bring the total close to sixty million."

"Sixty million dollars," said Father. "You can't even picture that much money."

"Sixty million dollars to those thieves," said Ajax, "and the government wouldn't back Major Brown for ten cents. Every cent that's going into these steam wagons is his own money. This one here cost him six thousand, he told me, and another fourteen hundred to ship it out. Well, he won't lose anything by it. And if we can get the steam wagons running in time to stop that sixty million dollar steal, there ought to be statues of Major Brown in every city, town and hamlet of the West twenty years from now."

"You know how much land they calculate to give the railroad?" asked father. "I mean all told."

"They estimate it at thirty-three million acres," said Ajax, grinning.

"Just can't picture it," said Father. "Thirty-three *million* acres."

"Well, let's figure it this way," said Ajax. He took an old envelope and a stub pencil from his pocket. "There are six hundred and forty acres in a square mile, aren't there?"

"Six hundred and forty makes a section," said Father. "That's right."

Ajax ciphered rapidly on the envelope. "Six hundred and forty goes into thirty-three million—let's see . . . Five, one—hmm, hmm, hmm, . . . it'd be fifty-one thousand five hundred and sixty-two square miles. Just about what I thought."

Ajax held up one finger and looked intently at Father. "From my elementary-school days in Watertown," he said, "I remember definitely the area of York State. Including the inland waterways," he droned, "New York State contains forty-nine thousand two hundred and four square miles. In other words, let's see—" Again the pencil scribbled. "Let's see. Yes, the government will give the Pacific Railroad Company two thousand three hundred and fifty-eight square miles more than all of York State!"

"By grab," said Father, "that can be blocked when they see they don't need a railroad, can't it?"

"I'm sure it can. You see, they certainly can't turn all that land over to the company until they get their surveys run, at least. Until then they wouldn't even know what land the railroad wanted."

"No, they couldn't, could they?"

"They may get a good wad of money, but certainly nothing like the whole loan."

"Wouldn't seem that they could. By grab, I never heard of anything like it." Father lifted me up behind Frank's saddle and swung up himself. Ajax mounted Bob and we trotted up Main Street.

"I calculate," said Father to me, "that we'd better go

to the Seymour House, after all. Costs more, but that's where things will be happening."

So we put the horses in a livery stable and Father carried our saddlebags up to a room in the hotel. Then he made me wash my hands and face and we went to a barbershop where he got a shave and a haircut and I got a haircut and the barber slicked it down with perfumed grease.

III

At the banquet they had one long table in the hotel dining room where the speakers and important men and their wives were seated, and many smaller tables for the others like Father and me.

When Major Brown and his engineers came into the room with Ajax and J. Sterling Morton and Kicking Bird Reynolds and several other gentlemen, there was great cheering and everyone crowded around to shake Major Brown's hand and tell him how proud they were to be in Nebraska City at such a time.

We crowded up too, and Major Brown's blue eyes were sparkling and he raised his bushy eyebrows at me when he shook hands, and he slapped Father on the back and asked him if he was satisfied with his farm on Medicine Creek.

"Satisfied?" said Father. "By grab, I'm delighted."

"Ajax wrote me about you and about the buffalo hunt," Major Brown said. "See here, as soon as we get this thing operating right, I've got to go buffalo hunting myself."

"Drop me a line when you're ready," said Father. Other people were crowding up.

"I'll do that," said Major Brown. "And I'll see you later."

We went back to our table and the tablecloth was

heavy and shiny under the glittering pendants of the chandelier.

The dinner was wonderful—cucumber pickles, piccalilli, huge platters heaped up with fried beefsteak and cream gravy; new potatoes and peas, scalded lettuce with vinegar, mustard and sugar over it; green apple pie and strawberry shortcake with big pitchers of thick cream, and wine for the grownups and coffee for everyone.

After the dinner J. Sterling Morton stood up at the center of the long table and rapped on his water tumbler with his knife. Then, looking very handsome in his shiny stiff-bosomed white shirt and high, flaring collar, Mr. Morton made a speech, telling what a great day this was in the history of Nebraska City, in the history of the West and of the entire nation.

"You will be happy to know," he said, "that a committee has been named to assist Major Brown and to further the interests of the Steam Wagon Road to Denver. The committee is composed of H. H. Harding, J. F. Kinney, J. Metcalf, William H. Taylor and William L. Boydston."

There was a volley of handclapping.

"The committee and we all," said Mr. Morton, "want to tell Major Brown that we have the fullest confidence in the entire future success of this great enterprise and we believe the time is not far distant when our city will be brought within a transit of two days' travel to Denver."

Then everyone in the room clapped and cheered and shouted, "Hear! Hear!"

"The committee," said Mr. Morton, "and I am sure all of us join them, will make a request to the county commissioners of Otoe County that an appropriation be made at once to establish at public expense a good, smooth road of suitably low grades from here to the flat prairies to ensure the complete success of this great enterprise. Now I want to ask you all to register a rising vote of thanks to that great inventor, that great public-spirited citizen, Major Joseph R. Brown."

Everyone stood up cheering and waving napkins and Father let go an ear-splitting whistle. They cheered for a full minute and then Major Brown, who was standing up smiling, held up his hand.

Finally the crowd sat down again and quit rattling their knives and forks and plates and water tumblers and Major Brown began to speak.

"My friends," he said, "my tongue cannot find words to express the emotion I feel at your kindness to me. This demonstration is payment in itself for all the dark hours I have spent in laboring over the trying details of my steam wagon. It is payment for the thousands of dollars I have spent. It is payment for the many discouraging obstacles we have been forced to surmount in building this improved steam wagon and bringing it to Nebraska City.

"My distinguished friend, J. Sterling Morton, anticipates a trip to Denver from Nebraska City in two days. I hope, however, you will not be too optimistic about that. At present we must be more reasonable in our hopes.

"Someday Mr. Morton's predictions will be realized, without a doubt. But not in the very near future. First, we must build much better roads than we can hope to build at present. When that has been done we shall build faster steam wagons.

"At present it is necessary to sacrifice great speed for power—power is necessary to pull the loads we must pull over the stiff grades, rough roads and seasonal handicaps of mud and snow.

"Our present engine is not speedy. But it *is* powerful. I am sure it can negotiate any grade that will confront us, with power to spare, and transport at least fifteen tons of freight.

"In a few days, as soon as the engine has been thoroughly tested, in and near Nebraska City, we shall start our first voyage to Denver. This will be merely a trial trip. We will endeavor to establish some stations along the route and even to strengthen bridges where that is necessary. I anticipate this trip will take six or seven days—possibly even longer.

"We shall learn a great deal from this first adventure. We shall learn positively just what problems confront us. It is quite possible that we may reveal weaknesses even in this engine—which may be corrected in the next model.

"Then, when we return, I shall order six more steam wagons constructed immediately, and some of them will be lighter, faster engines for passenger travel."

When the cheering died down Major Brown continued: "I don't believe I am too optimistic when I say I am confident that we can establish regular passenger service between Nebraska City and the Rocky Mountains next spring and that we shall make the trip in a maximum of four days. When the roads have been improved and our fuel and water stations are well established, I am willing to predict that we shall make the round trip from Nebraska City to Pikes Peak in six days.

"I have been asked what we shall do for fuel when crossing the Great Plains. I am happy to tell you, my friends, that the quantity of fuel necessary to operate this steam wagon is so small as to present no serious obstacle to our plans.

"Now I want to offer a toast to Nebraska City, the new metropolis—the gateway to the Great West."

Then there were toasts to Major Brown and his engineers and to J. Sterling Morton and to the committee and to everyone the toasters could think of.

IV

The next morning we were out early and the engineers, Osborn and Sloat, had the steam wagon together and properly oiled and greased and a fire roaring in the furnace.

Major Brown came down the hill in a hack and greeted everyone jovially. "How much steam have you now, Charley?" he asked.

Sloat looked at the clocklike dial on the boiler.

"Twenty-five pounds, major," he answered.

"I want to try her first with only thirty pounds. Less pressure, the more economy."

The crowd was small this morning and we had opportunity to look over the huge engine, looming up as high as a cottage, and its red-painted drive wheels swelling up twelve feet in diameter and two feet across the studded boiler-iron rims. Inside the big wheels were smaller wheels, about six feet in diameter, with cog knobs that fit into grooves in the drivers, and these six-foot wheels in turn were cogged and meshed into small gear wheels and the small gear wheels were on a shaft that was connected with the steam engine.

The front wheels were about six feet in diameter and were hooked up with the ship's pilot wheel, which was at the front of the machine directly behind the big oil headlight. There was a red-painted roof over the whole of the wagon, except the top of the boiler, and the floor was nearly five feet from the ground. Iron guard rails ran along the sides of the wagon, hip-high on a man, and other iron guard rails flared out and down from the boiler, shoulder-high, giving an elegant, racy effect.

Major Brown came up to us. "What do you think of her?" he asked.

"By grab," said Father, "she looks exceptional."

Osborn threw more wood into the firebox and there was the smell of hot new metal and a faint hissing of steam.

"It's a powerful machine," said Major Brown. "We tried her out briefly in New York and it's stupendous."

"When you going to start for Denver City?" Father asked.

"Not for a few days yet. We want to test her pretty thoroughly here. We want to get the gears worn to each other before we put any real strain on her. There might be some weaknesses. You never can tell about that in any new machine and it'd be a lot handier to have the weaknesses develop here than out on the prairie. We'd have a chance to repair them right if it happened here."

"Oh, major," Sloat called down from the engine. "There's thirty pounds pressure in her."

"All right. Try to take her part way up the hill easy and then come back. You look after the engine, Charley, while Dave steers."

Osborn swung himself up to the front of the wagon and took his stand at the helm. "Let her go," he called, grinning.

"I'm trying her out with very low steam pressure first," Major Brown said. "Probably won't perform so well with only thirty pounds, but I want to see what she'll do."

Sloat pulled one long lever back and pushed another long lever forward. Then he pulled a short horizontal lever slightly back. Immediately there was a loud hissing of steam and a shrieking clank of metal and the gigantic drive wheels began to move very slowly forward.

"She's going!" someone yelled.

The big steam wagon seemed to come to life and lumbered awkwardly out into the middle of the street. Then, as Dave Osborn twisted the steering wheel, she swung up the Main Street hill as fast as a man could walk. Each time one of the knobs on the six-foot inner wheels meshed into the grooves of the bigger wheels there was a scream of metal. The engine moved not only to the puff-puff-puff of steam exhausts, but also to a decisive clank-clank-clank.

Major Brown ran out into the street. "Take it easy, Charley!" he called. "I think those gears need more grease."

Sloat pushed in the little lever and the steam wagon slowed down. "Shall I stop her?" he asked.

"No. It's all right. Just don't open her up. Run her half way up the hill and then back again."

Sloat waved his hand and pulled the lever again. The crowd was running along beside the engine cheering, and the hissing steam engine waddled up the steep grade easily, turned in a broad circle and rattled and clanked down the hill again. When it came to a halt in the vacant lot, Major Brown walked up to the machine and Sloat swung down from the engine.

"How's she seem?" Major Brown asked.

Sloat nodded his head. "She's all right, major. But I *do* think Dave and I better go over those gears and smooth 'em up a little with a file. Don't fit any too good, but they'll be all right when we smooth 'em up and slap some more grease on 'em."

"Seemed pretty noisy."

Sloat nodded his head. "Yep, she *was* noisier than I'd like, but you got to expect that with a new machine. They'll break in all right and we'll take a couple buckets of grease along to slosh on the gears every few miles."

"I think," said Major Brown, "you and Dave better see what you can do with files."

"Yep. We'll get right at it."

Sloat and Osborn worked on the steam wagon for two days, trying it briefly down at the foot of Main Street.

Then word was passed around that Major Brown was going to give it a real test through the streets of the city.

It was Saturday and the city was crowded with farmers come in for shopping and to see the steam wagon—even though it was in the midst of wheat threshing. After all, it probably wouldn't rain, and this was an occasion that came only once in a lifetime. This was seeing history in the making.

Major Brown had five freight wagons hitched to the engine. The canvas covers were taken down from the first four wagons and they were draped with flags and red, white and blue bunting. In the first wagon was the Nebraska City brass band. The next three wagons had been fitted with plank seats and they were filled with Nebraska City women and girls, very gay and excited and holding up their ruffled parasols against the blazing sun.

Steam was up in the engine before the ladies were helped aboard and men and boys were clambering into the last wagon until it was overflowing.

"By grab," said Father, "they're going to get such a load that nothing on earth could move it. That's what they're going to do."

Major Brown climbed on the engine and Ajax came up, trying unsuccessfully to hide his own excitement.

"Come on," he said huskily to Father, "let's get on the side of the steamer."

"Think she can pull all of that?" Father waved his hand back at the string of heavy wagons.

"We'll soon find out. Come on before someone beats us to a place."

Major Brown reached down a hand and helped me up as Father and Ajax swung up by means of the hand rails.

"Strike up the band, boys!" called Major Brown, and the red-and-yellow uniformed band burst into "Hail! Columbia."

"Better get a good grip on that rail," Father advised

me. "Don't want to fall off and get run over by this thing."

Major Brown nodded his head to Charley Sloat and the engineer pushed and pulled his levers—very gently on the short horizontal lever, looking back anxiously at the line of freight wagons. Steam roared and the floor under us quivered. The gigantic red wheels began to move very slowly. There was a slight jerk as the slack was taken out of the first wagon's hitch and the lead cornetist cut in with a shrill, gratuitous trill. Dave Osborn spun the steering wheel quickly and the slack came out of the second wagon's hitch while the women and girls shrieked clear above the blare of the band and the roar of the steam wagon. Ajax looked down at me, grinning.

We were well out into Main Street and inching up the hill when the last white-covered freight wagon moved into line. Then Sloat pulled the lever again and again, half an inch at a time. And each time he pulled the lever the engine quivered and responded with a louder and quicker WHOOSH-Whosh, whish-whish, and the clank of gears took up a faster rhythm and the line of wagons behind us were banging and rattling over the bumps in the road and I could see sweat glistening on the faces of the band members as they blew everything they had into their horns. By the time we were halfway up the hill we were traveling as fast as an ordinary horse would trot. Panting men and boys running along beside us were losing ground and as they dropped behind, the women and girls waved handkerchiefs and little flags at them.

Before we reached the top of the hill the street was lined with cheering people and men were frantically getting their frenzied teams off Main Street. Major Brown, holding to the rail with one hand, was doffing his beaver hat with the other, smiling and waving and bowing in response to the cheers.

As we passed the Seymour House some men fired revolvers in the air and Sloat blew a deafening blast on the
steam whistle. Then he pulled the lever back until we
were roaring along at least ten miles an hour. A block
away a man in a light buggy essayed to cross Main Street
and his horses, catching sight of the approaching mon-
ster, leaped in the harness and ran away with the buggy
careening and bounding behind them.

Three blocks more and, while Sloat closed the throttle
only slightly, Osborn steered far to the right and then
swung the steamer to the left into the side street. The
rattling wagons lurched after us, each one cutting a little
farther to the left until the last one had scant clearance
from the left corner lamppost.

Osborn looked back and grinned at Major Brown. He
put one hand to the side of his mouth and yelled, "These
streets none too wide for a train this long." Then he
swung clear to the right again and cut to the left into
Otoe Street. There were shrieks from the women as the
wagons careened.

"Hey, there," Father called, "better take those corners
a little slower. You'll be throwing somebody overboard
back there."

"The wagons have got to have momentum," Major
Brown said. "They've got to have enough momentum to
carry 'em up to the turn or they'd be dragged off the
road to the left."

Again we swooped around the corner and Sloat blew
the whistle like a railroad locomotive to warn traffic off
Main Street before we turned right.

We roared down Main Street and then, shutting off
steam, we drifted up in front of the Seymour House
where the ladies were helped down. Then everyone who
could get in went into the hotel for refreshments and to
drink to Major Brown's health and to the magnificent
steam wagon.

Major Brown didn't stay long. Charley Sloat said, "You know, major, we only brought a few sticks of wood along and unless we take her back pretty soon we'll be out of steam—unless we go and get some more fuel."

So Major Brown excused himself and Ajax and Father and I went with them. On the way down the hill it seemed that we were traveling almost as fast as a railroad train and we pulled off the road into the vacant lot with the whole crew very elated over the successful trial.

"Couldn't be better," Ajax proclaimed.

"Well," said Major Brown, "I'm not quite satisfied with the sound of those gears yet, Charley."

"Neither am I," said Sloat. "Dave, I think we'd better bush 'em up some more before we start for Denver."

"When you starting?" Father asked.

"Well, tomorrow's Sunday," said Major Brown. "I'd thought we would start Monday, but I believe we'd better smooth 'em up a little more. Can't work tomorrow, so we'll start Tuesday morning."

"Going to take any freight?" Ajax asked.

Major Brown smiled. "Don't get impatient, Ajax," he said.

"Just wanted to know," said Ajax. "You know, after all, I'm a newspaperman and I'm looking for news."

"Well, no," said Major Brown. "No freight this time. We'll take three wagons with supplies and tools and a gang of workmen. We'll probably have to do more or less work on the road here and there and maybe put a bottom to some of the fords. That contraption's heavy and we don't want to get stuck in the mud. I had that happen to me up in Minnesota with my first steamer."

He turned to Father. "Can you have some wood cut and ready for us at your place?"

"You bet your boots," said Father.

"And maybe a couple barrels of good clean water for the boiler?"

Father nodded his head. "I've got a couple of good whisky barrels."

"Well, you have them filled with water and our men will dump them into our own barrels. Good idea for you to keep those barrels of yours on hand."

I looked at Father in dismay. "Listen," I said, "aren't we going to stay here and see her start? Can't I ride out to our place on the steam wagon?"

Ajax poked me in the ribs with his thumb.

"Well," said Father to Ajax, "I *did* practically promise to see if he couldn't do that. But it's no hurt. He's just had a fine ride on the steam wagon and he can ride it enough in the future. No, Clinton, you'll have to be grateful for what you got. We've been here a sight longer than I expected now. Can't possibly stay here until Tuesday."

"Well, jeepers," I said.

"I know. But we got a lot of work to do. Not only got to get up the wood and water for the steam wagon, but we've got threshing too. Can't lose our wheat."

"Aw," I said, "John Peterson will be threshing it."

Father nodded his head. "He'd better have been threshing wheat instead of just mooning around Eliza or I'll take his hide off. But John can't thresh it all."

"How do you thresh out here?" Dave Osborn asked.

"Have to flail it out this year and that's a big job."

"I should say so."

"Expect to get a horsepower threshing machine next year, though, when these steam wagons bring me a lot of business. Lots of settlers coming in and there'll be more when the Homestead Act takes effect. I'll get a threshing machine and make money renting it out. Well, son, I expect we'd better skedaddle. It'll be dark before we get home."

"Well, we'll see you Tuesday," said Major Brown.

"About what time can we expect you? Can we look for you in time for dinner?"

"Don't count on it. If we get there in time we'll take pot luck with you. But we may have a lot to do with the road, and it might rain too. Don't hold up your dinner much past noon."

"You coming too, Ajax?"

"No. I'd like to, but I've got work to do."

"Oh, *what* work?" demanded Major Brown. "I suspect that newspaper would come out whether you were there or not. And the subscribers will want to know what happens on this first trip. You've *got* to come as special correspondent for the Nebraska City *News*."

"Just waiting to be coaxed," said Ajax. "All right, Mac, it seems I'm coming. Tell your wife to put on one more potato for Ajax."

So we rode on home, reaching there under the bright July stars. And the next day, as Father did not hold Major Brown's reluctance to break the Sabbath, I helped John Peterson flail out wheat, which was hot and disagreeable work, and the chaff got down my neck and in my throat, making me cough. Father cut and split a pile of wood that Mother said would run the steam wagon clear to Denver City and on Monday he drew water and filled two empty whisky barrels, which he placed in front of the house and covered them with the old barrel heads.

That night John Peterson and Eliza took a walk and Father and Mother had a discussion.

"I don't like," said Father, "the idea of John seeing so much of Eliza."

Mother was darning socks in the kitchen while Bertha Peterson was waiting on some bullwhackers in the living room. Mother didn't say anything.

"But John's a fine boy," Father went on. "Maybe he hasn't got any too many brains, but he makes good use of them he's got. He's a fine worker and I don't like to hurt his feelings, so I don't like to tell him to keep away from the girl."

"No sense doing that," said Mother. "Tell him to keep away and they'll start sneaking off. Nothing but bad ever comes of anything like that."

"Maybe so. But he's got this idea of getting married in his head and he's a stubborn Swede."

Mother looked up and started to speak, but closed her lips when Bertha came in and got another platter of fried potatoes.

When Bertha went back in the living room Father said, "The whole trouble is he's got this getting married business in his head so strong. Too bad there ain't any women of marriageable age hereabouts. Ain't right for a man to be thinking about a little girl that way."

Mother shook her head. "I'm afraid Eliza ain't a little girl any more."

"What you mean?" Father demanded.

"Well, I just mean she's been growing up. She's nearly sixteen."

"That's still a little girl."

"I wasn't eighteen yet when we got married."

"Well, that was different." Father scuffed the heel of his boot on the floor. "You were a woman grown, no matter what age you was."

"It wasn't different at all. You were just different. You act like it was just John in this case. But Eliza is just as bad as he is. Worse, as a matter of fact. I haven't noticed that John can't do his work like he ought to. But Eliza's been mooning around for months. Don't know scarcely what she's about half the time."

"By holy dang, woman," said Father, "what're you talking about? You mean you think it'd be all right to let that child get married?"

"Not right now, no. But I think it'd be better to let

'em get married than to have 'em run away. We've had *one* child run away and that should ought to be enough."

Father scuffed his heel and looked at the floor.

"I don't know," said Mother, "as it'd be such a crime when she's sixteen. She argues and he argues they could get a homestead right close by if they were married and it just seems like to me *that* would be better than to make them wait a couple years and then they'd be living way off in the wilderness someplace where we couldn't look after them, and their land wouldn't be as good as it is here and—"

"Great holy jeepers," said Father. "Woman, you amaze me."

He kicked both feet out in front of him and put his hands in his pockets.

"But," he went on, "a long time ago I told you I was going to bring up the boys my way and make men of 'em. I told you to keep hands off the boys when I was bringing 'em up the way I thought they should ought to be brung up.

"Well, at the same time I told you I'd keep hands off Biddy so's you could bring her up the way you thought a woman should be brung up. Well, all right. I made you keep hands off when I thought I was right and you thought I was wrong. I think time will show I was right even if the war did step in and get Alan. Now I say to you I think you're wrong, but I'll keep my hands off. If you think it's right and proper and fitting for that girl to marry John Peterson next winter, all right. That's going to be your business and all I can do is hope you're right."

"I just want my children to be happy," said Mother. "I just want them to be successful and happy. I would rather Eliza didn't get married so young. But if it seems like they can get a better start in life getting married this winter, I don't want to say no and then have them get a poor homestead way off someplace in a couple of years and have them blame me for it all their lives."

Father took his hands from his pockets and slapped his thighs. "All right, wife," he said. "It's you for it."

V

Tuesday morning was hot and cloudless. Father looked at the sky and observed, "Well, there's no rain in sight to delay 'em." Then he worked with John and me, flailing wheat and throwing scoopfuls into the air so the breeze could carry the chaff away—or down my neck.

By eleven o'clock we all were adjourning every now and then to gaze eastward on the road for a sign of smoke. But there was nothing in sight except an occasional ox train of freighters.

Mother was agitated over the importance of her expected guests and didn't know what to have for dinner.

Father passed that off airily. "They won't be expecting any banquet," he said. "They're probably tired of banquets anyhow. Just have ham and eggs. They're always good and you can cook 'em after they get here, whether it's high noon or midnight, and I'll pass out a good stiff drink of good stiff whisky and after that they won't notice much *what* they're eating."

Noon arrived with the sun quivering above and still no wisp of smoke on the burning horizon. Half an hour later Father said, "I calculate we'd better eat dinner. Could see that smoke a long way off and there's no telling. They may not get here until midafternoon."

But at midafternoon there still was no smoke in sight and Father was getting nervous. He kept drawing water from the well and drinking deeply. Before supper we all gazed for a long time eastward and once I thought I sighted smoke. But when it drew no closer and finally

faded away, we decided it was only the sun glinting on
dust an ox wagon had raised.

Father sat up until midnight waiting, but at last decided they had camped for the night farther east and
went to bed.

He was out early Wednesday morning gazing down
the road, but still there was nothing to be seen but ox
and mule teams laboring slowly through the dust. The
farm work he left entirely to John and me while he
stayed close by the house to "look after business."

One party of freighters stopped to buy some ague cure
and chewing tobacco and he asked them what news they
had of the steam wagon. They hadn't heard that it had
started for Denver. They had left Nebraska City Sunday.

Shortly after noon the stage bumbled by westbound
and Father tried to flag it down. But the driver, a surly
fellow whom we did not know, merely waved his whip
and kept on his way.

"Do you suppose," I asked at dinner, "that they could
have gone right on by like the stage only when you
weren't looking?"

Father shook his head. "No," he said, "they wouldn't
have done that. They'll need water and wood, and besides they'd stop to see us."

"And besides," said Aunt Christine, "your father
hasn't done anything but watch since yesterday morning.
How could they have got by him?"

Evening came with the usual number of freighters for
supper and, as Aunt Christine said, Father was fit to be
tied.

"By grab," he said, "I'm getting alarmed. If they ain't
in sight by eight o'clock in the morning I'm going to
saddle Frank and ride back to see what's the matter."

"Can I go along?" I asked.

"No. You've got to stay here and help John with the
work."

"How long you calculate to be gone this time?" Mother asked.

"According to how far I've got to go. Won't be gone long, anyhow. Probably home by night, but not later than Friday night at the most. I just want to find out what's the matter and see if maybe I can help. Well, perhaps they'll get here in the morning."

Again Father was out early, scanning the eastern sky for smoke. He did his chores silently and after breakfast went out in the road and stood there for a long time with his hands in his pockets and a quill toothpick in his mouth. Then he went back to the threshing floor and swung a flail viciously for half an hour.

Presently he looked up. "Clinton," he said, "I've got to go and see what's what. Possible I may meet 'em down the road a piece and it's possible I won't be able to keep up with 'em coming back. If that happens, you see that they help themselves to the wood and water and insist on 'em coming in the house for a snack and a drink of whisky."

"All right, father," I said. "I wish I could go."

"Well, you can't go. You ought to be able to see that. Now, can I depend on you to look after things?"

"I guess you can."

"Don't want any guesswork now."

"Well, I'll do what you tell me to do."

"All right, then. And see that you do. I'll be back just as soon as I can get back."

He went into the house after his good hat. Then he walked out hurriedly and I heard him in the barn swearing at Frank because Frank apparently was swelling out his belly against the saddle cinch. Presently Father swung out of the barn on Frank and into the road on the gallop.

"Your pa," said John, "been pretty upset about that steam wagon thing."

"Well," I said, "it's pretty important. Maybe it's

blown up and killed everybody or something and then there might not be any steam wagons and the railroad will come through here and the government will give the railroad all the land and then where'll you be?"

John looked thoughtful and finished sewing up a sack of grain.

"Guess that's right," he said finally. "There wouldn't be any more homesteads then, maybe."

"Not many, I calculate. And they'd be way off where nobody would want because you couldn't grow anything on 'em—like where we was buffalo hunting."

"I guess," said John, "this steam wagon's pretty damn important."

"You bet your boots it is," I said.

Father got back late Friday and seemed very tired. I ran out to the barn where he was taking the saddle off Frank.

"What happened?" I asked. "Didn't blow up, did it?"

"No," said Father. "Didn't blow up. Just broke down."

"Can they fix it? What happened?"

"Of course they can fix it. Just hold your horses and I'll tell the whole thing at supper. Can't be telling it over and over."

So, after food had dulled his hunger sufficiently, Father began to talk.

"I kept looking ahead all the time I was riding," he said, "and I kept thinking I'd see her over every hill, but I didn't see anything and finally I got to Nursery Hill. So I stopped there and asked if anybody knew what had happened to the steam wagon and an old man says he heard tell she had broke down and they'd traded her off for a yoke of oxen.

"So I went on and on and still not seeing anything but freight wagons until I got maybe seven mile from Nebraska City and there, setting all by itself by the side of the road, was the steam wagon."

"What was wrong with it?" I asked.

"Well, I got off Frank and looked her over and I couldn't see anything wrong, so I rode on to Nebraska City and went to the *News* but Ajax was out someplace. So I went on and finally met Dave Osborn on the street.

"I says, 'Dave, what on earth's the matter?'

"He says, 'Well, those gears wasn't right in the first place. I knew that as soon's we tried them, but Charley thought we could bush 'em into shape. We did the best we could but one of 'em busted on the road and we had to take it off and leave the steamer there until we can get a new gear.'

"I says, 'Then you can fix it all right.'

"And he says, 'Why, sure we can fix it. It's not important, only it's going to waste a hell of a lot of time. Major Brown's gone back to New York with it, but he'd have to go anyhow because he's getting six more steamers built.'

"I says, 'He's not discouraged or anything, then?' "

"And he says, 'Discouraged? By grab, no.' "

"Father," I said, "Did Dave Osborn say, 'By grab?' "

Father scowled at me and went on: "He says, 'Heavens and earth—why *should* he be discouraged? Everybody's wild about the steamer. Russell, Majors and Waddell are going to give us all their freighting to Fort Kearny and Fort Laramie as well as the Denver business. The county commissioners are going to improve the road clear to Fort Kearny, maybe.'

"I says, 'Well, Dave, that's what I wanted to know. I just wanted to know the whole shebang hadn't been dropped.'

"That sort of horrified Dave Osborn. 'Listen,' he says, 'this little accident don't amount to a hill of beans. It's nothing at all. We'll be running regular trips by fall.

Nothing to worry about. You should ought to have seen the old steamer roaring over those hills west of town before the gear broke!'

"So," said Father, "that's why the steam wagon didn't get here and I calculate it won't get here until maybe September. Not until Major Brown gets back from New York with that gear thing, anyhow."

"That," said Aunt Christine, "may not be before next year."

Father shrugged his shoulders. "It will be," he said. "But just suppose it don't. What of it? We're getting along all right, ain't we? And the first of the year I'll nail that hundred and sixty down up there for our new house. We'll build up there in the spring."

"How," asked Mother, "can you be so certain about getting that land? Suppose the railroad comes and they get it?"

"Wife," said Father, "that's one piece of good news I picked up. Ajax and the other folks in Nebraska City ain't so sure it's good news, but it is for *us* just the same."

"You mean—"

"That's right. I mean Abe Lincoln has selected Omaha for the east end of the Pacific Railroad. So the tracks won't run anywhere near us—even if they ever run near any place."

"I thought," said Aunt Christine, "you and this Harvey man were so very sure President Lincoln never would pick Omaha."

"We were just sure it would be *foolish* to pick Omaha. That's all we were sure about."

"Well, I don't see— If it's foolish to pick Omaha, why are you glad?"

Father sighed. "Listen, Chris," he said. "You've heard this all before. But now you think real hard and see if you can understand what I'm going to tell you. It's a good thing they picked Omaha because now they won't be running any surveys through here and that railroad company won't be grabbing all the good public land in sight hereabouts. They won't ever get a railroad through to the Pacific, but they may run it a ways. And more than likely they'll get their hooks on an almighty lot of land unless Major Brown gets back with that gear pretty quick and gets the steam wagon line operating.

"There was one thing," Father went on, "that we didn't know about when we felt pretty sure Omaha wouldn't be picked. Ajax just heard about it lately. Seems Abe Lincoln was out this way in '59 and bought some town lots in Omaha. Man that owned property in Omaha wouldn't likely pick Nebraska City for anything, would he?"

Aunt Christine nodded her head and smiled in a wise way.

"When," asked Mother, "do they expect to really get the steam wagon running now?"

"Ajax says they'll be running weekly trips by November. They've got it all worked out. By the first of April they'll have two new wagons and special cars and the new steamers will be geared for two hundred miles in twenty-four hours. I swanney, the railroads can't beat that much for speed. These new steam wagons are going to have the power of seventy horses, according to Ajax, and I calculate he knows what he's talking about.

"So when they get the new steamers along the first of April, they'll start running two trains a week to Denver until the middle of July. Then they'll get two more steamers and there'll be a train every other day both ways."

Father grinned. "By that time, wife, we'll be living in a mansion up there on the hill."

"Jack," said Mother, "you talk suspicious like you had put money in this thing. Have you?"

"Money!" Father snorted. "I ain't had a chance. What

would Major Brown want with any of the little money I
could invest? Ajax tells me the telegraph carried news
from New York that the success of the steam wagon here
is a sensation back there. Ajax says Major Brown now
could get millions in backing in New York if he'd take it.

"Listen, all we've got to do for the steam wagons is to
have wood and water ready for 'em when they stop. For
that they'll make me a rich man."

Toward the last of August Father got a letter from
Ajax. The letter contained a clipping from the *Scientific
American* which told a great deal about Major Brown's
steam wagon. It called the trials in Nebraska City a
"spectacular success" and predicted that by spring the
thousands of oxen and mules on the Overland Trail
would have given way to the steamers.

But the letter itself was not so cheerful. It quoted from
a letter written Ajax by Major Brown from Henderson,
Minnesota.

On the way to New York Major Brown had been in-
tercepted by a telegram in Chicago. Sioux Indians were
on the warpath in the Upper Agency of Minnesota. His
family had been taken captive. His home, his grist mill,
his store all had been burned. He had joined the forces
of General Henry Hastings Sibley to run down the Indians and he had rescued his family safely. But he must
remain with the troops until the warring Sioux had been
subdued.

"I pray," Major Brown wrote, "that this may be soon.
But my property is virtually wiped out by the Sioux outrages. I may have to resort to financing the steam wagon
line in New York when I finally get back to my affairs in
Nebraska."

"This is terrible news," Ajax wrote. "If this campaign
is at all long it will give the railroad promoters opportunity to get what they want with no real opposition. We
can only hope that Brown gets out of this campaign

safely and soon. I am terribly shocked that he has lost his property, of course, but that in itself is not so serious. With his steam wagons he can recoup his losses quickly out here and he'll have no trouble in financing his affairs in New York."

Father was badly depressed. "This could be the end of everything," he said.

"Well," said Mother, "it could be worse. You have no money invested."

"I've got enough money and time invested in this place here, haven't I?"

"Well, yes . . . But, after all, we're doing pretty well. We're getting more money, twenty times over, than we ever got before. We could get even more if you'd settle down and work the farm."

Father twisted his mouth and scratched his chin. "Wife," he said, "there's a bare possibility you may be right."

Aunt Christine was not depressed at all. She had received a long letter from Casper Diercks and, while Casper as yet had not found his mountain of pure gold, he at least had a claim which he declared showed all the earmarks of being worth a million dollars. He told Aunt Christine he would be coming back for her next summer and that they would go to Paris on their honeymoon.

A month later the *News* published an account of the battle of Birch Coulee and told of Major Brown being seriously wounded while leading his men against the Sioux.

VI

Chauncey Loud was a good schoolteacher. He apparently never had heard of the York State rule of "no licking, no learning," and during the several years I went to his classes I never saw him take a switch to a child.

If some boy became unruly or indolent Chan Loud
would say in his slow way, "Now, young man, you apparently don't care for an education and in that case I
don't believe you should be forced to have one. But I
can't have you interfering with those who *do* want to
learn something, so I shall have to send you home with a
note to your father."

Then he would sit down at his tall, rough pine desk
and make out to be writing the note. And the refractory
pupil would begin to beg, "Oh, please, Mr. Loud, I
won't ever do it again. Please don't send me home that
way. Pa'll skin me alive if you do. I promise—I want to
get an education, honest."

And Chan Loud's thin, smooth face would smile and
he would put up his pen and say, "Well, I'm glad to see
you make that decision. Of course we all enjoy having
you here and I'm glad to help you all I can when you
want to be helped."

It wasn't often that he actually had to resort to sending
the pupil home. Once he did send Harry Phillips and
Sime Phillips took the end of a tug to Harry with such
effect that Harry came back to school the next morning
and made a little speech, declaring he was going to be a
good boy and study hard, and he apologized publicly to
Mabel Striker for tying her pigtail to a nail in his desk.

The schoolhouse had but one room and that was about
sixteen by twenty feet. The door faced the road to the
south and on each side of the door were nails for us to
hang our wraps.

Mr. Loud sat at the other end of the room facing us,
with the painted blackboards and a picture of George
Washington at his back. His desk was on a raised platform and directly in front of it was the recitation bench.
In the center of the room, east and west and just behind
the recitation bench was the round stove and the desks
ranged back on each side of the stove.

There were just two rows of seats and desks which Albert Striker had built and only three desks in each row, but there was room for about four more desks behind us as a provision for the future.

Martha Bergstrom sat by herself in the front seat of the east row and young Albert Striker and Pete Bergstrom were together behind Martha and Ole Bergstrom and I were in the last seat, behind Al and Pete.

In the other aisle Susie Striker sat alone in the front seat. Behind her were Tish Phillips and Mabel Striker and in the rear seat Willie Bergstrom and Harry Phillips.

Behind Ole and me was a stool with a wooden water bucket and dipper. We boys took turns carrying the water from our well, which was quite a chore, for it was about a hundred rods away.

The woodpile was behind Willie and Harry. The men who had children in school took turns cutting wood at the creek and would haul it up in a wagon or bobsled and dump it in front of the building. Then Mr. Loud and some of us bigger boys would split it up and carry it inside.

The building wasn't any too weather-tight and during storms some of us in the rear of the room would wear our wraps while Martha and Susie would be baking up near the hot stove. There were times when the water bucket even got a scum of ice on it right behind Ole and me.

After school we boys kept pretty much to ourselves and the girls kept pretty much to themselves, except that we sometimes would let them in a game of fox and geese after a light snow. Our recess play usually was some adaptation of the Civil War with snowballs for weapons. The girls would build snow women on the other side of the school. It was easier to make snow women than snow men because the women needed no legs.

On Saturdays and Sundays I traveled around mostly

with Ole Bergstrom and Harry Phillips, Ole being only
about a year younger than I and Harry a year older.
Harry also had a shotgun and we went hunting for rabbits and prairie chickens and quail and, in the spring and
fall, for ducks at a slough a mile down the creek. Once
Harry and I even brought home a couple of great
Canadian geese that were all we could carry.

This slough had been left by the creek when it had cut
through years before to shorten its course. We went
there in spring and summer to fish for bullheads and
perch and to wallow in the mud and dog-paddle in the
deeper holes.

In winter we coasted down the hill, or rather the
double hills that rose back of our place, down toward the
freight road. Sime Phillips first had made Harry a splendid sled with iron runners and Father hired him to make
me a similar one for my birthday.

There was one day early in that first winter of school
when a sleet storm followed snow and covered everything with a sheet of thin ice. Harry and I went up to
the crest of the hill with our sleds and came down side
by side with the speed of a railroad train. We whipped
past our barn and house, crossed the road and ended between Phillips's blacksmith shop and their house.

Tish Phillips and Susie Striker came running around
the house.

"Come on and give Susie and me a ride," Tish said.
"Oh, come on, Harry. Let us ride down the hill with you
once."

Harry looked at me.

"Well," I said, "just once. I'll give Susie a ride and
you take Tish."

Susie was a rather pretty girl about a year younger
than I. She had curly hair the color of new rope, but she
was thin and had little red in her cheeks. She had very
large blue eyes that had a friendly expression something

like that of old Don, the shepherd, only old Don's eyes
were brown. She was long-legged for a girl and wore
thick, black yarn leggings. This day, too, she was wearing a red knitted hood and a red muffler and red mittens.

So Harry and Tish and Susie and I climbed back up
the hill and it was hard climbing because it was so icy
and sometimes there would be a soft spot in the crust
which one of us would break through. The sun was getting low and clouds on the horizon already were taking
on a faint pink tint. The distant hills were very blue and
there were cold blue tints also along the edges of snow
hummocks and the trees along Medicine Creek were
stark and bare.

I looked down west instead of south and there was a
spot near the road where the trees and brush had been
cleaned out and I could see the blue of the icebound
creek where the snow had been blown away. It was very
quiet, but when a rooster crowed in our barnyard it
sounded far away.

Harry got on his sled in front and Tish behind with
her arms around him. He put his feet on the crossbar
and she gave a shove and away they went south down the
hill with the end of her yellow nubia sailing back over
one shoulder and fluttering very bright against the snow
while she screamed and the snow powder sifted up from
the runners and glittered in the waning sun. They went
very fast and threw up a cloud of snow when they crossed
the road and they passed the blacksmith shop where
Sime Phillips was hammering away on his anvil, and they
went out of sight behind the building.

I looked west again and got an idea. The snow seemed
to cover the bank down to the creek and it looked as if
it would be smooth. I thought I could steer through the
opening between the trees down to the ice and, as the
creek bent to the west there, I thought I could swerve

the sled downstream and have enough momentum left
to travel many rods on the ice.

"I'm going to give you a *real* ride," I said.

"That'll be lovely," said Susie. "Tish must have had a
very fine ride."

"No," I said, "that wasn't anything. This is going to
beat that all hollow. We'll go down the hills that way."
I pointed southwest toward the creek. "Then we'll hit
the ice and go whooping downstream."

Susie looked worried. "Oh, dear," she said, "you think
that'll be safe?"

"Oh, sure. I can steer this old sled anyplace. When
you get on, you put your feet on these runner braces
here and hold on tight. We'll have a real ride."

I sat down on the front of the sled and wrapped the
ropes firmly around each mittened hand while I kept my
heels stuck in the snow. Susie sat down behind me and
I looked to see that her feet were held properly against
the runner braces. Her arms were around me and her
red mittens were holding tightly against my stomach.
Contemptuous as I was of girls—or as contemptuous as
I pretended to be—it gave me a comfortable glow to
have Susie holding me that way.

"All ready?" I asked.

"I reckon I am," said Susie. "But I'm kind of scared
to go down on the creek that way."

I laughed. "I'll take care of you," I said. "Here we go."

I gave a shove with my feet and, as the sled started
down the incline, I jammed them solidly against the
crossbar and away we went with the polished iron runners sizzing over the crust and the wind whistling sharp
and cold on my face.

The double hills were much longer this way and with
Susie's added weight the sled quickly was traveling faster
than I ever had gone before. Susie squealed and clung to
me desperately. Particles of ice and fine snow flew up on

each side of us like spume from a fast boat and the trees along the creek were rushing toward us at an alarming rate.

I steered for the left toward the opening in the trees. The sled responded slightly, but not enough. I put down my left heel, scraping the crust, and hard snow stung my face. We veered and almost upset, but now I had the sled headed directly for the opening while we darted down with the speed of a swallow and Susie's shrieks hurt my ears.

Dead sunflower stalks and elderberry brush flashed past on both sides. We hit the creekbank and plunged down so precipitously that it took my breath. The sled actually left the earth and we hurtled through the air for half a rod, banged down again with a bone-shaking shock, crashed through a small bush, banged again on the blue ice, skidded sideways an instant and continued our wild flight downstream while a flock of alarmed junco birds fluttered across the creek with the white feathers each side of their tails glowing against the dark ice.

Ahead a smear of snow lay across the creek. I tried to steer around it, but the runners refused to respond on the ice and we were into it before I even could put down one heel. The snow sprayed up each side of us and instantly there was a roaring crash-WHOOSH and the searing impact of icy water in my face.

I was strangling and off the sled, threshing in water that was so cold it seemed to numb my soul. When I gained my footing I saw the water was only a little more than waist deep, but Susie still was struggling and splashing behind me. I pulled her upright and her curls were wet and black and stringy. Her mouth was open and her eyes were the most frightened eyes I had ever seen.

"Jeepers," I said.

She just stared at me.

"Jeepers, let's get out of here. You ain't hurt, are you?"

Susie screamed shrill and loud. She screamed again and again.

"Well," I said, "there's no use yelling now. Let's get out of this creek."

I helped her up on the ice and then to the bank. She stood there gasping and shivering while I went back in the water after my sled. Before I recovered it Susie began to scream again.

I was half frozen myself and her screaming made me mad. "Look here, Susie Striker," I shouted, "you quit that damn yelling or I'll slap your face. By gol, I'm just as cold and wet as you and you asked for the ride in the first place. Now you shut up and we got to get home quick and get on dry clothes."

She began to cry in short jerky sobs. I took hold of her arm and began hustling her up the first hill toward her house. She was sobbing and shaking so she could scarcely walk and ice began to stiffen our clothing.

"Clint," she cried, "I just can't go on any farther. I'm going to lay down here and you run and get Papa."

"You ain't going to do anything of the kind," I asserted, "You get really moving and you won't be so cold." I danced around her and swung my arms. "Do this," I said. "Jump and swing your arms and it'll warm you up."

My own teeth were chattering so badly I could hardly speak.

"I can't do it," she sobbed. "I can't do that and I won't." She sank to her knees in the snow.

"All right," I said. "Here, get on the sled and I'll pull you home."

Her face was bluish-white. Her lips were blue and her teeth clicked like a woodpecker rapping a dead limb. I had to help her on the sled and then I tried to run, pulling her to Striker's house.

Susie's clothes were solid with ice by the time I helped her into the kitchen.

Mrs. Striker was stirring a kettle of something on the stove. "What on earth!" she gasped.

Susie began to cry again. I said, "We broke through the ice on the creek. She's about froze."

"Oh, you poor darling," Mrs. Striker said and began to work on the muffler, which was stiff as a plank.

I left and ran home, crackling and rattling with ice, and Father took me in hand, making me soak my feet in a bucket of scalding mustard water and fixing me a mug of hot water, whisky and sugar. After I had sweat profusely, he rubbed my whole body with whisky and made me go to bed.

The next day I was little the worse for my experience, but Susie was away from school for three days. She didn't hold it against me, however. When I told her I was sorry, she said I couldn't have known about the air hole in the ice and that it was a dandy ride anyhow until we broke through into the water and asked me if I would take her for a sled ride again someday, but down the other way.

VII

Eliza was married to John Peterson in mid-December, a week after her sixteenth birthday. At Mother's insistence, Father drove to Nebraska City and brought back Reverend Arthur Chisholm who performed the ceremony in the living room. The living room was closed to freighters that day.

Father argued it would be better for the wedding party to go to Nebraska City to the preacher and have a wedding supper in the Seymour House.

"I always claim," he said, "that it's easier to take a cow to the creek than bring the creek to the cow—espe-

cially when you got to take the creek back after the cow
is through with it."

But Mother felt they should be married at home
where our neighbors all could attend. So it was a great
party with guests present from as far as Nursery Hill, including Harry Irving, a shy little youth with his fiddle,
and Harry played for the dance following the wedding
while Sime Phillips, the blacksmith, called off.

The party lasted until five o'clock in the morning—
hours after I had lost all interest in the festivities and
gone to bed. Even before I retired, several men had
given in to fatigue and Father's whisky. They would lie
down in a corner and go to sleep. And that was a signal
for Father to rouse them and assist them to the freighters'
big bedroom upstairs.

The next day Father spoke of his hospitality to Mother
and seemed pretty proud. "Not only," he said, "did we
feed 'em and pass out maybe fifty dollars' worth of liquor
free, but I didn't even charge a cent for them to sleep in
the freighters' room."

John had picked out his quarter section, directly back
of Father's selection and on the section line. He felt so
certain he could get this land that he already was doing
some work on it in his spare time. In the fall he even had
broken a few acres of prairie.

Aunt Christine shook her head over this. "Can't help
thinking that's bad luck," she said. "Take *anything* too
much for granted and it's bad luck."

"That's sluff talk," said Father. "What can happen
now? Railroad survey's not coming through here. *They*
can't grab the land."

"Nevertheless," said Aunt Christine, "and notwith-
standing, when you get counting your chickens before
they're hatched, I think it's just asking fate to show you
that pride goeth before a fall."

"Oh, jeepers," said Father, "John's not proud about

his homestead. He's just a good enterprising young man and getting some work done while he has a chance. And about counting chickens before they're hatched, how about you sewing on clothes and all for when Casper Diercks comes back next summer? Suppose he never comes back?"

"That's different," she said.

"Don't see a lick of difference."

"Well, if you must know," said Aunt Christine, "I've consulted the spirits and they told me Casper can be depended upon."

"Well, of course that's a horse of a different color," said Father, looking at the ceiling.

"And," went on Aunt Christine, "I have been told there is trouble ahead regarding those homesteads."

Father shook his head. "If you were smart, Chris," he said, "you'd file on a homestead yourself. Then you'd have some land whether Casper shows up or not. It'd be pretty nice for you to have a hundred and sixty acres of land to live on. Casper probably would appreciate it."

"Do you think for one minute," she said evenly, "that a cultured man like Casper Diercks would bury himself on a homestead for five years for the sake of raising a few bushels of corn and some hogs?"

"Well, by holy dang, when he gets through digging up all the Rocky Mountains, I'd think he might be grateful to dig up some good soil for a change. Maybe you can't find gold in the mountains, but you can always trade good provender for gold. That's something."

But we were all apprehensive when Father and John rode off on the cold morning of December thirty-first with red mufflers tied high and Frank and Doug breathing clouds of steam. Not only was there a chance of them not being able to file on the land they wanted, but there was a real danger of blizzards.

The weather, however, remained cold and clear New

Year's Eve and all the next day. On the second day the sky was overcast and in the afternoon sudden gusts of wind would bring flurries of fine snow.

Soon after dinner I was in the barn looking after the stock when I heard a horse's hoofs and came out to see a pony trot up with a blanketed Indian astride. The Indian slid off the pony, dropped the rawhide reins in Mother's frozen pansy bed and strode in the front door. I ran around the house and followed him into the living room to find him standing with blanket outstretched in front of the stove.

"How," I said.

"How," he said, without changing expression. "Indian cold. Catchum get warm. All right?"

"Help yourself," I said, edging around so I could flee upstairs after my rifle if necessary. "How's the Indian business?"

"Humph. Go long way." He stretched his arm north. "Go long way to Ponca country. Big cold maybe come."

He pressed the sides of his hands to his stomach. "Maybe got meat?" he asked.

"You bet," I said. "You sit down there. Pretty quick I bring you meat."

He sat down at the freighters' table and I went to the kitchen.

Mother was baking pies. "Ma," I said, "there's a hungry Indian out there. Can I give him some cold beans or something?"

She looked startled. "An Indian!"

"Oh, he's all right," I assured her. "Just a poor, cold, hungry Indian without much clothes and he's got to go way up north."

"Where's your gun?"

"Upstairs. But he's all right, ma. I'll take care of him."

Mother took hold of my shoulder. "You dish up a plate of cold pork and beans out of the buttery," she said, "and get some corn bread and a dish of sorghum for him. I'll pour some hot water in the teapot and you take that and a cup in to him. You watch him every second and if he starts to do anything or to take anything, you scream and I'll be right there with Father's rifle. Now mind what I say."

"Well, ma, there's no use being scared. He's a good Indian."

"They say," she said, "that there's no good Indian but a dead one. Now get a move on."

So I got the beans and corn bread and sorghum and tea and took it to the living room. The Indian no longer was sitting at the table. He was across the room standing before a showcase.

"What you want there, Indian?" I demanded. "Here's some grub for you."

"Likeum big knife," said the Indian, pointing to a butcher knife in the showcase.

"No. Big knife costum lots of money. Good grub here cost nothing. Eat."

"Likeum big knife," he insisted.

"Well, you no likeum good grub I take it back."

"Humph," grunted the Indian, and came over to the table and sat down. He wolfed the cold pork and beans, picking up chunks with his fingers and mopping up the sorghum with the corn bread. He ate all the beans and bread, then wiped the plate clean and the sorghum saucer clean with his fingers and licked them off carefully.

"Good grub," he said, nodding his head. "Now you catchum whisky?"

"No whisky. Now you catchum grub and catchum get warm. Now you go. Good-bye. Hope you have a nice trip."

"Likeum big knife," said the Indian.

"Big knife cost three dollars. You got three dollars in your pants?"

"No got dollars. Likeum big knife, skinum deer, scalpum Sioux."

"You Pawnee?"

"Me Ponca." He went over to the show case. "Likeum big knife," he said.

He had taken off his blanket and I saw slung on a thong around his shoulder a beautifully carved red stone pipe, so highly polished that it gleamed.

"All right," I said, "I likeum pipe. You give me pipe and I give you big knife. All right?"

The Indian unfastened the pipe and held it in his two hands looking at it. He did not change expression, but one hand stroked the smooth red bowl lovingly. Then he looked at me.

"Likeum big knife," he said. "Here."

He held out the pipe and I took it and laid it on the showcase. Then I went behind the showcase and took out the knife. I stayed behind the case and handed the knife over to the Indian, ready to duck behind and yell if he made a move toward me. But he took the knife and held it in his two hands as he had held the pipe. Then he raised his fierce black eyes to me.

"Likeum knife," he said.

"All right," I said. "You go now. You puckachee."

His lips drew down at that last word.

"Likeum grub," he said. "Likeum big knife. Now I go."

He wrapped his dirty and tattered blanket around him and stalked out the door, leaving it open. I followed to the door and saw the mangy pony still standing with head down in Mother's frozen pansy bed. The Indian picked up the rawhide reins and leaped on the pony's back. Then he rode at a lope northward without looking back and disappeared over the hill against the gray sky.

Mother came from the kitchen looking pale. She was carrying Father's rifle.

"My stars," she said, "whatever possessed you to give that Indian a knife?"

"Well, jeepers," I said, "he wanted it. And look what I got for it. Ain't that pipe something fine?"

Mother scarcely glanced at the pipe. "When you handed him that knife," she said, "I thought he'd cut your throat with his very next move. Why, I'm still trembling. I was right there with the door open a crack and all ready to shoot him if he made a move at you."

"Well, I knew that all the time. I was all ready to duck behind the showcase and I knew you'd shoot him all right if he started after me. Anyhow I knew he was a good Indian. He wasn't any Sioux, and besides he said he liked your cooking fine."

Mother sank wearily into a chair with the rifle between her knees. Then Aunt Christine and Eliza came into the room, both looking pale.

"Well, look at you," I said. "All of you women scared white from one hungry Indian. By dang, it's a good thing none of you showed up in here or he might have done something. I'll tell you something to remember about Indians. I'll tell you something I learned out in the Sioux country. An Indian is just like a strange dog. You act scared of the dog and like as not he'll bite you. You act scared of an Indian and like as not he'll scalp you. Now take me, this Indian knew did he make a false move I'd knock the ears off his head and—"

"Oh, shush," interrupted Mother. Then she began to laugh.

"Look how he cleaned up the dishes," I said. "Won't even have to wash 'em." They looked at the dishes and exclaimed and then we all laughed.

Father and John rode up before dark and to show they were grown men and not excitable, they took the horses to the barn and unsaddled them and rubbed them down before coming to the house. But when they got in the house John grabbed Eliza and hugged her and kissed her. "We got a farm of our own, honey!" he shouted. "We got a farm of our own."

"Could you get *our* farm?"

"You bet your boots."

"No trouble at all," said Father. "Just got to get up early in the morning to pick up the things you want in this world."

We all crowded up to hear what happened.

"Well," said Father, "we just got up at four o'clock this morning and hustled right down to the land office and it was a good thing we did because there was half a dozen galoots already there. So we got in line and stood stamping our feet in the cold and more galoots kept coming and we waited there nearly four hours before they opened the door and then there must have been a hundred or more in line.

"But we weren't worried a mite. Never had seen the fellows before that were ahead of us, so we knew they couldn't be after *our* land. So finally we got in and paid our fourteen dollars and a half and they made out our papers and marked us down on a big map. That was all there was to it."

Eliza and John danced around the kitchen and then Mother told Father about our Indian. I brought in the pipe to show them and Father examined it closely.

"Pretty job of work," he said. "Clint, I think you did a middling good job of trading, except that maybe you should ought to have took his blanket in payment for the meal."

I shook my head. "I couldn't have done that, father," I said. "He'd have froze to death without his blanket."

Father roared with laughter and slapped me on the

back. "You're a real Macdougall," he said, and that made me happy.

VIII

With spring there came a rush of homesteaders, many of whom were immigrants from the East where the war drafts were causing no end of trouble. A dozen new families settled in our vicinity on or near Medicine Creek.

Nearest to us was Lucius Clark, who took a homestead just across the creek in a part-log and part-board house with his family of two girls and a boy and who immediately passed out word that he was an expert cobbler and ready either to make new boots or to repair old ones. Then there were the families of Axel Nelson, who took land next to the Bergstroms, and Tom Ferguson and Emerson Frisbee and Frank Wallace and Webster Schultz.

Webster Schultz was a carpenter of sorts and Father hired him with Albert Striker when we started building our big house on the hill. It was to be a very fine house, all weatherboarded and with a high mansard roof adorned with elaborate lightning rods and fancy grilling.

Traffic on the road was increasing day by day and Martha Nelson, grown daughter of Axel Nelson, was engaged to help Bertha Peterson in cooking and serving meals to the freighters and emigrants. Joe Wallace, eighteen-year-old son of Frank Wallace, also was hired to help Father and John.

John now felt that he must put in a good deal of his time working on his own homestead where he and Eliza had moved to a one-room board shanty. John had a yoke of oxen and was working early and late breaking prairie and getting in his first crops. But he and Eliza walked

down to our place every evening for dinner and to help
out with the freighters.

One Saturday evening Father came back from Nebraska City with supplies, including a new barrel of
whisky, and John ran out to help him with the barrel.

"Pshaw," said Father, "I can handle this thing all
right."

"No use straining yourself when I'm around to help,"
said John. "What's the news?"

"Oh, nothing's really happened since Hooker was
licked at Chancellorsville. Down south they're yelling,
'On to Washington,' but that's just slang. This war's
going on and on until the North finally wins and you
can thank your stars you ain't back east. You'd be just
more cannon fodder. Lots of trouble in New York City
over the drafts. Probably more trouble coming up."

John shook his big blond head. "I don't want none of
it," he said seriously. "Don't think I'm a coward, but
don't see why I should go and get killed in this war. If
I was down south and somebody comes around trying to
take my homestead, that's different. I'd want to fight
plenty about that."

"Open that kitchen door, Clint," said Father, "and
hold it open until we get this barrel in."

I held the door and they carried the barrel in between
them, John panting from the weight and Father laughing at him.

"Whew!" said John after they slid the barrel in place.
His face was red and he rubbed his hands on his jeans.
"You hear anything more about this Major Brown?" he
asked.

Father shook his head. "Not much. Ajax Harvey got a
short letter about a month ago. Brown's got over his
wound and is back with General Sibley trying to run
down the Sioux. Says the steam wagon will have to wait
until he performs his duty. He thinks he should ought

to get back by fall, but it ain't doing that steam wagon any good setting out there beside the road. She looked rusty in places when I went by her today."

"He better hurry up," observed John, "or they'll have that railroad track built and then where'll he be?"

Father slapped John on the back. "Don't need to worry about that," he said. "They're not even *planning* to build any railroad. Just a big hoax. They'll keep pretending they're going to start building it, but you notice they haven't done a lick yet. They'll keep pretending because they'll want to get more money out of the government."

Father and John tested the new whisky and pronounced it up to standard. Then they went outdoors just as a light covered wagon pulled by two rangy mules creaked up. A slim young man in a long-tailed coat came over the front wheel and walked with measured stride up to Father and John. He was a serious young man and pale. His long upper lip failed to cover his enormous front teeth even when his mouth was closed. He smiled sadly and spoke in a rather high voice. "Brother Macdougall?" he asked.

"My name's Jack Macdougall," said Father. "What can I do for you?"

"I am Reverend Melvin Powell."

"Glad to know you, reverend," said Father, putting out his hand. "This here's my son-in-law John Peterson and my son Clinton."

"Pleasure to meet you all," said Reverend Powell. "My wife and I are moving west from Illinois, looking for a likely community to serve and, wherever we may be, we usually give services each Sunday to people who ordinarily don't have the advantage of spiritual guidance. We have a small organ in the wagon and my wife is an accomplished organist."

"Kind of got a company, eh?" said Father.

"You might call it that." Reverend Powell smiled. "Well, tomorrow being the Sabbath, I was wondering if it might not be well to hold services in your house and you could invite the neighboring settlers?"

"Fine and dandy," said Father. "Wouldn't hurt most of 'em to hear a sermon, I calculate." He looked up at the cloudless sky. "Another thing—it's been an uncommon dry spring. Don't say it would do any good, but it wouldn't hurt any to have an expert prayer for rain."

"I'm sure it would help."

"Fine and dandy. I'll call my wife and we can put you up for the night in my daughter's old room. Glad to have you. Just you help Mrs. Reverend down and I'll get my wife. Clint, you drive Reverend's mules back to the barn and pitch 'em down some hay and give 'em a measure of oats apiece. John, you see can you help Reverend with his carpetbags or whatnot."

So Reverend Powell and his wife were ushered into the house and Father and John carried the little cabinet organ into the living room and Father dispatched me on Bob to inform all the neighbors there would be church services in the morning.

The next morning virtually everyone in the district was in our living room, including a few freighters and an emigrant family. There were not nearly enough chairs and benches in the house, so a good many of the children were seated on empty boxes from the store shed and about a dozen men stood up around the walls, dressed in the best clothes they had.

Mrs. Powell was a washed-out little young woman with mouse-colored hair and shy blue eyes and a little voice that reminded me of a baby chicken peeping.

She pumped on the organ and Reverend Powell, looking as stern as he could look, waved a lead pencil and led the crowd in singing, "Shall We Gather at the River," and "How Firm a Foundation," and "Blest Be the Tie that Binds," and "Old Hundred."

Father's voice may have been off key sometimes, but it roared above all the rest even when he didn't know the words and resorted to la-di-daing.

In between hymns Reverend Powell made a prayer, asking God to "bless these courageous pioneers in this new clean land with a good rain that their harvest may be bountiful." It was a pretty good prayer, as Father said afterwards, but not particularly emphatic and it didn't call the Deity's attention to the fact that rain was an immediate need which should be given attention ahead of practically all other business.

Then, with Aunt Christine's cherry-wood table as a pulpit, or at least as something to rest his Bible on, Reverend Powell began to preach.

I was standing up by the wall next to John Peterson and John whispered behind his hand, "It been a good joke if Aunt Chris's spirits make that table begin to jump now." And I had to stuff my knuckles into my mouth to keep from laughing out loud.

Old Pete Peterson was standing right behind us. He leaned over a little and went "Shhh" at us. Old Pete had been eating onions.

Reverend Powell was saying very sternly, "I the Lord thy God am a jealous God, visiting the iniquity of the fathers upon the children unto the third and fourth generation of them that hate me.

"When the Lord sayeth, 'Thou shalt have no other gods before me,' He means just that, brothers and sisters, and woe unto him who disobeys. When the Lord sayeth, 'Thou shalt not make unto thee any graven image, or any likeness of any thing that is in heaven above, or that is in the earth beneath, or that is in the water under the earth,' the Lord means what He says. He doesn't mean that He is forbidding only the worship of a golden calf such as the erring children of Israel constructed, or a golden bull or a cast iron whale fish. The Lord says *anything* and the jealous Lord will strike down with woe any and all who disobey. And when the Lord says *any* graven image, that, brothers and sisters, certainly includes even the graven image of Mary, the mother of Jesus.

"Brothers and sisters, in every Romanist church in the land you will find the graven image of this woman, Mary. Oh, she was an excellent woman, brothers and sisters, a hallowed woman. But Mary is not God and the Lord thy God is a jealous God who wants no other gods before Him, who wants no graven images before Him.

"Oh, I say unto you, my friends, the wrath of the Lord soon will be visited upon these iniquitous Romanists, these idolaters.

"I have been told that thus far this new community has escaped the curse of Rome. Let me warn you then to keep it so. Let me warn you to keep the Romanists out. God will lend you the strength of His right arm to force them to move on should any Irish or other tools of the Pope try to settle in your midst. For let one spawn of Roman deviltry settle amongst you and there will be more. They attract more even as cockroaches attract more cockroaches and before you know it there would be a Romanist church in your midst and with it priests and black-robed nuns sworn to celibacy. Sworn to celibacy, I say, but by an oath of lies, for if you only knew the terrible things that take place in the darkened confessional of the Roman Catholic Church, if you only knew of the ravished maidens and the murders, yes, the murders, that are committed in these ghastly, candlelit rites, you would be horrified that such things could happen in nineteenth century America. But that isn't all. That isn't near all.

"You have heard of the draft riots in New York. Perhaps you have heard of rioting Irishmen there. But do you realize that these Irishers who are fighting against the authority of the United States government are in reality fighting for Rome?

"How many of you know, as I know, that these unspeakable Irish have their orders direct from the Pope, passed on to them by their Romanist priests? I have information from men whose word cannot be questioned that papers have been found on some of these Irishers showing they have been ordered to stir up riots against the draft.

"And not only this, my friends. I also have information from those in a position to know, and backed by the confessions of reformed Romanists, that every Roman Catholic Church in the East is an arsenal and the Romanist youth have been in military training for years, plotting the overthrow of the United States government. There is proof in the hands of the Secretary of War at this moment that the rebellion itself was instigated by the powers of Rome. Did you know that Jefferson Davis and Robert E. Lee are Romanists? That is not generally known, but it's a fact. They are Romanists and under direct orders from the Pope himself.

"Now how can we combat this menace? Well, one way is developing in the East. There is a growing campaign to exclude Romanists from employment. More and more often you see signs, 'Men wanted—No Irish need apply.' That's a splendid system. Drive them back to Ireland or to Rome where they belong. Trust an Irishman or any Romanist and you'll find a knife in your back some dark night.

"These Irishers—some of them at least—will be fleeing westward. Be prepared for them, my friends. Make 'No Irish need apply,' your motto.

"I even would advise putting up a sign on the road here reading, 'Irishman, don't let the sun set on you here.'"

"Excuse me, reverend," said Father loudly. He had stepped forward from the back of the room where he had been standing.

Reverend Powell paused with his mouth open, staring at Father. Father's face was red.

"Excuse me," repeated Father. "I wouldn't think of breaking in on a preacher when he was praying. I calculate I wouldn't break in on him no matter *what* he was saying in a prayer. But now you're just talking. You ain't even preaching. You're just talking and, by grab, you're talking sluff talk. And it ain't the kind of talk I'll stand for in my house, preacher or no preacher."

I looked at Mother sitting on a bench with Aunt Christine and Mrs. Peterson and Mrs. Bergstrom, and Mother was looking at the floor and blushing as red as Mrs. Bergstrom's dress.

"I'm trying to tell you the truth," blurted Reverend Powell. "I'm trying to warn you and save you from destruction."

"You're not warning anybody," said Father. "You're not preaching the gospel. You're out spreading a gospel of your own of 'No Irish need apply.' Well, that slang don't go here. We've got no Irish in this community and we've got no Romanists here yet, but nobody will put up any signs like you say while I'm in this community."

Reverend Powell started to interrupt. "Wait a minute," said Father. "You've had your say and now I'm going to have mine. I don't care whether a man's an Irishman or Dutchman or darky so long's he's a man, and I don't need any sweet-scented hairpin to tell me different. We want good honest settlers in this district and we don't care a whoop what kind of religion they've got. We don't care what religion they've got or what race they belong to, and that's in the Constitution of the United States too.

"Maybe you, reverend, know something about the

Roman Catholic Church and maybe you don't. I doubt
if you do. I once knew a Romanist priest in Rochester,
New York, and, by grab, he was a man. I had a drink
with him several times, and he didn't talk hate like you.
He talked Jesus Christ and he talked sense.

"There's a town getting started here on Medicine
Creek, reverend, and because I started it she's going to
be called Macdougall, Nebraska, and because I started it
I'm going to have something to say about what goes on
here—for a while, anyhow. I think maybe we should
ought to get a church started here pretty soon. That's
why I took you in my house and had all my friends and
neighbors come to hear you preach. I got an idea maybe
it's good for women and children to go to church and
that maybe it don't hurt men, either."

Reverend Powell's long front teeth were bared in a
patronizing but angry smile. "You really think *that*, do
you?" he said.

"But," went on Father, "I've heard enough out of you
to know we don't want *your* kind of church."

"Do you think you're king or something out here?"
demanded Powell.

"Not king, no," said Father. "I just elected myself
spokesman for the decent folks. And I've seen and heard
enough liars in my day so's I can spot one inside of an
hour or so—whether he's wearing blue jeans or a black
coat."

Sime Phillips clapped his big hands with a bang like
slapping two boards together and in a moment practically every man and a good share of the women were
clapping their hands too.

"Much obliged, folks," said Father, "and I want to
apologize for bringing you over here to hear this excuse.
Now, Powell, we've heard about enough out of you and
you can go and hitch up your mules. Maybe somebody

will help you carry that wheeze box out to your wagon. You don't look strong enough to do it by yourself."

Men began to crowd up and slap Father on the back. Reverend Powell picked up his Bible and glanced plaintively at his little wife, who looked frightened.

"Listen," he called, "I haven't taken up any collection for the foreign missions yet."

"Should have done that before you started talking," said Father. "We fed the foreign missions' mules and bedded the foreign missions down for the night and give 'em supper and breakfast. That's about enough unless that prayer of yours is bringing rain. Clint, run out and see is it clouding up."

I elbowed my way to the door and looked up at the burning sky.

"Not a cloud in sight," I called back.

"All right," said Father, "God don't think any more of your talk than I do. You'll have to get your dinner some other place."

Sime Phillips and John Peterson carried the little organ out to Powell's wagon and Reverend Powell carried his own carpetbags. He was white with anger. When he had his mules hitched and had helped his frightened wife to the seat and had climbed up himself, Reverend Powell shook his whip at Father.

"The Lord will punish you for this," he said bitterly.

Father laughed. "If the Lord," he said, "takes orders from you, He ain't God."

"Git up," said Reverend Powell, and slapped the lines on the mules' rumps.

Then we went into the house and Mother looked at Father sadly and shook her head. "I've got a chicken dinner all ready for those poor folks," she said. "We can't eat it all."

"Well," said Father, "there's Lucius Clark and his

wife. They look kind of chicken hungry. Let's invite them."

IX

The hot, dry weather continued and the corn was looking wilted and listless in the fields. The wheat was heading prematurely. The potato vines were wilted and drooping and the dirt in the fields was powder dry and gray. Despite my work carrying water from the well, our vegetable garden was practically burned out and Mother's flowers were withered and dead. Dust from the road lay over everything. The roof of the house was covered with it each day, even though the hot winds came up each afternoon and whisked it off like snow banners.

A week after Reverend Powell's visit Father came into the house from hopelessly scanning the sky. "By grab," he said, "if it don't rain pretty soon there won't be any crops at all. That's going to about ruin some of our homesteaders who didn't have enough ahead for only one crop."

"You know," said Aunt Christine, more than half seriously, "Reverend Powell said the Lord would punish you."

"Stuff and nonsense. This drouth started out before Reverend Powell crossed the Missouri River. Besides, if that galoot had any influence with the Lord, we'd have got rain. He prayed for rain, didn't he?"

"Then he changed his mind."

"I guess," said Father, "you can't countermand a prayer very well. When you've made a prayer you've made it. I guess you can't pray once for something and then send up another prayer and say, 'Oh, God, I've changed my mind. I'd like to exchange that husband I ordered for a mule instead.' I guess you can't do that."

"Jack Macdougall," said Mother, "you're positively sacrilegious. And I'm not fully satisfied this drouth ain't a judgment."

"It's hitting others worse nor it's hitting us," observed Father.

"The rain," said Aunt Christine, "falls upon the just as well as upon the unjust. I suppose drouths work the same way."

Martha Nelson came into the kitchen and said there was a man in the living room who wanted to see Father. I followed Father into the other room and a slim, middle-aged man was standing by one of the showcases. He was almost entirely bald and was minus even eyebrows. His face was seamed and lined with strange, fine wrinkles that ran in directions not usually followed by wrinkles. He blinked his blue eyes nervously.

"What can I do for *you?*" Father asked.

The man smiled. "I," he said, "am Professor Ivan Lewis."

"Glad to meet you. My name's Jack Macdougall."

"See you've been having a bad drouth hereabouts."

"That's right. If we don't get a rain pretty quick there'll be no crops in this country. It'll ruin a lot of folks."

The man smiled again. "That's why I'm out here," he said.

Father's eyes narrowed. "Well," he said, "there was another fellow through here a week ago last Sunday that prayed for rain. Haven't even had any dew since that."

"Mr. Macdougall," said Professor Lewis, "everything in this world is cause and effect. If there's an effect, there's a cause for it. The thing to look for is the cause. When you find that maybe you can do something. The Lord helps those that help themselves and I aim to help you people. I am a scientific rain maker."

"A *what?*"

"A scientific rain maker. I go to the cause of the drouth and correct that. When I correct that you get rain. If I get you a crop-saving rain you pay me. If I fail to get you a crop-saving rain you pay me nothing."

Father stared at the man. "Set down," he said. "I don't know if I altogether catch on to what you're talking about."

Professor Lewis sat down in the big splint-bottomed chair and crossed his lean legs. His face twitched. "It won't take me long to tell you," he said. "But first, you tell me why it hasn't been raining here."

"I swanney," said Father, "you don't want me to tell you much, do you? How should I know why it ain't been raining?"

Professor Lewis's eyes blinked rapidly. "Well, you usually have rain this time of year, don't you?"

"Have for two years."

"Have you any idea why it rained then?"

Father half laughed. "By grab, I don't know what you're getting at, professor. But when it rains a cloud full of water raises up and lets go. But there just ain't any clouds now. There's no water in the sky to come down."

"That's what I was getting at, Mr. Macdougall. It appears there's no water in the sky this year. But that's only appearance and appearances are sometimes deceitful."

"How can there be any water in the sky when there's no clouds?"

"Well, Mr. Macdougall, there's got to be water in the sky. There always is. How does it get there, ordinarily?"

"The sun sucks it up."

"All right, the sun sucks it up. Then when the sun's blazing down hotter than usual, you'd think it would suck up more water, wouldn't you?"

"Maybe so. But it don't seem to be doing it."

"Well, look at it this way. Is there as much water in

the creek down here as there generally is this time in June?"

"Jeepers, no. Not half as much."

"The water has gone someplace, then, hasn't it?"

"Well," said Father, "I just calculated it was drier because there hadn't been any rain."

Professor Lewis shook his head. "Of course that has something to do with it. Of course that's true. But the sun has been sucking up more water than usual too."

"Well, if the sun's sucking up more water, what becomes of it? Is it all burned up?"

"Oh, no. Not at all, at all. There's never a time when there isn't enough moisture in the air to make a good rain. There's enough now right up in that sky to save your crops—if we could just get it."

"Haven't seen a cloud in more than two weeks."

"That's all right. Now look, this is the way we scientists figure. This is what we know by actual tests. Hot air holds moisture better than cool air. If you get the air hot and keep it hot, it's pretty unlikely that any rain is going to fall for a long, long time. That's what is wrong in Nebraska Territory right now. The air has been hot up in the sky so long that it's not going to let go of its moisture.

"Now, when the air is cooled off the moisture makes a mist and when you see the mist up in the sky you call it clouds. But the tiny drops of water in the mist will stay up in the air because the hot air rising from the earth will hold it there. But suppose you cool off the mist a little more. If you do the drops of water gather together. They get bigger and too heavy to stay up in the sky. Then you're going to have rain."

"That sounds sensible," said Father, "but how you going to cool off the air?"

The professor picked up a palmleaf fan from the table and fanned himself. "Ever cool yourself off like this?"

"Of course."

"You cool yourself off by agitating the air. That's the way you can cool off the upper air—agitate it. Mr. Macdougall, I got my idea from the war. It seems almost always after a big battle there comes a heavy rain. The banging of the cannons agitates the air clear up into the sky and the agitation cools the air and makes the mist and cools the mist some more and down comes the rain."

"Well, I swanney," said Father. "You may be talking sense. What you calculate to do?"

Professor Lewis smiled and his eyes blinked half a dozen times before he answered. "I plan," he said, "to agitate the upper air with bombs thrown into the sky with a mortar. That is, I shall if the people in this vicinity are interested enough in getting rain to make it worth my while."

"You want," asked Father, "for us to pay you money?"

"I'm not in this business entirely for my health, Mr. Macdougall. Of course I *do* get a lot of satisfaction out of breaking drouths and saving farmers from ruin. But after all, Mr. Macdougall, my horses need grain and my family back in Iowa needs a roof over their heads and food to eat."

"All right," said Father, "that's all very well, but how do we know you can make it rain that way? You *say* you can, but how do we know it ain't just sluff talk?"

"You don't, Mr. Macdougall. And I'm not asking you to take my word. All I'm asking you to do is to sign an agreement with me and to allow me to use a field for my experiment. If I don't bring at least half an inch of rain within thirty hours you pay me nothing. If I do bring at least half an inch of rain within thirty hours you pay me a hundred and fifty dollars."

"Hmm. A hundred and fifty dollars is pretty steep for shooting a few bombs up in the air."

"It'll be more after people know more about my system, Mr. Macdougall. You see, I have spent a long, long time studying weather and the causes of weather. Only now am I beginning to harvest a little. I plan to charge five hundred dollars for producing a rain after I have more testimonials. As a matter of fact, I have only started on this career and at present I have only one testimonial. You see, I'm letting you in very cheaply.

"Consider this, Mr. Macdougall. You don't have to pay all of the hundred and fifty yourself. You have neighbors around here."

"And most of 'em are poor as Job's turkey."

"They'll be poorer if they don't get rain soon."

"That's so."

"Well, consider this. If you don't get rain within a couple of weeks the crops hereabouts will be practically ruined. Isn't that so?"

"Probably won't get much over half a crop, all things considered, no matter if the drouth is broken right away."

"Well, consider the value of half a crop compared with no crop at all. You surely can raise a hundred and fifty dollars in this community for a rain."

"Oh, I can raise it all right."

"Can't see, then, Mr. Macdougall, where there's any argument. A good rain would be worth thousands of dollars. You can get a good rain for a hundred and fifty dollars or I pay for my own gunpowder and time. If you don't get a good rain it'll cost you nothing."

Father rose from his chair. "All right, professor," he said. "You just make yourself at home and I'll go visiting and see can I raise seventy-five dollars from the neighbors on that proposition. If I can, I'll stand the other seventy-five myself. Clint, you help the professor put up his team and wagon and show him the stock. I'll saddle a horse and go around to the neighbors."

Shortly before suppertime Father came back. "It's all

right, professor," he said. "You just go ahead tomorrow morning and see if you can squeeze a little water out of the sky. And I'll get a bucket and mark off half an inch on it to measure the water you get—if you get any."

"That's fine," said Professor Lewis.

So Father went out to the store shed and came back with an old wooden mackerel bucket.

Professor Lewis shook his head. "No, sirree, bob," he said. "That's no good, Mr. Macdougall."

"Why not? It's plenty big enough."

"Big enough, yes. But it's wooden and that wood absorbs too much water. I've got a can in my wagon that's all marked off with inches."

"Rather have my own, if you don't mind."

"All right. But get something with straight sides. Anything with sides sloping in would be to my advantage, not yours."

Father looked up from the mackerel bucket. "That's right. Well, I'll tell you, I'll borrow one of my wife's frying pans. They've got reasonable straight sides."

"That would be all right."

So Father got one of Mother's frying pans and he and Professor Lewis measured half an inch up its black inside and scratched marks at that point.

The hot wind droned through the house and at supper the dishes were hot to the touch. Even though we kept the butter in a bucket down the well, it would melt after it was drawn up. It was necessary to use a spoon to dip it from the butter dish.

Everyone and everything was tired and listless. The birds had ceased singing in the creek grove and sat silent amongst the dry, dusty leaves. Old Don, the shepherd, spent most of his time in a cool hole under the house. Only the big purplish flies were active and they buzzed around so annoyingly that Martha cut a copy of the Nebraska City News in strips, tied the strips to a stick and stood by the table, waving it gently over our heads now and then to shoo them away from the food.

The next morning Chauncey Loud, our schoolteacher, drew Father aside. "You're not paying this man anything unless he gets rain, are you?" he asked.

"Not a red penny. Why?"

"Oh, nothing. But I'm glad you're not. Maybe I'm just a doubting Thomas, but it doesn't sound reasonable to me."

Shortly Sime Phillips came across the road and John Peterson and his father arrived and Web Schultz and Al Striker and Ole, Willie and Peter Bergstrom with their father, and we all helped Professor Lewis carry his paraphernalia up the hill back of where our new house was building.

There was a light cannon with a heavy base and a flaring barrel that pointed straight up. There was a keg of powder and a basket of bombs. The bombs were roughly round and about four inches in diameter. They had slow matches attached.

Father and Sime Phillips carried the cannon between them. John Peterson carried the keg of powder and Professor Lewis insisted on carrying the basket of bombs himself.

"They're very delicate and won't stand handling," he said. "I made 'em myself and I don't want to take a risk on anybody else touching them."

The rest of us were following along empty-handed but full of conversation when Father turned his head back and shouted. "Hey, there, Clint—go on back and get that rain-gauge frying pan."

I ran back to the house and got the frying pan and by the time I got up to the brow of the hill Father and Sime Phillips had set the cannon down and Professor Lewis was digging a foundation for it with a short spade Al Striker brought from our new house.

I put the frying pan down at a good level spot where it would be held solid by some clumps of grass, and then watched Professor Lewis load his mortar with a generous scoop of powder from the keg. He rammed old paper solidly down upon the powder. Then he gingerly let one of his bombs down the barrel. The bombs seemed to be made of brown paper cut in strips and pasted one upon another. While they were generally round in shape, the bomb surfaces were not smooth, but irregular, almost like a hickory nut.

Professor Lewis knelt in the grass and attached a slow match to the aperture in the base of the cannon. Then he straightened up. "Will somebody please carry that keg of powder back a few rods?" he asked. "And everybody please get back out of harm's way."

John Peterson carried the keg of powder back and we all scattered in a semicircle half a dozen rods away. Then Professor Lewis struck a lucifer and applied it to the slow match and ran stiff-legged back to join us. The match smoked down to the cannon and the cannon roared and the smoking bomb went sailing up into the glistening sky until it was only a flyspeck against the blue. Then it burst into a white flower of a cloud and the boom of the explosion struck my throat. It was almost as loud as a thunderclap, but sharper.

Professor Lewis took another scoop of powder from the keg and reloaded and sent up another bomb, but by the time the second white cloud burst loose in the sky the first one had drifted away. He fired four bombs in all. Then he said to Father, "That'll do for awhile. We'll wait a few hours and see what effect this has."

"Let me get this correct," Sime Phillips said. "Ordinarily thunder jars rain out of the sky. You make artificial thunder to jar it out. Is that the idea?"

Professor Lewis smiled and his eyes blinked. "In a way," he said. "That's not exactly it, scientifically speaking. But in a way I guess it's true. Let's all go back and wait awhile."

"Leave the cannon and things up here?" Father asked.

"Well, can I depend on everyone letting them be?"

"It's on my property," said Father, "and nobody will touch it. Listen here, folks, I don't want anyone to get within ten rod of this stuff while the professor ain't here."

"Nobody's going to bother it," Sime Phillips said. "Come on."

So we went back to the house and Father passed out drinks of whisky to everyone who wanted a drink of whisky and they drank to a "gullywasher."

"Here's to Jupiter Pluvius," said Professor Lewis.

"Nothing to do but wait now, I reckon," Al Striker said. "Come on, Web, we might as well get a little work done on Macdougall's palace."

So they went back to hammer on our new house and Sime Phillips went back across the road to hammer on his anvil and most of the rest went home. Chauncey Loud stayed awhile and it was easy to see he had little faith in the business.

"How long you going to wait?" he asked Professor Lewis.

"All depends. If a mist starts to form I'll agitate the mist with another volley. If it doesn't, why, I'll wait until tomorrow morning. It's better to fire your first volley in the morning."

"Why?"

"Well, it just is. Conditions are better in the morning."

Mr. Loud half smiled, but he didn't say anything more.

Every few minutes Professor Lewis would go outdoors and look at the sky. Then he would come back into the house and fan himself.

Right after dinner he took a short nap in the splint-bottomed chair. Then he went outside, looked at the sky from horizon to horizon and called Father. "Mr. Mac-dougall," he said, "the situation is beginning to look pretty good. A mist seems to be gathering."

Father gazed upward and the brilliantly blue sky really had lost some of its color. Now it was more of a dirty, washed-out blue. And while it seemed hotter than the day before, if anything, the sun had lost some of its vicious quivering. Its blazing light seemed to be more diffused.

"Well, by grab," said Father, "it *does* look different than it did. But I wouldn't remark that it looks like rain."

"It looks about ripe for another volley," Professor Lewis said. "Let's see what we can do for it."

So we sweated back up the hill and the professor fired four more bombs into the sky. By the time he had fired the first shot Al Striker and Web Schultz had deserted their carpentering and were on hand. By the time the second bomb blossomed in the sky Sime Phillips had arrived and the Bergstroms were hustling across the fields.

"Think you're going to get it?" asked Phillips.

"Looks good," said Professor Lewis. "I think we'll get something before dark. Ought to have half an inch by morning."

So we carried the professor's machinery back to his wagon which, instead of having the conventional rounded canvas top, had a square frame and was covered with black oilcloth. He declared the shiny black oilcloth repelled the sun's rays and kept his store of bombs and gunpowder from getting too hot.

At that Chauncey Loud looked at me knowingly, shook his head and walked away.

"Just possible," said Professor Lewis, "that it won't

work even now. In that case I'll have to agitate the welkin again in the morning. But I suspect we've done the job already."

So we went about our business and the heat bore down even more oppressively.

About four o'clock in the afternoon I was hoeing in the vegetable garden and I heard a low bumbling rumble. I looked off across the road and beyond the tired trees that bordered the creek and saw blue-black clouds piling up in the southwest. As I looked, a flash of lightning bisected the bank of clouds and the rumble came again.

I dropped my hoe and ran for the house. "Father!" I cried.

Father was in the living room with an open case of chewing tobacco he had just carried from the store shed. He set the case down, mopped his face with a bandanna and stared at me. "What ails you?" he demanded.

"It's coming. The rain. Go out in front and look southwest."

Father ran outdoors, took one look at the clouds, which were noticeably higher now, and yelled in the door.

"Hey, Lewis! Wife! Everybody! The rain's coming hell for leather!"

In a moment Mother and Aunt Christine and Bertha Peterson and Martha Nelson and Professor Lewis all were standing out by the road watching the approaching clouds. Sime Phillips heard the commotion in his shop across the way and joined us.

"Say, Lewis," said Father to the professor, "that cloud looks almighty like hail. Suppose you get us a hailstorm that ruins everything. What then? By grab, you'll be responsible for the damage."

"Can't hold me responsible for an act of God," said Professor Lewis.

"For an act of God? Well, I swanney, if hail's an act of God, so's rain. If you're responsible enough for the rain so we've got to pay you a hundred and fifty dollars for it, you're responsible enough for the hail so you've got to pay for the damage."

Professor Lewis's face twitched and he looked at the ground. "Well," he said, "you signed a contract for the rain and I *didn't* sign anything about paying for hail damage. But I don't think it's going to hail to amount to anything."

A gust of cool wind came roaring down the road bringing a great cloud of gray dust. The women ran for the house and we turned our backs to the blinding, choking cloud. By the time the dust had passed the sun was blotted out. Lightning crackled and the thunder banged an answer to Professor Lewis's bombardment that made his shells seem puny by comparison.

Then the rain descended—huge spattering drops at first that sent the dust rising from the road in little puff explosions, then a steady drumfire, then a near deluge with little wind and no hail.

We stood out in it, bareheaded, rejoicing in the delicious wet coolness, exulting in the sweet smell of new mud and in the clammy clutch of our wet shirts and overalls.

That night when the rain ceased, we went up the hill with a lantern and checked on the frying pan. There was nearly an inch of water in it.

So the next morning Father paid Professor Lewis his $150 and shook his hand. "Lewis," said Father, "you're a great man. You deserve to get rich and I hope you do. And I'd like to know where I can get hold of you if we ever have a drouth like that again."

Professor Lewis gave Father his address in Hamburg, Iowa, and drove on west through the rich mud.

We learned that our splendid crop-saving rain had not

extended more than twenty miles each side of us. And we learned later that Professor Lewis had attempted to bring rain to the parched regions in the west, north and east of us, that he had bombarded the cloudless skies with scores of bombs but never again was able to bring down a single drop of rain.

Chauncey Loud asserted that Lewis was a quack scientist and that his subsequent record had proved there was nothing to his theories. But Father was not convinced.

Lewis had brought us rain when no rain would have meant ruin for many of our neighbors.

He fired his bombs and the rain came. There had been no rain except in our immediate vicinity. "What more proof you want than that?" Father asked Mr. Loud.

Several years later Father tried to get hold of Professor Lewis again when a severe drouth was upon us. But the letter was returned from Hamburg, Iowa, unclaimed.

X

Before winter our new house was completed, as was the new barn and two wells. The one well was under the kitchen and Father established a marvel of modern convenience—a pump over an iron sink right in the house.

The house itself would not have been out of place on one of the better streets of Nebraska City, with its gables and glittering lightning rods. And our furniture for the parlor was beautifully upholstered in black haircloth—a haircloth sofa, very sleek and slippery, and a big armchair and two smaller chairs to match. Then there were two more armchairs with caned seats and a new parlor stove, very elegant with nickel and isinglass windows.

There was a marble-topped center table with clawed feet and on this table reposed our family Bible and a new marvel Father had purchased from a peddler—a device called a stereoscope which showed pictures of Niagara Falls, the Mammoth Cave of Kentucky, the Dismal Swamp of Virginia and of the Holy Land in three dimensions, fully as realistically as if you actually were looking at the scenes themselves, if not more so.

We had a new red carpet tacked down smoothly over a layer of clean straw and there were pictures on the wall of Edinburgh Castle and "The Lovers' Quarrel" and a portrait of George Washington.

The old crayon portraits of Grandfather and Grandmother Macdougall were moved to Father's and Mother's room. They occupied the downstairs bedroom and Aunt Christine, Martha Nelson and I had rooms upstairs, leaving one for honored guests whom we shouldn't want to bed in the old house.

Father was inordinately proud of the place. "I bet a shilling," he said, "that this place is the finest homesteader's house in America." Certainly it was better than any we knew, for most homesteaders considered themselves fortunate if they had a log house or plain board shack rather than a sod shanty.

Aunt Christine was still with us. Not only had Casper Diercks failed to come for her and take her on a honeymoon to Europe, but now she had not received a letter from him in two or three months. She pretended not to be worried, however. She said Casper had written her that he was going farther into the mountains on a new prospecting jaunt and that if he and Bass Muller made a strike they wouldn't come back to civilization until they were rich. Therefore, she believed no news was indeed good news.

Moreover, Tom Brooks had given his unqualified support to the cause of Casper.

Mother was present at this séance and told Father about it. "Tom told her," said Mother, "that he didn't want her to spend her entire life pining away for him."

"Pretty good sense, coming from a spirit," Father commented.

"And," went on Mother, "he said Casper is a fine man and one who will make his mark in the world."

"Maybe so," said Father. "But I always calculated he was a little afraid of work or he'd have got himself some fine land here and settled down instead of going off on a wild-goose chase after gold. You can't tell about galoots of that kind. Clever enough fellow, but I doubt an almighty lot that we'll ever see hide nor hair of him again. Maybe he's already tied up with some Indian squaw or somebody out there in the mountains. Can't tell."

"Now I don't think any such thing," said Mother.

"Don't say I *think* it. It just might be. Anyhow, I do think Chris should ought to get herself a good homestead before all the good ones are snapped up. Then she'd have something to offer a man. She ain't so young as she once was."

As winter came on, Major Brown still was in the Northwest, pursuing the Sioux with General Sibley, and the steam wagon, now definitely rusty, still stood waiting beside the road.

That December they broke ground for the Union Pacific Railroad in Omaha. This, however, didn't worry Father and it didn't worry the Nebraska City leaders, either.

Father came home from Nebraska City with the news one evening and expressed the general opinion of the move. "They've finally got around to dig a hole for that railroad," he said. "Well, that's something. They'll have a hole to bury it in when Major Brown gets back next spring."

That winter our community suffered its first death. Mrs. Jenny Clark, plump little wife of Lucius Clark the cobbler, died of lung fever. When it became evident that she was critically ill, Father rode to Nursery Hill after Dr. Utley. But it was twenty hours before they could get back through the storm and when they did arrive Mrs. Clark had been dead more than an hour.

The funeral was held in our old house where almost everyone could attend. And to preach the funeral sermon Sime Phillips brought Reverend George Addison from Osborn. Sime went for him on a bobsled.

After the funeral and after Mrs. Clark was buried on their farm, Lucius Clark went back to his house with the Clark children, to keep house and care for the children and run his farm and to cobble boots for the community.

XI

In the spring of 1866 Ajax Harvey, then a member of the territorial legislature in Omaha, wrote Father a letter. Ajax had just heard from Major Brown and Major Brown was back home in Henderson, Minnesota, back from the Indian wars.

But Major Brown feared it would be some time before he could return to Nebraska and take up his plans for the steam wagon line. His resources were gone, wiped out by the red man's torch. He must re-establish himself in his home before he even could go to New York and seek to raise money for new steam wagons.

"I am starting action in Nebraska City as soon as I get home," Ajax wrote, "to try to raise backing for Brown here in the West. They have the Union Pacific tracks extended sixty miles now and they claim they'll be running trains as far as Fort Kearny before the summer is over. Of course the farther the railroad runs the more difficult it will be to finance the steam wagon. But I still feel there is going to be no end of trouble when the railroad workers get out in the Sioux country. Mac, I am

positive that we yet shall see our steam wagons crossing
the prairies.

"New crimes are being mounted upon the old crimes
of this railroad project. They are denuding the Missouri
valley of the finest black walnut timber in America to
split up into ties—timbers to which they spike the iron
rails. Black walnut is the finest furniture timber pro-
duced in North America and cottonwood would serve
almost as well for railroad ties.

"But the thieving works both ways. The government
sent a commissioner here to Omaha to inspect the track,
a man named Wendell. This public-spirited official had
to give his approval before the government would continue making loans. Wendell's report was to ensure
honesty.

"So, when he arrived in Omaha, Wendell informed
the railroad chiefs that he wouldn't stir toward inspect-
ing the work until he was paid personally $25,000 in
cash. I have it on the best of authority that the railroad
paid the blood money, so we can be assured that Wendell's report will be favorable."

Ajax enclosed a clipping from an Omaha newspaper
which read:

"Nebraska City is ahead now, to be sure, but just wait
two years until our Pacific Railroad is done and
Nebraska City can support only two or three shops to
supply a little country trade while Omaha will be the
greatest city in the West."

Ajax had scribbled on the margin, "We are to be anni-
hilated. Boo-hoo-oo-oo!"

Despite the long delay in the steam wagon business
and despite Omaha's bounding optimism, Nebraska City
was far from depressed at this time. Eighteen new brick
buildings were under construction in the city, including
a fine big courthouse on Main Street.

Steamboats were putting off more freight there than at

all other Missouri River points combined. In the previous year more than 100,000 tons of freight were carried westward from Nebraska City by wagon. More than 8,000 men were engaged in freighting from Nebraska City and they were using more than 7,000 wagons, more than 50,000 oxen and more than 7,000 mules.

And this increase in freighting business, naturally, brought an increase in our business on Medicine Creek.

Father had enlarged our old house and turned it into sort of an informal hotel and restaurant. He had put up another large building close by, which was a general store. In the store was the post office, for, with the assistance of Ajax Harvey, Father had obtained official recognition of our settlement as Macdougall, Nebraska, and got the appointment as postmaster.

In our immediate vicinity there were some 250 residents. Father had persuaded a young Nebraska City physician, Dr. Tom Andrews, to put up his shingle in our community. He did that a month before Eliza's baby girl, Laura, was born. There was a small weatherboarded Methodist Church presided over by a mild young man named Reverend Dave Dewitt, formerly of Council Bluffs, Iowa. And we also had a weekly newspaper.

Father was half owner of the Macdougall *Enterprise* and that came about in this manner:

One day early in the spring of 1865 a slim, blond young man and his equally slim and blonde young wife drove up to our old house bound for the Rocky Mountains. The young man said he planned to establish a newspaper in the gold fields. In his wagon he had an old hand press and a few fonts of type with which he expected to make his fame and fortune.

The young man introduced himself as Howard Sebury of Quincy, Illinois, and asked Father what the Indian situation was ahead.

Father shook his head. "Haven't heard of any outrages

in the last few days," he said. "But I declare I'd think it was pretty foolhardy to start out across the plains alone that way. You better wait here until some more emigrants come along and join up with them. I don't think it's safe to get out past Fort Kearny now unless you've got anyhow twenty wagons and a lot of armed men. Nebraska City *News* here says Abe Lincoln will take a hand in a few days now."

"How's that?" asked Sebury.

"Well, I've got the paper here. I'll read it to you. Wait a moment. . . . Here it is. Listen to this: '*Terrible! Indian Barbarity!*

" 'News reaches us that Indians near Julesburg have killed and scalped an American citizen of African descent. Heretofore they have only murdered common white folks and the government has treated them ever so tenderly.

" 'Now that the redskins have actually killed a nigger, we think Abraham will see palliating circumstances in Colonel Chivington's case and release him and order the aborigines to receive a tremendous threshing. The government will soon teach Mr. Indian that though he has, during the past few months, slain with impunity several hundred white persons, killing a nigger is a serious crime.' "

Sebury laughed a little.

"I think," said Father, "this piece was written by a man named J. Sterling Morton. His family owns the paper, but a good friend of mine named Harvey is the editor. I don't think Harvey wrote this piece because he knows too much about this Colonel Chivington."

"Who's Colonel Chivington?"

"He's the man mentioned in this piece. He's arrested up in Colorado for abolishing a tribe of Indians and I have a feeling he *ought* to be in jail. He used to be a preacher in Nebraska City, but he don't act the way I calculate a preacher should ought to act."

"How do you mean?" Sebury asked.

"Well, this John Chivington, this Reverend Chivington, had about a thousand mounted men and they gallop in on a sleeping town of Indians at a place called Sand Creek last winter along in the middle of the night. They killed about five hundred of the Indians, mostly women and children and old men, they tell me. Just a massacre. Caught them while they were asleep and unsuspecting and mowed them down. That don't strike me as any way to teach Christianity to Indians or anybody. I sort of give the government credit for arresting Chivington. He sent a report that they had a glorious victory, but I don't think that's the kind of glory he used to lead the congregation singing about."

Sebury shook his head. "No," he said, "I shouldn't think the government would stand for that sort of thing. But, you see, I'm somewhat in a hurry to get out there. Pretty soon now the soldiers will be mustered out and thousands of them will rush for the West. I want to get established before that happens. You really think it would be dangerous for us to drive alone to Colorado now?"

"Downright foolhardy," said Father. "The redskins will be wanting to get even for the Sand Creek affair, you can depend on that. Can't tell where they'll strike next. Last month they burned the telegraph office and the stage company warehouse in Julesburg. If you want to go to Colorado you better stay right here until you can join up with a party.

"But listen, young man, what you want to go to Colorado for? Right here is the coming country for a young man with get-up-and-git. Miners are an ignorant bunch. Good share of 'em I see going through here can't even read or write. What good will a newspaper do a man that

can't read? Whyn't you stay right here and grow up with
Macdougall, Nebraska? There's still fine homesteads
open within a mile or so of town. You and your wife
could take out a homestead and run the paper here in
town."

Sebury smiled. "Not much business here to advertise
in a newspaper," he objected.

"There's *going* to be a lot of business. And I'll tell you
what I'll do, young man. I always thought I'd like to be
connected with a newspaper. You settle here and I'll go
partners with you. I'll build a shop right near the hotel
here and you put in your machinery and we'll gather all
the news around the country on whose cow had a calf
and who is digging a well and who went to Nebraska
City and what freight trains went through and all that.
And we'll run advertisements on what I got to sell in the
store and I'll make other people advertise and we'll sell
the paper to freighters who stop and have a lot of fun,
and make money too. We'll advertise Macdougall, Nebraska, and make the town grow. Then, by grab, we'll
make a lot of money."

Young Sebury looked at his wife. She smiled. "Mr.
Macdougall," he said, "it's a deal. Shake hands with your
new partner."

So Father put up a little one-room shack for the newspaper office and helped Howard Sebury carry in his
Washington press and type cases and boxes of type and
bundles of paper.

The *Enterprise* was a small four-page paper full of
gossip and Father's opinions. For the first two weeks it
was given free to all the homesteaders. Then Father
virtually forced everyone to subscribe at a dollar a year.
And, using Father's methods of refusing to take no for
an answer, I sold two or three hundred copies each week
to freighters who stopped on Medicine Creek. The price
was five cents a copy.

Not only were there weekly advertisements for the "Macdougall House," as Father called our hotel, and for the "Macdougall Emporium," which was the name of our store, but Father saw to it that there were ads also for Sime Phillips, the blacksmith, and Dr. Jim Welch, the veterinary, and for Bill Watson's slaughterhouse, down the creek, and for Lucius Clark, the cobbler. Father never was able to convince Dr. Tom Andrews that he should advertise, however much he argued. He pointed out that often there was sickness and wounds among the freighters and that the freighters bought the *Enterprise* but that they naturally would think the nearest doctor was at Nursery Hill unless Dr. Andrews ran a small notice each week. But Dr. Andrews wouldn't listen. He said it was not ethical for physcians to advertise.

So the town of Macdougall grew and Bill Watson opened a butchershop right in town to sell the meat from his slaughterhouse. He put up a small building next to our store on a lot he rented from Father. And Father went into partnership with a miller from Minnesota named Frank Dunleavy. They dammed the creek below our homestead where the banks were high enough to make a millpond, and they built a small grist mill.

Then, when winter came and the millpond froze over, giving us the first skating we had seen since we left Canandaigua Lake, Father was not content. He expanded the partnership with Frank Dunleavy by providing the lumber while Dunleavy built an icehouse and cut and stored ice against the coming summer. The Macdougalls and Dunleavys, besides making a good profit on the ice we sold, also traded enough of it to Bill Watson to keep us supplied with fresh meat.

One warm evening soon after Father had got the letter from Ajax, I came in after helping Howard Sebury set type for the *Enterprise* and found Father sitting in the kitchen with his shoes off, reading the Nebraska City *News*.

Aunt Christine and Lucius Clark and Martha Nelson and Eliza and Mother were in our fine parlor. Mother was rocking little Laura to sleep and the others were busy with Aunt Christine's cherry table. Lucius Clark had formed a habit of coming over often in the evenings because Aunt Christine was bringing him messages purportedly from Mrs. Clark.

I went back to the kitchen. "What's the news, pa?" I asked.

"Well, by holy dang," said Father, "this is a disgraceful howdydo. They have a fight in the city between a wildcat and a bulldog. Dog's named General McClellan and the cat's named General Grant."

"The wildcat win?"

"Oh, by grab, they had the cat half tied up with chains, but he scratched the bulldog's nose and the dog grabbed the wildcat and the wildcat couldn't get his hind legs working on account of the chains and the bulldog killed it. That makes me mad."

"Well," I said, "you don't care so much for U. S. Grant."

Father looked at me scornfully. "That ain't got anything to do with it. I don't care much for General McClellan, either. What makes me mad is chaining up that poor wildcat. If they're going to have that kind of a fight, why don't they have it fair and square? If they admit in the first place that the wildcat can lick the bulldog, why have any fight? And if they just want to kill the wildcat, why didn't they shoot it? By grab, what kind of sweet-scented hairpins would pay money to go and see that kind of a spectacle? What's this country coming to, anyhow?"

"Anything in the paper about the steam wagon?" I asked.

Father shook his head. "Kind of discouraging," he said. "We come in here five years ago when it seems like it'll be only a few months before the steam wagons are running regular. We get all ready for 'em and spend lots of money getting fixed so we can take care of the business. And still they're just as far away as when we first came here. Farther, if anything. If it ain't one thing, it's another. I've got to go to Nebraska City pretty soon and see what's what. Got to see how they're coming with this business of raising money for Major Brown. Maybe I should ought to invest some myself. Was figuring on buying some land with spare money, but it might be a better idea to put it in the steam wagon, if I get a chance. We won't get anywhere out here until the steam wagons are running, that's certain."

"Well, listen, father," I said, "you're complaining over the way things are going, but it seems to me you're doing pretty good. You've got a town started and you own a lot of property all in five years. That's certainly better than if we'd stayed in York State."

Father slapped his big stockinged feet on the floor. "Ho," he said. "This ain't a circumstance. Of course we've been making a living by hard work and seeing that every sixpence does a shilling's job. But when the steam wagons get running we'll get rich and we'll have a *real* town here with lots of stores and saloons and what not. And they'll mostly be on my land because the town'll be mostly on this side of the road. Well, I calculate I'd better put on my boots and go down to see how they're making out with feeding the freighters. Business picked up a lot since we can feed 'em fresh beef from Bill Watson's."

Father stomped his boots on, put on his hat and left by the back door so he wouldn't have to pass through the parlor. I went in to see how the séance was progressing.

The table was thumping merrily in the dim light of one oil lamp.

"Shh." Eliza scowled at me and I sat down by Mother and poked my finger at the sleeping baby.

The table stopped thumping. "Well, my land," said Eliza, "can you imagine that?"

Martha giggled and I looked up to see Lucius Clark and Aunt Christine both blushing very red.

"What was it?" I asked.

"Oh, mother," Eliza cried. "It was Tom Brooks and he said—imagine this, mother—he said, 'Christine and Lucius could make each other very happy. It would make me happy to see them happy.' "

"Well, I declare," said Mother.

Lucius Clark and Aunt Christine snickered, but didn't say anything.

"Oh, I've got to go," said Eliza. "John will be getting home any minute now."

"Clinton," said Mother, "you go with Eliza and carry the baby and she can take a lantern."

"Dear me," said Martha, "I got to go and set my bread."

So we all went, leaving Aunt Christine and Lucius Clark in the parlor to work out their own destiny.

Eliza and I walked up the section line, she with the lantern and I carrying the sleeping Laura.

"First time," I said, "I ever heard of a spirit playing Cupid. Wonder if Aunt Chris or Lucius was making the table tip that way."

"Hush," said Eliza and giggled.

"Spirits have anything more to say about Casper Diercks lately?" I asked. "I thought Tom Brooks said Aunt Chris should marry Casper. Seems Tom has changed his mind or something."

"Looks that way, don't it?" said Eliza.

In Eliza's little kitchen she set the lantern down and

lit an oil lamp. Then she took Laura from me and I
picked up the lantern.

"*You* should ought to have some idea on this business," I said. "Who was making the table say those
things? Was it Aunt Chris or Lucius?"

Eliza laughed. "Hush," she said, "you'll make me wake
the baby. And I can tell you it wasn't either one of
them."

So Father and Mother gave Aunt Christine a fine wedding in the church and we had a big party in our house
later.

Aunt Christine looked almost like a girl in her bridal
veil and we all were happy that she at last seemed to be
happy. She took the cherry table over to Clark's with her,
but Father observed he didn't believe she would be using
it so much now.

"I calculate," he said, "that poor Tom Brooks may get
a rest after fifteen years and, God, he ought to be glad.
After you're dead and rightly could expect to get some
rest, it must be pretty rough to have to get up at all times
of night to go someplace and bump a cherry table
around. If I was Tom, I'd take a long trip to Jupiter or
Saturn or someplace and I'd be hard to find now if Chris
tried to call me up again."

This time Mother didn't scold Father for such a
speech. She just smiled. Perhaps Mother herself was getting a little tired of Aunt Christine's table tipping.

XII

As the railroad progressed westward the Indians became
more savage. Repeated attacks were made on engineering
parties and graders and in more than one instance workmen abandoned their jobs and refused to return unless
given ample protection by troops.

Fierce old General Grenville Dodge, who was in command of forces guarding the engineers, made demands again and again for more trained soldiers. As many workmen were standing by with rifles as were swinging picks and shovels, but these guards usually fled at the first approach of a Sioux war party.

Then the Indians began attacking not only the railroad workers but the old established stage stations, looting and burning everything at Fairview and Sedgwick, and General Dodge sent another warning to Washington.

"The mail will stop unless we get sufficient troops to put down these warring Indians," he telegraphed. "Men will not run these stage routes with scalping Indians along them unless there are troops to give protection."

So more troops were sent and the troops killed many Indians and the Indians killed numerous soldiers and the railroad construction went on.

Father said, "Biggest advantage of having the United States army out guarding the track is that the taxpayers foot the bill. The company gets the army free. They got to pay regular men for standing guard just the same as running a plow or scraper."

One day of that summer of 1866 Father went to Nebraska City for supplies and to see the new McCormick self-raking reaper and mower that was supposed to "mow, rake, reap and save all the grain." Father thought he should have the Macdougall agency for this marvel—if it actually worked as the manufacturers claimed.

Although I had much to do in our store and helping Howard Sebury on the *Enterprise,* I went along because I needed new clothes and boots. I was becoming more particular about my dress. Perry Lawson and Susie Striker were responsible for that. Perry Lawson was a young barber for whom Father had built a little shop next to the *Enterprise* office where he cut hair and shaved faces on Saturdays and five evenings a week. On Wednesday evenings Perry Lawson conducted a singing class in the schoolhouse and I had been taking Susie Striker.

So I was driving our beautiful new span of black Hambletonians to Nebraska City and Father was sitting next to me singing, "Darling Nellie Gray." When we mounted a rise and the old steam wagon came in sight Father stopped singing.

The steam wagon now was quite rusty. Dirt and gravel had washed up around its faded red wheels and a vine had twined up one of the huge drivers. The red roof was sunken and smeared.

"Giddap," said Father to the Hambletonians.

"You think they'll ever get steam wagons running over this road?" I asked.

Father looked at me with wide-open eyes. "Well, by grab, why not?" he asked. "Ain't they more practical than railroad trains in this country?"

"I guess they are," I said. "But it looks like they're getting that railroad built. When they get it finished they'll have to run trains over it, won't they?"

Father sniffed. "One thing to build a railroad in this country," he said, "and another to keep it built. What's to hold those Sioux from tearing up the rails and wrecking the trains?"

"Maybe they'll keep soldiers out along the track."

"Soldiers! They can't keep enough soldiers along the track to protect it for two thousand mile, can they? Suppose they put out only one soldier for every rod along the track for two thousand mile. How many soldiers would that take?"

I scratched my head with the butt of the whip. "Well," I said, "there's three hundred and twenty rods to a mile and two times three hundred and twenty is six hundred and forty. They'd need about six hundred and forty thousand soldiers."

"See," said Father. "And they're not going to send out six hundred and forty thousand soldiers just to keep that track nailed down."

"Maybe they wouldn't need a soldier for every rod."

"By grab, they'd need more than that. They'd need a round million soldiers to protect that railroad, they would. And they can't get a million soldiers for that—let alone pay for 'em. No, Clint, that railroad is one of the biggest follies in history. Unless they get some smart and honest men down there in Washington pretty soon this country is going bankrupt. I swanney, it's pretty near bankrupt now."

Our Hambletonians trotted in on Main Street past the nearly finished courthouse with its white-arched windows. They were building a high wooden cupola on top of the brick building and a scaffolding of raw boards was spiderwebbed around it.

In front of the courthouse a group of men were standing on the sidewalk talking excitedly. As we passed I heard one of them say loudly, "Well, they'll hang the son of a bitch right enough." On the corner another group was talking earnestly.

We drove around to Lambert's livery stable.

"Going to the boardinghouse or to the Seymour?" I asked.

"Well," said Father, "I calculate it ain't so good for a postmaster to go to a boardinghouse in the city. Calculate we'd better uphold the dignity and honor of the United States Post Office Department by going to the hotel."

Father had been paying more attention to his dignity of late. As a concession to dignity, he even had laid aside his gold earrings.

At the livery stable a cross-eyed youth named Jerry Van Buren took our horses by the bridles.

"Howdy, Mr. Macdougall. Howdy, Clinton," he said. "Hear they caught that Cash?"

"Who's caught what cash?" Father asked.

"That murderer. Caught him over in Iowa. Caught him in Plum Hollow, Iowa."

"Who'd he kill?"

"Gol, didn't you know? Killed a little shaver name of Willie Hamilton three mile southwest of the city. Oh, it's going to go hard with that fellow, I'm here to tell you."

"What'd he kill the boy for?" I asked.

"Well, this boy was herding cattle for his father and this Cash comes along and kills the boy and throws him in the creek and run off with the cattle. Druv the cattle here and sold 'em to a dealer name of Hays down't the lower end of town and then he took the ferry across the river. Another fellow with him. Hays didn't ever get the other fellow's name."

"I swanney," said Father. "You say they caught him?"

"Yep. They caught him, all right. Reckon they'll be bringing him back tonight or tomorrow morning."

We went to the hotel and all the clerk could talk about was the murder. The victim was eleven years old. When the boy failed to come home in the evening a searching party went out and found his body in a stooping posture in the creek, his feet buried in the mud. He had been shot three times—twice in the head and once under the right arm.

After we put our carpetbags in our room we went down to Steve Robinson's to find out something about the McCormick self-raking reaper and mower. But Steve Robinson could talk of nothing but Cash and his victim.

Steve had been listening to a man named Finch who had served on the coroner's jury at the inquest. The jury brought in a verdict that the Hamilton boy came to his death from pistol balls supposedly fired by a man named Cash. Finch, Steve said, was anxious to serve on another body—one that would hang Cash as soon as he was brought off the ferry. "They're talking lynch all over town," Steve said. "Wouldn't be surprised if that ain't what will happen. Well, it'd serve a dog like that right and proper."

We went to the *News* office and found Ajax with carpet-slippered feet propped on his desk.

"Suspect I'll have to get out and make a speech," he said. "Or maybe I'd better get Sterling to do it—he's a better orator. If a mob breaks loose and hangs this fellow without a fair trial, it'll just give Nebraska City a bad name. Just make more talk back east about the West."

"Yes," said Father, "I hear from emigrants all the time about how rough and dangerous it is out here. Well, back in York State I got forced into fist fights every little bit. Calculate I had a knockdown and dragout fight about once a fortnight on the canal. But I've been in the wild West more than five years now and I haven't had a single fight that you could call a fight. Maybe I have to shake up a drunk bullwhacker once in awhile, but that don't count. Nearest I ever come to having what I'd call a fight I regret I didn't have. That was out in Beatrice with that Duck Bill and Wellman. Should ought to have knocked the brains out of both— only I calculate Duck Bill didn't have any to knock out."

Ajax's eyes opened and he held up one finger. "Mac," he said, "I was reading a piece about this Hickok in *Harper's Monthly* the other day. I saved it at home for you."

"What'd it say?"

"Well," said Ajax, "it seems that Duck Bill goes under the name of Wild Bill now. He's been bullying around Kansas and has even been a marshal—in Abilene, I believe. It appears he's quick on the trigger and he's killed a number of outlaws—or a number of folks he *said* were outlaws. In this piece I'm speaking of he tells of killing the outlaw McCanles at Rock Creek stage station."

"Why, that son of a bitch," said Father.

"Called him McKandles, though," went on Ajax. "Spelled it with a 'K' and put a 'd' in the name. Oh, it was a great article. Hickok said he was guiding a party of Union cavalry south and had almost reached the Kansas line when he stopped to call on an old friend, a Mrs. Waltman, at the stage station."

"Wellman, you mean?" asked Father.

"No, he said Waltman."

"Well, great holy jeepers, Duck Bill wasn't in the army. He wasn't guiding any cavalry. He was a stable hand and had been working there five or six months."

"I know it. Hold your horses, will you? I'm just telling you what this magazine piece says. If you don't want to hear it, wait until tonight and you can read it yourself."

"Oh, go ahead. What did it say?"

"Well, Hickok says he went up to Mrs. Waltman's house and Mrs. Waltman came to the door and screamed, 'My God, Bill, run. They will kill you!'

"And Hickok says, 'Who do you mean will kill me? There's two what can play at that game.'

"And Mrs. Waltman, as he calls her, says, 'McKandles knows you're bringing that Yankee cavalry and he swears he'll cut your heart out. And right now he's out there back of the stable dragging poor Parson Shipley around the ground with a lariat around his neck.'"

"Ajax," said Father, "if you're making all of this up out of your head—"

Ajax held up his hand. "I swear before God, Mac. Of course I can't remember the words exactly as they were, but I'm giving you the sense of the article and probably just about as it was written. I've got a pretty good memory for that sort of thing."

"Well, hell's ablaze. What they mean—dragging poor Parson Shipley around with a lariat. There wasn't ever any parson down there. Dave McCanles was the nearest thing to a parson they had. He did the preaching on Sunday. And even if there *was* a parson, what'd anybody be dragging him around for?"

Ajax shook his head. "Don't think I'm trying to explain this thing. Personally, I imagine there's a liar someplace, but I'm only trying to tell you what this article said. I'm trying under the handicap of a great many interruptions.

"Anyhow, Hickok said just then the woman cried out that McKandles and his gang were coming up the lane and that he stepped into the house just as he heard McKandles yell, 'There's that blankety-blank Yankee, Wild Bill's horse. He's here and we'll skin him alive. Surround the house and give the devil no quarter.'

"So Hickok says he saw a rifle on the wall and he took that down and he laid his own pistol on the bed and just then McKandles stuck his head in the door. Hickok says, 'I yelled at McKandles, "Come on in here, you coward. Come on in and fight me." '

"Then he says, 'McKandles jumped inside the door with his gun level to shoot, but my rifle bullet went through his heart and he fell back out of the door still hanging on to his rifle.' "

"Dave didn't have any gun at all," said Father.

"Curious he wouldn't have a gun," said Ajax. "Why, Hickok says McKandles was captain of a gang of desperadoes and horse thieves and murderers who were the terror of everybody on the Kansas border. He said he knew them in the mountains where they pretended to be trapping, but really were hiding from the hangman."

"What sluff talk," said Father. "Dave McCanles never was in the Rocky Mountains in his life."

"Also," went on Ajax, "Hickok says he once threw McKandles at back-holt and threw him so hard that McKandles swore he'd get revenge."

Father laughed bitterly. "Dave could have thrown that half-wit with one hand."

"Well, wait a minute. You haven't even heard the start of this bloody battle. Hickok says the cutthroat McKandles had nine men with him and now all nine rushed through both doors at him. But Hickok had his revolver and he says, 'I never aimed more deliberately in my life. One, two, three, four—and four of the desperadoes fell dead.'

"But *that* didn't stop the gang. Two of them fired at him with shotguns and filled Hickok's hide with bird shot. Two more got in close to him with their eyes glaring at him out of the clouds of smoke and he knocked one down with his fist and shot the other. The others rushed in on him and threw him across the bed. One of these outlaws was choking him so Hickok casually broke his arm. You know—just snap, and broke his arm." Ajax snapped his fingers. "And Hickok got to his knife and fought the remaining outlaws around the room, cutting and slashing until they were all dead.

"Hickok admitted he was in pretty bad shape after that fight, though. Says there were eleven or thirteen shot in him and he was cut in eleven or thirteen places, all of them bad enough to let the life out of an ordinary man. But the doctor pulled him through safely after what he says was a siege of many a week in bed."

"Well, well," said Father. "Peculiar there wasn't a mark on him when I saw him three days afterwards. Peculiar that he seemed pretty healthy there at the hearing before that Judge Coulter."

"Oh," said Ajax, "did I ever tell you about that Coulter?"

"Don't remember you telling me anything."

"Well, Coulter was elected treasurer of Gage County only a few months after that affair. Don't remember just how long he served, but they finally arrested him for embezzlement of county funds. He escaped and made his getaway. Hasn't been seen since. Maybe he's down in Kansas with Hickok."

"That's no surprise to me," said Father. "But there's one thing I'd like to know. What was that Union cavalry doing while Duck Bill was fighting the whole Confederate army singlehanded?"

"That," said Ajax, "is something *Harper's Monthly* didn't take up."

Father looked at the floor,. "Well," he said finally, "there's one good thing, one almighty good thing about that piece. Nobody anywhere could read that and not know Hickok is a damn liar. It just don't ring true. When a murdering coward sets out to lie himself into a hero he generally spreads it on so thick *anybody* can see he's lying. Ain't that so?"

"Usually, Mac."

"Anyhow, he'd better keep out of Nebraska. If I ever hear of him in my territory, I'll run him down and wring his neck. That's what I'll do, by grab, I'll wring his neck."

"He seems to be a bad man with a pistol, Mac."

"Probably shot all of those men in the back. I'm not afraid of his guns."

"Neither was your cousin," said Ajax. "You'd better watch your step if you ever run across him."

"Well, I won't worry about that until the time comes. Anything more about Major Brown? How you making out raising money for the steam wagon road?"

Ajax shook his head. "Mac, it doesn't look very good.

Major Brown is back in the army. He's up at Fort Wadsworth, Dakota Territory, as Indian agent and chief of scouts. About raising that money—I don't know. The government certainly is behind this railroad business for all it's worth. Looks as if they're willing to throw everything behind it—the army as well as the treasury."

Ajax paused and shook his head. "Mac," he said, "personally, I'm convinced."

"You're convinced!" Father's jaw dropped. "Don't tell me you're convinced a railroad is better than the steam wagon?"

"No. No, I don't mean that at all. I'm convinced they're going to put the railroad through no matter what happens. I'm not saying they'll keep it running once it's put through, but I do believe they'll lay the rails to the Pacific coast now and I believe they'll run some trains to the Rocky Mountains—if not through them."

"Ajax," said Father, "you amaze me."

"No, Mac. You mustn't let your prejudices influence your judgment. We've got to keep our eyes open and be willing to admit it when we're licked. It isn't smart or anything to butt your head against a stone wall."

Father got up and stomped across the room. "By holy dang," he said, "here I settle out there in the wilderness, working and waiting for these steam wagons to get running for five years. Everything I do and plan for is hooked up with the steam wagons. I'm bending every tarnal thing in that direction. Practically everything I've been living for is to get my affairs arranged right so I can be a part of the steam wagon road. Now, just because there's a little difficulty, the whole thing will be thrown over. By grab, what ails you, Harvey? Ain't you even trying to raise some money? I know I'm willing to invest and there's probably hundreds just like me."

"Now what's the use of talking like that? You haven't lost anything on account of the steam wagon business.

You got right on the main freight road in an excellent location and, as near as I can figure, you've made yourself practically independent in five years."

"It ain't the money. It's the principle of the thing," said Father.

Ajax laughed and slapped his plump thighs. "All right, and you know as well as I do that the steam wagons would have been running years ago if it hadn't been for the Sioux breaking loose in Minnesota. And I'm not saying it's hopeless now. I *don't* think so. I still doubt a hell of a lot whether the Pacific Railroad can be made practical and profitable. The government can't keep pouring money into it. Well, it's our job to play a waiting game now. If the railroad is a financial failure and the government shows signs of getting tired of pouring more and more money into it, then we'll form a corporation with Major Brown, if he wants to come down, and if he doesn't want to, we'll buy his patents and form a corporation without him. Then we'll take the business from the railroad."

Ajax thumped on his desk with a forefinger. "Now," he said, "just suppose the railroad turns out to be successful."

"Just suppose the moon's made of green cheese," said Father.

"Well, all right. But, Mac, I'm only trying to tell you how fortunate you are. You don't know. Have you heard that the new capital is going to be somewhere in either Saunders, Seward, Lancaster or Butler county?"

"What of that?"

"There's a whole lot to that. And I can tell you that the new capital is going to be in either Lancaster or Seward and that it'll either be on the Steam Wagon road or very close to it."

Father looked at him with his jaw jutted forward. He plainly was not highly impressed.

"We Otoe County legislators," went on Ajax, "made a deal. Of course we were standing out to name the new capital Douglas City, so the federalists up around Omaha finally said, 'Well, we'll consent to moving the capital south provided it will be called Lincoln City.' They thought we'd balk at that, but we fooled 'em. The Otoe delegation held a powwow and we decided that, inasmuch as Lincoln is safely dead, we were willing to let the city be named for him—provided we got the city down here.

"Do you see what that means? No matter where the capital is located now, it'll be pretty near you. It's going to be laid out as the perfect city. It's going to be one of the most beautiful, if not *the* most beautiful city in America. Well, suppose the Pacific Railroad should turn out to be a success. Now, hold your horses. Just *suppose* it is. In that case, it wouldn't be a year before there'd be a railroad to Lincoln City—probably along the Steam Wagon route, right through Macdougall, Nebraska."

"Ajax," said Father, "you're getting old and soft and fat and you've lost your manhood and there isn't a lick of fight in you."

XIII

The next morning Father and I were out early and the town was electric with excitement. Crowds were hurrying east on Main Street at the report that Cash was being brought back. We joined the crowd and passed Benham's "Bull of the Woods" mule train with its fancy trappings pulled up at the side of the street. It was abandoned by practically all the freighters who had joined the throng, and there were twenty-four wagons, each drawn by four mules, and no one watching them except eight or ten half-grown boys.

Milling men and boys jammed clear across Main

Street and overflowed into the vacant lots and levee. The steamers *Majors* and *Omaha* were tied at the dock and their upper decks also were filled with people gazing across the river where Captain Bebout's ferryboat was steaming away from the Iowa shore.

A long-haired man with protruding blue eyes came running with a limp down the hill. He carried a coiled rope on his arm.

"I've got a rope with a hangman's noose all ready for the murdering bastard!" he yelled shrilly.

"Wait a minute, there," someone deeper in the crowd shouted. "Don't get so fast there with your God-damn hemp. I was here first with my rope."

"Where'll we string him up?" another shouted.

The long-haired man hitched himself hurriedly over to a cottonwood tree and threw his rope snaking over a limb. "Bring him over here!" he shrieked. "Bring him over here when you get him. Got the rope all ready." He stood looking up at the limb and pulling both ends of the rope to test its stability.

The ferry was waddling across the current, her stern wheel paddling up foam, a haze of wood smoke hanging over her smokestack. On the broad deck was a wagon and horses and a crowd of men standing closely around it.

It seemed that every one of the thousand or more men on shore was talking at once and the mumbling roar was almost frightening.

A small man with a high flaring linen collar climbed into an empty wagon and tried to talk to the mob, but his voice was lost in the general yammering confusion. No one paid any attention to him.

Father was holding tightly to my arm. "That fellow," he said, "is trying to talk some sense into 'em. Wait right here."

He elbowed his way to the wagon and vaulted up

beside the speaker, towering almost a foot above the
little man.

"Wait a minute, you!" Father bellowed and held up
his hands. His voice roared like a steamboat whistle and
the mob noise strangely diminished to a mumble. "Listen
to me a minute," he shouted, "before you do something
you're going to be sorry for."

"Who asked your opinion?" a voice called.

Father paid no attention. "There's a murder been
done and maybe somebody should ought to be hung
for it. That's all right if the right man is hung. It's
almighty wrong if the wrong man is hung."

"The posse is bringing back the right galoot," somebody cried, "and we're going to hang him higher'n Haman."

"Listen to me!" roared Father. "You think the posse's
got the right man. I hope you're right. But *I* don't know
and, by grab, *you* don't know. In this country a man's
supposed to have a fair trial no matter what crime he's
done. If you grab this fellow and hang him before he's
had any kind of a trial it's going to give Nebraska City
and all of Nebraska a bad name. And that's whether he's
guilty or innocent. If he's guilty he can be hung legal
and everything will be all right. If he ain't the guilty
man you're all going to be pretty damn sick if you hang
him before you find out certain. I don't know anything
about this fellow they're bringing across the river."

"Shut up then," somebody yelled.

"And," went on Father, "*you* don't know any more
than I do. All that I'm asking is that you calm down a
little and let the court decide whether this fellow is
guilty or not."

"Court takes too long," a man with a bushy red beard
shouted. "Suppose he breaks out of jail before the court
ever gets around to try him?"

"The courts do take an almighty time sometimes,"

said Father. "Well, why not make the court try this fellow right away? There's enough of you here and, by grab, I'd help you do that. Let 'em take that man right up to jail and then demand the judge to get a jury and start trying him right now. No sense waiting until the next session of court. If he's guilty you can find out today and he can be hung by sundown."

"This man's talking sense," the little man next to Father piped.

"You don't even have to wait for a regular judge if you don't want to," said Father. "Who is a judge, anyhow? He's just a man elected by the people to boss a lawsuit. You can elect a judge or a court president right here now. You can elect a special prosecuting attorney and a lawyer for the defense. They can pick a jury from among you folks and go right uptown and hold the trial in that park in front of the new courthouse. Then you can find out what's what."

Another man climbed laboriously into the wagon. He was a fat man with immense jowls and someone in the crowd yelled, "Hurray for Tod Wilson!"

"My friends and neighbors," said Tod Wilson, "I personally think it would be better to hold the prisoner until the next term of court."

"No! No!" the crowd yelled.

"But I certainly would prefer this man's proposal than an out-and-out lynching. If you want to do it the way this man says, I propose the name of D. J. McCann for president of the court. All in favor signify by saying aye, contrary nay."

There was a roar of ayes, then a scattering of nays.

"All right," said Wilson, "the ayes have it. D. J. McCann is elected president of the court. Mac, come up here and take charge of the meeting."

A wiry, middle-aged man with iron-gray hair pushed

through the crowd and climbed into the wagon amid cheers.

Someone in the crowd began to sing, "We'll hang killer Cash to a cottonwood tree!" and a score of other voices took it up.

"Wait a minute here! Wait a minute!" McCann shouted. "You elected me president of this proceeding, and if I'm going to be president there's going to be order. Shut off that singing there."

The singing ceased. "Now I want Dan Lauer for secretary. Where are you, Dan?"

"I'm here," a husky voice called.

"All right. You get up here with me and we'll all march uptown with the posse. We're going to conduct this thing calmly and deliberately. This is going to be a decent, honest trial and the prisoner is going to be given every chance to present his case—if he's got one. I'm going to put up some names of lawyers for you to vote on for prosecutor and defense attorney. Here comes the boat now, and I want you men to act like civilized American citizens. Mind you, now. And we meet in front of the courthouse after the prisoner is lodged in jail."

"We're with you, Mac!" a man yelled.

I looked over at the cottonwood tree and the lame man had pulled his rope down and was coiling it on his arm.

The ferry bumped into the dock and stevedores made lines fast. The gate opened and the posse of a hundred or more men armed with rifles and shotguns marched out grimly, surrounding the wagon. Six or eight more armed men were in the wagon around a disheveled, broad-shouldered man who seemed more embarrassed than frightened.

This man's ruddy face looked strangely familiar to me. Father came down from the empty wagon and I took hold of his arm as the crowd jammed forward to follow the posse and prisoner. The morning was getting hot and in the close-packed ranks of the crowd above the odor of perspiration there also was a curious smell of excitement.

I stared again at the bareheaded prisoner in the wagon. He was tight-lipped and looking straight ahead, apparently oblivious to the shouts of the crowd. Every now and then a cry would go up—"You murdering bastard, you're going to find out!"

"Father," I said, "I think I've seen that fellow Cash someplace before."

"Yes," he answered. "He's Casper Diercks."

"Holy jeepers," I said and looked again. Then I saw he really was Aunt Christine's Casper. A somewhat older and heavier Casper Diercks, but unmistakably it was he.

"Did you know—before?" I asked.

"No. I'm glad I did what I did, though."

"Do you suppose he killed the boy?"

"Can't tell. He's a clever fellow and I'd hate to think so. Wish they could wait to hold his trial until the excitement has petered out. But I suppose he's lucky not to get hung right down there at the river."

The crowd followed the posse to the jail, and when Casper was locked up and twenty men stood guard outside, the crowd assembled again on the grass in front of the new courthouse.

From somewhere men carried up a large table. Others brought a score of chairs and as McCann and Lauer sat down behind the table a man brought two yellow-backed lawbooks and deposited them on one end of the table, apparently to make the proceedings look official. Another came up with a large Bible which he placed on the other end of the table. Still another had an umbrella which he opened and lashed to the back of McCann's chair to protect him from the blazing sun.

A dozen chairs were arranged for the jury in two rows to McCann's right and more were placed in front for the counsel.

Carpenters working on the courthouse cupola left their scaffolding and came down to join the crowd, which now filled the park and blocked the street.

McCann pushed his umbrellaed chair back and stood up. "My friends," he said, "we are going to conduct this trial in an orderly, legal and fair fashion. We are going to give the prisoner, Cash, a fair trial. I want you people to regard this as a regular courtroom and to conduct yourselves accordingly. Now nominations are in order for prosecuting attorney."

"Mr. President," a loud voice called, "I want to nominate Phil Stevens."

"Second the nomination," another shouted.

"The nomination of Phil Stevens has been made and seconded," said McCann.

"I move the nominations for prosecutor be closed," the first loud voice said.

"Second *that* nomination," another yelled.

McCann smiled and the umbrella brushed the back of his neck as he stepped back. He moved the chair farther away. "All right," he said, "all those in favor of Phil Stevens for prosecuting attorney say aye."

There was a roaring chorus of ayes.

"Contrary nay."

Two or three weak nays responded.

"All right. Phil Stevens will prosecute. Phil, you'd better come up and get your witnesses and all together. Now, it's within the province of the court to name an attorney for the defense, and the court nominates Fred Bacon as defense counsel. Any objections to Fred Bacon?"

"No!" a dozen voices yelled. "Bacon's all right."

"Don't you think," Father called, "that the prisoner should ought to have a chance to pick his own lawyer?"

"My friend," said McCann, "there's no better lawyer in the territory than Fred Bacon. Not knowing our legal talent, the prisoner isn't competent to pick as well as this court. Bacon will do everything in his power for the defendant. You can count on that. Now, Fred, you'd better go back to the jail and confer with your client. The court will now recess for thirty minutes to allow counsel time to prepare their cases."

XIV

Before the recess was over carpenters who had been working on the cupola carried a pile of timbers and new lumber to the west side of the little park, eight or ten rods from McCann's table, and were digging holes in the turf and sinking the timbers. They were aided by numerous willing hands.

When the half hour was up Fred Bacon, a dapper little man with a gray stovepipe hat, came around from the jail followed by a guard of a dozen men armed with rifles. The guard surrounded Casper Diercks, whose ankles were bound together with heavy clanking leg irons and whose wrists were manacled with big hand-cuffs. In jail Casper had found time to comb his long hair and to smooth his wrinkled clothing a little, but he still was unshaven and weary-looking.

The guards pushed Casper into a chair and stood in a semicircle back of him with their rifles resting on the ground. Bacon brought up a chair and sat next to Casper while Phil Stevens, the prosecutor, seated himself in a wobbly chair a few feet distant.

McCann pounded on the table with a carpenter's hammer and the crowd pushed in closer. McCann now was sitting in the umbrella-shaded chair. "This special court," he said, "now is in session to try John Doe Cash on charges that he did with malice aforethought and with felonious intent willfully kill and murder one William Henry Hamilton in Otoe County, Nebraska Territory, on August fifteenth, eighteen sixty-six."

"Your honor," said Fred Bacon, standing up, "I move that this indictment be dismissed as not applying to this defendant, whose name is not John Doe Cash, but Casper Diercks, and on the grounds that there is no whit of evidence connecting this defendant, Casper Diercks, either with John Doe Cash or with the cause before the court."

"Motion overruled," said McCann. "The secretary will amend the indictment to read John Doe Cash, alias Casper Diercks."

"Your honor," said Casper in a clear voice, "I wish to protest the unseemly haste with which this so-called trial is being conducted. To me, at least, this case is of paramount importance, and I wish time to assemble my witnesses and to prepare my defense."

"Your attorney," said McCann, "will make the motions for the defense."

"All right, your honor," said Bacon, "I move for a continuance of this case to give us time to assemble witnesses for the defense and time for prejudicial passions to subside. I protest that this court is not an authorized court, that this court was not selected in a legal election by a majority of the electorate of Otoe County, that any action of this court cannot possibly hold the status of legal jurisprudence."

"Motion overruled," said McCann. "The defense has had as much time to prepare its case as the prosecution."

"The defense saves exceptions to the court's rulings," said Bacon, "and I move that at least those jury chairs be moved to face the other direction on grounds that sight of those workmen erecting a gallows would be prejudicial to the defendant."

"The court," said McCann, "will grant that motion. Will some of you men move those jury chairs over there to face east instead of west?"

Twenty men pushed up to move the dozen chairs. And by this time the carpenters had two tall six by six timbers erected with a cross timber nailed across the top.

"All right, Mr. Lauer," said McCann, "call off some names for jurors."

Lauer called a dozen men up who swore to judge the case on its evidence and they were seated in the chairs for examination by Stevens and Bacon. The prosecutor excused one man because he had once served a jail sentence for stealing chickens and another because the man expressed himself as unalterably opposed to capital punishment. Bacon excused one because he declared himself satisfied already of the accused's guilt. Both lawyers accepted the three new men called up by the secretary.

Then McCann thumped on the table with his hammer. "The court," he said, "would like to call the attention of all, and particularly the attention of the defendant, that the jury which will decide this case is composed of old and influential citizens of Nebraska City. Every man on this jury has a high standing in the community. That in itself is assurance of a fair and just trial and verdict. You may proceed, gentlemen."

Stevens rose to address the jury, but the carpenters were making such a racket with their battalion of hammers that he had difficulty in making himself heard. He turned to McCann, frowning.

"May I ask the court," he said, "to do something about that noise? To order those workmen to halt their activity on that gallows until after the trial? After all, your honor, I can't make myself heard."

"Motion granted," said McCann. "Bill, will you and John tell those carpenters to hold up on that hammering until after the trial is over?"

The guards pushed their way through the crowd with their rifles and presently the hammering ceased.

Then Stevens went on with his opening address, saying that the prosecution would prove the Hamilton boy was slain with premeditation by Casper Diercks, alias Cash, and that the purpose of the murder was to steal cattle the boy was herding, that the prosecution would demand the death penalty for this crime.

Henry Hamilton, father of the dead boy, was called to take the witness stand, and he told of his son failing to return home and discovering that both boy and cattle were missing. He brushed tears from his eyes with the backs of his gnarled hands as he told of identifying the body, and he told of identifying the cattle then in the corral of Bert Hays in Nebraska City.

Bacon cross-examined. "Mr. Hamilton," he asked, "had you ever seen this defendant before today?"

"No. But I wish I'd had a gun and seen him two days ago."

"I object to the witness's last statement, your honor," said Bacon.

"All right," said McCann. "The jury will forget about Mr. Hamilton wishing he had a gun and all."

Then members of the searching party told of finding the child's body sunk in the creek with his feet buried in the mud. But none of them had seen Casper Diercks before except Floyd Gunther, who had been a member of the posse and naturally had seen him at the time of the arrest in Iowa. Gunther said Casper had no firearm in his possession when apprehended at Plum Hollow.

Dr. J. C. Campbell told of examining Willie Hamilton's body and finding three bullet wounds, any one of which would have caused death. And he, questioned by

Bacon, said he never had seen Casper Diercks before and that he personally knew nothing which might connect the defendant with the murder.

Then Bert Hays, the cattle dealer, was called to the stand and he identified Casper as the man who had driven in the Hamilton cattle and sold them as his own. "Another man was with him," Hays said. But he declared the other man remained in the background and gave no name. Casper had said his name was John Cash.

"The prosecution rests," said Stevens.

Fred Bacon then made his opening statement to the jury. "There seems," he said, "to be some evidence here of cattle stealing, or at least of receiving stolen property against the defendant. But receiving stolen property or even cattle stealing is not murder. I insist there is not one scintilla of evidence to prove that Casper Diercks murdered the little Hamilton boy and I ask you to protect the fair name of Nebraska City and Nebraska Territory by not giving way to your passions and prejudices and to mob excitement. I urge you to acquit this man of the charge of murder. The cattle stealing crime is another charge. He can be tried on that later in a regular court of law."

Bacon then called Casper to the stand.

"Did you kill William Hamilton?" he demanded.

"No," said Casper in a loud voice.

"Did you ever see the boy, William Hamilton, in his lifetime?"

"To my knowledge, no."

"Were you ever on the land of Henry Hamilton, the father of William Hamilton?"

"I suppose I was."

"Did you drive off some cattle that did not belong to you and bring them to Nebraska City?"

"Yes. I sold them to Hays."

"Was there a boy herding those cattle when you first saw them?"

"No. There was nobody herding them. That's why I took them. I needed money desperately."

Bacon waved his hand at Stevens and the prosecutor rose, sneering at Casper.

"You admit you stole Mr. Hamilton's cattle?" he asked.

"I stole somebody's cattle. I suppose they were Mr. Hamilton's."

"And you didn't kill the boy?"

"No, sir."

"Who do you suppose did kill Willie Hamilton?"

"I have no idea. I never saw the boy at all."

"That's all."

"Your honor," said Bacon, "in this short time I have been unable to assemble any other witnesses for the defense. If the court will not grant us a continuance, the defense will be forced to rest."

Father elbowed forward. "Wait a minute," he called.

Stevens, Bacon and Casper turned. Casper's eyes opened wide as he recognized Father. Otherwise his expression did not change.

"Do you know anything about this case?" Stevens asked.

"No," said Father. "But I know something about this prisoner and I hate to see a man in a place like this without a soul to say a word for him."

Bacon stepped up to Father and put out his hand. "What's the name?" he asked.

"Jack Macdougall, postmaster of Macdougall, Nebraska."

"Will you please take the stand, Mr. Macdougall?"

Father was sworn and seated himself in the witness chair. He took off his hat and wiped his perspiring forehead with a blue handkerchief.

"Will you please, Mr. Macdougall," said Bacon, "tell

us what you may know about this case and this defendant?"

"Don't know anything about the case, except what I've
heard. All I know is that Casper Diercks stayed at my
home for some days once when he was held up by high
water, and that he seemed like a clever, honest fellow.
Was on his way to Colorado for the gold mines and was
held up by high water. One of the last men in the world
I'd ever pick for a murderer. I'd say he was a man you
could trust."

"You know anything about his family?"

"No. He said he came from Holstein, Germany."

"And you say he's one of the last men in the world
you'd pick for a murderer?"

"That's right."

"That's all, Mr. Macdougall."

Father started to leave the chair.

"Just a minute, Mr. Macdougall," said Stevens, "didn't
you make a speech to the crowd this morning down at
the ferry landing?"

"That's right."

"You urged the people to give this man a trial and
not lynch him?"

"That's right."

"Well, that's very commendable, Mr. Macdougall. But
if my memory serves me right you declared down there
that you didn't know the prisoner."

"Well, yes, I did, but—"

"All right. Now you say you do. It seems as if you
have considerable interest in this case, Mr. Macdougall."

"By grab, I don't like that insinuation. They said the
prisoner's name was Cash. I didn't know he was Casper
Diercks until I saw him in the wagon."

"You got up there and pleaded for this man without
knowing he was an old friend of yours?"

"That's exactly right, by grab. And—"

"But you really don't know very much about this Diercks or Cash or whatever his name is?"

"I got pretty well acquainted with him while he was at my house."

"How long ago was that?"

"I disremember exactly. Must have been four or five years ago."

"And you haven't seen him since that time? Or have you, Mr. Macdougall?"

"No, I haven't."

"You're sure of that. Well, Mr. Macdougall, where were *you* on August fifteenth?"

"I was at my home at Macdougall, Lancaster County, Nebraska."

"You could prove that, I suppose?"

"Why, damn your eyes, of course I can prove it! What do you mean—"

McCann hit on the table with his hammer. "Careful, Mr. Macdougall," he warned.

Stevens grinned. "May I ask this, Mr. Macdougall," he soothed. "Would you have picked this Casper Diercks for a cattle thief?"

"Not by any means."

"You were surprised to hear the defendant admit he stole the cattle?"

"Yes, I was. Surprised and shocked."

"And you're more surprised and shocked to learn that he killed a little boy in order to steal the cattle?"

"I can't believe he did it," said Father.

"That's all, Mr. Macdougall," said Stevens.

Then Stevens made a stirring speech to the jury, demanding death for the "worst cold-blooded murderer ever to enter the territory," in order to serve warning to other criminals to stay away from Nebraska.

And Bacon pleaded with them not to take a fellow man's life while there was a shadow of doubt of his guilt.

And he urged them not to be influenced by the excitement of the moment and to be calm and deliberate as they considered their verdict. And as Bacon closed his talk a man on the outskirts of the crowd yelled, "Hang the son of a bitch and get it over with!"

Casper looked around at that and his lips tightened and muscles worked along his jawbone.

McCann hammered on the table. "The jury," he said, "can go up there in the courthouse corridor to deliberate."

So the jury got up, looking self-conscious, and filed up to the new courthouse and inside the door. Within five minutes they filed out again and came down to their chairs.

"Gentlemen," said McCann, "have you reached a verdict?"

"We have," answered a brown-bearded man with a broad-brimmed straw hat on his head. He cleared his throat and then spoke loudly. "We reached a verdict and we found the prisoner guilty of murder in the first degree. That means hanging, don't it?"

I looked at Casper and he didn't move.

"Yes," said McCann, "it means hanging. John Doe Cash, alias Casper Diercks, stand up."

Casper stood up, his leg chains clanking.

"John Doe Cash, alias Casper Diercks, it is now the duty of this court to sentence you to be hanged by the neck until you are dead, dead, dead, and may God have mercy on your soul."

Casper bowed and sat down.

"Let's hang him now!" someone yelled.

"Naw. The gallows ain't finished yet."

"Hang him to a tree. What the hell you need of gallows?"

"No. Hang him right. Hang him from the gallows."

A slim man in a long black coat had moved up by the

table and McCann beat on the table with his hammer. "Quiet, quiet, there!" he demanded. "Reverend H. F. Davis of the Methodist Church has got something to say."

The preacher turned to the crowd and held up his hands.

"I beseech you," he said, "to be calm in this sorry moment. If the law says a life must be exacted for a life, I can say nothing about that. But at least you can grant this poor wretch a few hours to make his peace with God. If this execution must take place, let it be as orderly as possible. I beg of you to give him until six o'clock this evening at least. Give him this little time, my neighbors, for prayer and repentance."

"Mr. President," a man called, "I move we hang this son of a bitch immediately if not sooner."

"Second that motion," another shouted, and a roar of cheering followed.

"It has been moved," shouted McCann, "it has been moved and seconded that Diercks be hanged immediately and not be given a chance to make his peace with God."

"He never gave the boy a chance to make his peace with God, did he?" a man yelled.

"All in favor of the motion signify by saying aye," called McCann.

There was a roar of ayes.

"Those in favor of not hanging Diercks until six o'clock and making this an orderly, civilized execution signify by saying nay."

The chorus of nays seemed to outroar the ayes.

"Take the prisoner back to jail until six o'clock," said McCann. "Court's adjourned."

Casper was led clanking away and the catcalling, howling mob began to spread. Immediately the hammers took up their pounding on the scaffold.

"By grab," said Father, "this is awful. I need a drink."

"So do I," I said.

Father looked at me. "Clint," he said, "I always declared I'd lick you if you started drinking before you're eighteen at least. But this is for medicine and you're bigger'n an eighteen-year-old cub has any right to be. Let's go to a barroom."

Thus, with Father, I had my first drink of whisky. And I didn't like it. The barroom was very crowded and noisy with members of the mob. Father took three quick drinks of whisky and then we went around to the jail to try to see Casper.

On the street we ran into Ajax Harvey and told him our mission.

Ajax nodded. "The poor wretch will be glad to see somebody he's known," he said. "I was just talking with him and I can get you in the jail, I think. Reverend Davis and Fred Bacon were with him and Bacon just drew up Dierck's will. He's leaving a thousand dollars to Davis's church and twenty-four hundred to a brother in Philadelphia and two thousand to a Nebraska City woman named Jenny Graves."

"Who's Jenny Graves?" Father asked.

"Prostitute he's been living with."

"By holy dang," said Father, "Christine better not find that out."

"She kind of sweet on him?"

"I should remark. They were going to get married. Then he just quit writing from Colorado."

Ajax whistled. "She don't know how lucky she is."

"I should say not. Well, she's happy married now, so she wouldn't take it so hard. But I calculate we'll tell her the hung man was named John Cash and we won't let her read the Nebraska City *News* when it comes. She and Clark read our copy of the paper, but we'll lose this one."

"Good idea. Well, Mac, I was late getting down to the

dock and I only heard the end of your talk to the mob. But others told me all about it."

"I thought I was doing the right thing."

"Well, I was impressed by how you handled 'em. I never could have done it, I know. Of course we could wish for an orderly trial, a regular trial instead of that farce, but in the circumstances I suppose that was impossible."

"I calculated," said Father, "it was either that or a lynching."

Ajax pulled his side whiskers. "From the standpoint of the man's constitutional rights," he said, "that trial wasn't much better than a lynching. But at least it wasn't as bad for the city's reputation. That's something."

Father shook his head sadly.

"Oh, well," went on Ajax, "I don't suppose there's any doubt of this fellow's technical guilt anyhow—even if his partner may have done the actual killing."

Ajax led us through the crowd around the jail and introduced us to Sheriff Hail. The sheriff reluctantly unlocked the iron-barred door and permitted us to enter.

Casper smiled when he saw us. He rose and held out both his hands, which no longer were manacled. I took one and Father took the other.

"Jack Macdougall," Casper said huskily, "that was a fine thing you did for me when I deserved it so little. I'll go to my death thanking you for a kind act."

"Wish it could have had more effect," said Father.

Casper hung to my hand and kept squeezing it. "How's Christine?" he asked.

"Fine," said Father. "She's happy married to a good man named Clark."

"Oh, I'm glad. I treated her so scurvily. She's a fine woman and deserves happiness. Will she have to know about—about this?"

"No," said Father. "Pretty sure we can keep her from knowing."

"Oh, I hope you can. Maybe she could just think I was killed in Colorado or something. I really did love her, Jack, but I was unworthy. I have lived a very unrighteous life. I have sinned, but Reverend Davis here thinks I may be forgiven if I spend my remaining few moments of life in prayer."

Casper's blue eyes roved restlessly. His face was red.

"Well," said Father, "I calculate you want to get to your praying. Clinton and I wanted to come and shake hands with you and tell you you've got our sympathy."

"It was kind of you. God bless you both. And I do hope Christine never finds out." He seemed excited— almost elated with excitement.

"Good-bye, Jack. Good-bye, Clinton, and let my end be a warning to you. Never make the first misstep or the next one will follow easier. God bless you both and I hope I'll see you in heaven."

When we were outside the jail and beyond the crowd Father looked at me and raised one eyebrow.

"Don't seem much scared, does he?" I said.

"No," said Father. "You'd think he was sort of enjoying the attention he's getting. By grab, I need another drink. But you can't have any more, so let's go to the hotel and lay down for awhile."

We were back on the courthouse lawn a quarter of an hour before six and already at least two thousand persons were assembled around the bright pine boards of the scaffolding. From the crossbar a new yellow rope hung, swaying slightly in the breeze. In the end of the rope an elaborate noose had been tied.

McCann, Lauer and several other men were standing on the scaffold talking and once in a while admonishing some small boy who attempted to climb up on the platform. Guards with rifles stood around the rough stairs

on the south of the platform and now and then a guard
or one of the men above would take out a watch, open
it, take a quick glance and snap the case shut again.

A man near Father and me was talking loudly to several men and women.

"Naw," he said, "that's the pity of it. Don't hurt a
bit. That big hangman's noose goes behind the ear.
When he drops that knot snaps back hard and breaks
his neck clean as a whistle."

"I've heard tell," another man said, "sometimes it
don't work like that. I've heard tell sometimes their neck
don't break and then they just strangle to death slow."

"Just hope," said the first, "that this one will be like
that. I'd enjoy seeing a bastard like that strangle slow."

On the platform McCann looked at his watch, snapped
it shut and put it in his pocket. "All right," he called.
"You guards clear a way. It's time for 'em."

The guards pushed people with the sides of their rifles.
"Open up there. Clear the track," they kept saying.

And presently there was a commotion and a move-
ment of heads and at least twenty guards with rifles came
pushing along through the crowd and the clank of chains
could be heard and there was Sheriff Hail holding to
Casper on one side and Casper holding to the arm of
Reverend Davis with his other hand. The preacher
looked as pale as if he himself were to be hanged. Casper
looked almost cheerful.

Three guards went up the steps, then Casper, then
the preacher, then two more guards.

McCann held up one hand. "Quiet, please!" he called
to the crowd. "Quiet, please." He turned this way and
that repeating it. "I ask for quiet."

Then, as the crowd quieted, he spoke loudly: "John
Doe Cash, alias Casper Diercks, you have been convicted
of murder in the first degree and sentenced to death by

hanging to pay for your crime. Have you anything to say before you meet your Maker?"

There still were no manacles on Casper's wrists. He reached up one hand and took hold of the rope.

"Holding as I do," he said, "this rope which is to send me to eternity, I declare that I am guilty of the larceny of the cattle, but of the murder I am not guilty."

"Who killed the boy, then?" someone in the crowd shouted.

"I don't know," said Casper. "I suppose he must have drowned in the creek."

"Where'd the bullet holes come from, then?" another yelled.

"I suppose," said Casper, "the fishes must have eaten them."

That brought a chorus of catcalls and two guards seized Casper's arms and began to bind his wrists behind his back.

"I want to say this much more," went on Casper. "I have led an unrighteous, sinful life. I hope my sad fate here will be a warning to young men to mend their own ways lest they also sink step by step and die as I am dying on the gallows. May God have mercy on my soul."

McCann came up to Casper with a large handkerchief and started to blindfold him.

"No," said Casper, "I'll go to eternity with my eyes open."

Two guards placed the rope over his head and tightened the big noose back of his left ear.

Then Reverend Davis held up his hands, one holding a Bible, and in a quivering voice shouted, "I'm going to ask you, my friends, to join me in a prayer for the salvation of this poor sinner's soul.

"Oh, Lord, Jehovah, have mercy on this poor repentant sinner who is about to be gathered into Your fold. Unto You, O Lord, we commit his spirit. His ways have

been sinful, but he is repentant and he has been baptized
in the name of the Father, the Son and the Holy Ghost.
Forgive him his trespasses as we hope Thou wilt forgive
ours.

" 'The Lord is my shepherd; I shall not want. He
maketh me to lie down in green pastures: He leadeth
me beside the still waters. . . . Yea, though I walk
through the valley of the shadow of death, I will fear no
evil; for Thou art with me; Thy rod and Thy staff they
comfort me . . .' "

Casper suddenly leaned forward and gave a mighty,
frantic surge on the ropes that bound his hands. His
face was contorted and crimson. He leaped writhing into
the air and surged on the ropes again and again.

"Spring the trap!" shouted McCann.

A knife flashed. And with a crash the section of platform flooring that held Casper swung downward and
Casper swung down with it, still yanking hysterically at
his bound wrists.

The new yellow rope creaked screamingly as Casper's
weight thumped down and stretched the hemp and
Casper, with mouth open and eyes staring, contorted and
spun and danced.

I turned my back, sickened by the sight.

"Holy Christ," said Father, "let's get away from here.
Let's drive home *tonight*."

We walked hurriedly toward the hotel and the street
was almost empty. Two blocks down we came upon Ajax.

"You at the hanging?" he demanded.

Father nodded his head.

"I'm ashamed of you," said Ajax. "Did you enjoy it?"

"God!" said Father. "Let's get a drink."

We went to a saloon. "You know those bequests he
made?" asked Ajax.

"Yes," said Father, tossing off a glass of whisky.

"Well, Diercks didn't have a dime except what he got for the cattle, and of course that goes back to Bert Hays."

XV

In November of 1866 we held an election in our town, with Sime Phillips being elevated to sheriff, Chauncey Loud to town clerk, and Father mayor and justice of the peace. Father took these responsibilities seriously and henceforth rarely went out without boiled shirt and frock coat, except when hunting or doing a little work around the farm.

By the following summer, 1867, the Pacific Railroad tracks were laid to the borders of Nebraska despite Indian raids. That one season the enraged Sioux were reported to have taken more than three thousand white men's scalps on the plains.

Trains were running on the railroad more or less regularly from Omaha to the new town of Kearney, which was across the river and east of old Fort Kearny. For $19 one could ride from Omaha to Kearney in comparative comfort and complete the journey in nineteen hours—if all went well.

Old Fort Kearny had been ordered abandoned. The new railroad town was being spelled with a second "e" to distinguish it from the fort and its notorious Dobetown. This came about when General William T. Sherman came out fresh from his torchlight procession across Georgia to see what should be done about the Sioux. The conqueror rode through Dobetown and got hisses and boos instead of cheers. So Sherman telegraphed Washington that the fort should be abandoned. Thus the Dobetown wantons and bullies were made to pay for insulting a general. And thus a historic island of refuge was closed before its period of usefulness was over. From the time the railroad approached the Sioux country, Fort Kearny had been the last safe outpost. Troops required westbound freighters and emigrants to halt there until they had at least fifty wagons in their trains before moving into the danger zone.

In February, 1867, Nebraska was admitted to the Union and in July of that year a committee headed by Governor David Butler selected the site for Lincoln City on Salt Greek in Lancaster County.

Ajax Harvey was appointed to survey and lay out the Lincoln City townsite and frequently, while on this job, he came to visit us over the weekend and we would ride out for bird shooting.

On one of these visits Ajax told Father he should send me east for a formal education. "You can afford to give that boy a chance," he said.

Father shook his head. "Don't believe in too much education for a cub," he said. "Just spoil him for hard work, and this cub's got a lot of work ahead of him. He can cipher and write and tell you Columbus discovered America in fourteen-ninety-two and he knows the value of a shilling. What more can a man want of schooling? It's what he learns outside of a schoolhouse that does him good in this world. Give a cub a lot of fancy education and he'd likely set around with his nose in a book all the time like Chan Loud."

"You're wrong, Mac," said Ajax. "Life is getting more complicated and you need an education to compete with it. A good education is the best thing you can give a boy. It's going to be a lot more important for the next generation than it was for us."

"Clint'll get along all right," said Father. "When he's twenty-one I'm going to take him in partnership. It'll be the Macdougall and Son Enterprises then, and he'll never have to worry where his next meal is coming from. Couldn't spare him to be away to college two or three years now anyhow. Need him in the store. Need him in the printing office. Need him a lot of places. By grab, though, I wish he *did* know something about bookkeeping."

Ajax shook his head and grinned.

"If," went on Father, "he knew how to keep complicated accounts, I'd start a bank. Yes, sir, Macdougall needs a bank. Too much trouble going to Nebraska City all the time and it ain't safe keeping a couple of thousand dollars or so around the house."

Father looked at Ajax. "Harvey," he said, "maybe you're partly right for once. I don't agree that the cub should go way back east to learn what poet wrote which. But I *will* send him to the academy in Nebraska City to learn about bookkeeping. Then I'll start a bank. I'll be president and make Clint cashier."

So I went to the academy in Nebraska City and took a business course during the winter of 1867-68. And the next summer I was eighteen and cashier of the Macdougall State Bank.

The next year the Union Pacific Railroad was pushed across the Rocky Mountains and joined with the California line at Promontory, Utah.

Freighting by ox and mule team had been falling off alarmingly on our road ever since steam trains began moving from the Missouri River to the Rocky Mountains. And when the rails were opened clear to the coast, whole days would pass without a wagon train coming by Macdougall.

These were hard times. For a while Father was confident that the railroad never could continue to operate, that it would be closed in the face of the many difficulties confronting it, but when the hotel business dropped to a point where there was practically no business at all, he became gloomy indeed.

Then for some unknown reason, a spurt of traffic

would return to the old freight road and Father would
turn cheerful again. "We've just got to set tight," he
would say. "Business will be right back where it was in
a month or so. These shippers realize and know they
can't trust a railroad to get their stuff through."

Then the spurt would die down and Father would
pace around restlessly, having little to say to anyone,
until another flow of traffic developed on the road.

One morning after an especially long dull period,
Father stalked into the bank. He looked over the accounts and then sat down and gazed out the window for
a few minutes. Then he said, "Clint, it looks like the
government's going to keep that Pacific Railroad running in spite of hell and high water."

I looked up at him in surprise.

"Yes," he went on, "it looks that way. Don't matter
what it costs—just looks like the government's going to
keep it running—out of spite, if no other reason."

"Well, maybe so," I admitted.

"Freighting on this road's gone to hell in a hand-
basket," he said. "Yes, Clinton, you've got to look facts
in the face. No other way. Take my advice, boy. I've
lived longer than you and I've had loads of experience.
You *think* that you think freighting is coming back on
this road and that the railroad is going to peter out and
that we'll finally get the steam wagons running. But you
don't really think it, Clint. You just wish that would
happen and wishing it makes you think that you think
it's so."

Father shook his head sadly. "I know how it is with
you youngsters," he said. "You get counting on something and it's hard to give up when it's not coming, but,
as I say, you got to look facts in the face. Maybe because
I've had loads of experience I can see things that ain't
plain to you. And *I* can see this freight road is all
through and finished if the government's going to keep

that Pacific Railroad running, and it's getting plainer every day that the government is going to do just that. You know what that means, Clint?"

"Well," I said, "I don't know, but—"

"All right, I'll tell you. It means, by grab, that Macdougall, Nebraska, has got to have a railroad itself or it's going to dry up and blow away."

By 1870 Father was as ardent a railroad enthusiast as he had been a supporter of the steam wagon ten years before.

"Of course it costs a lot of money to build a railroad," he would say, "but you got to spend a lot of money to make a lot of money. Build a railroad and you've got something. You've got something real and something permanent. You've got a smooth track that you can run a mile a minute on, rain or shine, and it takes an almighty snow to hold up a steam locomotive."

This was about the time the Midland Pacific Railroad was being promoted to run from Nebraska City to Lincoln and Father leaped at the proposal like a hungry cat at a can of fish.

He went around the countryside talking to settlers, businessmen—everyone who would listen, beating down opposition by force of argument or sheer lung power.

"We *got* to get this railroad," he declared. "If we don't get it, this part of the country might as well fold up and die. Might as well give up our land and homes and business and move up north on the Union Pacific. By grab, we'll starve to death down here."

In 1871 the Midland Pacific was built from Nebraska City to the capital. And it passed through Macdougall, just to the north of the Steam Wagon Road, and they built a fine yellow depot just a few rods from our hotel on land purchased from Father. It seemed the natural thing for the railroad to pass through Macdougall on the way to Lincoln. And besides, Ajax Harvey was the surveyor.

Major Brown's old steam wagon still stood on the edge of J. Sterling Morton's farm, brown with rust and forlorn with its once-red wheels slowly sinking into the ground. When he was driving by there now along the Steam Wagon Road—as everyone called the old freight trail—Father would slap the lines and go past on a trot.

Once when he and Mother were driving to Nebraska City in our new surrey he flicked his whip at the steam wagon. "Wonder," he said, "how long they'll let that thing be an eyesore there?"

XVI

Soon after the Midland Pacific Railroad built its yellow depot and water tank, Father put up a grain elevator next to the track, just west of the tank. This tall, gray elevator, like most of Father's enterprises in Nebraska, proved profitable.

When trains began coming into Macdougall with shrieking whistles and clanging bells and with the metallic clicking of the telegraph sounding from the depot, our frontier home suddenly seemed no longer on the frontier. It was the railroad and the telegraph that made our community seem to be an actual town.

Here is a picture, as well as I can describe it, of the way Macdougall, Nebraska, looked at that time.

Our old house, now the hotel, had been enlarged to twice its former size. Once our guests had been the roughest of freighters and gold seekers who were glad to sleep on the floor. Now neatly dressed drummers complained over the accommodations in their separate rooms, which were fitted with real beds and mattresses.

In the days of the freighters the house had faced the

road, but with the coming of the Midland Pacific Father had a new and larger door cut in the back of the building, facing the depot. There now was a porch on that side and a slightly crooked sign reading "Macdougall House" above the porch. There was a hitching rack and a watering trough on the east side near where Mother's pansy bed used to be. All of Mother's flowers and plants were gone now, but the cottonwood saplings we had planted were grown to such a spindly height that their quivering leaves could be seen over the hotel roof.

Inside, our old living room now was the lobby and the addition on the west held a barroom. Except for Sime Phillips's open-faced blacksmith shop across Main Street (once the freight road), the hotel was the only log building in town, and its construction was only about half log.

West across Medicine Creek and opposite the hotel was Lucius Clark and Aunt Christine's old house, which now was converted into his boot and shoe store and cobbler shop. Their new white weatherboarded house was a few rods farther west.

East of the hotel and of the depot ran Coach Street. It was a graded road which Father had named for Coach Street in Canandaigua and, although now it had no sidewalk except a path of gravel and ashes, it bid fair someday to rival Main Street in importance.

Across Main Street south on Coach Street were the blacksmith shop and Phillips's new white house on the west. A few rods east of the street on Sime Phillips's land was the Methodist Church and the church horse shelter and privies. The church wasn't very big, but it had a respectable steeple and a bell which sounded very cheerful on Sunday mornings. Some cottonwood trees were making a good start in front of the church and there were shrubs and cannas set out in the yard. The church itself was painted brown and the congregation was fond of singing "Little Brown Church in the Dell," although this church was in no dell.

Going north on Coach Street, to the west there was our hotel, of course, and then the tracks and the depot with its freight and baggage platform extending clear up to the gravel sidewalk. Then there was a section of our orchard, which wasn't doing so well, and then Dr. Andrews's house which he had built on a lot he bought from Father. His house was small, but neat and white and with green shutters and two tall lightning rods.

On the east side of Coach Street, but fronting on Main Street, was the *Enterprise* office, where I often worked evenings helping Howard Sebury. The building was painted green and it had a tall false front which was supposed to make it look two stories high. It had "The Macdougall Enterprise" in big black gothic letters across the false front.

Just north of the newspaper office was Perry Lawson's barbershop with a new red, white and blue barber pole topped by a gilt ball. Perry had sent to Chicago for this pole and he was proud of it. He used to wash the dust and mud spatter from it with warm water and castile soap.

Then across the railroad track was Watson's butchershop with a board porch in front so ladies could get out of carriages and wagons there without getting their feet muddy. And beyond the butchershop was Father's big, unpainted shed where he kept his McCormick reapers and binders and other implements too big to stand on the floor of the Emporium. The south side of this shed was covered with bright posters of elephants and lions that a gang of men put up the year before when the circus showed at Lincoln City. That was all of Coach Street unless, of course, if you went on up the hill there was our new house with its gables and grilling and lightning rods and a horse block in front and a grass lawn and evergreen trees looking thrifty—the finest house for miles around.

But back on Main Street and going east, next to the *Enterprise* office was the bank where I put in most of my time.

Then, walking along the wooden sidewalk, you went up two steps and were in front of the Emporium, which covered as much space as the hotel and looked fully as high because of the false front. The Emporium was filled with everything from nails and hatchets to ladies' hats and from kerosene to coffins. There were three hitching racks in front of the Emporium and the sidewalk was high enough here so a woman could step easily from a carriage. Ole Bergstrom and Harry Phillips were working for Father at the Emporium together with a young man named Barney Black who came out from Nebraska City looking for a job.

After the Emporium there was nothing more on Main Street until you came to the school, which was sixty or seventy rods away and between the Emporium and the school there was a gully on Sime Phillips's land where people had taken to dumping old tin cans and other junk, despite a sign Sime had erected reading, "No Dumping Aloud."

West of the creek and south of the road, however, there was considerable business. First, there was Father and Frank Dunleavy's icehouse on the mill pond and then the mill and still farther south Bill Watson's slaughterhouse, which was very handy because you could stop there for a piece of liver for bait when you were going fishing at the slough.

That's all there really was to the town, although the whole countryside now was filled with settlers and there was absolutely no open land left for many miles.

These homesteaders made the business for our town and made it possible for Father to acquire three more farms. On speculation, he also had bought six town lots in Lincoln City (on Ajax Harvey's advice), one of which he sold a year later for twice what he paid for all six. So father felt rich enough to build a neat farmhouse for Eliza and John and to make John a present of a reaper and binder.

Father was forty-seven, but there was only a touch of gray at his temples and his waist had thickened little. He still walked with the spring of youth. Boundless vitality still snapped from his black eyes. And he kept me hustling, particularly at my work in the bank.

Father was immensely proud of being a bank president. It was a tossup whether he was prouder of being a bank president or of being mayor.

The bank itself was not much to look at. It was simply a small, one-story wooden building with a false front and a fancy scrolled sign on the Main Street windows reading "Macdougall State Bank" and iron bars on the side windows.

Inside the main room we had a counter topped by an iron grilling. There was one teller's window in the grilling with gilded bars and an opening at the bottom about five inches high. The counter stretched more than three-quarters across the room and then a wooden railing met the counter and ran back to the rear wall. There was a hinged gate in the railing.

Behind the counter and railing we had our big iron safe that required two keys to unlock, and my high desk and bookkeeper's stool where I wrangled with figures and wished I had learned more at the academy and where I also attended to business at the teller's window.

Father had an office in the rear room where he kept all his accounts and where in a smaller safe we kept our farm mortgages and other paper.

Early one hot afternoon when I was busy over my

ledger, Father came into the bank and went directly to his office without entering the railing gate.

I had been to a dance the night before with Susan Striker and I felt drowsy working in the afternoon heat. As I wondered vaguely what Father was after, there was a clank of spurs on the floor and I looked up to see a tall, broad-shouldered man entering the bank. He was dressed as a cowboy, with broad-brimmed hat, overall legs tucked into his boots and a cartridge belt around his waist. Beyond that I did not notice, except that he did not stop at the teller's grilled window, but came around to the far side of the railing.

I got down from my high stool and the seat of my trousers stuck briefly to the hot varnish. I jabbed my pen into the metal holder and walked to the railing.

"How do you do," I said.

The man's face was deeply sunburned and his long, arched nose had been peeling. As I spoke he flashed a big white-handled revolver into my face.

"All right, sonny," he said, "open that safe and be God-damn quick about it. I want gold—none of your greenbacks."

"But—" I began.

"If you want to live, open that safe."

I remembered we had about $12,000 in gold in that safe and also several large sacks of silver dollars. I wondered if I could work off the silver on the robber and I looked at him and his blue eyes were cold slits and dangerous. The hammer of the long-barreled revolver clicked back and I went over to the big iron safe. I fumbled in my pocket for my key ring and took a quick glance at the back room, hoping Father would not come out.

I wished now that Father had not been so contemptuous of revolvers. I wished he had a gun with him so he might shoot this fellow while I busied myself with the safe locks.

But I knew Father had no firearm at the bank and I knew too if he heard this robber his impetuosity might lead him to do something rash and to get shot. I must work quickly, give this dangerous man our money and let him escape.

I knelt before the safe and the sweat ran down my forehead and dripped on the floor. Putting the first key in its keyhole, I turned the lock. The man was standing right behind me and I sensed the revolver was trained on the back of my head.

There was a quick scuffing sound and I turned my head to see Father vaulting over the railing, his long, black-clad legs spread. His black coat and tan waistcoat were off and his white, stiff shirt bosom gleamed in mid-air.

The robber whirled and his spurs jingled. His gun roared deafeningly and I scrambled to my feet just as Father's boots banged on the floor and his big right fist, swinging in a lightning arc, smashed into the man's face. The gun's roar, Father's feet hitting the floor and Father's fist hitting the robber came one, two, three, as fast as one would clap his hands.

The bandit hurtled backward violently and his head struck the iron safe with a sickening crunch. He quivered slightly on the floor, but I knew he was dead.

With feet spread far apart, Father stood panting and stroking his knuckles. He stepped closer and bent down peering at the grimacing face on the floor.

"Oh, jeepers," said Father. "Oh, holy Christ! It ain't him at all."

I looked down. The man's forefinger was looped in the white-handled revolver's trigger guard, but the gun itself was out of his hand.

"Ain't him?" I said. "Who? He's a bank robber. He was trying to rob our bank."

"I know that, all right. But I wouldn't have hit him that hard for it. I just saw the side of his face from the door. Just saw that nose and the side of his face. I'd have sworn it was Duck Bill Hickok."

"No," I said, *"that's* not Duck Bill Hickok."

"I can see it ain't now. But I'd have swore it was just from the side."

"Well," I said, "he was trying to rob the bank, anyhow. And it's a wonder he didn't shoot you—jumping in like that at a man with a cocked revolver."

"He *did* shoot me," said Father.

"What!" I looked and saw the red blood staining his white shirt at the side. "O God, father. Sit down there and I'll run for Doc Andrews."

Father sat down. "Don't think it's bad," he said. "Don't feel bad except for a stinging in my side. Almighty lot of blood running down, though."

Several men came tearing in the door, attracted by the shot. Among them were Howard Sebury and Paul Henderson, who worked for Howard on the *Enterprise* next door.

Howard sent Paul running for Doc Andrews.

"Better get Sime Phillips in here too," said Father. "He's sheriff and he'd better be looking over this bank robber. By grab, I'd never taken a chance like that with a plain bank robber. I'd have sworn it was Duck Bill."

"Who's Duck Bill?" Howard asked.

"Old friend of mine," said Father. He squinted his eyes and looked at his hand. "I swanney, I've busted my fist. Look there. That knuckle's pushed clear back. Never hit anybody that hard before."

"I'd hope not," said Howard. "But this one had it coming to him. You're a hero, Mac."

Father laughed and blood dripped from his saturated shirt to the floor.

I got a dipper of water and Father drank deeply. "Maybe you'd better go get me a good snort of whisky," he suggested.

"Oh, no," said Howard. "Wait until Doc Andrews gets that blood stopped. Whisky would only make it bleed faster."

"Maybe so."

It really took only a few minutes, but it seemed an hour before Paul Henderson came back with Doc Andrews and Doc got Father's soaked shirt stripped off.

Doc Andrews sponged off the blood. "You're not hurt so badly," he said.

"Who said I was?" demanded Father. "But there's no sense setting here and bleeding to death, is there?"

"Mostly a flesh wound," said Doc Andrews, "but you've probably got a cracked rib. Bullet hit you glancing and bounced off the rib."

"What a man," observed Howard Sebury. "Even bullets bounce off him."

Doc Andrews cauterized the wound after cleaning it and was bandaging Father's body when Sime Phillips came in the bank.

"Hey, Sime," called Father, "we've caught a bank robber for you. What's the good of having a sheriff if the citizens got to do the sheriffing?"

Sime's eyes opened wide. "God, Jack," he said, "you get hurt?"

"Just shot a little. When you going to get that dead bank robber out of our bank? He reminds me of somebody I don't like."

Sime scratched his head. "Gol," he said, "I can't very well put a dead man in jail. It ain't a sheriff's job to look after corpses. That's a coroner's job and we got no coroner."

"Howard," said Father, "as mayor I appoint you coroner."

Howard Sebury scratched his nose. "No, thanks," he said. "That's one public office I've got no wish for. I don't care for dead people. But I'll be coroner pro tem long enough in this case to hold a quick inquest and declare John Bandit Doe came to his death by butting his head into an iron safe during the commission of a felony."

Doc Andrews laughed. "Guess that'll cover it," he said. "Now, listen, Mac, you go home and lie up in bed for a couple of days. There's going to be a shock from this wound and you don't want to take cold in it."

"Go to bed for a little nick like this? What're you talking about, man? I've got business to look after, if some of you fellows will kindly carry that corpse out of here. Tired of looking at him. Ouch!" Father looked at his right hand. "Doc, can you do something about that?"

Dr. Andrews pushed the knuckle back in place as best he could and strapped up the hand on a shingle. Then Father went back into his little office and some of the men carried the dead robber out. I took the white-handled revolver for a souvenir.

The dead man was partially identified as Frank Crotin of Cheyenne and buried on the prairie. Father ordered his horse and saddle sold for taxes.

Howard Sebury sent accounts of the attempted holdup to the Nebraska City and Omaha newspapers, which made much of Father's attacking the armed robber with his bare hands. The Nebraska City *News* especially went to great length, describing Father as a hero, using most elegant language to tell how he had moved to the uninhabited country on Medicine Creek and in the short space of a decade had built up the community and established a thriving town.

"Mayor Macdougall," said the *News*, "is an example

of the best type of patriotic American citizen, fearless, honest, extremely industrious and endowed with extraordinary vision. When his sense of righteousness is outraged, as it was outraged at sight of this desperado robbing the bank of Macdougall of money entrusted to him as president, Mayor Macdougall has ever been quick to throw himself into the fray with an energy that overwhelms all opposition."

Then they told of Father's part in Casper Diercks's hanging, elaborating and glorifying his speech from the wagon to the mob bent on lynching the murderer. They declared Father thus saved Nebraska City from a "blot on her fair escutcheon by convincing the angry citizens with masterful oratory that they should give the accused a fair trial."

Newspapers all over the United States took to printing articles about Father, and each one seemed to make him a little greater man than the last.

Despite Dr. Andrews's warnings, Father refused to "take it easy" until he recovered from his wound. He did take cold and for almost the first time in his life he was sick in bed with a fever. There was some congestion in his lungs and Dr. Andrews, frankly afraid of pneumonia, called at least twice a day. He characterized Father as the most impatient patient he ever saw.

During this period Howard Sebury brought bundles of "exchanges" over with stories about Father from coast to coast. Father read them with tremendous satisfaction —especially those parts that described his acumen and vision.

One night his fever mounted alarmingly and Mother called me. "Clinton," she said, "I think you'd better go and get Dr. Andrews right away."

"Right away, mother," I said, and dressed hurriedly. But by the time I was ready to go, the fever had broken.

"I ain't got any fever," Father protested. "I'm cold. By grab, I want a snort of whisky."

"Oh, Jack," said Mother, "you know you can't have any whisky in your condition."

"Wait until Dr. Andrews gets here," I said. "If he says he can have it, all right."

I dashed out the door and down the section line road for the Andrews house. Only half dressed, Dr. Andrews hurried up the hill with me, carrying his satchel. He was grim and plainly worried.

But when we got in the house, Father was half sitting up in bed reading a Chicago paper by the kerosene lamp.

"Hello, doc," he greeted. "All tarnal foolishment getting you up here this time of night. I'm all right."

I looked at Mother and she was flustered. "He wanted," she said, "me to go get him some whisky and of course I wouldn't do it. And while Clinton was gone he just got up out of bed and I couldn't hold him and he went and drank almost a water glass of whisky."

Father laughed. "I knew what I needed," he declared, "and, by grab, I wasn't going to die for need of it—not when it was right in the house."

Dr. Andrews shook his head sorrowfully and took Father's temperature and pulse. "Well," he admitted, "he's better. By all rights he ought to be dead. But he's better."

A week later was Father's forty-eighth birthday. He still was a little pale and gaunt-looking, but we had a party. It wasn't a big party, but only Eliza and John with little Laura and the baby, Jack, and Aunt Christine and Lucius Clark and the Clark children and the Seburys and Strikers.

It was practically a family party, as Susie Striker and I were going to be married in the fall, and as the Seburys, as business partners, had been virtually adopted by the Macdougalls. So there was a great deal of jollity and what

Father called "codding" back and forth—more than there ordinarily would have been because we were so relieved at Father's recovery.

"Chris," said Father, "looks like that cherry-wood table of yours has lost its power. Why didn't it give you a warning for me that I was going to get shot?"

Aunt Christine looked down with embarrassment while we all laughed. "Well," she said, "maybe it would have if I'd given it a proper chance. But I declare, we've been so busy I don't believe I've touched that table in more than a year, except to dust it."

We were all sitting around the parlor with the big center light glinting through its crystal pendants, Father holding baby Jack, when the doorbell clanged and I answered it to find Ajax Harvey and a man named Sam Grove on the porch. They had just come in on the train from Lincoln.

Martha Nelson brought them glasses of wine.

"What's all this nonsense I've been hearing?" demanded Ajax of Father. "I expected to find a sick man."

"Sick man!" Father blurted. "Where'd you hear that sluff talk. Never felt better in my life."

"Well," said Ajax, "the main reason we came down was just to see you. But there was another reason too. We're sort of ambassadors from the Democratic party state committee. You've been getting almighty famous of late, Mac, and getting a reputation for being a man of vision and a backer of railroads and a fearless fighter."

"You've known that all along, haven't you?" said Father.

"Of course, of course. And the Nebraska Democrats feel we need a man with a reputation like that to run for Congress. Sam and I are instructed to feel you out. Would you consent to run?"

"You're not codding me?" asked Father.

Mother looked frightened. "You don't mean Congress in Washington, D.C., do you?"

"Of course," Ajax laughed.

"You mean of course you're codding me?" bristled Father.

Sam Grove bellowed with laughter.

"No," said Ajax. "Of course we're *not* codding you. I meant of course Washington, D.C."

Father shook his head. "Don't see," he said, "how I could move to Washington, D.C. Got an almighty lot to look after here."

"You wouldn't have to put in all your time in Washington," said Ajax. "Just need to be there when Congress is in session. Live in a hotel while you're there. And speaking of your business here, what's this big overgrown cub good for? He's probably looking after most of your business for you now."

"Any public-spirited citizen," said Sam Grove, "has to make some sacrifice to serve his country and party. Nebraska needs a man of your type, Mr. Macdougall, to represent her. Nebraska needs an honest man and a fearless man such as you. Nebraska needs a builder, a man of vision and not only does Nebraska need you, but the whole nation needs you. And, believe me, the people will not be slow to reward you if you prove to be the sort of legislator I am positive you *will* make."

"Hear, hear," said Ajax.

"You know, Mayor Macdougall," went on Sam Grove, "it isn't such a long step from the halls of Congress to the White House itself."

Father rubbed his chin. His wide-open black eyes glittered in the lamplight. He looked at me. He looked at Mother, who was gazing thoughtfully at a rose figure in the carpet.

"By grab, gentlemen," said Father, "I'll take the job."

The End